PART I

JUNIOR THOMPSON

The Day Lee Surrenders
April 9, 1865, near the end of the Civil War
(Carlisle, Pennsylvania)

SOLDIER'S HEART

by

MICHELE MCKNIGHT BAKER

SOLDIER'S HEART BY MICHELE MCKNIGHT BAKER
Published by Heritage Beacon Fiction
an imprint of Lighthouse Publishing of the Carolinas
2333 Barton Oaks Dr., Raleigh, NC, 27614

ISBN: 978-1-941103-69-2

Cover design by Elaina Lee
Interior design by AtriTeX Technologies P Ltd

Available in print from your local bookstore, online, or from the publisher at www.lighthousepublishingofthecarolinas.com. Also available for order at www.soldiersheartnovel.com

For more information on this book and the author visit: MicheleMcKnightBaker.com

Brought to you by the creative team at Lighthouse Publishing of the Carolinas: Eddie Jones, Rowena Kuo, Ann Tatlock, Brian Cross, Meaghan Burnett

Library of Congress Cataloging-in-Publication Data
Baker, Michele McKnight.
Soldier's Heart / Michele McKnight Baker 1st ed.

Printed in the United States of America

Praise for *Soldier's Heart*

When I read the first sentence of Michele Baker's *Soldier's Heart*, I knew I was in for a rare treat—every sentence is delicious. Baker's storytelling conjures up a land long past; yet it's driven by a subtext still pulsing in our culture today. At times, Baker waxes from poetic to prophetic. I could feel the ground shaking under the fragility of her perfectly wrought characters.

Don't let *Soldier's Heart* be overlooked in your reading this year. You will treasure every word and not want to give away your copy, but keep it on your bookshelf for the treasure it will bring to your library. Michele Baker is a gift to modern literature.

~ **Patricia Hickman**
Author of *Tiny Dancer* and *Fallen Angels*

Inspired by a true story, *Soldier's Heart* follows the plight of two families, one black (the Thompsons) and one white (the Hendersons), as seen through the eyes of their young sons, Junior Thompson and Web Henderson, who live in Carlisle, Pennsylvania during the Civil War. Reminiscent of Faulkner's *The Unvanquished*, descriptions of daily life are brilliant. Skirmishes and battles are just miles away, while readers witness the economic, religious and social consequences for the two families who represent two very different worlds. The women and children must fend for themselves. The only thing the women have in common is their fear of war: Maggie Henderson, for the safety of her family and property; Sarai, for their loss of freedom. Their escape in search of sanctuary is absorbing.

~ **Betty J. L. Curtis**
Women's Army Corps Veterans Association

A Civil War period novel that touches the true drama of families forever haunted by the effects of war. A great read, factually based, that draws you into war-torn Pennsylvania, pitting family member against family member and neighbor against neighbor as all try to find a foothold for survival and understanding. *Soldier's Heart* brings an insight into the effects of war not usually discussed. A must read novel for the Civil War enthusiast.

~ **Andy Anderson**
Expert collector and owner, Paper Trails

With an intriguing mix of historical fact and fiction, *Soldier's Heart* stirred a few pleasant and unpleasant memories of my own. It took me back to my boyhood from bullying and playfulness to sincere friendships with my childhood friends. It reminded me of the challenges of race and relationships even in my adulthood.

Michele Baker's novel has many moving parts, none so direct and subtle as its language and dialogue. *Soldier's Heart* will grab you and hold on until its end. It will change you, maybe move you to action.

~ **Michael Newsome**
Business and community leader

Inspired by letters and photographs from her own family history, Michele Baker has crafted a haunting and intimate novel about the Civil War. This is the behind-the-scenes story. This is what it was really like for two families, one black and one white, who struggled to maintain friendship, family and sanity as the battlefield moved closer and closer to their Pennsylvania home. A compelling read.

~ **Susan Breen**
Author of *The Fiction Class*

Michele Baker's *Soldier's Heart* has that perfect ingredient necessary for a historical novel to work - authenticity. That quality no doubt comes from her own family tree and runs through this story of friendship and reconciliation in one of our nation's toughest moments. The author paints scenes that put you there with the characters. She writes with passion that makes you care about them to the book's last page - and long afterward.

~ **James McClure**
Historian and editor, *York Daily Record/Sunday News*

"Now *this* is beautiful writing," I thought as I read the first pages of *Soldier's Heart*. As one who loves not just a good story, but one that is lyrically and intelligently written, I've found a new favorite in Michele McKnight Baker's remarkable debut novel.

~ **Ann Tatlock**
Award-winning novelist and children's book author

Michele is an amazingly articulate writer. She skillfully transported me back in time. I feel as if I know each character personally. I was spell-bound by *Soldier's Heart* from start to finish.

~ **Barbara Cole**
Area Coordinator, Moms in Touch International

Soldier's Heart is a beautiful telling of both anguish and tenderness side by side during the Civil War. Chronicling a town and its relationships, the conflict of a national disaster is reflected in a parallel tale of relationships that are sometimes strained but reconciled, sacrifices that prove and deepen already existing love.

~ **Lt. Colonel Allen Satterlee**
Editor-in-Chief and National Literary Secretary
The Salvation Army National Headquarters

To Marcus and Marguerite
and all forebears dedicated to reconciliation

❖

I wonder if a soldier ever does mend a bullet hole in his coat.

—Clara Barton

TABLE OF CONTENTS

Gettysburg Thunder

1863, refugees (Carlisle and Lancaster, Pennsylvania)

Wilderness

1863–1864, later battles (Pennsylvania, Virginia)

PART III

At Home

1864–1865, as the War ends (Virginia and Carlisle)

~the day Lee surrenders to Grant, April 9, 1865~

What the Child Saw

My name's Junior Thompson. I'm twelve years old today.

My pap's called Chance and my mam's name is Sarai.

I'm telling you this story because it's your story, too.

Outside the church after it all happened, his mam told him to hush and whispered, "Forget this. You're too young to understand." Junior thought, *She means she doesn't want me to. But I know what I seen.*

He walked to church a few steps behind his parents, Chance and Sarai Thompson. It was past winter, on the cold edge of spring. The last snow was all shoved up at the corners of streets, melting into grand puddles that looked like chocolate soup. Junior dropped behind just a bit and timed his foot's arrival to a puddle to match the arrival of a silly schoolgirl who wasn't paying attention anyway. When his mam heard the squealing, she looked around quick but all she saw was a gasping girl with a muddy dress front and face and Junior walking all purposeful-like. She made a face at Junior and kept walking.

They walked to the church at the center of town just like they did every Sunday. Theirs was the biggest church in Carlisle, all rough and gray on the outside, all light and shadows on the inside. Junior's mam and pap paid for their pew seats. Others with brown skin sat high in the gallery, when they could find a seat. Once Junior asked Pap why they were the only colored family paying for their own pew. "Sometimes it is necessary to be the only one," he said in a way Junior knew meant he would get the same answer if he ever asked again.

Things were not as proper here as they seemed, Junior thought. *Secrets and stuff. Like the name of our town. It's got an "s" inside, but you're not supposed to say it.*

The Thompsons sat in their back row box pew as usual, right behind Junior's school teacher, Teacher Brumbach, and her daughter Abigail. Junior looked at them but turned his head quick when Abigail looked his way. *Widow Brumbach, that's what grown-ups call our teacher. Nobody sets next to them because they're German and Abigail's mam's never really been married. That's why at school we call her just plain Teacher Brumbach.*

Junior's folks knew he liked sitting close to the center aisle. Which usually he got to do, if he hadn't splashed too many girls on the way. He liked sitting there because, when Preacher Wing walked up the aisle in his big coat that looked like a dress and was the color of blood, Junior could stick his hand out so that the edge of it flowed over his fingers. *Like that lady who touched the hem of*

Jesus' coat and power flowed right outa him. Junior covered a sly grin with his hand, remembering one time when his foot had gotten stuck out there along with his fingers and Preacher Wing flew. *Almost fell on his face!* Teacher Brumbach, leaning in the aisle, broke his fall with her ample bosom, and when Preacher came up for air he looked straight at Junior and did not look unhappy.

Junior liked running his hands along the smooth dark pew wood because his pap helped make them and you could not find a catch or splinter anywhere. Junior looked around, watching people put their Sunday faces on. Preacher stood at the high pulpit. Junior liked squinting his eyes at one or the other of two deep windows where sunlight came slanting in like a pathway for angels. Junior thought he'd see the angels if he squinted long enough. One time he did see a glow overtake Preacher. One blink and it was gone. Later he told Preacher about it. Preacher laughed and said, "Shucks."

There was the usual boot scraping against bare brick and floorboards and clicking of watch fobs and rustling of petticoats while people got settled in, still smelling winter damp and musty. Junior could hear the coal fire hissing, and, by the time the church filled up, he did not feel the wet cold anymore.

They began singing "Stand up, Stand up for Jesus," the church's favorite song because the son of one of the old preachers wrote it. Folks in the gallery started a marching foot stomp and, when the congregation sang "… ye soldiers of the cross, lift high his royal banner, it must not suffer loss," all the children in the place stuck their hands up holding pretend flags.

Preacher Wing talked at the people for a while from the deep and the wide and the Oh Holy Ghost. "Mend the deep wounds in our churches," he prayed. "And would Our Father please heal and strengthen the re-union of our states?" He told what everybody else already knew, that Richmond fell, and how General Lee's Army was surrounded. And how our guest speaker was elected a representative in the State House in Harrisburg for a while, before the war. And how he went from captain to brigadier general during the Rebellion on account of his heroic actions. And how he still served the Republic and Pennsylvania as Provost Marshall. Then Preacher came down from that little mountain of a pulpit and shook the hand of General Henderson, the man in the sharp blue uniform sitting with his family in a pew up front and on the other side of the aisle from the Thompsons.

Junior fastened his eyes on the Henderson family. He felt squirmy with anticipation, his heart full-up proud. Some people called him General but most everybody still called him Representative or else Attorney. Beside Mrs. Henderson sat their son, Junior's best friend Webster and his baby sister Lizzy. General Henderson's father, with his big lion's head of white hair, people called The Old Colonel because he fought in the War of 1812. That old man's eyes stuck to his son General Henderson like he would never look at anything else. *Like that little smile my pap gets when he's proud of me,* thought Junior.

Preacher sat down on the pew in front and General Henderson climbed up to that pulpit like he was mounting his war horse.

Junior liked hearing his friend's pap speak. General Henderson had one of those voices that hooked you and took you along with him. He took his listeners to the battlefield along with the Grand Army of the Republic. Junior saw his own pap and other veterans nodding their heads, remembering. In his heart Junior became a Union soldier too, marching where General Henderson marched, fighting where General Henderson fought. Bravely fighting to win the War of the Rebellion.

Everybody was listening so hard, nobody but Junior heard the soldier come in the door, heard the click of the door latch that sounded like a rifle cocking. Then Junior saw his Rebel gray coat with brass buttons and thought, *Oh there will be trouble*. The soldier wore a sidearm and carried a stick Junior had seen before. *I gave that stick to him!* The man walked down the aisle slow and quiet and wide in the leg, like a gunslinger biding his time. Junior thought the soldier was looking at him but then he walked right by the Thompsons' pew and Junior could see his gaze was fixed on something a thousand miles away and directly behind General Henderson.

Abigail Brumbach squirmed around, stuck out her finger at the man in gray and whispered, "Isn't that Web's uncle, the General's brother?"

Web's Uncle Nathan. Junior nodded his head. *They do look like copies of each other, sure enough. 'Specially how they hold themselves, straight and strong, like oaks that refuse to bend in the wind.*

At the front of the sanctuary, the soldier stopped and held the stick up until it was pointing straight at the General, who stopped talking. People started rustling in their seats, uncomfortable at this odd way of saluting. *That ain't no salute.* Junior knew what it was. General Henderson looked hard at his brother, waiting for him to sit down. Junior got up real quiet and stood in the aisle so he could see all of what was happening.

Web's Uncle Nathan turned suddenly and looked straight at Old Colonel, sitting off by himself in the corner up front.

"Look at me, Father," said the son.

Old Colonel just kept looking straight at General Henderson. His other son. Everything was oh, so quiet. Junior could hear the brother in gray breathing sharp, like he was hurting from an injury.

"Look at me, Father. I'm your son, too."

Old Colonel just sat there, stern as stone.

At first Junior thought that Nathan Henderson started laughing, but he turned fast to face the whole church and he was crying hard, eyes screwed shut, mess coming from his nose. He dropped his stick, his hands at his waist, fiddling with the buttons. Then he started to lift his hands like he was asking for help, but his hands went to his pants again, and he shoved the pants down.

What Junior saw looked like a map with angry red scars instead of roads, running up and across that man's lower body. *I never seen a naked white man 'til now, but I seen scars before.* Junior felt sick when he saw what was missing. *No male parts like I have between my legs! Naught but a rough looking bump and nub. That map of skin, seamed and stretched tight.*

Men's voices started to rumble, while ladies whimpered. Mrs. Henderson stood up in front of Nathan Henderson, turned her head away, and spread her skirt a bit wider so nobody could see that awful map. She had a white handkerchief in her hand and she lifted it toward him so gentle Junior thought about how his mam wiped tears from his face gentle when he fell. *I bet that handkerchief smells good like Mam's, too.*

Nathan Henderson sighed like he was letting go of something. General Henderson started stomping down those curved steps from the pulpit, when all of a sudden the soldier grabbed his pistol from its holster and lifted it up in the air. People's voices rose and Junior heard how the ocean must sound right before a gathering wave crashes down on some helpless ship. Men rushing forward, but Dr. Cook, a tall man and quick, got there first. Nathan cocked that gun at his own head, but Dr. Cook reached out with his long arms, grabbed Nathan Henderson's wrist with one hand and pulled the gun away with the other. General Henderson got there. When he saw his brother from the front, the General's head reared back like somebody punched him hard. Junior heard the General yell, "Are you insane?" Nathan pulled up his pants and began to fasten them. Men rushed up with rage on their faces. Dr. Cook stuck his long arms up in the air and shouted, "Stop! Stay!" like a herd of wild dogs was coming his way. Those men did simmer down for Dr. Cook, but Junior felt sure they also saw the blood and fire in the General's eyes.

It got almost quiet except for ladies' whimpers. Dr. Cook spoke strong. He said, "This man suffers from Soldier's Heart. We'll attend to him."

Mrs. Henderson spoke softly to Nathan while he wiped his face. Then General and Mrs. Henderson, with Web and little Lizzy, hurried Nathan out the side door up front.

Preacher said a fast blessing and told everybody to go home. Church folk started hurrying out. The ladies in their hats, pulling their young ones by the arms, the men herding their families along, armed with gilt-edged Bibles. Junior's folks turned to leave. Junior's pap looked at him, hooked his eyes toward the door. But Junior hung back.

"Crazy man!" Teacher Brumbach spat the words as she stormed past Junior, red fury in her face, yanking Abigail along and Abigail looking at Junior funny as she flew past, along with everybody else.

Except Web Henderson's grandfather, Old Colonel. He lit a cigar. Right there in the sanctuary! Junior could smell the tobacco afire, saw glimpses of the old man, in between people rushing by, set off by himself. He smoked it slow and never mind the ash crumbling to the floor.

~after church, April 9, 1865~

Junior

Outside in the glare of day, families hurried their separate ways. Web and his family were already gone, so Junior could not hang around to play as they usually did. Nobody called out to Junior "Happy birthday," but that's how it usually was. In Junior's family, your birthday was the day you could eat your favorite meal, and the one day you didn't have to do your chores. Maybe he did hope his twelfth birthday would be different. And sure enough, there was a surprise. Just not the kind Junior had hoped for.

He caught up to his mam and pap. He had questions, but that's when his mam whispered, "Hush. Forget this. You're too young to understand." His folks walked so fast he had to hustle to keep up. They were whispering to each other, too, with their shoulders close in so Junior couldn't hear, though he tried. His pap put his left hand at the small of his wife's back, half guiding, half protecting. His other hand was stuck deep in his coat pocket. Junior studied his parents. *They walk so straight together. Mam comes just to his shoulder. She looks strong for someone so tiny.* He heard his mam say, "Nathan surely must of got soldier's heart."

Junior tugged on Mam's skirt. "What's soldier's heart?"

His mam gave him a squinty look. "That's when a soldier leaves his true heart on the battlefield, comes home with one that's weak and fearful. Now stop pulling at my skirt, Junior." She went back to whispering with her husband.

Loud enough so they could hear him, Junior said, "Poor Web. That must be some carriage ride home!" They didn't turn around, so Junior kept himself company. *Hope people aren't talking bad about them. Bet my folks and other folks with children saying, 'Mercy! The war's hard enough and why'd our children have to see that?'* With both hands Junior patted down his shirt front and pants, relieved to know what was underneath was like it was supposed to be and that everything was all there.

Junior stopped walking, but his folks didn't know. He felt his fingers clenching up. *What if it was me saying, "Look at me Father, I'm your son," and my pap wouldn't see me? What if?* His parents had crossed the street and were already halfway up the next block. Carriages came fast, so when Junior saw a break he hurried across the street, too.

At times when Junior felt jumpy, or if there was something he wanted to get out of his head, he gave himself something else to do. Like a challenge or a dare. There was a long straight block ahead, so he decided to try walking it backwards. He turned around and swung one foot behind himself. And that's when he noticed.

People were still coming out of the church. Faces pale, shaking their heads, walking toward home. Then of a sudden the faces changed. To brown and black. The colored faces came out in a thin row and crossed the street catty-cornered, to the other part of town, where they lived. They all looked scared. In that instant, Junior knew why. It was as if he could see them through the stone wall of the church, standing on the rickety wood steps leading down from the gallery. Standing on those stairs, waiting in place because they can't cross the river of elbows and pale faces shoving their way out first. *Packed into that stairway so dark and so tiny, even my mam would have to bend a bit.* Their faces wet with heat and worry and scarce enough room to breathe. Just standing and waiting. *Like they're not even there.*

Junior's brain was so full up with questions. Swirling and pressing down, one on top of the next. Then one came up like the sick he'd been swallowing to keep down and it came rushing up to his lips and out of his mouth like a roar.

"FIRE!"

Just one word did he spit out and it did not sound like a question.

Junior never heard his voice so loud before. That thin line of colored folks scrambled faster and they kept their heads down. But the white folks stopped walking. Some even stopped in the middle of the road. Carriage drivers had to pull up on reins to keep horses from tramping them. They stopped walking and they were just staring. Right at Junior.

Junior turned and ran. He caught up to his folks, who stood waiting where the road curved toward their woods. He felt their surprise as he ran past them. His pap caught him by the shoulder, spun him around.

"Why, Son?"

Junior knew that was not his whole question either. But Junior had questions of his own. "Why'd Web's uncle drop his pants in front of everybody?"

His pap's head went back, his right hand stuffed in his pocket, his mouth in a straight line, thinking his answer. But Junior couldn't wait for one. All his questions came spilling out at once.

"Why the old Colonel get to smoke in church and why he ignore his son Nathan like that? Why we the only black people get to leave church with the white folk? What if there be a fire? And then who's gonna die? Why do you walk around with your hand stuck in your pocket all the time? It's stupid!"

What Junior meant was, *It's all stupid.* Not just his father's hand in his pocket. But again his words got ahead of his meaning and before he could correct himself his pap's hand came out of his pocket as a fist and smashed into the side of Junior's face.

His mam screamed, "ROBERT!" Her husband's real name, which she almost never said. Junior landed on his backside, gravel dug into the palms of his hands. He could feel his cheek puffing up already. Blood trickled warm from his mouth to his chin. He felt out the inside hurt with his tongue, pushed one tooth and it wiggled a little. *First time my pap ever—ever—hit me.* Junior's brain was numb. All he could think was, *Some birthday present.*

Chance Thompson looked like he'd seen a ghost. He thrust his fist back in his pocket. He tried to help up his son with his other hand, but Junior shook it off. He got on his feet and walked fast, then ran. Junior ran and ran until the palms of his hands hit the front door of his house and he dropped onto the top step, his lungs burning for air.

But he had time to get his breath back. It seemed his folks took their sweet time getting home.

When they finally arrived his mam said, "Let me see that."

Junior let her fuss over his cheek while he watched his pap's back walk to his workshop. Junior said something low enough like he meant to keep it private but loud enough so his mam could hear: "Seems like ignoring your son is becoming a epidemic round here." For a quick moment she looked like she was going to smack him, too. But she kept her hands to herself.

Junior was sitting in the kitchen, holding a cold wet rag to his cheek, watching his mam work. *It will take her a while to finish my birthday dinner.* She was at it already. Rolling out crust dough on the floured table near the woodstove, her cheeks puffing with every shove of the pin. She grabbed the bowl sitting nearby and punched the dough that was rising in it. She slammed down the lid on the stew kettle where the meat and vegetables were bubbling and shoved it back on the stove so there was room for the kettle of lima beans. Things were happening in the kitchen louder than usual. Plus Junior already had a good bit of noise in his head.

"I'm gonna go see Web now, okay?"

"No!" Sarai's face got all red, not just from kitchen heat, and her eyes squinted hard at Junior. "Them folk need their privacy."

Junior was thinking, *That's not what Web and me need,* but he didn't want to sass her.

"Can I, uh, may I wait outside, Mam?"

"Yes, but …" she looked out the window with a worried expression. "Don't disturb your father. You know he likes his peaceful alone time after Sunday services and Lord knows he don't get many moments of blessed quiet."

Junior walked outside the house and tried to take his mind off things in his usual way, by looking all around for stories that may be hiding, waiting to be told. But his mind kept bringing back things he didn't know how to think about.

Web's house sat on the other side of the creek and cornfield, his family's field. It was all stubble now, just waiting to be. But in Junior's memory he could see the tasseled stalks sway in formation—*Wind showing its whereabouts*—like a battalion of dressed-up Army men. When Web and Junior were little, before the war, they made a game of moving through summer's cornfield without being caught. Summer was some months off. *Anyways, we way too big for that now.*

Junior tested his weight against a footbridge Web and he had made with sapling pine logs. *To connect our two lands.* In summertime if they weren't working, they met at this bridge almost every day. They had a slap shake they did when they met in the middle. *Secret, so we have to look around 'fore we do it.*

One time Web had said, "My land is your land, your land is my land." *Sounded righteous, like God talking. We looked at each other and started laughing. Now it's part of the hand slap. Sometimes the best stuff comes to you like a happy surprise.*

Junior squatted down on the footbridge and looked over to the cleared path Web and he beat through his field. He looked up and could see the roof of Web's house. Junior imagined his friend standing right in front of him. *That orange hair and freckles. Generally he's a stay-abed, so most Sundays and schooldays he's got his hair all stuck up in the air, his mam be trying to pat it down with her hand.*

Bet he wishes he stayed abed today.

Junior felt his own hair. *Fleecy, like the boy-king David's sheep. His black sheep anyways. My hair'd stick up too, if Mam didn't keep it nice and trim.* Junior bounced on the bridge logs just until they touched the creek face, to see how the water bubbled up through the cracks, cool and clear.

Junior picked up a rock from the creek bed. He felt the weight of it in his left hand. "That's the hand I use to do things, not the one Pap uses," Junior said out loud but mumbly low. His fingers closed onto the rock, into a fist. He threw that rock hard as he could. It whipped through the woods, through air and dead leaves. Scared out a turkey vulture. *Now there's a nasty bird. Color of a black eye with a red beak as hooked as his claws.* It flapped its big crooked wings and mounted the air real slow. Took its perch high in the empty branches of the oak tree that Web liked to climb. Fixed its beady eye on Junior and sat there watching, like it was the boss.

Then the vulture swooped down and away, racing the LeTort Spring to the Conodoguinet Creek, from there to the Susquehanna River, and from there to the sea. *Same river my ancestors took to reach the places where they hunted and farmed and buried their dead.*

Junior saw another gray rock. It fit nice in his hand. A fine oval, the best shape for throwing. He decided to throw it at the target on the tree by his pap's workshop, a target Junior and Web had carved. Junior had never tried a throw from this far back. *You got to squint, wind up your body, like a spring-loaded gun, take aim with your arm and eye together. My hand is a messenger with a rock-message for that old tree.*

WHAP!

The stone found its mark and echoed through the woods like gunshot or good news. *That's a keeper,* he thought, and went to retrieve the rock.

Junior noticed his pap had left his workshop door open a crack. *Wait 'til I tell him about this bull's eye. Surprised he didn't hear it!* Then Junior felt his cheek throb. Anger came with it. He thought about lobbing one of those stones at his own pap. *That's a first. If getting older means having thoughts like this, maybe I just stay eleven. Forget the birthday, Junior!*

He heard his pap talking to somebody and slipped a little closer.

His pap was alone in his workshop, stooped down on the floor, his Bible open beside him. *His face is all—it's wet with tears! Pap cryin'? Can't be!*

Junior thought, *Pap, what you beggin' God for?*

He crept closer, until he could hear his pap's voice clearly. Chance Thompson moaned, "They should punish me. Punish *me!*"

Punish you for what, Pap? Junior felt so weak in the knees he fell down. *Seeing my Pap cry's worse even than seeing that naked white man.* Junior could hardly see, his eyes stinging. *He mustn't see me, shameful like this.* His fingers clawed at earth in fistfuls, until he could push himself to his feet.

Junior scrambled back across the bridge and through the cornfield. To where his Mam told him not to go.

Junior stopped running when he was halfway across Web's back lawn, almost to the brick wall at the little spring-fed pond where before the war they used to feed Web's big geese with handfuls of dried corn.

Now there were no geese and the pond looked lonesome. *Web should be looking for me and be outside by now.*

The back porch wrapped all the way around the house and became its front porch, too. A stone wall wrapped the streetside front of the house, low enough so folks inside could see what was going on in the lawn from its big windows. Yet the wall was high enough that other folks couldn't see what was going on the other way. *House looks dark and closed. Feels funny walking up to the back porch by myself.* Junior went up the back steps on tiptoes.

This big empty porch made him feel cold and lonely. The double doors had glass windows with lace curtains. Junior cupped his hands around his eyes, looked through the window, and could see all the way through to the front porch door. The hairs on the back of his neck pricked, as if to say *Why you looking in somebody's house?* Then Somebody grabbed Junior's shoulders.

He jumped, banging his nose on the glass and yowling. Somebody spun him around and Junior stood face to face with old Yancy, who worked for the Hendersons. Yancy was frowning but did not look angry.

"Family's not back yet. Master Web, too."

Junior rubbed his nose. "Reckon I'll come back later?"

"No. Best not." Yancy bent down, squinting at Junior's swelled-up cheek. He straightened up, looked fierce into Junior's eyes. "Boy, why you say that?"

"Say what?"

"You know what. That thing you say in town. Fire! Peoples talking about it."

Junior's hand dropped to his side. His whole body felt strange.

"Let's walk, boy. We got to talk about this."

Yancy walked Junior across the lawn slowly, one hand still on Junior's shoulder. Yancy had a stiff leg and a loose one. *He walks like a see-saw. He's wrinkled as his clothes but tough and watchful and black as the guard dog at the jail in town.*

"My ears is waiting," said Yancy.

"Well I reckon ..." Junior's thoughts came to him slowly because there was a whole herd of feelings coming the other way. "Reckon I saw how dangerous it was for folks setting in the balcony and not able to get out. 'Specially since Old Colonel—"

"Stop right there. I get your meaning. Don't say that last part. Don't say it to nobody, understand? Words have two meanings. What you mean and what other peoples hear." Yancy was looking toward Junior's house, popping his fingers against his lips as if he was pretend smoking.

"Talk to your folks about this?"

"Nnnooo." Junior's stomach sank low. It guessed what Yancy was going to say.

"I know your folks." He was looking at Junior's cheek again. "Talk to 'em."

Junior took his time going back through the field. When he got to the woods, he heard his pap calling his name. Junior had to take another long minute before he followed the voice back to the house. Even then, he did not feel ready.

Sarai Thompson had the table loaded up with food. The smell of fresh-baked apple pie made his empty stomach give a hurry-up rumble, reminding him he is twelve today. Chance spoke grace. Junior kept his eyes open during the prayer, eyeing those brown loaves of bread, crackled and crisp on the outside, so warm and soft inside. He watched steam rise off the crust of his meat pie, knowing what good things hid inside. *Pulled and dug out the carrots and potatoes myself from last year's garden.* After the Amen, he poked a big hole in the meat pie crust so it would cool faster. He jabbed some lima beans onto his fork, rolled them in pie gravy, and stuck the whole pile of them in his mouth. *Awwwwmmmmgood.* Junior saw his pap looking at him. Chance picked up his fork, but before he ate anything, he put it down again. *Mam looks like she's warning Pap about something.*

"Son, I want to talk to you about what happened."

Junior kept eating like everything was fine, even though nothing was fine. He could not look at his pap directly. His cheek still hurt.

"Junior, please stop eating and listen to your pap. He trying to tell you something." Sarai cast a warning look at Junior. He put down his fork. Chance waited until Junior glanced up at him.

"Web's Uncle Nathan was fighting in the war a long time." His pap was still looking at Junior's cheek while he talked. "Stayed in longer than Web's father and me. Nathan did not even want to go to war at first. Then when he wanted to go, his brother made him wait and go with another company. You remember the middle brother, William Jr.? Remember how he came home, sick with fever? After Willy died, Nathan fought with a grudge in him. And now you know he got hurt bad. He saw some terrible things. We all did." Chance Thompson cleared his throat like something was stuck.

"It's going to take a long time to understand. Maybe take our whole lives. Maybe not even then.

"It's okay to ask questions, Junior. You ask good questions. But they are questions with several answers each and take a long time to understand, like I said. Except one. The one about my hand being in my pocket. And I think you already know the answer to that one. So tell me why you asked that question. I'll give you a good, straight answer."

"Never mind, Pap. It's not important."

"Yes, it is important. And I do mind. But not how you think." He pushed toward him, his face close up to Junior's. "Listen , Son. It's like you yelling 'Fire!' At first I didn't understand why you did it. But deep down, of course I do."

He waited for Junior to say something. When he didn't, Chance said, "I promise never to hit you again. I should never let my anger best me like that. Especially with you. I'm sorry, Junior."

Junior's hand was on the table. His pap put his right hand on Junior's, the one that used to be his stronger work hand. The one he usually kept hidden in his pocket. It was the first time he had touched Junior with that hand since he came back from the war. *Well, second time, counting him punching me.* That hand felt strange. The heaviness of a man-size palm but with fingers light as feathers. *'Cause there ain't any fingers nor thumb above the first knuckles, just nubs. Aren't any, I mean. All cut off.*

Junior pulled his hand away like he had been bitten and folded his arms tight against his chest, hands tucked in. *Safe.* That sick feeling came back, grumbling in his stomach.

"It's okay to ask questions?"

His pap nodded.

Junior braced himself. Made his face blank against the sight of that gnawed-off hand. "Then I have another one. Why did you tell God you should be punished?"

Air wooshed out of his pap's mouth like March wind. He scratched his head with those awful knobby knuckles. Junior thought he looked like a skeleton. Face all thin, no young man fat left on it. Hair stubble coming in gray on his bark brown chin. Head bald, and sunk-in cheeks. Clothes too big on his body. *Practically every meal, Mam say, "I'm a gonna fatten up that war-body of yours."*

"That's enough for now," his mam said, in a tone that warned them both.

Junior pushed away without being excused.

It's disrespectful, I know. But I'm so full-up tired of grown-ups, secrets, and my birthday being ruined.

Junior walked out the door. Nobody said "Stop."

Junior sat outside on the tree stump where his mam liked to rest. The sky's blue had deepened before he heard the door shut. His pap sat down on the ground next to Junior, picked up a stick with the nubs of his thumb and first two fingers and started scratching something in the dirt. *Knowing Pap, that hand isn't never again going back in his pocket.*

"Your mam has some birthday pie for you."

"Not hungry right now."

"She told me to come out here and do what I've been itching to do since I woke up this morning."

Junior could make out what he was scratching. The letters were a little wobbly. But no mistake, he spelled out JUNIOR.

Chance dropped the stick and put his right hand behind his back. "I know it hasn't been much of a birthday. Have a gift for you, though. If you want it."

Junior didn't say, either way.

With his left hand, Chance pulled a shriveled up rubber thing from behind his back. He winked at Junior, fiddled with the thing, then started blowing into it.

"Why Junior, your eyes look half the size of your face!" His mam came to stand next to Junior. She forced a giggle into her voice. "It's a ball!"

Junior stood up slow. He couldn't believe what he saw. A real rubber ball! He had heard of them but never touched one before. Did not know anyone who owned one. At school, the boys played with a pig gut they had to blow up with their own breath. Those balls were odd shaped and not so steady in flight. A pig gut ball lasted just a few games before it broke. Then the boys would have to wait to play ball until someone got another one.

Chance raised his eyebrows but said nothing as he puffed. As the rubber stretched and smoothed, Junior felt his own heart swelling so big in his chest he thought it might explode. His pap capped the hole, pressed to check that the ball was nice and firm, and handed it to Junior.

"A real ball? This mine?"

"Don't know," his pap scratched his head again, all serious. "We better check to see if it works."

Junior and his pap separated. Sarai took a seat on her stump to watch them.

Chance threw the ball to Junior and he held onto it. Had to convince himself it was real. Chance started jumping up and down like a kid, so Junior finally tossed it back.

Chance ran with the ball, egging Junior to get him. Junior rushed and threw his arms around him. He made it out to be a roughhouse tackle, harder than he meant to. *Or maybe not.* They fell down on the ball.

"Pap! Did it break?" Junior's stomach took its own dive.

Chance rolled over and held up the ball like a prize.

My beautiful, perfect ball! Junior backed away from his pap and ran to his mam. He threw his arms around her waist, buried his head in her lap. He tried to make it look like a tackle too, but gentler, and not a babyish hug.

"Thank you, Mam."

"Thank your Pap. It's his hard-earned money got you that ball."

"Thank you, Pap." Junior said it stiff.

When he stood, Chance planted the ball in Junior's arms, slapped an arm around his shoulders. Junior shrugged it off. His pap's arm felt uncomfortably heavy.

"Let's take a walk into town, Son. To the playing field."

Junior stepped back, shaking his head.

"Come on. We can spread out more in the big field, see how far it'll fly."

"Better take the lantern!" Sarai said.

As they reached the playing field, the sun was setting and spitting gold fire through the trees. Junior recognized Web's pap, General Henderson. He looked like he was waiting for something, or someone; smoking a pipe, not a cigar like his father, the Old Colonel. Not smiling, but not angry like the Old Colonel, either. Junior saw Web running toward him. Some other boys were also standing around as if waiting for something. When they saw Junior, they ran toward him, too.

Junior felt Chance's hand on his shoulder, heard his pap whisper in his ear, "Have fun with your friends," and, before Junior could shrug him off again, Chance let go.

Junior got mobbed by a clatter of boys. They boosted him up in the air and carried him all around, cheering and whooping. Junior floated above them, holding the ball high with both hands so that it floated above everything.

When they finally let Junior down, it did not take long for the boys to stack two piles of rocks for end goals and organize into teams. Two mobs of boys formed, kicking the ball and catching it and rushing each other, shoving and grunting their way toward their goals.

The sun slipped away. The boys turned into shapes and shadows and shouts. They couldn't tell who was who and it did not matter. Junior looked over and could see the two fathers, still watching the boys, standing a certain space apart.

I know about that space, he thought. *It's the sort that's not so big, yet somehow you can't close it. Like the one I have now, deep inside my chest.*

~evening, April 9, 1865~

Night Walk

Later Junior knew his pap would blame himself for letting Junior walk home alone. *But I wasn't alone,* Junior would say. *I was with Web.*

Chance Thompson and General Henderson walked ahead of Junior and Web. Chance held the lantern. The way the light wrapped around the two paps made them look extra big. They walked stiff, tense about whatever conversation they were having. Being about the same height and build, in the lantern light they changed to shadows, looking like two matching book weights. Web and Junior joked about it because they knew their paps looked opposite-different by days' light.

Junior wanted to ask Web about his Uncle Nathan. He wanted to tell Web what he heard his pap say. He wanted to tell his friend what he shouted in the street. But they needed to be alone for Junior to open his mouth on those subjects. Junior could see Web wanted to talk privately, too. They were still so excited about the ball, they talked about it like there was nothing else to talk about. Even though they both knew there was everything else to talk about.

Web's pap coughed deep, a painful sound, like gravel in his chest. About then the night sky opened up in a strange and beauteous way. A full moon rose from its hiding place behind clouds and shed a Hosanna-to-the-Highest path of light all across the road and field between the boys and the woods near their houses. They stopped just to look. It put Junior in mind of the Holy birth. He even listened for heavenly host song. Instead, his ears filled with pure silence.

Web ran out several long paces back toward the field and waved for Junior to throw the ball. Which he did.

"Can we throw a bit more!" Junior said to his pap loud. He said it, did not ask it.

Chance Thompson shook his head slow. "Long day , Son." Junior could hear the tired in his voice.

"Just twelve more throws. One for each year. No? How 'bout six?"

Web ran up, gulping his breath. His pap said in a low voice, "To be a boy again." Junior's pap nodded like that was some sort of secret message he understood.

"You go on," Junior said to his pap. He wanted to sound grown-up because it was his birthday, but it was almost over and some begging sneaked into his voice instead. "We'll take just five throws, then home."

"Yes, Father, please!" said Web, his voice rising to a squeal. Web would be thirteen soon and his voice was changing. Just about the only time it got high like that anymore was when he was excited.

The two paps looked at each other. "Should we . . . ?" Web's pap asked with his voice and his eyes, like Junior's pap was the boss.

Chance smiled. Even his smile looked tired. "General Henderson wants me to tell you that General Lee surrendered today."

Web and Junior stared at each other, their mouths flapped open. Then they shouted and whooped and hollered and danced around and smacked each other on their arms and backs. Web's pap and Junior's looked at each other like they wished they could jump around, too.

"Cause for celebration," said Web's pap.

"I suppose a few more ball tosses would be all right," Junior's pap answered.

Web and Junior crowed, raised their arms, clapped their bodies together and danced a victory jig.

The way to their homes divided near that spot, Junior's dirt lane splitting from the main road. Junior's house was visible as pinpricks of light through the trees, with moonlight showing the short way across the field. His pap would take the lane home and Web's pap would keep walking by the main road, around the curve to the stone and iron gate entrance and up the gravel lane. The moon lit the whole path. Book-weight Paps looked at each other. Junior's pap passed the lantern to Junior. Still looking at Junior's cheek.

"Five throws, then home."

Their paps nodded goodnight and walked their separate ways. Web ran out long again, in the direction they had just come from, back toward the field. Junior put the lantern down and gave the ball a mighty heave, watched it arc sweet through the moonlight right to Web. Then Junior saw something strange. His eyes couldn't entirely make out what it was.

Three shadows glided from the trees by the road to where Web was. *Like night moths. Only big.*

Junior took up the lantern and started over to see. Then he heard Web cry out. Something said to him, *Put the lantern here, behind this rock.* So Junior did and started running, hard as he could.

Those wings flapping be arms. Those three shadows be boys. They wrastling for my ball? Web cried out again, a sharp pain cry, then moaned, regular on a beat. *They're beating him!*

Junior recognized the "they" were three older boys, known to all as bully boys to be avoided. One was holding Web down by his shoulders. The other two, their backs to Junior, were using their boots and fists to hurt his friend. Junior leaped onto the back of one, screaming in his ear. "Get offa him!"

He threw Junior like he was a rag doll. The bully turned. Junior saw the ugly snarl on his face. Like a dog showing his teeth. "Our beef ain't with you today." He turned back to kick some more.

He was still turning when Junior jumped on his back again, his legs spinning out, thrashing toward one of the other ones. His fingers clawed at the bigger boy's eyes. His teeth sank into his neck. The bully yelped, tried to shake Junior off. Junior's teeth stayed sunk. His feet hit what must have been the other boy's head. Junior felt it snap back. The fellow groaned and fell. The other bully came from behind and grabbed Junior's shirt, yanking him off, throwing him to the ground. He bent over Junior, fierce, breathing heavy.

"Can't you hear? Our beef ain't with you today. We figure his uncle must really love the enemy to wear that uniform and do what he done in church. So this boy's gonna get what's coming. Don't you know Union boys died for you, nigger boy? We'll come teach that lesson to you some other day." He turned back to the beating.

Junior couldn't take them all by himself and no more sound was coming from Web. That frightened Junior more than anything. He looked around for help. Saw the flickering lantern behind the rock. Junior filled his chest with night air and fury. His roar voice came out even louder than when he yelled FIRE.

"You boys so evil, the DEVIL COME FOR YOU—Look!"

The bully boys looked up and saw the shadowy flicker, like the Evil One fast overtaking them. Their eyes got wide and they fell on their backsides, rolled onto their feet, and ran loose-legged, as only cowards can.

"Webbie!"

Web's mouth, busted and bloody. His nose, busted. Both eyes swelled shut. Web's arms were squeezed tight cross his chest. One leg looked angled oddly. His voice came out small and slow through those broken lips, like it was hard to talk.

"They got your ball, Junior. I tried to keep it."

Junior's eyes burned. He growled, wiped them hard with his fist. He reached down and lifted his friend's arm. "Easy there, Web. Can you stand up?"

Web straightened one leg. He got up on it somehow, Junior lifting, until his arm was slung over Junior's neck, his weight resting on Junior. Every move hurt Web, Junior could tell. *No way I'll get him home. I'm taller, but he's heavier.* Panic rose in Junior's throat with the last of his birthday supper. He swallowed it down.

"Come on, Web. Walk with me to the lantern."

They struggled along until they got along the roadside. Then Junior felt Web's weight go dead against him.

He saw a carriage coming their way, oil lanterns swaying. Junior stuck up his arm and stumbled with Web to the roadside. The horses turned their heads toward the two boys. The carriage slowed. *Thank you, Lord!*

When they got to Web's house, everything but hell broke loose. Web's pap scooped him up, a most awful look on his face. He knew the carriage driver, barked, "Bring the doctor!" He disappeared into the house, door flung wide open, all that yellow light streaming out. Junior sat in the pool of light on the floor, just inside the door. His heart was beating so fast. Junior told it, *Don't worry, Doctor's on the way.*

He heard Mrs. Henderson scream. It sliced right through his panicky heart. He couldn't help it; tears trailed down his cheeks.

He felt a hand on his shoulder. *Yancy*. He looked up the stairs but was talking to Junior. "Come on, Son. I'm gonna take you to home."

"Can't leave Web!"

He pulled Junior to his feet, firm but not mean.

"Maybe your folk heared that scream. Reckon they be worried anyway, by now."

Yancy walked Junior to his doorstep. He spoke to Junior's mam and pap about what happened to Web.

"I want to go back! Web needs me!"

Junior's pap shook his head. His mam's face froze. "I told you something like this gonna happen," she whispered to Chance.

Chance thanked Yancy before he left. Then he pulled his son into the house. Into his arms. Junior stayed right there because he felt too weak to hold himself up. Junior started sobbing. His pap's shirtfront got soaked.

Junior's parents walked him to his bed, helped him into it. But first his pap slipped off Junior's shoes and outer clothing. His mam checked him all over, covered him up, asked him if anything hurt.

"No," Junior said.

Yes.

No way they gonna let me go to Web's house tomorrow.

No way they gonna keep me from it.

Junior lay awake, listening to the whisperings of his folks. They were sitting at the kitchen table. He didn't know how long. He must have drowsed a little because his head jerked when he heard his pap's voice go sharp.

"But I killed Graysom!"

That's not what he said, Junior told himself. But his mam hushed his pap so loud, Junior knew different.

He heard his mam whisper his name, "Junior," then "worships." Then her whisper went too low.

An unsteady quiet settled in the house. Junior heard a chair scrape, footsteps toward his bed.

~late evening, April 9, 1865~

Sabbath Rest

Sarai brought the lamp across from the kitchen side of the room to Junior's bed and pulled the bed curtain aside. She must have seen his eyes were closed; Junior was pretending to sleep. She tucked him in tight.

"Guess that's the last time for that," she murmured, as if everything was all normal. "I mean—now you a young man of twelve and all. And on the Sabbath, no less."

Junior wanted to hear her voice a little longer so he opened his eyes and grabbed her hand and quickly asked the first question that popped in his head that he thought she would answer. "What does Sabbath mean?"

"It means 'day of rest.'" Then her face changed.

"You thinking about this morning? About what happened at church?"

"No! Now hush , Son, don't talk about that."

"About Web?"

She looked down. "No."

"Then what?"

"I was just remembering." She pulled her hand away. "Another Sabbath, long time ago." She looked so far away, Junior caught her hand again and gave it a squeeze, a gentle one. She shook her head, gave Junior a wobbly smile.

"What Sabbath you thinking 'bout, Mam?"

She stared at Junior. Her face went so hard she scared Junior, but he was more curious than scared, so he stared back. Just when he was about to blink first, she started talking. "I guess you are old enough." She pulled her hand away again and disappeared into the other room. Sarai came back, dragging her rocking chair. She pulled it to Junior's bedside and dropped into it with a thump. She began to rock. Junior sat up in bed so he could see her better in the half-light of the woodstove fire. He could hear the tea kettle water humming. She cupped her hands in her lap, like she was holding a secret. "You know who Hettie was, right? Your grandmam. My mam. This be her story. Hers and mine.

"I had a hat back then. . . . Whatever happened to that hat?" She rocked and hummed along with the tea kettle. "I wore it that day. I loved my hat more than any other thing in the whole wiley world."

She rocked as if she was rocking away from Junior, so he asked, "What's so special about some old hat?"

"Oh, Junior. It had a white crown and a open weave along a fine wide brim. Why, I can feel it frame my face even now. Made me feel so pretty and grown up! That hat was the onliest part of my Sabbath outfit I was allowed to touch on any other day." She rocked, smiling at something in long-ago time.

"In the summer I gathered wildflowers and plaited them in the open weave. Mother put my hat at the center of our table on grand display. My wee heart near burst. In the wintertime I would just look at that hat and dream of summertime."

"What day you dreaming about now, Mam?"

Her rocking slowed, flattened out, like her voice when she spoke again.

"Under the flesh of my five-year-old chin I could feel the knot of my hat's satin ribbon, tied in a bow."

Mam stuck her chin up, remembering. And then she began to speak.

Hettie lifted up the chin of my brother Zechariah. She spoke to him in that way she always had to let the rest of us children know she was a-speaking to us, too. "Keep thine eyes straight ahead. Look at that stall door, not at any person. Keep thy hands folded in thy lap. Do not smile, or frown, or laugh. Or cry. Sit still. Do not talk to each other. Keep thy chin up. The. Entire. Time." She emphasized each of them last three words by dropping her voice to a whisper in such a fashion that it chilled us to our tiny bones. We would obey. There weren't no Or Else.

This was my first time in the barn on a Sabbath morn. Big double doors open on each end, light spilling through like glory hallelujah. We set there, all up in our Sabbath best, the four of us setting on a church bench carried in earlier that morning, twixt Hettie, our mama and our papa, James. Mama set with her fingers clenched up. My fingers itched to touch that satin bow. 'Course I kept my hands in my lap, folded, just like Mama said. The bow did its work of keeping my hat nice and still on my head.

This Sabbath morn rang in feeling just nigh of summer. And just after the Sabbath of all Sabbaths when the earth cracked open and out come the Risen Lord. We talked about that one time, us four, when we be digging a hole for the Missus McGuire. Zechariah, he said, "Savior come back to life with that creamy stuff all over his body like newborn babies have." Jamie, he laughed and said, "You fool! He's all beat up and scarred. You forget the part about the cross? Them nails? Like old Sol, that real old slave limping around. His scars be so thick all over his legs, tain't any regular skin left."

Zechariah looked not too happy 'bout being called a fool. He stared hard at Ester. She looked sick to her stomach. "What you think, Ester?" he said. Ester swallowed hard. "Boys shan't speak of the Savior that way, 'tain't right." Now Zechariah he's mad cuz he wanted somebody to agree with him. He looked at me, said, "Sarai, what you think?"

Being Hettie's youngest, I said, "I don't know I only five."

Something important's 'bout to happen. I remember thinking that, wiggling my toes in my shoes. Nothing else was allowed to move, but Mama didn't say nothing about our toes staying still. One church bench set front of the stalls on one side of the barn, all filled with us. Another church bench set on the other side, too, all empty though. Table set up in the middle. Four empty chairs. *Preacher gonna set there?* I wondered that, mainly cuz I never seen a preacher set still when he's preaching. *So who the other chairs for?*

Well, I found out who soon enough. Four men came in. Mr. Turnbrough came in first. Next, his brother by marriage, Mr. Webster, with a wee girl trailing.

Guess who the wee girl was? Family name's a hint. Who you know named Webster? That's right, the wee girl's your friend Web's mam, Margaret, married name of Henderson. But she be a Webster then. And also our master, Mr. McGuire came in, and a Mr. Fisher, with papers under his arm. They set down in this fashion: Mr. John Skinner Webster set on our side, with his back to us. Wee Margaret, her red curls bouncing, she wandered over to the fartherest stall. She looking for her pony but all the animals elsewheres. Mr. Turnbrough sets across from his brother-in-law, Mr. Webster, so's we see his face. Master McGuire sets next to Mr. Webster. Across from him sets Mr. Fisher and he starts spreading out them papers.

For a long time my clear memory stopped right there. Until just now, when you asked your question, Junior, and I saw your sweet gift of a face. Then memories started coming, fast.

Mr. McGuire and Mr. Fisher was spreading out them papers while we set still. Hay smelled so sweet and light, barn earth smelled so dark and secret. The mens talked low while we set still. Mr. Fisher began to read, sing-song, like a preacher beginning his theme. Now I only knew this next part cuz not too long ago the Hendersons gave me a copy of them papers. Your Pap read them aloud, over and over. Now I know every word by heart. Anyways, I thought maybe somebody gonna get married that day. Maybe somebody gonna have a baby. How'd I know, being only five?

Mr. Turnbrough leaned over, said something to Mr. Fisher. He nodded his head. Mister Fisher read the words on the paper. He had a curly bit of mustache on his lip, bobbed up and down. I watched it move with words sounding so, so grand.

> "Know all men by these Presents, that I, Scott McGuire, of Baltimore County, in the State of Maryland, for and in consideration of the sum of Nine hundred thirty four dollars to me in hand paid by Joseph Turnbrough and John Webster as and before the sealing and delivery of these presents, the receipt of which is hereby acknowledged, have granted bargained and sold and by these presents do grant bargain and sell unto the said Joseph Turnbrough and John Webster, their executors administrators and assigns the following named Negroes to wit:"

Mr. Webster say, "James Tilghman."

That my father's name and I felt proud inside, wondering what special thing he done. I kept my face straight ahead and moved my eyes just enough to see my father. His face looked stone hard. *Why?* That brim of my hat started to tremble. Mr. Turnbrough say, "Zechariah Tilghman."

Zech stood up, walked over to the empty pew on the other side of the barn, Mr. Turnbrough's side, and set down. He whimpered like a pup. I look over at Zech as he set down, seen his eyes all shiny.

"Why?" Word was out of my mouth before I could stop it. And Jamie whispering, "He got the bad master."

Mother said in a whisper-cry, "Hush."

Mr. Webster say, "Ester. Jamie."

I heard air spill outa Jamie like a bird in flight. I kept my eyes straight ahead. My stomach flipping I didn't know why. Next Mr. Turnbrough say, "Hettie Tilghman. Sarai."

As I walked I looked at our new master, Mr. Turnbrough. His face, his eyes, looked like the first slip of ice on winter water. My insides froze up just like that. Mama and I walked over and set next to Zech, refolded our hands. I saw a tear dried on his smooth brown cheek. Mr. Fisher read:

> "To have and to hold until such time as the males under forty years of age attain the age of thirty and the females under forty years of age until the age of twenty five, said Negroes thenceforth to be free. In witness whereof I have hereunto set my hand and seal this tenth day of April in the year of our Lord one thousand eight hundred and thirty six. Signed, sealed and delivered before us."

Them three masters set to signing them papers while Mr. Fisher watched. Mr. Webster said, "Margaret" and the wee girl climbed in his lap. I looked at Margaret and she be looking straight back at me. I wondered, *What she know about me now and will it be for ill or good?* And she the very same age as me, turns out.

'Cept on that day I be a child no longer.

Master Turnbrough got up and waved his hand. Zech followed and our mama Hettie, they still looking straight ahead.

I know I'm supposed to follow. Gust of wind came from behind through them open barn doors made my hat flap like it want to fly free. In that moment I couldn't bear for one second more the feel of that hat on my head, mocking me, ribbon on my chin, choking me. I yanked it off by its brim and dropped it right in front of me on the stable floor. I stepped forward and my foot crush down on the crown of that hat. And I kept walking. A sigh comes outa Mama's mouth but she bit it short.

Don't need to look back to know it's ruined for good.

By the flicker and shadow of firelight, Junior could see his mam trembling, especially her hands, still clenched, still guarding. His tongue felt too heavy to talk. Words died on it, too weak even to put themselves into a question. Until, "Does Pap know?"

She put a finger to her lips, dropped her voice to a whisper. "There be different kinds of knowing, Junior."

She was trembling so hard her voice wobbled, too.

Junior's body felt too big for his child-size bed, and blazing hot. He noticed his feet stuck out at the end. *Do something*, they cried out. So Junior threw off his quilt, the one his mam had made for him, with tufts of red and green and blue yarn he used to love to wind around his fingers—*What a babyish thing to do!* He stumbled over to her, thinking, C*omfort her*.

Junior stretched out his arms toward her. Sarai clapped her hands over her mouth, shrinking into the rocker, eyes blinded and wild, as if telling herself, *Don't scream!*

"Mother," Junior said, his voice deeper. That was the first time he ever called her that. His grown-up arms just hung there, strong and stupid, like they didn't know what to do. Powerless to get back what's gone forever. He pulled the quilt from his bed, carried it over to her slow. Junior thought of the time his pap and he found a lamb stuck in briars. They had to talk and touch so slow and gentle, elsewise that poor thing struggled and hurt itself worse.

Junior gentled his voice. "Mam, you look cold." She leaned forward slow so he could slip the quilt over her shoulders. He hooded it to cover her head and gathered it close around in front. Junior held it there for her, letting the warm sink in. "How's that, Mam?"

"You will be cold." Her voice sounded so tiny, like it was coming from her cupped hands.

"I'm fine, Mam. You know how I'm always too hot."

One of her hands, so tiny, peeked out from underneath the quilt. It reached up, felt the hood on her head. She paused at a tassel, wound its colorful yarns around her finger. Then her hand slid down, found Junior's hand and patted it. He tucked the quilt into her folded hand, nice and snug. Junior sat on the edge of his bed and started rocking the chair. Lullaby gentle. Her eyes calmed down.

"Thank you, Junior."

The rocker made little sighs, wood against wood. Sarai blinked, tilted her ear to another sound: hiss of the tea kettle, almost boiled dry.

"Thank you, Junior," she said again. Junior watched her get up slow and walk over to the stove and the hissing kettle, the quilt dragging on her clean wood floor.

Mam's rocker sat empty. *Mam used to rock me to sleep in that chair.* He wanted her to rock him to sleep again. *I'm too big for it now*. He dropped into the chair, numb. His feet reached the ground with plenty of leg left over. *Now I'm keeper of this knowing.* Junior rocked back, then forward. Back. Forward. His bedroom space shrank down so tight, he barely fit into it. Chill night air seeped in through the wall, frosting his breath, but he didn't shiver. There was a hot anger inside of him, burning through the numbness. It grew bigger, like a living thing.

His mam and pap went to bed. When the house was quiet but for his pap's snoring, Junior pulled his schoolbook sack from under his bed. He took his books out and put some clothes in, got dressed. He made his way noiseless to the table where his mam had left the last of the apples and bread, already wrapped with a white cloth. He put them in his sack. He cupped his arms over his sack, holding it tight against his chest as he went out the door.

Holding secrets that couldn't be kept.

Webster Henderson

1860, in the year prior to the Civil War
(Carlisle)

~July, 1860~

Teacher Brumbach

The woman and girl had sat there for who knows how long, before Web happened by and saw them waiting on the steps of the schoolhouse one steamy afternoon. The woman called out, "Who do ve see about se schoolteacher job?"

Webster stopped in his tracks. His owl eyes widened with frank curiosity as he examined these two strangers, looking hot and sipping lemonade from two jars. Finally he said, "The superdetendent. My father is friends with him. I know where he lives." He pointed down the road. "Other side of town. My name is Webster. Who are you?"

The woman winced as she rose to her feet. She turned heavily toward the girl. "Daughter Abigail." Pointing to herself she said, "Frau Brumbach." She hesitated, and in that moment, Web understood that she had decided to take a young boy, a stranger, into her confidence. She drew herself up and lifted her chin as she spoke. "I am Margaretha Brumbach, a niece in se family of Friedrich Ancillon, tutor of King Frederick William IV."

As Web looked on, Frau Brumbach and Abigail screwed the lids back onto their lemonade jars, wrapped them in tea towels and tucked them, like sleeping babies, back into their wicker baskets, between dresses and undergarments and other belongings. The woman's most valuable possession, judging by the way she clutched it, seemed to be a bunch of papers.

"What are those papers?"

"Letters of recommendation." She drew a deep breath. "From se schools in Lancaster vhere I taught. All say, 'Goot! Frau Brumbach ist goot teacher!'" Abigail stood behind her mother, rolling her eyes and grimacing.

Web shrugged his shoulders. "It won't be too hard to best the last one. Ready? Follow me!"

Townspeople gawked at the mother and daughter trudging across town in thick soled shoes, following Webster. Abigail, a sallow, angular girl with black knotted hair that grazed her limp collar, half-dragged her basket with both hands; and Frau Brumbach, graying hair in a strict bun, gripped her basket in one fleshy hand and the fistful of papers in the other. Web beamed as he led this singular parade, his eight-year-old voice singing out directions.

Townspeople called her Teacher Brumbach, or Widow Brumbach. For weeks afterward, her march across town and application as schoolteacher remained a prime topic of conversation. Web had overheard his father say she was the successful supplicant for the teaching position. And, truth be told, the only one.

~September, 1860~

School

Webbie Henderson held tight against his chest a canvas sack containing his schoolbooks, a cool jar of lemonade, an apple, and a sandwich wrapped in stiff butcher's paper. He stood at the portico near the lane, in the yawn of space between the front door and the barouche that would take him to school. Webbie was pleased that his father had told their driver to prepare the carriage. Pleased, and a little nervous, because he and his father would sit face to face and because the school year was still new.

He watched Yancy adjust the horses' halters. Yancy moved at an old man's speed with a young man's pride. His hands, shiny as the tack room leather he polished, danced along the trusting forms of his horses. He had worked for Webbie's parents forever and occupied many of the boy's earliest and happiest memories. Webbie never tired of observing Yancy. Finally, brush in hand, the old man waved Webbie over.

"Books?" Yancy raised an eyebrow.

"Oh." Webbie bounced onto the carriage step and plopped his sack onto the seat he would occupy. He scrambled back to Yancy and held out both hands. Yancy put the big brush in Webbie's hands and lifted him to the nearer horse's mane. Webbie held the brush horizontally with both hands, huffing with the effort of each firm, sweeping stroke.

"Tell me more about the war, Yancy."

Yancy Swonger's stories had become another part of their school-morning ritual. "War of 1812. Brits never seen a Yankee sailor dark and tough and mean as me. Yancy's a fancier way of saying Yank, that's why they called me Yancy. Never catched me. No, sir. I be sixteen then. Fast on the oar. But mind you, Lake Erie water cold. Very cold. We work quick, now. Your daddy be out here soon. I already done the insides."

Yancy carried him around to the other horse. Webbie brushed its mane smooth. Yancy lowered Webbie and received the brush. The boy scrambled into his seat and looked over just in time to see the door open, his father touch his mother's cheek, and kiss her mouth, and to hear him say, "My rose of Sharon."

When his father, Representative Robert Henderson, came toward Webbie, he seemed to loom so large as to fill every space—doorway, portico, carriage opening. Henderson swung his leather folio and suit jacket onto the carriage seat across from Webbie before settling himself onto the seat so that he faced his son. From a high driver's seat, Yancy watched for Representative Henderson's nod, then flicked the horses into motion with expert reins and tongue-clicks.

As they sailed down the winding drive, a fresh September morning greeted them. Dewed grass, pines, garden licorice and mint mingled with Robert Henderson's aftershave. They rolled past the brick gateposts of the estate's entryway, its wrought-iron arch lifted high, with the word SHARON. He lifted his face to the open air. As his imagination took in ripening fields, he saw Yancy and other seafaring soldiers rowing through their drifts.

"Third grade, second day. Eh, Webbie?"

"Yes, sir."

"You will have to walk home again today. I have business in Harrisburg and need Yancy to take me there today. And all this week." Webbie's father folded one long leg over the other. "What book do we have here?" Books were spilling out of Webbie's bag. His father picked the thickest one from the pile. He opened the book to its title page. "*Moby Dick*?"

"I like the picture." Webbie pointed to the blank inside cover page.

"What picture, Son?"

"I can see him." Webbie squinted, concentrating.

His father leaned over to study the blank page with him, dimpling into a smile. "Ah, I see him now. The fearsome whale!"

Webbie sighed. "I want to read it myself but I get flustrated."

"Frustrated?" the father gently corrected. He tapped the book with his index finger. "Shall we read it together, starting this evening?"

"Yes!" The same dimpled smile echoing on the son's face, plumping his freckle-rashed cheeks. "I know how it begins! Mother told me!"

"Call me Ishmael," their voices bumped together, high and low, which made them laugh.

A flash of something caught Webbie's eye. "Look, Father! It's the new boy at school!"

"Where?"

Webbie pointed to a line of trees, backdrop to the blur of a fast-running boy. "Do you see him?"

The boy ducked into the woods on a shortcut to the schoolhouse.

"Oh. He's gone now." Webbie strained to see any hint of the schoolhouse through the trees. "Do you think he'll get there first?"

But Robert Henderson's brow was already furrowed over papers from his folio.

Webbie trotted along the dusty lane from road to schoolhouse in time to see the new boy emerge from the woods. A girl standing alone, watching other school-boys play with baked clay marbles, also must have seen the new student because she bent, cupped a hand to her mouth, and the boys sprang up from their circle. They spread out, various ages and heights, forming two rough lines leading to the school's door. The girls, whispering, giggling nervously, ran over to the school's front steps and waited.

The new boy tried ducking away, but his nearest schoolmate grabbed him, punched him, and shoved him toward the next boy on the opposite line. That one pulled a board from behind his back and smacked the new boy across the back of his legs, then shoved him back across to the next boy on the other side. And so it went, the new student getting shoved in a zigzag path, each boy delivering a punch or kick or shove, all the way to the school steps, where the girls stood in a gaggle. Webbie noticed that the new boy did not fall once. Indeed, he seemed taller with each shove, and he mounted the steps to the children's taunts without even wobbling or looking back. Webbie doubted whether he could manage the same feat. He wanted to try. However, by the time he reached them, the boys had dispersed and were also entering the schoolhouse.

Webbie took his seat at a desk by the window, on the boys' side of the room. He lifted the hinged desktop and stuck his sack into its hold, redolent of maple wood, shaved pencils, yesterday's forgotten apple. The first square of slate blackboard bore something new since yesterday: "Rod Rules." The points of Teacher Brumbach's printed Vs and Ws looked extra sharp.

1. Soiled clothing, neck, ears, fingernails; bare legs or arms = chore during lunch
2. Writing with left hand = 1 knuckle rap
3. Talking in class = 1 whack
4. Chewing tobacco or spitting = 7 whacks
5. Damaging school property, fighting, lying, or cheating = Expulsion

Webbie shifted his gaze to the desk directly ahead. Teacher Brumbach had moved it to the front corner of the class yesterday, had turned and angled it so that its occupant would be in full view of her and the rest of the class. She had told the new student to sit there. He was seven and should be in the second-grade level, she had told the class, scowling. She had waved her rod as a threat while she scolded him about his parents keeping him home from school for a year, as if it was the boy's fault. "Ach, so I must treat you like first-grade schtudent!" Teacher Brumbach had fussed, smacking the rod into her palm. "Because you must—catch—up!"

The new boy, Junior, sat there now, writing. He had a swollen ring around one eye, Webbie noticed and wondered which boy had caused it. Webbie looked around the room to see other students jostling into their desks, talking, laughing.

The schoolyard bell clanged its warning. The job of ringing the bell was an honor Teacher Brumbach reserved for the previous day's best-behaved student who was tall enough to reach the bell's knotted cord. Webbie glanced at Teacher Brumbach, waving latecomers through the door, then looked back at Junior. Webbie grinned at him conspiratorially; whispered loudly, "You look caught up to me."

Junior kept writing and seemed not to hear him.

Teacher Brumbach sidled up along the center aisle to the slate board, her striped shirtdress ballooning against desks on either side.

"Take out pencils. Und paper. Se spelling primers, first blank page. No laughing." She began to print words on the slate board, chalk screeching with every stroke, provoking Webbie to grit his teeth. She wrote words in a neat stack, the words growing longer toward the bottom of the board.

"It is alvays goot to learn from each udder vhen vee can." She held a pointing stick to the board, her eyes sliding to the corner desk. "Who can use sis vord in se sentence?"

No hands raised.

"Riot. Sis vord ist new to you?" Teacher Brumbach looked doubtful. She moved toward the new student's desk. "Vas your fasser in se riot of Forty-Seven?"

Junior looked up at her, expressionless. "Vas he?" she prompted. He shrugged his shoulders.

"Vhat ist your proper name?"

"Junior."

"Your full, proper name."

"Junior Thompson."

Teacher Brumbach ignored the snickers. "Ya, but Junior ist se nickname."

"Everybody just calls me Junior."

"Vell then. Vhat about sis vord." She moved back to the board and tapped the next word with her chalk. "Who can use sis vord in se sentence?"

Teacher Brumbach's daughter, the same girl who had whispered in the schoolyard, raised her hand. "Slave. The old slave worked hard."

"Vell done, Abigail." She turned again to Junior. "Vas your papa ein slave? Your mama?"

The boy shook his head.

"Are you sure? Tell us. Vat ist slave?"

"I don't know."

The class erupted with laughter. Teacher Brumbach clapped her hands for order, lumbered to her desk, called over her shoulder, "I sought you could tell us some goot schtories. But no." She moved on to the other words, none containing Ws, Teacher Brumbach's least favorite letter—*apple, school, summer, marbles, silence, remember*. She called on students with raised hands, heard their sentences, instructed all to use the edge of their primers to fill the paper with lines drawn evenly, and to neatly print the spelling words five times each onto those lines.

Their pages filled with lines and spilled with words: *riot, riot, riot, riot, riot, slave, slave, slave, slave, slave, apple, apple …*

Teacher Brumbach lumbered up and down the aisles, slapping her rod against the palm of her hand.

When he heard the new student lay down his pencil, Webbie looked up from his paper. Junior had already finished the assignment. He sat with his hands folded over his paper, watching the others work.

At the lunch bell, the girls and boys filed out into the midday sun. Some ran home to eat. Webbie left his apple in the lunch sack but stuffed his sandwich into one pocket and felt the other pants pocket for his painted clay marbles. With both hands, he carried his jar of lemonade out to the play yard.

A ring of boys had already formed. One boy made space and motioned Webbie over. He grabbed Webbie by the arm. Webbie's sandwich fell from his pocket and into the dirt. The lemonade jar fell and shattered, darkening the earth to mud. A boy on the opposite side of the circle thrust his hand into Webbie's pocket and pulled out a fistful of marbles. The other boys hooted their admiration. They shoved Webbie to the center. From there Web spotted Junior standing on the outside, arms stiff at his side, with an odd wrinkled expression Webbie had never before seen on any child's face. Beyond him, the girls had gathered to play some other game. Except for Abigail, who sat observing all from the top of the schoolhouse steps, on lookout—either from, or for, her mother. Teacher Brumbach remained sequestered in the school's shaded interior. Webbie wanted his marbles back. But he liked being included in the boys' rough play and felt satisfaction in guessing at the game they had planned.

"Oh, the 'What Color Is It?' game!"

"That's right, Webbie, my boy," shouted the student who had grabbed him. "You know the rules. Call the color while it's still in the air and you get the marble back."

The second boy held high between his thumb and forefinger a colorful marble, smooth and round. The other boys cooed with envy. He tossed it across the circle.

"Red!" Webbie shouted.

"Sorry." The boy who caught and pocketed Webbie's marble shook his head in mock sympathy.

Another marble flew past Webbie.

"Blue!"

"Sorry." Another.

"Green!"

"Awww! Wrong! Again!" The boy held up what Webbie counted as being the last marble. *One color left.* Webbie's chest filled with anxious hope. The boy whipped it high into the air.

"Smoke!"

Laughter rang round the circle of boys as the marble flew beyond them. Junior stuck his hand in the air, caught it. Junior looked only at Webbie, before pocketing the marble and walking away.

During the lengthening afternoon, Teacher Brumbach's temper shortened. At the back of the classroom, an older boy named Evers Johnson was whisper-bragging about how he talked his younger sister into doing his chore of feeding their plow horse, an orange-spotted bay. Teacher Brumbach whacked the slate board with her rod. She pointed the rod at his chest, fired her piercing warning of a gaze, bellowed, "Tank you, Evers! Dass vill be our sentence for schtudy." When she had silence, she turned back to the board and wrote in loopy cursive:

The little girl feeds the orange spotted boy.

A whinnying laugh filled the void of her mistake. Webbie jumped up, pawing the ground with one leather hoof, grinning and neighing. Laughter mounted from other students as they recognized his play-acting as a horse. Webbie bobbed his head toward a smiling girl in front and pranced to her, nickering for a snack. The girl was still pawing in her book sack for something to feed Webbie when Teacher Brumbach caught him by the arm. With one firm yank, she laid him prone over the corner of her desk and with another yank, she bared and began beating his backside. He writhed, grabbing for his pants with one hand and trying to protect himself with the other. The room fell thickly silent, but for the awful cracking sound of rod against flesh. Web looked too surprised to cry.

"But that's me!" he protested, his face so flushed its freckles seemed to pop. "Didn't you mean … aren't I … the spotted *boy*?"

After school, Webbie trailed some other boys toward the main road to look for his father's carriage. Then he remembered what his father had told him about walking home. He looked back at the woods where he had seen Junior emerge. Junior was already disappearing into the foliage. Webbie walked to the small clearing at the woods' edge, paused, and plunged in.

~September, 1860~

Boys' Secret

Webbie caught up with Junior Thompson easily enough. Junior was taking his time walking home. He stopped often to examine whatever interesting thing he spotted in the woods. Webbie managed to walk silently, without being noticed, until his foot caught on something and he lurched forward. When he saw what had tripped him, Webbie jumped even farther away.

At the rustle and twig-snap of human feet, Junior, who had been squatting to examine lichen at the base of an ancient tree, grabbed a rock, turned, and stood in one fluid motion.

"Wait!" Webbie called out, trying to sound brave, even as he hugged a tree, his orange hair sticking up, his eyes wide with alarm.

Junior lowered his arm and released the rock. "Oh, you're the boy got spanked."

Webbie nodded, but he was staring down at a turtle almost the breadth of his two trembling hands.

"Don't be scared," Junior said. "It's a box turtle."

Webbie's face flushed. "I'm not scared. Just careful."

"Careful." Junior nodded his head. "It's a big turtle, true enough. Won't snap you, though."

"You sure?"

"See? Junior bent down, lifted the turtle at an angle, showing Webbie its orange undermarkings. "And that jaw won't hurt anyone." Junior pointed at the creature's head, but the turtle pulled into its shell so fast both boys burst into laughter.

"*Real* dangerous!" Webbie said, and the boys laughed again. Webbie squatted next to Junior to play with the turtle.

"Eight," Junior said. "That's how many whacks you took."

Webbie said nothing.

"A whole new rule for Teacher Brumbach's blackboard!" Junior whispered loudly. "You look caught up to me!"

Webbie's whinny of a laugh escaped. "I *thought* you heard me!"

They watched the turtle extend its head just far enough to see them. Blink its wise eyes at them.

"Your name's Junior, right? My name's Webbie."

Junior puffed his chest out, imitating Teacher Brumbach. "You mean it's not Vebster?"

Webbie snickered. "Naw."

"Webbie, when the boys were tossing those marbles, why didn't you know your colors?"

"I *know* my colors. I just don't *see* them."

"What? You mean you can't see the yellowy orange marks on this turtle's tummy and back? You can't even see the orange of your own hair? Now that's a shame, 'cause your hair is some sight to see!"

Webbie rocked back on his heels. "Fact is, I know more colors than most boys. My mother's always teaching me new ones."

Junior smiled. "Like 'smoke'?" He pulled the marble from his pocket and handed it to Webbie.

"Where do you live?" Junior asked.

"Over there." He pointed past the creek and the cornfield behind the Thompsons' house.

"You live just on the other side of that field, Webbie? But I've seen you take the way by the Pike before, with the other boys. That'd be the long way round."

"I know." Webbie scraped his upper lip with his teeth. "I'm not 'sposed to be here."

"Why not?"

"Because this land belongs to your family. I'm not 'sposed to walk on land that does not belong to my family." Webbie wiggled his finger at the turtle, trying to tempt it to stick its head out further.

"Does the Pike belong to you?"

"No."

"Well."

Webbie rubbed his nose, thinking about this. "Some places are private. Like the privy, or land that doesn't belong to you. There's another word about the Pike. I forget it though."

It was Junior's turn to think. "You mean 'public'?"

"Buplic!" Webbie squealed his laugh.

"And what you gonna do when you get to the cornfield?" Junior asked.

Webbie grinned another grin that showed he was caught out. "Walk through it, I 'spose."

"You smile a lot for a boy who got the rod eight times." Junior raised and lowered the turtle again, gauging its weight. "That's a pretty big field. You might get lost." Junior's words wiped the grin off Webbie's face.

"I have an idea," Junior said. "This turtle's looking for water I reckon, and there's a creek right by that field. Let's take the turtle there and we can figure out how to get you through the field safe to home."

Webbie stood up and brushed the dirt off his pants. Junior tried lifting the turtle by himself, but it was wiggling and awkwardly heavy. Web pulled a deep breath, and offered to help.

When the boys reached Junior's land, a massive bloodhound ran to greet them. He stuck his black nose into each of the boys' chests. Tan folds of fur drooped from his wistful sloe eyes.

"Our dog Blood," Junior said, making the introduction as he scratched behind the eager dog's ears. Blood flopped one of his long ears across his eyes in pure delight, his humming whine so puppy-like, both boys hooted with laughter. Junior's pap stood outside his workshop and started teasing them about turning the turtle into soup.

"He's kidding," Junior said.

"How do you know?"

"Aw, Pap's just working up to one of his stories." Junior shrugged and added low, "Oh brother, we don't have time for this."

"I don't think a story would be so bad," Webbie said, still worried about the turtle's fate.

Junior's father said his name was Chance Thompson and shook Webbie's free hand. Then Mr. Thompson pulled several flat stones into a circle and squatted down with the boys and their turtle. He settled the largest, flattest stone onto a smooth straight stick, put the turtle on a path toward it, and began his tale with a question.

"Fellows, how many rocks do you think this old turtle can lift?" He launched into a tale about a boastful giant and a brave shepherd boy named David with strong faith, who would one day become a king.

It was a familiar story and afterward both boys agreed they would rather be David-clever than Goliath-strong.

"Pap, I think it's time to put Turtle in the creek." Junior elbowed Webbie as he said this.

"Are you trying to get rid of me, Son?" Chance grinned. "Some serious plans, eh? Well then, I best be back at work, too. Have fun." He chuckled as the boys picked up their turtle. Then he turned and ducked back into his workshop with Blood.

The boys found a spot along the creek where it narrowed and deepened and curved around the tallest oak tree.

"I know what let's do." Webbie looked up and down the oak tree. He pulled his shoes off. He grabbed the lowest branch with one hand while he found toeholds on stubs along the trunk. Webbie pulled himself up to the next branch and disappeared into the oak tree's lush upper reaches. He could see Junior standing close to the trunk, peering up after him into the mass of green leaves.

"For a big fellow you surely can climb!" Junior called out.

Webbie yelled down, "Don't you love how the bark smells like earth and green together?"

Webbie saw Junior feeling the tree's brutal skin with both hands, his face wistful, yet terrified.

"Wow! You can see everything from here!" Webbie let his voice float down. "Come up!"

A too-long pause before Junior responded, "I can't."

"Why not?"

Junior's face tilted up in terror. "I'm being … careful."

"Ah!" Webbie's voice shifted directions. "I see my house! Junior, watch while I shake this limb. It's pointing right to my house. Then we will know which way to go."

"I hear you. But I can't see you. Shake harder!"

Webbie grunted as he adjusted his position. It took more grunting and all of his body weight to ride his stout branch until the tree rustled and shuddered.

Junior's voice sounded tiny. "I see now. Don't crack it, you'll fall!"

Webbie squealed with laughter as he scrabbled his way down. He jumped the last few feet, smiling at Junior's astonishment.

"Now we know which way to walk! Plus we'll be able to see the oak tree all the way to the other side of the cornfield!" Webbie's grin dissolved into a frown. "How are we gonna get across the LeTort? Some parts are deep and the rapids run fast between the rocks."

"Let's build a bridge!" Junior slapped Webbie's back. "See those fallen trees in the woods?"

Webbie hesitated. "How 'bout you pull from water, I push from land?"

Junior was already tugging on the first slender log, as he stepped from rock to rock all the way across the LeTort while Web stood on the near bank and pushed the log into position. They worked five logs into a snug fit. The boys found flat-edged stones suitable for digging. They dug around the ends of the logs and pressed them into the softened creek bank until they were satisfied the logs would stay put.

They stood back to survey their work. Junior said, low, solemnly, "That's our bridge now, yours and mine."

"And our oak tree." Webbie lowered his voice too. "And field."

"Our field. Our oak tree. Our bridge. Let's not tell. Our secret."

"I can keep a secret," Webbie pledged.

Turtle seemed to like the spot too. It slipped right into the creek and lay there soaking. The boys tested the bridge carefully. Their mothers would not look kindly on wet, muddied school clothing. Just in case, they cuffed their pants to their knees. Junior, the taller, led. "See ya, Turtle!"

Webbie, the stouter, stepped gingerly. "Yes, see ya, Turtle!"

On the other side, Junior said, "Webbie, hold onto my shirttail and walk backwards. Keep an eye on that oak tree." Junior tramped through straggling weeds that managed to grow in the shadow of the cornstalks, sometimes having to spread stalks apart as he went. Web followed along.

"Next time, we'll take Pap's big knife along," Junior puffed, "and we can cut in a clear path. For keeps."

When at last they emerged from the field, sweat-soaked but relieved, and could see Webbie's back porch, he became so excited he lit off across the lawn toward it.

Then he stopped, turned around, and squinted at Junior. "You thirsty?"

Before they even opened the back porch door, the boys could hear Webbie's parents arguing.

"Blasted Copperhead!" his father's voice exploded.

Mrs. Henderson's voice was low but forceful. "Are you certain you heard him correctly?"

Webbie wagged a finger in front of his lips and tiptoed into the rear vestibule, waving in Junior. They stepped soundlessly through the formal dining room, skirting a long table. Their faces reflected in the mahogany sheen of the formal surfaces of the table and paneled room. They tiptoed past precisely folded linen napkins and a clock ticking its measure of each pause in the argument. A series of ancestral faces stared down at them from gilded frames. They passed a half-opened door leading to a kitchen spacious enough for a broad round oak table to occupy its center.

"You have two tables in one house!" Junior whispered.

They tiptoed down one corridor and turned, passing the front door, into a longer hall. With every careful step the voices grew louder, clearer. Webbie pressed against the wall near an open doorway. He motioned for Junior to join him.

"—knows where the Governor stands!" Mr. Henderson's anger vibrated through the wall, although all the boys could see was a book-lined corner of the room.

"Such bitter, factious opinions! A house so divided! How ironic, we call them parties." Mrs. Henderson's skirts rustled. "Peace seems impossible now, Robert." Her voice muffled, "Our world is cracking apart."

"The Volunteers are doubling up on drill sessions. Starting tonight."

Webbie flew around the corner and into the room, shouting, "Not tonight, Father! We're reading *Moby Dick* tonight! Remember?"

Junior remained alone in the doorway as Webbie clung to his parents, who were holding each other and did not see Junior. Mr. Henderson cupped his hand over his son's head, half buried in the folds of his mother's full skirt.

"You're right, Web, I'm sorry. The legislative session ended early today. Good news for dinner at home. Bad news for the country, most likely, as Pennsylvania voted for unity, which some other states no longer wish to honor. *Moby Dick* will wait 'til tomorrow night. Tonight I shall take you with me to the drills. There's no harm in your seeing a company of men organizing for conflict. Particularly since—"

Webbie looked up to see why his father stopped talking. His mother was staring open-mouthed and so, now, was his father. Webbie looked back over his shoulder. "That's my friend Junior Thompson. We're thirsty. Father, may Junior come to see the drills tonight?"

"Hello, Junior Thompson." Mrs. Henderson moved first, bent to shake Junior's hand. "I believe we know your father and mother. We must check with them first before we invite you to an, eh, *evening* event."

Frowning, Mr. Henderson sat down behind his desk and began arranging papers. Mrs. Henderson herded the boys back to the kitchen.

Webbie squirmed from beneath her guiding hand. "His parents are at home *now*! Can we check after we have some lemonade?"

The boys sat next to each other at the big round table in the kitchen, their hands wrapped around tall mugs. They sipped with noisy pleasure. Mrs. Henderson fixed a mug of lemonade for herself and was about to sit down when the front door slammed. She excused herself and ran out of the room.

"That's the first time I've seen a white lady run."

"My mudder runs all duh time." Webbie said this with his mouth full of toast, the look of it so funny and disgusting that Junior laughed, and then both boys snorted stinging mouthfuls of lemonade up their noses.

"What's wrong?" Web giggled.

"This!" Junior opened his mouth wide and gave Web a good look at its chewed contents. Webbie laughed with his eyes squeezed shut until his cheeks flushed pink.

Junior swallowed. "Why was your pap upset about a copperhead?"

"Oh, that's just a silly political party."

"What's a political party?"

"Well, it's not what you think." Web put his mug down and wiped his mouth with his sleeve. "Political parties are groups of grown-ups. They argue about how things should be."

"There's more than one?"

"Yes." Web sighed. "Some are dead, some are alive. My grandpa Henderson was the last Whig, and now it's dead. Not grandpa, the Whigs. My father's a Republican. They're alive and so are the Democrats and the Copperheads and I forget who else."

"Your parents argue a lot?"

"Sometimes." Webbie shifted in his chair.

"About whether there's gonna be a war?"

"Sometimes."

"Your pap's gonna go, right?"

Web nodded his head.

"Soon?"

Web shrugged his shoulders and took a big gulp of lemonade.

Junior nodded his head. "My pap wants to, but my folks don't talk about it. Or they wait 'til after I'm in bed. Your mam don't want him to go, right?"

Web rubbed his mouth with the back of his hand. "Sometimes she seems all proud. Other times she seems worried."

"What do you think? About a war?"

"You know our path through the cornfield? Like that."

Junior shook his head. "What do you mean, Webbie? That it's fun and exciting?"

"I mean, it looks like the short way home," Web spanked his hands free of crumbs. "But it's really not."

~September, 1860~

At Drills

Webbie sat on the floor cross-legged, watching his father and other men get ready for their drills practice. They had stacked and moved chairs to the far wall of a large meeting room in Marian Hall. Each man held a sword, the blunt-ended type that would not hurt anyone. Webbie's father had explained that these men were businessmen and friends, in a club called the Fencibles, with the Young Men's Christian Association.

Webbie wondered when he could have his own fencing sword to practice drills. Sometime when his father wasn't so busy, he would ask.

The men called his father "Captain," Webbie noticed. They lined up in four rows, four columns, with Webbie's father at the front, facing and directing them. Webbie had begun to count the men, when Junior came and sat cross-legged next to him. Junior's father stood in the doorway, long and straight, hat off, his hands folded over its rim.

Webbie's Uncle Nathan came and leaned against the other side of the door from Mr. Thompson. The two men nodded to each other, then turned to watch. Webbie waved and his uncle waved back. Webbie liked playing with Uncle Nathan because he smiled all the time and seemed young enough to remember being a boy. Webbie especially liked climbing onto his shoulders. With Uncle Nathan holding Webbie's legs tight, they would gallop all around the house and yard.

Now Mr. Thompson was holding his hat in one hand, working the other hand as if it had a bad itch that holding one of those swords would cure. The Young Christian Men paired off and were battling each other with their pretend swords. Junior whispered to Webbie, "We can do that. With cornstalks. Or some good, long, straight sticks."

Webbie nodded. The boys did not talk after that. They watched men parry and charge and march and stand at attention. They watched and remembered, so that they too could do all of these things with weapons of their own devising.

By the time his father guided their buggy into the carriage house, Webbie was dozing off at his side. Yancy met them with a lantern he placed on a wall hook to shed its watery yellow pool of light on their task of unhitching the horse.

Yancy led the horse as he walked alongside Captain Henderson, whose arms held Webbie, fast asleep.

"Preparing for war, sir?"

"Yes, Yancy. Looks like we're headed that way."

"How long?"

"Until war is declared? If Mr. Lincoln is elected, I would say mere months, if not weeks."

"And then how long?"

Captain Henderson stopped to look at Yancy. "You mean, how long will the conflict last? Not too long, I hope."

"Yessir, we hope." Yancy returned his gaze. "We had that hope in '12. Treaty signed in Feb'ry, 1815."

Rep. Henderson frowned, shifting Webbie to his other shoulder. "Against a rebellion, the Union states would already have a standing army. In addition, volunteer militias like ours are beginning to form all over the north. Any states in rebellion would have to raise troops and arm them. Create a government, mint currency. It's hard to imagine a rebellion lasting very long against such odds."

"Just thinking about provisioning for the family, sir." Yancy's gaze settled on Webbie. "If you be gone. Maybe we should hope for the best. Provision for the worst."

Captain Henderson stood silent for a long moment. The horse whinnied, pulled against Yancy's grasp.

"Point taken, Yancy." The father kissed his son's tousled hair and walked toward the house.

"Let's provision for the worst."

"Rocket's red glare, sir." Yancy said this low, squinting as he watched them disappear into the house. "Land of the free. Home of the brave."

Chance & Sarai Thompson

1850–1861, courtship and family

(Carlisle)

~June, 1850~

Dance

"Thompson!"

Even amid the voices of the rabble and thrum at market, Chance Thompson heard his best friend's greeting. Chance kept at sanding the edge of a small oak stool similar to the one he sat on and smiled without looking up at Quincy Graysom, who sauntered into Chance's booth and squatted on the stool next to him. Chance ducked as Graysom swung a banjo from his shoulder to his lap.

"Are you trying to kill me with your music?" Chance joked.

"Nope. You'll kill yourself working first." Graysom whistled and plucked a fragment of tune. "Market's crowded today. So how's business?"

"Take a look."

Graysom flipped open the hinged lid of a battered tin box. He whistled appreciatively. "Amazing. They ain't even painted nor shellacked. Other people's got every kind of color on their gewgaws and gimcracks."

"You calling my hand-carved stools gimcrack?"

"Naw, Thompson. Everybody knows you're a fine woodworker. Anyways, sell them fine furnishings fast, 'cause I got another opportunity for you."

"You going to talk me into spending my savings?"

"Nope." Playing a minstrel song now, Graysom smiled and nodded to passersby, his hat on the ground in front of him. Coins dropped in almost immediately. "Talk you into spending money? That never works. No sir, I propose a party. You think your daddy Ben Robert Thompson will let us use his property tonight?"

"Party? What's the occasion?"

Graysom hummed softly as he played "Old Folks at Home." "My friends from Maryland showed up today, in their hay wagon."

"Free or freed?"

"Freed. Quaker family from Baltimore. Two brothers. Here with their two sisters."

Chance, back to sanding, made no response.

"Yessir, two fine ladies." Graysom looked sideways at his friend. "I even have nicknames for them both."

Chance blew off a fine dust and held the stool high to inspect it. Immediately a customer lifted it from his hands and asked for the price. Chance tucked the money into his box.

Graysom nudged him. "Listen here: nicknames are Fire and Ice." He launched into a spirited rendition of "Camptown Races."

"My, oh, my." Chance pushed him off the stool and placed it on the front ledge of the market's raw-edged plank table that served as his booth. "Last two!" He called out. "Solid oak!"

"You see, Fire is a feisty, fast-talking, full-figured gal," he said under the music, into Chance's ear. "While Ice says nary a word. Tiny slip of a gal. But oh, oh, Oh!" Graysom slipped right into strumming "Oh! Susanna."

The next customer bought both remaining stools and dropped the change into Graysom's upturned hat.

Graysom whistled his admiration. "Now I take that as a sign!"

Chance shook his head as he packed up.

"Daddy Ben Robert, here we come!" Graysom crowed.

Ben Robert Thompson had a small farm with dairy cows. He was known to the white community for his smooth butter and flavorful iced creams. Now, he stood just outside his dairy barn, watching the two young men hurry down to a flat expanse of yard below and busy themselves with preparations.

Chance and Graysom scythed the grass extra short, for dancing. Dusk gave way to a clear night dense with starlight and the romance of a smiling quarter-moon. They set up a refreshment table and hung some oil lamps on nearby posts. Young people began arriving, by foot, by horse, and by wagon. The elder Thompson strolled past, sniffing the beverages and pointing his cane to underscore the rules.

"No booze, Mr. Thompson," Graysom confirmed, shaking his head with a schoolboy's earnestness.

"No cussing." Chance looked sidelong at Graysom. "And no ungentlemanly conduct."

Satisfied, Mr. Thompson started back toward the farmhouse. "Nothing wrong with a bit of dancing." He paused, winked. "Mrs. Thompson, rest her soul, could turn her heels. She surely could."

Chance and Graysom took their positions on a small wooden platform. Graysom tuned his banjo while Chance arranged items repurposed for percussion: washboard, bucket drums, saw, and a hand-made tambourine. They would play some popular music but preferred folk tunes and music of their own improvising. As guests began to arrive, Chance and Graysom started playing.

Several songs into the evening, Graysom sashayed across the band platform. "They're here!" He elbowed Chance. "Fire and Ice!"

Heads turned in the wake of the striking women and their tall and solemn-faced escorts. The ladies looked this way and that, nodding greetings. Chance had no trouble sorting out Fire from Ice. Fire wore a flowing white cotton dress gathered just below her shapely bosom. She had woven into her hair a fireworks array of ribbons: red, purple, green, yellow, blue. Her laugh lit up her face and spread among the people around her. Ice walked behind her, a sprite in a sea-green pinafore over a slim ivory dress with lace-beribboned sleeves. Her braided hair was tied with ivory lace ribbons that trailed down her back. Shy smile. Slender and soft as a pussy willow branch. *A pussy willow princess.*

Graysom, in Chance's ear, "Do you know you said that out loud?"

"Said what?"

"'A pussy willow princess.' You said that. Right out loud. Right when she walked past. Maybe she even heard you," said Graysom, laughing. "And you haven't played a lick since they showed up."

Chance resumed playing, reluctantly. Like the other male partygoers, he stared after they passed but lost his nerve and looked away when they turned and approached. In his callow youth, he had pressed his attentions on women in a way that shamed him now. This bewildered feeling was new. *What's wrong with you, Thompson*, he scolded himself.

"Talking to yourself again." Graysom looked irritated. He felt trapped too, Chance guessed. "And I see you looking, Thompson."

"I'm going to bang this drum harder to cover up your fool remarks."

"No one's asked them to dance. Better get out there, 'fore I beat you to the punch."

"Why don't you go, Graysom?"

"'Cause you're so slow, boy, I gotta give you a head start."

"Who's going to dance, with those brothers hovering like guard dogs?"

"Zech and Jamie? They're Friends. Harmless."

As if on cue, one of the brothers approached the bandstand with a sack slung over his shoulder. In one beefy hand he carried a high stool and set it down. He reached in his sack and pulled out a fiddle. "May I play with you boys?"

Graysom made introductions. "Zech Tilghman, Chance Thompson." Zech got right down to business. He played a country ayre.

Chance beat his drums like an enemy.

"Now you making us all sound bad! Just go!" Graysom growled.

"All right!"

"All right, what?" Fire stood grinning in front of Chance's table, hands on hips.

"As a dancer he's all right," Graysom butted in. "Just all right." Graysom changed tempo, firing up a rollicking quick-step.

"We'll just see!" Fire stuck out one hand and, laughing, swung Chance with her into the fray of dancers.

As they wove past the other dancers, Chance stole glances at Ice. She stood in the shadow between two pole lanterns, yet something caught his eye. As they danced closer, Chance noticed that sister Ice seemed to glitter. Her dress—or was it her skin?—somehow caught the starlight. Or was it light from that sly-grinning moon?

"That's my sister, Sarai."

"Oh!" Chance snapped to attention, embarrassed. "Excuse my poor manners. I'm Chance Thompson."

"Ester." She dimpled. "Ester Tilghman. We're from Baltimore. Tell me, does thy friend dance as well as he plays?"

"No." Chance smiled at her generous laughter before adding, "Better. He dances circles around me."

"That would be something to see. The two of you. Dancing. In circles."

"I mean …"

She shook her head to show she was teasing.

"Your brother's good at the fiddle."

Ester nodded. "He sings too. Thanks to Zech, I do believe I can get thy friend to join us now."

So it was Ester who circled round and pulled Graysom into the dance as smoothly as she had with Chance, so that Chance's two-stepping brought him directly in line with Sarai.

Focus on a goal, Chance told himself as he stared at her. *Or two. Find out what makes her sparkle like that. And try to get her to smile.*

As it happened, he managed to achieve the second goal first, by bumping into a whirling fellow, and falling over. Sarai appeared above him and offered her hand.

Shy, the hand.

Inviting, the smile.

~September, 1860~

Home

He squinted up the road. Still no Junior.

"Chance, did you hear what I said?" Sarai stood at his elbow. "I know she's a white teacher, too, but we could send him to Miss Sarah Bell's colored public school at the A.M.E. church."

"No way. I pity those poor children in that damp basement, and nary a book."

"What about the colored school in Miz Keech's house?"

"That's thirty mile, Sarai." His voice drifted in, as if from far away. "'Twouldn't be right for a boy his age to be traveling that distance. Even on a horse."

"He could board there. Come home and help here on the weekends."

"No." Chance Thompson shook his head. "No. He's fine. Besides, we've already taught him at home for one year, waiting for a better time."

She matched the corners of the linen tablecloth precisely and folded it against her waist twice, until it was a smooth ivory square the size of her lap. She carefully laid it in the basket. "He is the only one."

"Just like I was the only one. And my papa. And his papa. That's how I know. People don't get too worked up when there's only one."

"The other children are hard on him."

When Chance turned, finally, to meet her gaze, his wife could see he was straining to gentle his voice. "There are all different kinds of hard, Sarai. This one is not so bad."

"What if someone picks a fight? He will not even—"

"Sarai." He folded his massive hands over her shoulders and gave them a gentle squeeze. "Your upbringing was different from mine. Maybe not free, but sheltered. Freedom costs. I know all about that. Now he may be the *only one,*" he pitched his voice high in imitation, to get her to return his smile. "But he is not alone. Immanuel ..."

"'Our God is with us."

"Yes, ma'am, that's right. If God is with us, who can be against us?"

"Nobody." Her lip trembled.

"Is our son smart?"

"Yes."

"Is he learning?"

"Yes."

"Well then." Chance broke into a chuckle, his eyes bright. "Here he comes now. Through the woods. And what do y'know, he is not alone."

Two boys, aged seven and eight, walked with their heads huddled, talking and carrying something between them. Robert Junior, though younger, stood a few inches taller than the stockier fellow, a white boy. Suddenly the boys shrieked with laughter, arms rippling up and away from their bodies.

"Hmmm." Chance squinted, shielding his eyes against sunlight in a brilliant blue sky. He grinned down at Sarai. "Nothin' quite like a big ole box turtle to bring two boys together." He framed his mouth with his hands and called out, "Junior! Looks like a mighty fine SOUP turtle!"

The boys shrieked again. Chance's dog Blood loped over to investigate. Chance laughed and turned to wink at Sarai, before striding over to help them.

Sarai could hear the voices of Chance and the boys mingling from across the yard where they huddled. She sat on her stump, folding her linen tablecloth in just the right way, so that it would fit into the wooden box at her side. She tucked the tablecloth deep in her lap and carefully lifted the box to her knees, fingered the S carved into its lid. S for Sarai. Chance had made it for her. Her treasure box. She opened its lid slowly, as if for the first time, anticipating the luster of its contents. Sure enough, sunlight found the gold timepiece and chain, its glow illuminating the palm of her hand as she cradled it.

"Papa." She breathed. She slipped the timepiece back into the box and picked up a cardboard-mounted photograph. "I see you, Papa," she smiled. His hair looked wild. Illness had dulled and hollowed his face into a death mask, though his shoulders still bore their proud set.

After James Tilghman had been freed, he worked as a laborer, then as a bootblack and finally as a steward for the B&O Railroad until he took sick. After that he had come to Carlisle to live near Ester and Sarai, both newly wed.

She pressed her fingers to the corners of her eyes. "I'm not gonna cry, Papa," she whispered. "And I'm not gonna fuss about what you said the photographer's wife wrote on the frame. She's just an old fool." She tapped each word with her finger. "'James. Tilghman. Bootblack. A Character of Carlisle.' Like you always said, Papa, People see what they wants to see. Change comes slow. But change comes."

She chuckled. "Like here, Papa." She lifted the crisp edge of a new document from the box, admiring its official authority. "It's the deed, Papa. We got the deed!"

Sarai had marked the center of their land with an uprooted tree stump. She sat on it now. She looked up to see Chance and the boys squatting with the turtle by a pile of rocks. To her left, she saw the creek, and the neighbor's fields beyond. To her right, she saw their woodland and knew their own farmland fanned beyond it in neat and pretty rows. Her vision opened up a seam of time. She saw people walking through the woods, adults with children on their shoulders, strong young people leading the gray-headed ones. Future generations of her family, and Chance's family, she realized in awe, before the vision faded.

Her gaze settled on the covered wagon that became their home every weekend. Nearby, Chance Thompson's workshop, and their home rising up from a sure foundation on their very own land. It needed only a roof now, and finishing the interior walls and floor.

Land. Home. The words warmed her tongue. Luminous as Papa's gold watch, yet timeless. She watched Chance play with Junior and his new friend. "Play with a purpose," Chance always said. She could hear the bubbling of their voices, not the actual words. Chance sliding a stick under a rock. Stacking smaller rocks on one side. Now the turtle lifting itself onto the other side of the rock. She could guess at the teaching, part homily, with learning about some practical skill. "Build character and talents together," another of Chance's sayings. "No, not sayings," she corrected herself. "*Doings*. Robert Chance Thompson does what he says." She chuckled. "Sampson's story, that's my guess."

She smiled again, humming a half-remembered tune. Soon there would be other families, their friends, gathered here to help. The men had made a pact to help each other secure land and build homes. The women would revive their circle of campfires from the previous weekend and cook, while the men and boys took full advantage of remaining daylight. Then a delicious supper. *Why does food always taste better when shared?* And afterwards, campfire coffee, music and conversation while the children played tag by firelight. Then reluctantly, one by one, into their wagons to sleep under the stars, before rising with the sun.

Just a few campfire weekends left. The house was almost finished. Sarai tasted the bittersweet of one blessing soon ending, another beginning. *Both bitter and sweet,* she said to herself. *Taste them both. Favor neither*. Aloud she said softly, "Lord, Lord. Thank you, Lord." Sarai held this rare moment of contented reflection in her heart, savoring it.

~September, 1860~

Into Town

Junior wanted to go early to see his friend at the drills practice and pleaded, "Can we ride in the wagon, Pap?" *Sometimes it's healthier and wiser for a family like ours to walk,* Chance mused. *How do you explain that to a seven-year-old?* He answered, "No son, it'll be a nice evening for walking. Let's eat fast and get an early start."

As they set off, Chance couldn't resist the proud grin that grew as he observed his boy. Junior's eyes were the first feature anyone noticed, and the hardest to describe. Unblinking. So clear, so deep. Pre-dawn gray, shot through with rays of green and blue, even a hint of purple when angry. Junior wore his favorite blue shirt. Intense blue. It suited him. Knickers the color of summer grass in a dry season, more brown than green. His shirt was not tucked in, and why should it be, when you're seven? He wore a pair of shoes he had outgrown. Sarai had cut out the toes and the backs, handed them to Junior, and said, "A pair of sandals just like Jesus wore." His eyes had gotten big, as if he could see in a whole new way the past and future spread around him. Those sandals had already taken him on some good adventures.

Smart gal, my Sarai. Junior's got her smarts. Whatever cleverness I have resides in my hands. And I do believe my son has my hands, thank you, Lord. Junior's height was about right for a boy his age. His skin about five shades lighter than his mam's, about two shades darker than Chance's.

Bearing Junior almost killed Sarai. *Something amiss with her woman's organs. Pain so terrible I had to look away a few times.* The midwife had declared, "'Tis a miracle this child's even alive!"

What thundering, overwhelming joy! Chance had thought his heart would burst. He never knew he could feel joy like that. *His tiny chest working hard, his little circle of a mouth gulping air like a caught fish gasps for water. 'Til he breathed proper and became himself, his newborn baby skin took on the oddest colors, shades of purple and yellow.* Chance had held him up so an exhausted Sarai could share in the joy, see what her labors had wrought. But when she laid eyes on the baby, she looked at Chance in a way he had not seen before or since. Not joy. Shame? Disappointment? Anger? It was a riddle wrapped in a mystery. Chance rubbed his chin, remembering. The midwife had seen it too, presumed Sarai was worked up about whether the baby would live. She'd said, "Don't worry. I'll wrap and massage the boy, get his little lungs working good."

She started to take Junior from me. I said, "Wait. Let her hold her son."

They had both looked at Sarai. Her eyes closed. Arms crossed over her chest. The midwife looked at Chance, then walked off clucking and patting the baby's back. *Sarai doesn't like to talk about that day. Won't talk about it.*

"Pap, any bear in these woods?"

"No, Junior. All the bear got tired of being shot at and hurried their hides up into the South Mountains."

Junior studied the shadow ridges as if he had never seen them before. *That's how he is. Always looking for something new. The story behind the scene.*

"What about wolves, Pap?"

"People say there are no more wolves around here. I'm not so sure. See, now, a wolf's a sneaky animal. They'll steal into a farm, sniffing out chickens. If a careless farmer gives him half a chance, he'll grab a hen and run. He and his wolf wife and wolf son Junior have a nice chicken dinner."

"Do wolf parents love their wolf children?"

"Sure. Wolves are proud of their pups. And partners. Could as likely be a she-wolf at the henhouse door."

"Did a wolf ever come to eat our chickens?"

"Yes. She or he—I'll say, it—came by once when you were a babe and we started coming out here in the wagon. We just bought the land, so no hen house then. Just a few chicks and a low wire fence and some crates tacked together. I never thought I'd see one 'cause as I say, people figured they had all cleared out from these parts. One morning I climbed out of the wagon ready to greet the dawn and also relieve my bladder. There it was: Wolf. Ready to jump into that pen, but fixing its hungry yellow eyes on me."

"Do wolves eat people?"

"Wolves will surely attack to defend if you don't pay proper respect. I recollected what my papa Ben Robert taught me, as his grand-papa White Elk taught him. Wolves are grouchy, so don't look them in the eye. Speak to them in their language. When you hear them answer back with breathing more like a dog, less like a wolf, listen to what they say."

"What did you say? And what did Wolf say back?"

"Remind me, Junior, when we are in the woods, and I'll teach you all the wolf-talk I can recollect. For now, I can tell you the translation. I said, 'Greetings, what brings you here?' Wolf answered immediately, 'I am hungry.' My reply was, 'Why eat a little chick that's nothing but bones and feathers when I can toss you a nice hunk of salted venison?' Wolf replied, 'That sounds good. And how about a song?'"

"A song?" Junior laughed. "Wolves like music?"

"This one did. I said, 'Stay right where you are. I'll sing to you while I fetch the venison. When I toss it over your head, run and keep running. We want no trouble here.'

"'Fine,' said Wolf. 'It would be rude not to take it and share with my family. Besides, salted meat requires a nice drink of water.'"

"What song did you sing?"

"My favorite hymn, of course."

"Come Thou Fount?"

"That's right. I sang it to you from the time you were a babe. Now you know why. Want to sing it now? Like we're entertaining that wolf together."

Junior nodded. Chance started them out and Junior's voice chimed in, a bright clear thread wrapping around his pap's.

Come, Thou Fount of every blessing,
Tune my heart to sing Thy grace;
Streams of mercy, never ceasing,
Call for songs of loudest praise ...

"It's okay to sing loud, Pap?"

"Of course."

"Who's Ebenezer?"

"You jumping ahead to the next verse?" Chance mussed Junior's soft fuzz of hair and hummed his way to the proper lyrics.

Here I raise my Ebenezer,
Here by Thy great help I've come;
And I hope, by Thy good pleasure,
Safely to arrive at home.

"What meaning do you take from it, Junior?"

"That Ebenezer is a what, not a who?"

"Right as rain. An Ebenezer reminds us that God is real, and always close by."

"Do you have an Ebenezer, Pap?"

"That song's an Ebenezer for me. Just like it was for the person who wrote it. I do have other Ebenezers. You. Your mam. I see you both as promises to me God kept, in an overflowing generous way. And that knife I have, belonged to my great-grandpap, White Elk? That's an Ebenezer, too."

"I like the verse about wandering the best," Junior said.

"Why is that son?"

"I like to wander."

Junior's confession so stung Chance, he forgot to sing. "What sort of wandering do you think the song means, Junior?"

It was Junior's turn to hum through. "Just like it says, Pap. The going away kind of wandering." He began singing, loud and strong. Chance had trouble steadying his breathing. This time it was the father's voice that caught up and threaded through the son's melody.

Prone to wander, Lord, I feel it,
Prone to leave the God I love;
Here's my heart, O take and seal it,
Seal it for Thy courts above.

It took Chance a few minutes to find the right words for what he wanted to say to his son. And then he tried to time the words to their stride, so as to keep the anxious out of his voice.

"God's going to hold on tight to your heart, and He's not going to give it back because He loves you so much. More even than"—Chance stopped talking to swallow the catch in his throat—"More even than your mama's love and mine. Put together. Hard as that is to imagine."

Junior didn't answer right away. Chance could tell he was thinking this over. When he did, his voice sounded deeper. Older. "Yes, Pap."

They reached a rise in the road and the town appeared before them suddenly, spreading on a curve to the horizon.

"Here we are." They arrived at the door of a plain-faced brick building. Chance held the door open for Junior. Its interior closed in on them cavelike, their eyes preferring daylight. The rug underfoot felt thin, smelled of mildew. From some inner place, they heard men's voices and the muffled clang of metal instruments. They could smell exertion.

They followed the voices and metallic din to a large meeting space, its door propped open, as if inviting spectators. Junior raced in to join Webbie and sat next to him on the floor. Chance blinked. Was it only his imagination, or did those two boys have an aura about them? Something irresistibly beautiful bursting forth from their friendship? Some special bond that jumped right over curious or judgmental glances and made people look a second time, more carefully? *They make it seem so easy, so natural*, Chance thought. *Like they're saying, "See here, World: this is how it's done."*

Chance Thompson stood just inside the door. He let his shoulders ease back against the wall. He was still standing straight, just giving his wearied body a little respite. He watched the boys cutting up, the men lining up. As the Pennsylvania Volunteers began their maneuvers, Chance felt someone approach, looked over to see a much younger, fair-haired copy of Robert Henderson, leaning against the other side of the doorway. Chance had seen him before at the mill, though they'd never had occasion to speak. The younger man wore an easy smile. Underneath it though, he held himself tense. Almost like he had a watch coil inside, being wound tighter and tighter with every minute's worth of spectating. *How can a fellow that young be so tightly bound*? When Chance leaned across to introduce himself, the other man startled. Chance saw specks of perspiration on his upper lip.

"What—" he said.

"Name's Chance Thompson."

"Thompson?" He blinked hard, as if waking from a nightmare. "I know that name. How do I know your name? From the mill?"

"Yes. And isn't that your brother leading the pack? I'm overseeing the addition on his house."

He relaxed after Chance's "leading the pack" remark. And recollected his manners. "Nathan Henderson." He extended his hand, shook Thompson's briefly and firmly. "Yes, that's Robert leading, and in the back row, that's our middle brother, Willy, the one with the dark, full beard. Thompson, eh? You have a woodworking shop between Robert's place and our mill, right? Been meaning to pay a visit." The conversation ended there. Chance kept his thoughts to himself, though he might have shared them with the other fellow, had he been open to conversing. *Myself, I have trouble understanding the value of formal drills. But I could see myself going into battle alongside these men. They have determination, I feel it stirring in my soul. They too have families and a history they feel duty-bound to protect. But all this marching and about-facing and draw your weapons? Me, I'm a load-and-shoot man.*

Right about when Chance started thinking about summoning Junior for the walk home, Captain Henderson barked a "Halt!" The men froze facing forward. *Facing me? No, truly, facing Nathan.* The Captain moved toward Chance and Nathan, to the front of the four columns of men, and laid a hand on his brother's shoulder. Chance noticed how Nathan flinched under the Captain's grip. But he stayed put while the Captain explained the next thing.

"Gentlemen, we shall spend the remaining time in freelance maneuvers, as in close combat. Lieutenant McAndrews is distributing wooden handguns for this exercise. Thank you, Lieutenant. The fencing sword represents a bayoneted rifle. You all know Nathan Henderson, Willy's and my brother. Some men are born fighters. My brother Nathan is one of them. If you have hunted with him or competed against him, you know. Of course, if you want to ascribe that talent to defending himself against two older brothers, that's up to you!"

Captain Henderson waited for the laughter to die down before continuing. "You also know that this is Nathan's first time attending these drills. And that he is a private man. So let's address him as Private Nathan, shall we?"

Some men laughed like they weren't sure they were supposed to. The two brothers stepped toward each other, Chance saw them make fists and thought, *Looks like they're squaring off!*

Robert kept his eyes on Nathan when he spoke again. "I am going to volunteer Private Henderson for this next demonstration. Again, the scenario is combat close in, using bayoneted rifle and handgun. This demonstration's rules are simple. If he touches your hand or arm, you release the weapon that hand holds. If he touches your head or chest, you are down. Likewise, if you touch his hand or arm, his weapon goes down; touch his head or chest, and he is down. Private Henderson."

Nathan faced all those men, pale in the lantern light, staring at him. Fencing foils quivering straight up. Wooden guns pointing straight ahead. Looked so absurd yet frightful, Chance didn't know whether to laugh or run for cover. Nathan gave a sudden piercing shout and became a blur. Men's faces in the front row went to shock the instant before they dropped down. Nathan chopped at necks, slashed hands, kicked weapons out of hands, slugged opponents on the head with his gun. The rest of the company came awake, charging at him. Nathan grabbed the Captain and held him up like a shield, pushing his brother along over his struggling and shouts and still mowing down the rest with the rip-saw blur of his pretend bayonet. He shoved his human shield like he was playing duckpins, the man bowled into an entire remaining column that way. Chance had seen barroom brawls in his wooly youth, but this was way and away different. *The man's a killing machine.* Chance found himself wondering what Nathan Henderson's older brothers might have done to him, this brother in particular. Even though Nathan's weapons were fake, Chance saw the look of pure amazement on the faces of his so-called enemies. Nathan disarmed them with a surprise third weapon: his voice. He screamed and yelled, slashed right, left, right, knocking weapons out of hands, backing the rest of the company into a corner to finish his work.

"Halt! Keep your positions!" Captain shouted, picking himself up from where he had landed. Men lay all over the floor, some piled atop each other. All that was missing was blood. Nathan stood wild-eyed, breathing hard, his arms and legs akimbo, his weapons silvered with sweat, the Captain's flushed face a rock, hard to read. Around the mouth, twitches of pride in his brother's performance. In his eyes, extreme displeasure. His voice sliced the same deadly way his brother's sword did. Captain did not need to shout to devastate.

"We shall encounter surprise attacks. The advantage should last but a few seconds. Not the entire battle! We shall encounter opponents with skills equal to, or exceeding, Private Henderson's. If we succumb to intimidation, we have already lost! How can we gain advantage over the enemy?" He paused. No one volunteered an answer. "After the body is strong and ready, the real preparation is mental." His eyes swept the company of men and came to rest on his brother Nathan.

"Kill! Or be killed!"

Chance lifted Junior by one arm and hurried him out the door, Junior's feet scrabbling, his body trying to turn back.

"Pap, Pap!" Junior cried, loud enough so the whole room surely heard him.

"I gotta get me a gun and sword like that!"

~June, 1861~

Gift

Chance Thompson's bloodhound raised his head and sniffed the air. He sensed the stranger's presence well before his master did. Blood stood, alert, rumbling a warning.

"How do you manage such straight work with a crooked knife?"

Chance finished the cut before turning to the man standing in the workshop doorway, shadowed by a brilliant summer afternoon.

Thompson laid down the knife so that his visitor could see the handle. "I think I recognize your voice, but I can't see your face, 'cause you're standing in my light."

The visitor stepped into the workshop. "Nathan Henderson. We spoke at Marian Hall last year." He patted the dog's head as it nosed him.

"The drills."

"Yes, the drills my brother captains. Mr. Thompson, you have quite a reputation for woodwork and construction. You've done g-g-good work for my brother. And father. My father is not a man to hand out compliments. But I heard him tell someone our milling machines would not work, if he did not have Thompson making replacement parts for him."

Chance extended his hand in greeting. "Thank you for passing along that word. Your father is a clever businessman. I've learned from him." He nodded toward the knife. "My great-grandfather was Indian. He made that knife." Thompson picked it up and continued working as he talked. "You watched me use it so you know my thumb fits in this space and I pull the knife toward me. The crooked design keeps it level in my hand. The handle's carvings tell a story about its maker. I can feel the story in my hand as I work."

Nathan pulled a piece of paper from a pocket inside his jacket, but his eyes wandered all over the workshop interior. "You show the same care in all your projects. This shop looks like a fine piece of furniture in every detail."

"My wife Sarai says she loves cleaning this place over any other 'cause she doesn't get splinters when she dusts." Thompson chuckled. "'Course I don't let her dust here too often."

Nathan ran his fingers along the workbench, to the wall, to molding around the window. "It takes so much time to do things right, as my father says. All those projects though. How do you g-g-g—"

"I have some good men, teachable men, working with me." Chance silently scolded himself for interrupting Nathan. He remembered his own father's admonition, *Let another soul speak.*

Nathan spread out a drawing onto an open space on the workbench. "My brother Robert celebrates his tenth wedding anniversary this year."

"I'll be sure to offer congratulations. It's number eight for Sarai and me." Chance looked at the drawing as Nathan spoke. "Well, sir, this is a big year for anniversaries as we had two weddings in our family in 1851. My brother Robert's wife Mag-g-gie has a sister Becky in Baltimore."

"Never had the pleasure of meeting her sister," Chance said. "Met her brother though. Henry, right? I seem to recollect he's a friend of your brother Robert. Henry and Robert came in my shop one day, referred to me by your father. Made Henry's wedding gift for Mrs. Henderson, matter of fact. A lap desk. Brass inscription and lock laid in flush." Chance nodded his head. "That's right," he said, half to himself. "That was some fine cherry he brought from their parents' home. 'Twas a joy to work that wood."

Nathan nodded politely but was obviously anxious to move on to his drawing. "We shall g-g-gather for a g-g-grand celebration. Mag-g-gie—desires an autumn g-g-garden party. You are quite familiar with my brother's property, Sharon." He turned the drawing toward Chance. "The addition you're working on now, located here." Nathan pointed as he talked. "The house, here, of course. Straight pathway through the g-g-garden, here, and your addition, on the other side. Currently no outbuildings in the g-g-garden. There is space here for one, in the lawn, open to g-g-guests seated here, and the creek view beyond. Mag-g-gie's family home in Maryland has an outbuilding, looks something like this." Nathan pointed to a detail in his sketch.

"Yes, they're in fashion now, what do people call them, something like, 'I sees a 'bo ..."

Nathan laughed. "G-g-gazebo, same idea. Personally I don't see or g-g-gaze the appeal. 'Tis their party. In any case, I mean t' g-g-give it as my g-g-gift. However with less than four months' time, weather permitting. Would you have enough time?" He stood straight, folded his arms.

Thompson studied the plan. "The land is level here. Guests can walk from house, through garden, to this gaze-ebo? That right? Dimensions here correct, sixteen foot diameter? You show a round structure, we'd need to settle on the number of wall facets. Six? Eight? Eight it is. Raised floor? Bench? Tighter-fitting boards, so people don't trip and the lady's heels don't get ruined, yet some space for the wood to forgive changes in weather. Yessir, you have to think of everything. Latticework skirt around? White wash? You'd supply lumber, whitewash and materials—I mean ALL materials, so's I don't need to lay out my own cash? Good." He rubbed the close-cropped nap of his hair in concentration, picked up a stub of charcoal pencil and jotted a few numbers on a scrap of paper.

Meanwhile, Nathan picked up his drawing, puzzling through another question. "We need to include a layer of tar in the roof, in case of rain. How many people could stand there under cover, do you think? Twenty?"

"About that, seated. More standing." Chance Thompson cleared his throat. When Nathan met his gaze, Chance named his price. The drawing in Nathan's hand fluttered to the floor. He opened his mouth. No words came out, and he closed it.

Chance waited. This was a moment he enjoyed. He could look into a customer's eyes and see the reflection of angels' swords—not the angels themselves, but the flashing silver edges of their weapons which the Great Book says is sharper than any made by human hand.

"Well I suppose the best worker deserves to charge the highest fee. A smarter man would have saved my father's compliment 'til after neg-g-gotiation," Nathan said, looking rueful.

"You strike me as a man who's both smart and fair."

Nathan accepted the compliment with a smile. "Let's set a completion date of September 30th. Can we agree to completion of everything, including whitewashing, at least two weeks prior, to allow for weather? And could we further agree to the rate and not a penny more, come what may?"

Thompson thought a moment. "Barring damage beyond our control."

"Of course. Fire, flood, acts of G-g-god. Can't take it out on your hide, what nature causes."

Thompson did not blink.

Nathan inhaled deeply. "All right then. Shake on it?"

Chance took Nathan's extended hand. Nathan, crossing over with his other hand, reached for Thompson's free hand. "Feel the strength in that handshake? In the one hand, we have a deal. And in the other, a partnership."

"Yes, and I will also spell out on paper what we just agreed to," Thompson added. "For I find that the strongest partnerships have a clear writ of agreement supporting them. Including terms." Thompson stood firm, though he felt Nathan's grip loosening.

"Terms?"

"Those that your father's bankers taught him. And I, on the receiving end, learned by hard experience. How to ask for half the money up front. Then leaven the investment of time with even monthly payments on the balance so that when a job's done, a final payment is made with great satisfaction all round. With that first half payment due now."

Nathan returned his steady look. "Well then Mr. Thompson, Chance, I shall need my hand back to reach my wallet."

Chance grinned. "Mine as well, to receive your pay. Partner."

~June, 1861~

Sticks and Stones

Early the next morning, Chance Thompson walked with Blood to Sharon, Robert and Maggie Henderson's estate. He knew that he could not begin the gazebo project until he and his workers made more progress on the addition at Sharon.

Chance began every onsite work day in the same way. He sat down on the ground, letting his legs splay apart. The worksite tent was pitched behind him, plans spread on a portable wood table Chance had designed. His laborers would not arrive for another hour. Before every building job, he reserved this particular hour—the one in which daylight crept in and conquered darkness—to pray, and to review plans.

"Lord, you know how all things happen and what's to be. I got my matters writ down, but You got all your plans in memory. Must be nice not to need paper."

Chance chuckled and picked up a stick, scratched the property in miniature on the patch of earth between his knees. At this hour, he could still barely distinguish the outline of his own hand figured against the dark earth.

"'Course, when you became a man, and a man of profession similar to mine, you picked up a stick—like this one maybe—and scratched a note or two in the sandy earth." Chance wrote a name in the dust: HENDERSON.

His dog snatched the stick and pranced with it in his mouth, ready to play. Chance shifted his attention from the Almighty to the dog. "You remember Old Colonel Henderson, don't you, Blood? Gave me my first building job. Well, this is his eldest son's land." The dog dropped the stick and settled next to him, and Chance gave him a good scratching behind the ears. Chance's smile faded, remembering.

"How I hated his father, the Colonel. Fooled me bad on that first job. Said, 'Thompson, how'd you like to build me a barn on my Oakland property? Pay you a thousand dollars.' A thousand dollars! What man would say no to that deal? Least I had him write it down. Sometimes the writ word can hurt more than help. Learned that lesson for sure. Battling that rocky pick-ax soil. How I had to beg, borrow, and pay white folks for materials. How my workers had to choose between their regular farm employ or work for me. I had to pay them over and above just to keep them. Finished in the dead of winter. By some cold, hard miracle."

Blood whined softly, craned his neck. Chance exhaled a hollow laugh. "If memory serves, I prayed the whole time through gritted teeth! Barely kept my calm to collect that last payment. Largest pay, of course. Hungry, broke. Had spent my last penny getting that barn built. In debt too, at high interest. Colonel Henderson held that cigar between his fingers while he handed me the money. Not even a thank you.

"I counted the money while I walked. Stopped dead. Overpaid by $100! 'Now what, Lord?' I said. But the Lord held His tongue. The Colonel still standing there, waiting. 'Sir,' I said. 'There's too much money here.' That awful laugh of his makes you for a fool. 'How much?' he asked. I said, 'One hundred.' He waved me over. He took the hundred dollar bill. Pulled a roll of cash from his pocket. Peeled off another hundred dollar bill and added it to the first. Handed it to me. 'Thompson, know what a college education costs?' Not exactly, I said. He just laughed that ugly laugh, but I got the point.

"You should have been there, Blood. To help hold me back. *My* blood picked that moment to boil over. But I kept my voice even when I said, 'Then I overpaid, Colonel Henderson. That education was a journeyman's education, not a proper college education. See, 'tisn't enough to read, write, do proper bookkeeping, and keep your word as a man. That's what I learned. No sir, for the cost of a proper college education, I expect to know how the surveyor does his art. How the businessman deals with the banker and his suppliers. When to buy and when to borrow. How 'bout this, Colonel Henderson: these hundred dollar bills you fancy as your reward to a colored man for his honesty? How about you really deliver on the education you say you gave me? And when we're through, I'll give you back this money as a bonus?' Surely goodness and mercy, that man saw the hatred I had for him writ all over my face!

"What did he do then?" Chance brushed flecks of dirt from Blood's coat, admiring by first light the field all around him, glittering silver with dew. "Well, he looked me up and down. Dropped that cigar butt, ground it dead under his boot. Looked me in the eye and told me to meet him at his mill in the half hour before closing time on the following day. And every day after that, 'til all my questions were answered. Blood, I learned more and saw more than I care to recall. And not just about business. About that family, too. Robert, the eldest son, how straight-backed and favored he stood, apple of his papa's eye! Middle son Willy, a shadow, staying in the background. His eyes look haunted, constantly darting back and forth. How Nathan, the one with the halting speech, ne'er caught his father's eye. Not once."

Chance stood and stretched his legs. Blood rubbed against him. "Now here we stand, on the land given to that favored eldest son. Contracted to expand his home. 'Tis a detailed contract, sound and fair in all its parts."

Chance Thompson began to pray with his eyes open. "Father God. This is a lonely path You've got me on. No white man to fully trust. No black man to help me think and pray along the way. My pap's gone now and Graysom, well, he doesn't answer to you. You did give me a beautiful helpmate in Sarai. But some things weigh too heavy for her to shoulder."

In dawn's half-light, Chance could now see the markers delineating the foundation of the addition. He began to walk the boundary, praying with strong voice.

"Lord bless this land, and all who inhabit it. Bless the earth. 'Tis borrowed of you after all. Let the work be fit worship to You. Grant us safety as we work. Grant us favor against any untoward spirits. Jealousy. Greed. Bigotry." Chance paused. "Even such as shadows my own heart. Forgive my trespasses as I forgive."

Chance grinned at the sun glowing warm on the horizon. Just enough light to review the plans. He entered the tent, unfolded his canvas-seat chair, sat down and pored over survey, site drawings, material lists. Blood curled up nearby.

When Chance looked up, he saw his foreman and closest friend, Graysom, ride up on his horse. Others arrived. Chance stood to watch the daily miracle unfold: Graysom directing the journeymen, journeymen organizing laborers. The foreman and each journeyman had their own budgets and bonuses. They were Freemen, and they came unencumbered by other commitments. They came from miles around, drawn by Chance Thompson's growing reputation. Just when it seemed as if they could not absorb another walk-on laborer, another job offer came to Chance. *God's provision.*

"By the by, Lord, Mr. Robert Henderson named this place 'Sharon' as in, 'Rose of Sharon.' One of your nicknames, and I believe he means to honor You with it.

"'Course, You would know for sure."

One gray morning his foreman did not arrive as usual. Chance noticed that another person besides Graysom did not show up: Robert Henderson. It was the day of the month when Henderson was scheduled to visit the work site and give Chance the monthly draw.

Before long a journeyman loped toward Chance, yelling. "One of the men seen Graysom meet up wif Attorney Henderson!" Journeyman Andrew Clark was one of Chance's most dependable workmen. Everyone called him Clipper because he sometimes barbered hair for men by the evening campfire. Clipper was winded when he reached Chance. "Fellows are saying Graysom took the month's pay."

"I don't believe it!" Chance thundered. "Graysom would never do such a thing!"

Clipper held his hands up. "That's what I said at first, Boss, and I know he's a good friend of yours and all. So I run up to the road to check things out and I seen Graysom riding off. Now he's gone! Graysom's gone, Boss!"

Chance Thompson felt his heart go numb. *Dear God, not Graysom!*

"Hear me, Boss? I said—"

"Yes, I hear. Which way?"

Clipper waved a hand toward the northwest. "He's out of town by now. But he hasn't been gone long. Boss, you can ride my horse, she's all saddled. She'll get you to him."

Chance hurried Clipper into the work tent. "You be the foreman now, 'til I return." Chance gave Clipper a quick review of the plans, punctuating his review with questions, until he was satisfied that Clipper was prepared to oversee in his absence.

Chance grabbed his rifle and jacket. He kept his voice even. "Come nightfall, I expect a complete report. Writ in a neat hand."

Clipper nodded, then reached into his back pants pocket and pulled out a ragged black kerchief. "Boss, take this with you. Graysom dropped it on the road when he done rode away. Got his scent on it and his horse's. Let Blood get a good whiff."

Mounted on Clipper's horse, Chance followed his bloodhound as it raced across fields and through woodlands. Chance had acquired Blood as winnings in a card game. Rumor said Blood had been a slave trader's hound. Chance wasn't sure. When not working, his dog's eyes, its personality, revealed a temperament too gentle for such cruelty to humankind.

Is there a limit to how low man can sink? Chance wondered, his mind reeling. He imagined Robert Henderson's reaction to the news that Graysom had duped them. *No, duped me*, he corrected himself. *Graysom is my worker, my responsibility. Robert is a businessman. That's what he'll think, and he would be right. If I don't recover that money, it's out of my pocket, not Henderson's*. The humiliation burned in his throat, his stomach. Through his entire being. *Graysom! My oldest friend!* He kept up with Blood, who was following the scent of a man on the run.

Blood led them along a trail that took them several miles away from Carlisle, then looped back toward the Conodoguinet Creek. They entered woodland so dense its filtered light resembled dusk. Blood paused at the creek, whining his uncertainty. The dog crossed at a shallow part and Chance followed. Blood nosed along the bank and picked up the scent again, sniffing his way to a nearby evergreen tree. He clawed at its trunk, barking and howling into the dense screen of its branches. Chance thought he glimpsed a horse, farther in the woods.

Chance dismounted and secured Clipper's horse to a nearby tree. He cocked his rifle. "Graysom!" His voice was metal-cold.

Graysom dropped to the ground just beyond the baying dog and a few feet from where Chance stood.

"Stay!" Chance ordered Blood.

Chance's foreman lifted his hands, palms up, grinning with embarrassment. "Hear me out, Chance. It was debts from playin' cards. My luck's gone. All my money's gone, too. Did this on impulse 'n I'm ashamed already."

"You should be, Graysom. Those men look up to you."

"I know, Chance. Look at me, hiding in a tree like a fool. I just got scared when I thought what you might do. Put down that gun now, Chance. You're scarin' the piss straight outa me."

Chance kept his rifle cocked and aimed at Graysom's chest.

Graysom begged, "Come on now, Chance! Finally I did turn around! You must know I was comin' back, since you followed my trail."

"You bearing arms, Graysom?"

The man's shoulders slumped. He shook his head. "No."

"Toss what belongs to me on the ground between us."

Chance flexed his firing finger as he saw Graysom reach for the inside of his jacket. "Slow there, Graysom. You've done enough damage to the trust in our friendship."

Graysom pulled out a wad of wrapped currency and dropped it to the ground.

"Can you forgive me, Chance?"

"Forgive you for what?"

"Wanting money what belongs to you."

Chance lowered the gun. As he stooped to recover the money, Chance shook his head slowly in reply, once, twice. "No, wanting the money'd be forgivable, as I figured you had a reason for that. But what would possess you to break the trusting bonds of our friendship?"

Graysom toed the dirt, eyes down. He shrugged. "What you gonna do now, Chance?" His voice sounded tiny and high in relation to his hulking frame.

Chance peeled off several bills and threw them to the ground. "I figure this covers your wages and gives you some Get Out money besides. Look me in the eye, Graysom." It took a long moment for Graysom to comply. Chance's voice bore ice. "Don't you ever come back here. Ever."

Chance turned his back and, securing his gun to the saddle, began to mount the horse. He heard the breath and footfall of distance traveled before he could fully turn. Graysom leaped on his back, closed his fingers around Chance's throat, pressing hard on his windpipe. Graysom's voice hissing in his ear. "Leave town? How dare you order me around! Who you think you're bossing? Maybe I just leave town with Sarai. She belong with me, not with some uppity nigger—"

Chance pulled on Graysom's wrists and whipped his own body down into a fast crouch, throwing Graysom's weight forward. Graysom lost his grip and rolled toward the creek like a coin on edge. He landed, sprawled on his back. Chance grabbed a rock and rushed Graysom, who rose on one elbow, the other hand held up in defense. "How dare you even speak Sarai's name!" Chance roared. "The likes of you don't even deserve to know her."

Graysom's fear seemed to give way to the look of a man who has the upper hand and is about to play it. "Come on now, Chance. I knew that family way longer than you. Sarai's no saint. Why, who's to say Junior's even yours?"

Chance landed a solid blow of the rock to Graysom's temple. He fell back with a groan.

Hot anger flowed from Chance's chest to his fist and into that rock. By the time he stopped to catch his breath, he saw that Graysom's skull had become part of the stone-littered bank. The creek flowed red. Chance's hound whimpered, sniffing the substance of his name.

Chance dropped to his knees next to the dog. He howled, and Blood howled with him. No other thought, no other sound. Anguish engulfed Chance, clung to him like a shroud. He finally staggered to his feet. When he saw the blood covering his hands and clothing, he waded into the creek, submerging himself to his chin. He let the water flow over him until it ran clear and his flesh felt as numbly cold as his heart.

Dusk had crept up on Chance. Waterlogged, he dragged himself out of the creek. With a flat stone and his bare hands, he dug a grave in the softened earth of the creek bank, then laid his friend deep into the hole and covered him with earth. "Isn't that the devil's way, Graysom? We hurt those we love. Can't blame this one on the devil. No sir. All my doing. Thank God you're a single man, too. If I bore the guilt of a widow and children, I'd throw myself into the grave with you." Chance stood, dry-eyed. He kicked fresh dirt onto the stain remaining on the earth, watched the mud and blood swirling in the water's current, painting it rust. He yearned to do the same for the stain on his soul. "Jesus. This one's too big." He closed his eyes. "Too terrible."

Chance opened his eyes. Blinked. Just that fast, he marveled, the creek's waters already ran clear.

The next morning Chance greeted his workers in the usual way, but he saw in their faces they knew something had transpired. Maybe Blood howled the whole story during the night. Men have a way of finding out such things.

Clipper proved to be a reliable foreman. Chance maintained a distance such that close friendship was no longer a possibility with any of the men. They completed the gazebo well before the deadline, and the addition to Sharon would be complete before first snowfall. Chance divided the bonus even more generously than usual. Yet he knew that grace could not be bargained. And that in some sense or other, this side of eternity, loneliness would ever after be his portion.

~late August, 1861~

Sarai's Lament

Sarai sat on the stoop of their completed home, shelling garden peas into a bowl as she watched her sister Ester's girls, Vera and Inez, ages five and four, play with Junior in the creek. Ester and her husband Ned lived at the other side of the property, farmed the Thompsons' arable land, and shared the proceeds. They were bringing in the last of their harvest today.

Sunlight spilling through pine boughs cast a halo on the creek, the laughing children, and this precious spot of land they called home. Who knew how many more sunstruck days they would have before autumn's chill and winter's cold? Sarai hugged the wooden bowl, worn to familiarity, closed her eyes and lifted her face to the sun, eager for its warmth to penetrate deep, beyond her skin and marrow, to the very center of her shadowed being.

She opened her eyes and breathed in the intoxicating smell of fresh-milled pine boards, her new home. She had every reason to feel happy and content. When would it release her, this haunting emptiness?

She spread her skirt wide and fancied herself the princess of her realm. A silly fantasy from childhood, when she'd learned the meaning of her name; it almost always succeeded in cheering her. But not today. Not after yesterday. They had fought, Chance and she, just a small matter, and they quickly made up that evening. Still.

Her eyes traveled up to the blue ribbon of sky unfurled overhead. Indian summer. Why do folks use that name for a warm autumn? Why had she called Chance that name, an Indian? No, an *Indian-giver*. Yesterday he had given her a horse. A horse that had belonged to Graysom. "Why would a man go away so suddenly that he leaves his horse behind?" she had asked. It was a beautiful animal, sweet-tempered. She couldn't wait to ride it. Why hadn't she heeded the warning signs of her husband's silence and held her tongue? *I knew he heard me*, she scolded herself. *Why repeat a question he clear enough had no plans to answer?*

"But …" She asked the question again.

All light and warmth left Chance's eyes. In their eclipse, Sarai's mouth went dry. She had seen that look before in another man's eyes. Chance's gaze held such remote detachment, she felt the hopelessness of a victim, that terror just prior to a brutal act.

The table lifted as he stood. His chair fell backward. "Never mind," he called over his shoulder. "I'll give the horse to someone else."

"Indian-giver!" Words powered by anger and pain.

He spun. Another murderous look. She recoiled as he came toward her and he must have noticed her fear. His words came slow, soaked in that tone which made her feel worse than dead: Uneducated. Stupid.

"You. Got it. Exactly. Wrong." Then he had left.

That was it. A small argument. Or a big argument, but short.

On her dark-mood days, Sarai thought of her husband as better than herself. She never said this aloud. It shamed her to even think it. Still, she considered the Indian part of him unknowably foreign, and she found herself fuming when Chance filled Junior's head with his family's ancient stories. Chance had heard these stories at his own papa's knee, about an ancestor born in the pre-Revolutionary days, part Indian, known as White Elk. Chance thought of himself as a steward of his forefather's mystical powers. She did not doubt those God-given powers. Indeed, she herself had a bit of the visioning gift. Chance did dream strange dreams. And they did seem to fortify him from the slurs and frustrations of daily life. Furthermore, she had to admit, some whites seemed to recognize his moral fiber and were drawn to him, entrusting him with business and friendship. His childhood seemed gilded; set apart somehow.

Whereas her own childhood.... She startled to find bits of peas oozing from her clenched fist. She'd grown up belonging to someone, not cherished, but owned, as property. A careless observer of those years would have judged her to be a healthy and well groomed child. She had food, clothing, even some playthings of her own. She ground her teeth at the thought of her stupid mistress, so full of airs. What sort of woman does not know—or care—that her husband habitually defiles their marriage bed? Her heart seized up when she thought of her master. The strange feelings Master Turnbrough had stimulated in her blossoming body, frightful for a girl not even twelve years old. "Call me Papa," her master would whisper, before he touched her in that way. "For I am the only daddy you will ever truly know." How she had despised him. How she had yearned for him!

Ester appeared, walking slow on the path. Ester's childhood had been more like Chance's. Safer. Set apart.

"You're back early!" Sarai called out.

"A hireling showed. So Ned sent me home. Move over, I gotta sit."

Sarai made room for her older sister. A big-boned, confident woman, Ester sat down heavy, unloading her workday. She wiped her face with the kerchief she pulled from around her neck, the smell and heat of her body filling the space between them. She stuck her tongue out, panting like a dog. "Water!"

Sarai uncorked a glazed clay jug, removed the pewter cup looped around the jug, and poured water into the cup. She passed it to her sister.

"Shelling peas?" Ester gulped the water, letting it dribble down her chin. She tossed the dregs onto the back of her neck and sighed her relief. "Let me see some."

When Ester reached into the bowl to grab a pea pod, one of her fingernails dug into the back of Sarai's hand.

"Hey!" Sarai slapped Ester's arm. "Get your own peas to shell, Farm Lady. There's plenty of them."

"Who art thou calling Farm Lady?" Ester smiled, her teeth ivory against lips and skin so sun-darkened, she looked like melting chocolate. "Let me show thee the proper way to shell peas. Look, snap them like this, see? One quick move. Much faster."

"Show me nothing!" Sarai swatted away her sister's hand, angry now. "Look, you drew blood! Go play with your girls in the creek. Cool off. Get some of that grime and stink off you."

"Cool off thyself, Little Sister!" Ester was laughing now.

Sarai sucked on the back of her hand, shook it above her head to stay the tiny ooze of blood. "Think I will!" She shoved the bowl of peas into Ester's lap, almost spilling them. "You so fine and fast, job should go quick."

Sarai pulled off her flat shoes, shed her bunched-up socks, took the short distance to the creek barefooted and waded in, warning the children not to splash her. Broad, smooth stones carpeted this part of the creek bed. She stood erect, holding up her skirts regally with one hand to keep them dry. As might a young girl play-acting a childhood role.

Chance knew bits of Sarai's story. She could never tell him the darkest parts. Surely not *that* part. She must keep that most unlovable side of herself hidden and protect the love they have for each other. *Love is fragile and fleeting.* Uncharted. She had no map for her love with Chance, for the reckless way they wept and laughed together. Prayed and made love together. Sometimes a ray of grace would break through, and she would have an inkling of what real peace, real freedom might be like. "Pray through your troubles," Chance would urge her. "Lord," she prayed low, tentative, "You promise not to make our burdens too great to bear. That you will help us carry our load."

Sarai held her skirts higher and waded deeper into the creek. Ester stood on the bank, hands crooked at her waist. Sarai turned away from her sister and felt the sun—or was it Ester's nagging gaze?—burning her shoulders and back.

Sarai heard a torrent of water rise from behind, gasped as cold wet cascaded over her head. She whirled to see Ester crouched in the stream, grinning, calling out, "Doesn't that cool water feel so good, bubbling through thy dress?" Ester reached back with cupped hands for another volley. Sarai ran at her, or tried to run against the water's current, throwing her full weight against the solid wall of Ester's body.

"Ow!" Ester toppled backward into chest-deep water. Sarai flailed and twisted in her sister's wake, trying to regain footing.

Ester rubbed her wet dress front. "Why'st claw my titties like that?"

"How does it feel … getting … grabbed?" Sarai gasped, spitting out water. "I want you to … leave … me alone!"

Ester glanced at the children playing downstream. "What art thou talking about?"

Sarai's toes found creek bottom. She crept closer so she would not have to shout, staying two arm's lengths from her sister. Sarai had to screen her eyes from the sun's glare, amplified by water. "You treat me like a child!" She spit her words. "I was *never* a child!"

"Baby sister—"

"Stop it! I'm your sister, not your baby. Our mama's gone. Papa, too. I'm *nobody's* baby!"

Ester passed one wet hand over her face. Her puzzled expression remained. "That's right. Mama's gone. I look out for thee now."

"She didn't! How could she?" Sarai hissed. "Mama couldn't even look out for herself!"

"What?" Ester's face clouded over.

"You heard me."

The children's laughter and squeals floated to them. Junior was helping his cousins dig a shallow basin in the embankment and fill it with water. They sat in shallow water lobbing pebbles into their basin, shrieking each time water-spray signaled a stone hitting its mark.

Wearily Ester waved away a dragonfly. "Yes. We knew. Zech told us. We all knew. What that man was doing to thee. And Mama."

Sarai recoiled. She struggled to stand, water rushing from every fold of her dress and body. She crashed her way toward the creek bank. Ester rolled to one side, reached up and with one smooth motion caught Sarai's arm, pulled her down.

"Go ahead, splash!" Ester called over Sarai's flailing. Ester freed Sarai's hand. "Thou has both hands free now, have at it." Ester closed her eyes. Sarai grunted with every wall of water she heaved. Ester's buffeted body bobbed back each time. Sarai, tiring, fell forward and under the surface. Ester opened her eyes. She pulled her sister up, Sarai choking out tepid creek water. Ester wrapped her arms around Sarai and, in spite of her squirming, held her close. All their splashing had caught the attention of the children, who stood looking at their mothers. Ester waved. The children, judging the scene not sufficiently fun, returned to their own watery explorations.

"I blamed Mama," Ester said into Sarai's ear. "She knew I did. Thou blames me. All this blaming going around without finding its true mark. Even if it did, what good is that? Besides, Mama gave thee a gift. She made me promise not to tell thee. But it's time thou knew. After Master Turnbrough did that wicked awful thing to you, Mama went to his brother-in-law. You know what kind of courage that must have taken? Putting brother against brother? She could have been kilt! But John Webster said, 'Be patient. I will do something.' That's how thou wert freed same time as me."

Ester released her grip. Sarai still clung to her big sister, her cheek resting on Ester's chest, and gave a long, low moan. Ester spoke gently.

"I ever tell thee I saw thee being born? I was four, no five, just barely. Mama had a long, hard delivery. And a good-for-nothing midwife!" Ester made a spitting noise. "Well, thou came out and I could not believe my eyes, thou looked so mag*nificent!* All curled up in a smooth, deep gold oval. Like a shiny egg. 'Mama,' I yelled. 'Thou laid a golden egg!'

"Worn out as she was, our mama got up on one elbow to get a good look. Sarai, one look at thee and she glowed with a love I've never seen her give anybody else. And that's the way she looked at thee for the rest of her life. Did thou notice that special look she had for thee? No? Too bad. Sure? Think about it, baby sister.

"And think about this. Thou might wonder, when I saw that special love thou got from Mama, did I feel jealous? Only natural, right? Wrong. 'Cause when I looked at thee, I saw the very same thing she did. Felt the very same way. No. It's love, baby girl. All love." Their dresses ballooned to the surface and floated, colorful wings on the water.

"Sarai, what does thou think, that Ned and me want to live here, where the soil and the people are harder than any in Maryland? No child, we're here 'cause thou art here. I'm looking after thee now. Thou art my baby sister. Always was."

A shout and laughter. The children cavorted their way toward the women, pure delight splashing, overflowing.

"Always will be."

~October, 1861~

Reader

Jeweled leaves blew into the house along with Junior. It was late October, barely two months' worth of third grade for him. He enjoyed doing work with older students and had already blazed ahead of others his age. He had a trophy to show for it. Junior dropped his sack on the table, pulled out his prize, a book, and laid it on top, on display. His first grown-up book.

"Mam, look. Webbie gave me this book." A secret little smile wiggled onto his face, as he waited for her reaction.

Sarai worked to hide her feelings before they overwhelmed her. She wanted to grab the book, devour it, have it for herself. Instead, Sarai sat down in her chair and rocked, facing away from Junior and his book. With the to-and fro of rocking, she tried to soothe her pounding heart, ease it into a rhythm she could bear. She felt Junior standing at her elbow.

"Is something wrong, Mam? Are you sick?"

"No Junior. I'm just rocking." She attempted a smile. "How was school? I see your book."

Joy broke out on Junior's face. "It's Webbie's favorite book! He finished it and said I could have it. I can already read a lot of the words, Mam!"

"What's the name of the book, Junior?"

"*Moby Dick*! It's the name of an animal, not a person! Guess what kind of animal, Mam?"

As she looked at Junior, she could see the book on the table. Her vision swam. The blurred table and book began rocking. Was the house becoming a boat?

"A fish?"

"Yes, a BIG fish! A whale! How did you know that, Mam?" He floated to the table, grasped the book, floated back. "Did you read it before?"

"No, Junior."

"Would you like to read it now? Or how about I read it to you? You can help me with the bigger words I don't know yet." He began to climb into her lap.

"Wait, Junior. I have an idea. Bring your practice book and pencil, too. You can write down the words you don't know. It's a better way to learn."

Cheered, he scrambled into her lap with both books and the pencil. Junior put his pencil into the practice book to mark its first blank page. It sat in their laps like a shelf for the bigger book, Junior holding the right side, Sarai the left.

"Use your finger to show me where you are, Junior."

He swiped his finger over the cover. "Moby Dick," he read soberly. "Or the Whale."

"Whale," Sarai repeated, staring at the symbols his finger underscored. "Whale." Feeling the word in her mouth. Tasting it.

"Let's pretend, Mam. We're a ship at sea." Sarai rocked faster. Junior laughed his appreciation. She slowed again so that he could continue. "There's the fellow who wrote it. Herman. Mel"—Junior studied the name, remembered suddenly—"Melville." He thumbed through several pages. "Teacher Brumbach says it's all right to skip this stuff."

"Now." Junior drew a deep grown-up breath and read, finger blazing the trail.

"LOOMINGS." He looked up and sideways at his mam. "Teacher Brumbach says that means 'What's ahead and coming at you.' So, look out, Mam!" Another deep breath. "Call me Ishmael. Some years ago—never mind how long …" Junior paused. "Prekissly. Precissly. What's that word, Mam?"

"Write it down."

Junior sighed. Sarai held the book while he opened his journal, found the pencil, and carefully printed the new word.

"But what does it mean, Mam?"

"You'll figure it out, Junior."

"Aw." Another deep breath. "… having little or no money in my purse, and nothing"—He took several stabs before settling on "particular." His finger and voice started again—"particular to interest me on shore, I thought I would sail about a little and see the watery part of the world. It is a way I have of driving off the spleen, and reg-u-la-ting the"—Junior's brow furrowed—"Kirku—aw, that word's too long!" he complained, frustrated.

"I think you're doing very, very well." Indeed, the words had a narcotic effect on Sarai. She could rock and listen to him read for hours. Forever.

"But could you just help me a little, Mam?"

"I'll help by holding the book so that you can write the word down."

He sighed through the labor of re-opening the journal, spelling aloud as he printed, "c-i-r-c-u-l-a-t-i-o-n." Then he returned to reading, pausing in the middle of longer words. "When-ever I find myself growing grim about the mouth; when-ever it is a damp, drizzly Nov-em-ber—"

"Wait!" Sarai studied the page. "Where is 'drizzly' again?"

Junior pointed.

"See how odd it looks. And sounds. So different from the rest …" her voice trailed off.

"—a damp, drizzly November in my soul; when-ever I find myself in—" he looked at Sarai, pleading.

She smiled distractedly, opened his journal for him. "November's not far off …" her voice trailing again. Junior spelled aloud as he printed, "i-n-v-o-l-u-n-t-a-r-i-l-y."

Junior silently re-read their progress so far, until his finger found their place, his voice continuing, "… pausing before coffin ware-houses, and bringing up the rear of every fun-er-al I meet; and especially when-ever my hypos"—he craned again to look at her—"What are hypos, Mam?"

"I don't know," she said honestly. "Did you read something about coffins? Maybe this man Ishmael is afraid of something."

Junior looked greatly relieved to at last hear his mam express some opinion about their reading quest. He ventured forth with new energy, his voice popping off each word, his finger dancing along: "… get such an upper hand of me, that it requires a strong moral princ-ip-le to prevent me from de-lib-er-ate-ly stepping into the street, and—"

Without asking or prompting, he silently jotted into his book, meth-od-ic-ally.

Sarai lowered her left hand to her side and wiggled a finger for each word he had written down. "You have four words writ down, Junior." She gave him a squeeze. "That's good. You are a very good reader."

Junior puffed with the compliment. He sang the next passage, his index finger skipping to the beat: "… flourish Cato throws himself upon his sword; I quietly take to the ship. There is nothing sur-pris-ing in this. If they but knew—"

"What's this about Cato?" Chance stepped inside, pulled off his boots, and set them just outside the door, beneath the tiny overhang at their front steps. "And who is this expert reader? It's Junior! Really?" Chance's eyes widened with mock surprise. "You must have reading in your veins , Son. Imagine that! A boy—deemed a third grader, at that—reading an adult book." Chance pulled up a chair next to them and sat straddling it, his hands and chin resting on its curved top brace.

"Do you know Cato, Pap?"

Chance nodded. "Met him in a book."

"Who is he?"

Chance scratched his temple. "He was a Roman leader from long ago. What are you reading?"

"*Moby Dick.*"

"Ahhh!" Chance winked and smiled. "Call me Ishmael."

"You know Ishmael, too?"

"So do you, Junior. From the Bible. His papa was Abraham. What was his mama's name?"

"Sarai?"

Chance winked at his wife. "No, the other one."

Junior raced through the Bible stories he knew concerning Abraham. "Hagar?"

"Right as rain!" Chance tilted his head to see the page. "Read some more?"

"I'm getting tired," Junior admitted. "Read to me, Pap?"

"Surely. After supper."

Sarai's rocking slowed, stopped. "We can sit up in our bed and read. The three of us."

"I'm in the middle!" Junior called.

"The three of us," Chance repeated, studying his wife's face.

Late that evening, under cover of the whistling, regular breathing of her husband and son, Sarai crawled out of her bed and relit the table lamp. She eased a blank piece of paper out of the back of Junior's practice book and opened *Moby Dick*, paging until she found the beginning. She saw *Loomings* and copied that down. She spotted and copied several other words: *money, purse, drizzly*. *Moby. Dick.*

"Friends," she whispered. "I like the way you sound. And I do believe I'll recognize you when we next meet." Sarai folded the paper twice and tucked it into her canister of wheat flour. Then she slipped back into bed.

~October, 1861~

Woodpiles

"Two woodpiles set on our land. Two very different piles."

Pap was talking to Junior. But the woodpiles made his mind wander because beyond them lay the field of grass where Webbie and Junior liked to play. Where Junior learned about Webbie's secret about water.

It started at summer's end, when they had been playing Moby Dick, acting out all the parts of the preacher and Ishmael, Queequeg, Ahab, and Starbuck, even the great boat Pequod, and the even greater white whale.

"Oh captain, my captain!" Webbie had yelled.

Junior stopped. "Let's play in the creek. Moby's a fish. It makes more sense. And I'm hot."

"Naw."

"Why not?"

Webbie winked one eye, pirate-like.

"Come on, Webbie, let's cool off."

"Naw."

"You don't know how to swim. Is that it? Oh, I can teach you, Webbie. It's easy."

He made a stabbing motion at the invisible monster whale. But his heart wasn't in it.

"Or is it … are you … being careful?"

Webbie kicked the dirt with his shoe.

"You're joking me!" Junior was shocked. "But you love Moby Dick—you love the sea! You want to be a sailor someday, right?"

Webbie nodded his head real slow.

Creek swimming was one of Junior's favorite things to do. "You mean we're never, ever going to swim together?"

Webbie looked away. "Well, you don't climb trees, Junior." Still kicking dirt. "There's a whole other world up there."

"Listen, Webbie. We can stay in the shallows. We don't have to go into deep parts. Won't you try?"

He started easing toward the creek, scratching his elbows, all nervous. "After we do this," his voice sounded strange, "you climb the oak. Okay?"

"To the creek!" Junior yelled, running in circles around him. Webbie took off his shoes, then socks, while he walked, dropping them on the path like trail markers. His eyes stared even wider than usual. By the time he reached the creek bank, he had everything off except his knickers. Both boys wore them cuffed to above their knees. Webbie balled his fists, tensed his jaw, and walked right into the water. Junior splashed in with him. Webbie walked deeper, deeper, into the center of the creek where a swift current ran. Up to his chest, up to his neck.

"Webbie, wait!"

Webbie's head went under.

"WEBBIE!"

Junior waded then dog-paddled furiously to the spot where his friend had gone down. Webbie's hand flipped up in the air. Junior grabbed it and pulled. The other boy's head whipped up, water spouting out of his mouth and nose. Junior pulled harder, fell down, went under himself. Got up. Webbie surfaced again, this time head and shoulders leaping out of the water, hands and arms waving. Junior grabbed one of his arms and gave a strong yank toward shore.

"Ow!" Webbie struggled to gain his footing, his head just above water. A slow smile came across his face. "How was my Moby Dick?"

"You scared me, Webbie!"

"Sorry."

After they waged a fierce splash battle and declared a truce, the boys sat in the sun on the bank to dry.

"When we dry off," Webbie said, "we can climb that old oak."

"Nope."

"You tricked me!" Disappointment was writ so big on Webbie's face, Junior felt bad. But not so bad as to change his mind.

"Never agreed to it, Webbie," Junior shook his head. "Some things just do not come natural. Why, I'd rather die than climb that big tree!"

"You'd rather die, huh?" He spoke low, that secret smile running across his face. "I'll find a way. I'll get you up in that tree. Even if it kills *me*."

They went swimming plenty of times after that. Webbie said he was no longer afraid of water. Junior didn't mention the tree. Webbie didn't bring it up either, not for a long while.

Junior's pap moved closer to the pile set in the curve between the woodshop and their home. "Like I said, these two woodpiles are two very different piles. This one that stands high and narrow is all firewood, cut clean and uniform. First year wood, a rough clean white on each end. Second year wood looking yellowed and cured dry by time. Ready for burning." He cleared his throat. "The other pile, well, that's something special. I know you don't think so, Junior. I heard you tell Webbie it looks like a graveyard where old trees crawl to die."

Sheepish, Junior kicked a smooth stick, watched it roll.

Pap said slow, "These are not just any old trees, Junior. It's time for you to learn about wood."

Father and son wandered around the tree graveyard looking it over. "Think of them as our friends, Junior. All these different kinds of wood. Some keep us warm and dry. Help us cook. Some are so valuable we can sell them and buy food or clothing with the money. Or we can make them into something we can sell. Or keep. Like the wardrobe I made for your mam. Each kind of wood has a story to tell."

"Wood can't talk, Pap."

"Sure it can. All you have to do is listen. When we go to the workshop, I'll show you." Chance rested his arm on one of the logs and told Junior to do likewise. "Here. Let me show you a trick. Compare it to your arm. How much darker? Or lighter? How much bigger? Is it rough or smooth? Is it hairy like mine?" That last question made Junior giggle. His pap smiled but kept going. "Tell me what you see."

Junior studied his arm against the log's bark. "It's a lot rougher. Not hairy. The gray bark's darker than me. But here"—he held his arm next to the cut end—"The inside wood's the color of cinnamon, close to my shade." Junior put his nose right up to the bare end and sniffed. "Smells like ordinary wood."

Pap laughed. "Good description. I'll give you a few more clues before you try your guess." Junior followed him to the edge of the woods. "Look up," his pap said. "Now what do you see?"

"A very tall, straight tree."

"Yes. The straight trunk makes the wood more valuable. What else?"

"Leaves."

"What do they look like? And how many?"

Junior felt his eyes get big. "On the whole tree?"

"No," Pap smiled. He reached out to bend a slender green twig. "Just one stem."

"They're spikey. Seven on each side, one at the end."

"What else?"

"Nuts?"

"Yes. You've helped us get the nuts out of those big green hulls. Some are ripe and dropping now. One last clue. Mam uses them for staining things."

"Walnut!" Junior crowed.

"Right as rain!"

Junior rested his arms on the log. He liked seeing the cinnamon-brown of his own skin against the gray bark. And against blue, his favorite color, the color of his best shirt. And the sky…

"Junior! Where did you and your imagination just go?" Pap squatted so they were eye to eye. "Maybe we should start with the trees and work our way back to the woodpile. What tree you want to learn about next?"

Junior pointed to the tall, broad-limbed tree along the creek. "Webbie likes to climb that one."

"That's an oak. You boys climb that tree?"

"Just Webbie. I don't like to be high."

"Oh." Pap stood up. He guided Junior back over to the woodpile. "An oak tree's a good choice for climbing. It's a strong, hard wood. It won't let you down."

When his pap said that, they both laughed because it meant two things and Junior knew his pap meant both ways.

People all around knew about Chance Thompson's woodpile. If they had a tree on their property ready to pull down, they would call on Chance to take a look. When they would ride to one of his jobs, Junior sat alongside him on the wagon seat, pretending to drive, too, listening to the stories told by whomsoever else was along. Junior especially liked the stories of Mr. Graysom, before he went away, because his stories came from way back in Pap's childhood. Those stories would get them laughing so hard, they had to wipe tears away.

Junior liked his pap's stories the best. They made you see, hear, and *think*. Especially his tales about two wolves who lived with their pup named Junior in the South Mountains. They had adventures together, the sort that needed a clear and present faith to survive.

One day while they were working, Chance and Junior talked about the war, and how Webbie's pap had gone off to fight. Junior knew from Webbie that his Uncle Nathan talked about leaving soon.

Pap said, "We men who remain have to make sure things go well at home. Because conflict can happen at home, too." He considered his son's profile. "What sort of conflict happens at home during a war?"

Junior had to think about that. "We have to work harder?"

"True enough. What else?"

"Things cost more. Or there might not be enough sometimes."

"We've seen some of that already."

Then Chance did something he didn't do so often now that Junior was a bigger boy. He sat down on a stump and pulled Junior onto his lap. They listened to the wind tease, the squirrels complain. Junior breathed deep the good smells around him, fresh-chipped wood, oiled machines, Blood's coat and his skin warmed by the sun, even some flowers. All those good smells rubbed off on Junior's pap. Which meant his pap smelled best of all.

"Pap, will the war come here?"

"No, not here, Junior. That's not likely."

Junior had a question he didn't want to ask. But he did anyway. "Will you be going to the war?"

Junior could tell Pap didn't want to answer. But he did anyway. "If I'm needed. Yes."

After he said that, Junior was on the lookout for anyone showing up from the war with a message for his pap, saying he was needed. Nobody came. Except Webbie's Uncle Willy. But not to the Thompsons' door.

Willy Henderson, named after his father, Col. William Henderson. *He's a junior, like me,* Junior thought. *Or he was.* Willy had come home sick from the battlefield. Junior didn't see him, but Webbie said Army officers in a wagon had dropped Willy off at Oakland. He went straight upstairs to his old childhood bedroom, lay down on his bed, and slept for six days.

On the seventh day he died.

A few days after Webbie's Uncle Willy died, Mam brought out a big pitcher of cool, spring-water peppermint tea for Chance and Junior, who were hard at work. Pap asked Junior to fetch two pieces of ash from the woodworking pile. Together they would commence making a toolbox for one of his customers.

"Ash is a lighter weight hardwood and easier to work," Pap explained.

Junior wanted to choose well. He knew the second length would be needed for the finished piece or would serve as do-over if he made a mistake. He did not want to waste a fine piece of wood to the humiliation of a do-over.

Pap said, "Don't worry, Junior. We can make bowls from do-over wood."

Yet, out by the woodpile, Junior felt his nerves rise on the wave of his doubts, so he did a quick review in his head.

Walnut and pecan trees shed nuts; oaks shed acorns. It was his job to gather these, each in its season. "Leave the buckeye nuts for the animals," Mam always warned. "They'll make you sick to death." Junior stroked the shag bark of black cherry, easy to spot, rough to climb though, even for Webbie, when it's thick with leaves and a boy wants to pluck summer fruit before the birds beat him to it. Junior loved dipping his face into the fragrant soft quills of pine or fir boughs. *Too soft for burning, but strong in special ways.* His pap had used pine for some parts of their house because it didn't mind water.

Pap had asked Junior to pull two stout logs of ash. Without leaves as clues, Junior sometimes confused young ash with young hickory. Except shagbark hickory. Anyone could spot that flaky wonder a mile away.

He found a nice length of ash, finally, traced the raised diamond pattern in its bark with his finger to be sure. Its trunk was bigger around than his arms would stretch. He switched to the end with one sawed-off branch sticking out, grabbed it, dug in his heels, and dragged it toward his pap, walking backward. It took many short heave-hoes, Junior grunting the whole while. When his heel bumped into the workshop's stoop, his pap stood there waiting, nodding his approval.

"You are strong, Son. This one big log may do it."

Pap and Junior had made up a game they called *Watch, Listen, then Do.* Junior watched while Chance sawed and planed his way to the several flat, sturdy rectangles of wood they could use for the box.

"Hear that, Junior?" Pap said. "Did you hear the wood singing to the saw? Now can you hear it whispering when I sand? Like I told you, every one of them has a story."

Junior put his hand to the saw and made several cuts himself, some guided by Pap's hand, some done on his own. They secured in a vise each section of wood they worked. Junior liked the feel of his pap's big rough hand over his own as they worked the plane. He showed Junior the proper way to use sandpaper on wood. Junior worked at sanding the first side piece while Pap finished forming the rest of the boards. Their project took the whole afternoon. As the sun's last light glimmered through the workshop door, Pap and Junior sat side by side on the bench outside the workshop, the finished, handsome toolbox in their laps.

Pap invited Junior to feel the fine, smooth surfaces of their work. "Did I tell you which customer we did this for, Junior?"

"No, sir."

"How did I forget to tell you that?"

Junior could hear the grin, and the way it softened his pap's voice.

"It's for you."

Junior looked to see if he was teasing. "A real toolbox, Pap? For me?"

"Yes, indeed."

"With real tools?" Junior held his breath, let it out slow.

"Well, Son," his pap rubbed the stubble on his cheek, tired but still smiling. "Some things take time. Let's see, you're how old now?"

"Eight. Halfway to nine."

"Halfway, that's good. That means you understand the measure of a year. Tell you what." He clapped his big hands together, as if making a deal with himself. "Your first two tools will be a handsaw and an axe the right size for you. I saw you tug that big ash log today. You did it the smart way. I'll teach you the proper ways and means of cutting wood for the stove. And then that will be your job."

Junior swallowed hard.

His pap looked serious. "It's a man's job, Son. 'Course, I can understand if you would rather not …"

"I'm ready, Pap!" Junior started pulling up his sleeve. "I'm strong. See my muscle?"

Pap put a hand on Junior's arm. "I know you have strong muscles. Fact is, I can see them through your sleeves, that's how big they are."

Tired as they were, Pap showed Junior how to chop and split logs and haul them to the woodpile on a length of leather, sledlike. The next day, he showed Junior how to stack split logs into tight, airless cords of wood. In two weeks' time, Junior became expert at gathering stove wood. Chance thumped his son's shoulders in congratulations. The job now officially and only belonged to Junior.

On all those nights, Junior was the good kind of worn out and dropped off to sleep right away. One night he dreamed about being with his pap at the woodpile. In his dream both piles melted away, like spring snow.

In Junior's dream, it's the next morning, and his pap is gone.

Robert & Maggie Henderson

1850–1854, courtship and family
(Baltimore, Maryland, and Carlisle)

~late March, 1850~

Train Station

"Standing room only! On a train! Every holiday these cars get worse. Do I now look like a sardine?" Henry Webster joked, making fish lips and rolling his eyes. He stood at the back of the railcar with his law school classmate, Robert Henderson. A porter had to move sideways to squeeze past them and other standing passengers, stepping over baggage and dodging the elbows of seated passengers as he made his way back down the aisle.

"Perhaps a train should be added to the schedule," Robert said.

"That would likely require building another locomotive." Henry lowered his voice. "You remind me, friend, that I have some rail stock. It may be time to check the price and secure more."

"My family has always invested directly in land, and our businesses," Robert said, curious. "Would you tutor me in securities?"

Henry's receding hairline made him look older than twenty-four. Though he was the same age, Robert's smile and trim brown hair, with bangs that often broke free from their pomaded and carefully combed and parted form, made him look several years younger.

"My pleasure," said Henry. "Ah, the train slows for the station. Listen, I shall gather our bags. Whenever there are train delays, my sister waits in the station's tea room. Would you kindly locate her? I shall take our bags to the carriage and then find you both."

"I can see to the bags, Henry. Does she know I'm coming?"

"Probably not. Last minute arrangements and so on."

"But I want to—How will I know—?"

"Nonsense," Henry interrupted. "You are my guest, I will see to bags and porter. My sister is easy to spot. She will be drinking, eh, tea, of course. Ginger colored hair. Large green eyes. Her mouth—that's the giveaway."

"Her *mouth*? As in, beautiful? Or . . sassy?"

Henry laughed. "Both."

Robert scanned the station's crowded tea room and moved toward the only woman seated alone. Unmistakably green eyes. Ginger hair? Yes, tucked under a gray hat. He picked up a vacant chair at a nearby table and approached her.

"Excuse me, my name is Robert Henders—"

"Pardon?" The woman leaned forward against the din of voices and teaspoons at work. Her posture remained politely demure. Her eyes smiled, lively with curiosity.

"I said, My name is Robert Henderson and I—"

"Pleased to meet you, Mr. Anders." She offered her hand. "Margaret Webster. You were wise to bring your own chair! I am waiting for my brother, Henry. He likes to move quickly, so you shall soon have the table to yourself."

Robert sat down, suppressing a smile. "Actually we've just arrived from Carlisle—"

"Ah, then my brother shall appear at any moment, he attends law school there, just completed his studies, in fact. Perhaps you know him. He's an upright fellow, who will bring honor to that rag-tag profession."

"Rag-tag?"

"Mr. Anders, perhaps I speak too frankly. But do you not observe how lawyers seem to become increasingiy money-hungry and obfuscating?"

"Well, you may have a point, Miss Webster. I—"

"May I ask you something, Mr. Anders?" She leaned toward him confidentially. "I take by your accent you are from up north?"

"Pennsylvania, yes ..."

"Is the matter of slavery being discussed among your neighbors and acquaintances? Or is it solely a topic for politicians and journalists?"

My response to this Southern lady should be careful on such a volatile subject, Robert cautioned himself. "Slavery is an important topic of news and political interest to all sorts of folks, I would say."

"I am glad to hear it. Slavery is an abomination to humankind and an embarrassment to our nation. I cannot discuss the matter with my lady friends in Baltimore, as our disagreement is well-established. Northern ladies, in my experience, seem to prefer ... other topics. Ah! Brother Henry approaches, I shall introduce you."

Henry leaned over to kiss his sister's cheek. "Looks as if you have gotten past introductions with my classmate, Robert Henderson."

Margaret's teacup hit its saucer with a clank. "Your *law school* classmate?"

"Of course! What other school do you imagine I attend?" Henry motioned to Robert. "Shall we go? I'm certain food and drink will be lavished upon us when we arrive home."

Margaret caught Robert's eyes and mouthed, "Pardon!"

Robert shook his head and smiled his response, *No apology needed.* He spent the carriage ride in the facing seat, listening to the brother and sister catch up, all the while admiring her celebrated mouth.

~late March, 1850~

Wild Ride

Margaret Turnbrough Webster sat astride her horse straight shouldered, taking in the panoramic view of her father's land. She had chosen to bring their house guest to this hilltop location because it offered the broadest unobstructed view of the estate.

And what a glorious morning! The brilliant sapphire sky provided a dramatic backdrop to Maryland's finest emerald topography, fragrant and festive with cherry orchards in pink bud, and gold arcs of forsythia hedgerow. Margaret reveled in the neat geometry of early rye fields, rippling in the breeze, parsed by corrugated earth, freshly tilled and planted with tobacco. Nearby, a spring-fed creek cascaded over rocks in its rush to the valley and the Chesapeake Bay beyond. Birdsong punctuated the rustling applause of breezes through woodlands on these primordial hillsides. And from the highest promontory rose the stone façade of Mount Repose, its windows glinting a coded greeting to the rising sun.

She surveyed the scene with the pleasure of girlhood memories, mixed with the responsibility of a twenty-year-old woman, her father's youngest child. Mr. Webster consulted her rather than her older siblings on financial matters, most recently the railroad right-of-way dispute. She bristled just thinking of Briscoe, the railroad executive who tried—and failed—to bribe her father. As if cueing to her thoughts, a steam whistle sounded from afar, the B&O, heading west.

Margaret could feel the eyes of her companion upon her. He was their guest and now, to some unspoken degree, it seemed, a suitor. She smiled and smoothed her horse's mane but did not return the look.

Robert Henderson shifted his weight in the unfamiliar saddle. He could not break his gaze from this mystifying young woman. The visit's dynamics seemed to have changed overnight. Then again, he had to admit to himself that Henry had given him fair warning.

For weeks, Henry, who was recently engaged, had kidded Robert about still being single. His invitation to stay at Mount Repose had concluded with, "As you are thoroughly unattached, I might introduce you to my plain-faced albeit utterly fascinating sister."

The train station encounter had amused him and piqued his curiosity. As soon as they arrived at Mt. Repose, Margaret and her mother had excused themselves and disappeared up a grand winding staircase while the men sat to talk in the Websters' drawing room. Henry's father had just opened Robert's gift, a bottle of the best whisky from the Henderson family distillery, when Henry's ginger-haired sister reappeared. She swept into the room, embraced her father and planted a kiss on Henry's brow. She had changed from gray cap and cape to a sparkling emerald evening dress that flattered every curve of her figure and matched her eyes. Her hair, unloosed, swept provocatively over one shoulder. As they stood, Henry intoned, "And this, my friend, as you now know, is the irrepressible Maggie."

Maggie greeted Robert's dumbstruck gaze with laughter. "Did Henry tell you I'm plain? He tells all the single male visitors that. His obsessive need for full disclosure, I suppose."

Now Robert could not even remember any of his contribution—inane, no doubt—to last evening's dinner conversation. Each encounter with her felt as if they were meeting all over again. He had eyes only for the smooth curves of her hair, her cheek, her neck, her profile entire.

Yet, pleasing as that profile was, he hungered for a glance from her—those eyes! Warm and sweet as this sun-drenched morning, they melted his heart in a wildly exciting way. Or was it her manner, so independent and sharp-witted? *Must think gentlemanly thoughts*, he told himself, *Or I'll have no hope of comfort in this abominable saddle!*

She turned her mount to face him. "Ready to ride into the valley? We'll follow the creek trail past the planted fields, to that stand of willows on the far side. Do you see? We shall have to jump the creek at that point, but don't worry. Your gelding knows every groundhog hole and water hazard on this land. He'll serve you well."

Robert returned her gaze and smile with a nod.

She adjusted a linen scarf that had fallen from her head to her shoulders, exposing her hair, which was swept into a French knot. "Oh, by the way … will this ride be friendly?" Her smile dimpled. "Or for blood?"

"Wha—"

But she was already gone, her scarf floating off behind her. Robert had to scramble to grab it and then try to catch up to the trail of dust and laughter she left in her wake. "Maddening!" He growled through clenched teeth. "Irresistibly maddening!"

"How did you learn to ride like that?"

"Taught myself," she replied, smoothing the long pleats of her skirt as they fanned around her on their picnic blanket. "Started as a very young girl. I didn't ask for permission because I knew Father would say no. I also knew that if I just did it, he would be inordinately proud. I paid attention, watched the adults ride. Could not figure out how to manage the process with skirts. So I borrowed a pair of my brother's pants and stole out, early mornings, mostly."

"Impressive. And I gather you challenge all of your gentleman friends to a race when you first meet?"

"Well, yes, my *gentleman* friends, of necessity. Not one of my lady friends has yet to accept the dare."

"Ah, so it *is* a dare. You were coyly vague on that point." Encouraged by her smile, Robert added, "When you say that bit about, let's see … yes, I think it was, 'Friendly ride, or for blood?' you might try waiting for a response before actually taking off." Robert rewarded her laughter by pulling her scarf from his pocket and dropping it in her lap. "Another clever touch."

"Now you think I am both plain and a flirt."

"No. And yes." Robert leaned toward her, lowering his voice confidentially. "The race. Is it some sort of test?"

"A test …?" She bit her lower lip thoughtfully, as a child might. "No … but I daresay, that's not a bad idea." Robert reclined on his elbows, watching her. "Why not a test? The way the ancient Greeks and Romans tested each other. Tested their gods! 'Twas how they measured heroic action!"

"Ye gods, what have I done?" exclaimed Robert, in mock horror.

"I'm not kidding. It's a superb idea, Robert. We live in sobering times. Yet the young people I know all seem so … so complacent. As if their ease and good fortune were a birthright! As a generation, perhaps we should put each other to the test."

"What sort of test?"

She closed her eyes and tilted her face to the sun, mulling over the question. Robert made a study of her lips, thinking, *This is a beguiling sort of test.*

She turned an urgent face toward him. "What I have in mind has to do with our mettle. Our resolve. Our *courage*. Is there one thing you could do now, Robert Henderson, that might be unpopular in the short term but could have enormous long-term benefit? Tell me. Just one thing?"

Robert had never met anyone like this enigmatic Maggie. She was making his head and heart spin furiously in competing directions. He thought about responding with, "I am seriously smitten with you," and decided against it. Fleetingly, he considered proposing marriage but did not, for fear she might think he was joking. Or she might think he was not joking. A dilemma either way.

"Could I have some time to think about it?"

"No," she said firmly. "Have you heard the Transcendentalists say, 'The mind and heart know what they need?' I think you, Robert, already know that great and singular purpose God has placed in your soul. That thing that is bigger than the practice of law, or even our homes and families. If you don't think it too terribly presumptuous of me to ask, please Robert … tell me."

He held her gaze as he considered his response. "Well, our country's defensive power is in very poor shape. Pennsylvania, for example, founded by Quakers—as you well know—does not have much of a militia. Cumberland County has none. I have it in mind to develop a reserve corps of volunteers in Carlisle."

"'Tis true, your commonwealth was founded on the peaceable principles of the Society of Friends. As a Friend and Christian, I value peace. Do you consider maintaining an army essential to maintaining peace?"

Robert nodded. "I do. It is naïve to think peace can be kept without an armed force."

"Isn't it naïve to think a standing army will not eventually have to wage war?"

They sat in silence for a moment, stalemated. Then Robert asked, "And what about you?"

"What do you mean?"

"You mentioned 'we' … that 'we' as a generation should change. What is your purpose?"

She neither hesitated nor blinked. "My parents are former slave owners. I am an abolitionist. It took years, but once papa was convinced, he granted manumission to all of the slaves once they reached adulthood. Most of them chose to stay on as paid workers. At first, we struggled to survive financially. Now many of those former slaves are employed and able to benefit in the prosperity they help create. If we truly desire a just society, slavery in our country must end. And in its place, institutions such as free schools, and free libraries, for the common good."

"May that goal be achieved peacefully," Robert nodded soberly. "Using military force only as a last resort."

They measured the weight of their admissions in the eyes of the other. "Shall we shake on it?" Robert extended his hand.

Maggie took it, gently pulling him closer. "Nay, tests of this magnitude must be sealed with a kiss."

By the time they returned, Mt. Repose had taken in other visitors for an evening gathering, as household workers carried bags and attended to requests for pressing a shirt or shining a pair of shoes. Maggie guided Robert back to his room herself before she disappeared down the hallway, promising to meet him in the main parlor before the dinner party.

After he changed, Robert left his room and descended the central staircase, admiring how a grand crystal chandelier showered its glittering candlelight on elegantly attired guests passing through the foyer. He had barely set foot in that space when Henry and another gentleman approached him. Henry grasped his shoulder while the other pumped Robert's hand.

"Robert Henderson, I presume. Prepare yourself to be thoroughly examined as to your suitability to squire the young and impressionable Miss Margaret Webster—"

"Impressionable?" Robert interrupted.

The gentleman eyed Henry, then Robert, with mock sternness.

"Well, young, to be sure. Relative to you. Impressionable, in the sense that you seem to have made a favorable one and we have come to see for ourselves. My name, sir, is Philip Tyson. My comrade in this effrontery thou know well. I am described as the strong, silent, scientific type. Henry may not say so, but he is in perfect agreement with every word I utter."

Robert looked at Henry, who shrugged his shoulders and rolled his eyes.

Philip Tyson cleared his voice sternly. "Passing muster with Father Webster will be a cakewalk compared to the grilling we intend to inflict. You see, Margaret, Henry and I have been close associates since childhood. Henry and I have squired his sister to countless occasions, had many adventures together and do not intend to step aside lightly. Eh, Henry?"

Something in the next room had attracted Henry's attention. "Yes, yes. Many adventures," he said distractedly. "See here, Philip, are you quite finished?"

Philip's eyes rounded in mock horror. He cocked his head and studied Robert. "Quite."

Robert smiled at their farce. Maggie had warned him to look out for them in a way that left her meaning up to his imagination. He spoke to Philip. "I understand you're a scientist?"

"Newly minted, agricultural chemistry. I have just begun work for the state of Maryland. Geological studies. So I tend to the land while thou tend to the law of the land."

When Robert glanced at Henry, Philip smirked. "Did thee know we call him Preacher?"

"Preacher? I don't see why—"

"Have you heard him argue a case?" Philip narrowed his eyes but was grinning broadly.

"We call him Preacher …" came Maggie's voice from behind Robert, followed by a tantalizing whiff of her French *parfum*. When she stepped into their circle, Robert couldn't take his eyes off her. "Because he speaks of his work with such passion and conviction. He has volunteered his assistance to—"

"Good old Reverdy Johnson, a Maryland Whig!" Philip grinned. "Henry makes a great pair-up with old Rough and Ready."

Maggie continued with an exaggerated sigh. "Yes, to Mr. Johnson, our Attorney General, in his important work for Mr. Taylor, our President—"

"Of these United States," Henry said crisply. "And as Zach Taylor or any soldier will tell you, peace is the ultimate objective." He gave Robert a pointed look as if ready for his objection on an oft-argued topic.

"Robert is a soldier!" Maggie announced. "Or shall be." From the next room, her father called her name. She excused herself. "It appears I am holding up the evening's programme!"

"Well, not really a soldier. Henry and I are completing our law studies …" Robert saw Philip's curiosity dissolve to restlessness.

"Yes, yes. I considered taking up the law myself. The urge lasted no longer than a week." Philip began steering them in the direction Maggie had disappeared. "Thou will not want to miss this, Robert. The Webster sisters and their best female friend are on the docket, thee might say."

They entered a broad, high ceilinged room, sparkling with light and laughter and glasses refreshed by attendants. He lifted his glass, took a sip, and was pleased to discover it was the whisky he had brought as a gift.

Philip seemed about to comment on the drink when piano music began. His face settled into a broad grin. He winked at Robert and whispered, "That fine instrument is the Webster family's newest acquisition. From New York, crafted by the German maestro, Steinweg." The room fell into an expectant silence.

The pianist was Maggie. She played a popular tune, slow and romantic. Robert observed her in profile, surprised by the plainness of her features when she concentrated: her eyes downcast, brow furrowed to a frown, her nose slightly hooked, her lips pursed. He glanced past her, to a ceiling-high bookcase, its shelves lined with leather volumes. It was framed by silhouette portraits of the Webster family. He looked for each member amid the guests. Henry stood next to a seated young lady, his fiancé, Lizzie. "Our neighbor and my dearest, oldest friend," Maggie had enthused when introducing her to Robert earlier. Upon meeting Robert's glance, Henry lightly raised his glass in salute. Nearby, Philip stood stiffly, his arms crossed, studying his seated female companion, shimmering in a gold and silver brocade-patterned satin dress. Maggie's older sister Rebecca, or Becky, as the family called her. Maggie's parents sat together at the center of a high-backed sofa, their attention fixed on their daughter at the piano. Mr. Webster listened with his eyes closed.

When Robert looked back at Maggie he was rewarded with the smiling eyes of the face that had first captivated him. *I am utterly smitten!* he admitted to himself. *Her looks may have caught my eye. But it is her spirit that draws me in.*

The music's tempo had stepped up to *allegro*, her fingers racing playfully across the keys. Maggie's sister and their friend Lizzie sashayed to the piano and began to sing in a perfectly pitched harmony: Lizzie the soprano to Becky's alto. Their pleased listeners applauded. Robert noticed a change in the affect of his male companions. A smile played at the corners of Philip's mouth as if he were fighting an urge and losing. Becky returned his smile. Meanwhile, Henry grinned unabashedly, holding his glass high in silent tribute to Lizzie, a petite, fair-haired beauty in a sapphire satin hooped dress. Henry's other arm looped around a white column as if it was an anchor restraining him from flying to her. Robert returned his gaze to Maggie in time to see her wink at him. She looked mischievously enchanting in a long dress of purple velvet with an oval neckline of delicate silver braiding. Her fingers raced to the crescendoed finish with a flourish. Their audience rose to a standing ovation, cheering and applause. Henry jostled his way past guests, to Lizzie's side. Philip bowed to Becky.

So we are the three suitors, Robert said to himself as he made his way to a waiting, triumphant Maggie.

~June, 1850~

Hendersons at Work

Maggie resisted the urge to cover her ears against competing raucous sounds, the din of industry. From the dusty intersection of wagon roads, she could hear, but not see, the clang and bellow of the Henderson family mill, one of several enterprises. She admired its wooden paddle wheel, animated by the boisterous waters of the LeTort Spring. Robert pointed to a line of trees. He raised his voice to a level just below shouting. "The distillery is beyond those trees. The dairy is on the other side of the LeTort. My brothers help my father oversee all of the businesses. I handle the legal work, of course. Father keeps his main office here." Robert pointed back to the roadway. "As you can see, we have a steady stream of wagons to fill." Indeed, wagons going and coming lined both lanes of the tar-chip road as far as could be seen, their wheels clamoring for attention, competing with the shouts of drivers and thudding beat of horses' hooves. Some wagons bore the name HENDERSON emblazoned on their rear and side panels. It appeared to Maggie that she was the only woman around. She kept this observation to herself.

"Come. I'll introduce you to my father and brothers."

They led their horses to a tethering post and ventured into the mill. Morning light streamed through grime-filmed clerestory windows, bathing machinery and workers in a golden, oddly tranquil glow: a sanctuary for those who love noise and purposeful bustle. One man stood calm at the eye of activity, sleeves rolled up against the heat, absorbed in making notes in a ledger crooked in his arm.

Robert cupped his hands to his mouth and shouted, "Nathan! Where's Father?"

When the man looked up, Maggie caught her breath. A younger version of Robert's face, stunningly handsome, stared at her with the same unblinking aquamarine eyes. His hair the precise color of the golden wheat pouring through the mill's chutes behind him. Nathan slowly raised a stub of lead pencil toward a set of stairs topped by a windowed office. Maggie felt herself coloring under his stare.

"Nathan, this is the very Margaret I have been raving about," Robert shouted. "Now you will be raving about her, too, I can see." Robert chuckled as he punched his brother's shoulder. Nathan seemed uncertain how to respond. He blinked, finally, and extended his hand to Maggie, then thought better of it. He made a slight bow so stiffly that Maggie, charmed, had to suppress a laugh.

"Pleased to meet you." Nathan's voice was gruff with shyness. And something else, Margaret noticed. An accent?

"Robert shows me in the best light, as usual."

"Nathan, you look just as a mill proprietor should!" Maggie attempted to reassure though she heard her voice go too sharp as she spoke over the mill's thrum. "We arrived unannounced, I hope we are not interrupting. I asked Robert to show me the business workings. He obliged."

Nathan gave them a slow grin of forgiveness. "The Colonel is presentable. G-g-g-good to meet you." With a nod to Maggie, Nathan disappeared into a corner of the mill where men bent to the tasks of filling and stacking sacks of grain.

Not an accent, she realized. *A stutter.*

Robert pointed at the men and spoke into her ear, "The dark-mustached one next to Nathan is Will Jr.—Willy. Our middle brother. Nathan's a chatterbox next to him. Willy prefers work to talk." She nodded. Willy's brown hair looked a shade darker than Robert's. But it was Willy's eyes that gave pause: haunted as if they had seen something they could not erase from memory.

Robert escorted Maggie up the steps and opened the door for her. Cigar smoke met them.

"Greetings, Father! I wish to introduce Miss Margaret Webster."

As he stood, the broad black-jacketed form of Colonel William Henderson filled Maggie's frame of vision. He removed his cigar and swept his hat off his desk, adding a flourish to his deep bow. When he straightened, he appeared pleased, yet stern, his eyes squinting hard over a close-lipped smile. "Welcome to Henderson Mill." His voice rumbled, gravelly from smoke. Perhaps also slurred by whisky. Robert's jaw tensed, she noticed.

"We'll be staying until tomorrow. See you at dinner?"

Colonel Henderson nodded toward Robert but kept his eyes fixed on his son's guest, as he tapped cigar ash into a cast iron bowl with a flanged edge bearing the family name. Was this aggressive stare an attempt to intimidate her or simply poor manners? Maggie did not look away until Robert's father returned to his desk and Robert nudged her toward the door.

At dinner, four of them—Colonel Henderson, Nathan, Robert, and Maggie—occupied one end of an immense dining table, Willy having stayed late at the mill to oversee a repair. Robert had told Maggie his mother was deceased and avoided any further mention of her. Thus, Maggie looked for clues about the woman in the furnishings of the house, but outmoded curtains and wallpaper merely hid in shadows, faded with inattention. Colonel Henderson and Nathan both lived here, though they seemed to occupy different wings. No, different worlds. She took another small bite from unadorned meat and potatoes, the sort of meal bachelors would prefer. This house, she judged, was not a home.

Robert and Maggie did most of the talking. Nathan sat across from them. He kept his eyes on his food, although more than once Maggie caught him looking at her. Colonel Henderson, at the table's head, kept his gaze on Robert, occasionally leveling it at Maggie.

As Robert was recounting a Dickinson College story involving Henry Webster, Nathan stood suddenly, interrupting the tale with his raised glass.

"A … special night," he began. "Robert, with his intended. A toast for you both. Especially …" Nathan looked directly into Maggie's eyes for the first time that evening. “Marg-g-g—Margaret Webster. You are … both beautiful and … g-g-gracious.”

The others lifted their glasses. Maggie lifted hers and beamed her thanks. *What a gentle, sweet man.* She noticed the extreme contrast to the father’s manner, braced herself in the chill of the elder Henderson’s darkened expression.

Col. William Henderson snorted in disgust. “Is that the best ye can muster?” He downed his whisky. “Time for dessert.”

“No scenes, Father. Not tonight.” Robert’s voice was even, his jaw taut.

“That’s right.” The emptied glass landed with a thud. “No scenes.” The elder Henderson stood and strode from the dining room. In moments, a white-aproned woman appeared, carrying a silver tray glistening with three glazed strawberry tarts. Colonel Henderson did not reappear.

~August, 1851~

On Balance

Maggie looked up from the ledger when she heard her father approaching. *By his footsteps, he seems like a much larger man,* she thought. *They more accurately match his spirit. He has presence. Gravitas. People trust him.* She was proud of his reputation, which of course extended to the family's wholesale and retail enterprises. He wore his reading glasses perched on top of his balding head, white hair fringing his pate like a victory wreath. She knew how much he enjoyed surveying the store in the morning hours before opening. She watched with affection as he ambled down the long aisle toward the business office, peering down each row of retail space, visually checking for order, cleanliness. Given his years of experience, he could, at a glance, accurately estimate turnover and profit for the month. And it had been a very good month.

When he saw her, John Skinner Webster winked. "That prep school education paying off for us, Margaret?"

It was an old joke, as was her rejoinder: "Webster School of Business. We're doing just fine."

He leaned over her desk and studied the columns of numbers in her neat hand. "Eh, I was low. That's good." He gave her a cheerful thump on the back.

"Is Uncle Turnbrough coming?"

"Yes."

"May I stay for the meeting?"

Her father studied her.

"My idea," she said. "My work."

His face grew pensive; in that instant he looked older. More saddened than angry.

"We have been over this, Margaret. Thou must understand that thy hard work might be undermined by thy presence—"

"—which does not say much for me!"

"On the contrary. This is about Turnbrough's limitations, not about thy capabilities."

"But Father, he calls himself a Friend! That is shameful. Equal in the pew, but not the marketplace?"

"Thy gender is not the issue with Turnbrough. Nor thy age nor thy modern ways. Rather all of them together, the sum of which seems too difficult for him to factor." Her father sighed and dropped into an armchair by her desk. "Aye, 'tis shameful."

Her father's agreement opened a floodgate of self pity. "It is simply not fair!" She knew her mistake as soon as she said it.

He sighed, gazing at the activity outside. "I remember when these were mud streets. Could not call them dirt roads because Baltimore is too wet. Your Uncle Turnbrough and I grew up during those days. Everything required such effort. Adventuring together. We were like brothers even then, even before I married his sister." He turned to face her. "Not fair, you say? Can you imagine White Elk paddling all the way down the Susquehanna from trapping sites in northern Pennsylvania? Perhaps even New York. Not even your great-grandmother Alizanna knew to what great lengths he had to trek to make a living-wage quota of beaver pelts. Not fair, Margaret? Their daily work was … back-breaking. Treacherous." He stretched his arms wide, his face flushed. "Thrilling. Rewarding. Yet almost never fair. Not in thy sense of it."

Margaret returned his direct gaze. "Fair or not, I want to be part of that meeting because you have trained me for this work. Is that not Alizanna's legacy to her great-granddaughter?"

"Thou favors the expansion plan but dislikes the partner, I gather."

"Father, I do not trust Uncle Turnbrough. For years he has desired a partnership with you. You divided the farmland and have kept both family and friendship peaceable. But you have eluded the partnership. Why? Whatever your reasons, it is important for you to remember them now."

"All the more reason for thee not to attend the meeting, my dear. If I am going to disappoint an elder kin, both friend to me and brother to thy mother, better that it be without an audience.

Outside, Maggie had to labor to catch her breath in humid summer air, dense odors of horse droppings and sweat, commingled with the sweeter scents of saltwater and, through open doors or windows, merchants' spiced foods. She walked, aimlessly at first, along Lee Street and to the harbor. On any other day, she would exult in the colors and textures of her harbor town: red-brick facades of townhouses in neat rows; ships at harbor, their colorful flags snapping in the breeze; fragments of brilliant blue sky visible between the masts. On this day, she found herself studying the faces of women passersby. Even the privileged powdered faces shimmered with perspiration in the morning heat. She saw faces drawn with age or burdens or both. And round, young faces gazing at their beaux with coquettish eyes. Margaret heard people bellowing greetings to others in African and European dialects, with accented English ranging from pidgin to Queen's court. She observed faces and features in every shape, color, and description, all beautiful in the eyes of someone, somewhere. And in all, she felt the alien. Nowhere did she see a woman with whom she felt kinship.

She gazed at the water lapping the gritty shoreline below the corner of Lee and Light streets. A fresh breeze rippled over the harbor's water. She lifted her arms, felt the billowing of her azure linen blouse and slate-colored skirt—the colors of this day's sky and sea. A locomotive departed for Philadelphia with its haul in a display of steam and sparks. Ships left for London and other more exotic destinations, journeys her father had had the good fortune of completing.

Maggie walked farther along Light Street, to Barre Street, and the home of her sister. Becky and Philip Tyson had graciously invited Maggie to stay with them in the three weeks prior to her marriage, as her parents' home filled with visiting guests, and her mother's excitability worsened. Maggie arrived to find a letter waiting for her on the vestibule table and also a box from her seamstress. The long-awaited wedding gown!

The envelope featured her brother Henry's handwriting, elegant and flawless, addressed from Washington City. She missed him, and in her mood today, Washington City and Henry seemed especially far away. She pushed the twine-secured box aside and slit open the letter with her thumbnail.

> Dear Mag,
>
> I cannot look forward without fear and trembling, knowing that there may be evil at hand which no human sagacity can avert or even foresee, and which may come upon us at any moment.

Maggie shuddered, almost returning the letter to its envelope. Should she read it later, when, hopefully, she would be in a stronger frame of mind? Henry and Robert had become close friends and confidants, as evidenced by the decision Henry and Lizzie made to name their son Robert. Henry shared far more about the political mood in Washington with Robert than with Maggie. Robert guarded his tongue with her on the subject, uncharacteristically so. She read on:

> We see no visitors and hear nothing from the old folks at home or young folks either, except when one of Mr. Tyson's letters to me on coal, gold, or copper business contains an item or two in regard to family matters—and of these by the way he never omits to make some mention. Lizzie is particularly anxious to hear from you and says you must give her all the news. She sends a great deal of love to yourself and better half, in which I cordially join,
>
> Your affectionate brother,
> Henry

Maggie felt her cheeks grow hot with regret in spite of Henry's diplomacy. It was true, too much time had passed since she last wrote, and she rued the distance and time that separated her from her dearest friend. *My letters are too few and in them I tease Lizzie too much,* she fretted. *And why the teasing? Why not simply tell her I am lonely and I miss her?*

"Never mind," she told herself aloud. "The wedding is barely a month away and soon we shall all be together again." Robert and she had arrived at a compromise. Given their Maryland and Pennsylvania relations, they would host a week's worth of entertaining and parties at the Tysons' home and Websters' town residence in Baltimore. And then they would be married in Carlisle at the newly completed Sharon. Followed by a trip to some tantalizing destination Robert would only hint about. And then …

"Is that you, Mag?" Becky's skirts rustled against stair rails, her ringed hand skidding along the banister. "Is that your dress? Finally! Let me see!"

Becky ushered Maggie and her package into a sunny bedroom off the main corridor. She left the door ajar and opened both windows, ecru dotted swiss curtains billowing slightly in the summer heat. "Gracious, it's gotten steamy so quickly!" Becky said, as she opened her sewing bag and found a stuffed fabric strawberry bristling with steel pins. "Wait!" she fussed. "Before you open it, I want to bring in some gardenias and pink rosebuds I snipped. They're resting in a vase of water in the kitchen!" Becky hurried from the room, calling back, "They are for an idea I have, you'll see!" Maggie basked in her older sister's attentions and overlooked her bossiness. It was good to see Becky, normally so reserved, excited about something. Becky returned with a fragrant display of pink and white blossoms gathered in a vase in her hands.

"Ah, Becky, they are lovely!" Maggie inhaled deeply and smiled.

Becky led Maggie to a dressing screen and mirror, setting the vase of flowers on a small table. "Slip off your things; we shall try this for fit. Wearing a corset? Good." She freed the box from its twine with a tiny pair of sewing scissors and used the sharp tines to slice open the wrapping so that she could lift off its lid. "Look!"

Vanilla waves of lace and organza tumbled over the sides of the box. "Oooh, Becky, it's a gorgeous fabric confection!"

"Silly girl!" Becky clucked, grinning. "Here is a note from our seamstress. She profusely apologizes for the delay, et cetera." Becky slid a wooden box-step in front of the mirror and adjusted the mirror's tilt on its frame. The gown seemed to gather itself over Becky's arms in great swells. "Bend! Let me lower this over your head. Then step up so that we may have a better look-see."

Maggie's hands emerged from the sleeves, and when her face, pink-cheeked, emerged through the dress's oval neckline she glimpsed herself, the disheveled bride. She began laughing.

"I … I look as if I boxed three rounds—and lost!"

"Now Mag, you're making me laugh! Stop! Or I shall surely button you wrong or jag you with pins!"

It was not until Becky had fastened the last loop over its satin button at the back of Maggie's neck that her laughter finally subsided.

"Stay facing away from the mirror, toward me, Mag. Here is the veil. You see how fresh flowers can be inserted along here?" Becky gathered some blossoms from the vase and deftly inserted them into lace eyelets along the veil's band. "Now bend down again and let me place the veil—yes, just the right length." Becky stepped back, appraising. She broke into a wide smile. "See for yourself."

Maggie turned and caught her breath at the elegant, radiant reflection of herself. Her fingers flew to her lips in astonishment.

"Is that the door knocker?" Becky asked, distracted. "Were we expecting anyone?"

Becky and the bride-to-be turned toward the clatter of heavy bags dropped in the vestibule, then footfall in the hallway.

"No carriages for hire at the station!" Robert filled the doorway, flushed and breathing hard. "So I walked because I could not wait—" He halted, awestruck. Blinked.

"… to see you."

"Away with you!" Becky took his arm and began pulling him toward the door. "It's terribly bad luck to see a bride in her dress before the wedding."

"Wait!" Maggie hurried to Robert. She held his other arm. "Robert, I've been thinking. We never discussed my work."

"Your work?" Robert tried to turn.

"Out!" Becky, agitated, pulled harder.

"Yes, my bookkeeping work. My family's business. I've been assuming—" Becky grunted with exertion as Robert twisted back and forth in their grasp.

"For pity's sake, Becky, unhand my fiancé!"

Flushed, Becky let go and staggered back a few steps, arms slapping to her sides. "Fine! I will not be held responsible"—she stomped to the doorway, turned, glowered, hand on glass knob—"for the consequences!"—and yanked the door shut.

"Sorry, my dear." Maggie kissed his cheek.

"What kind of kiss was that?"

"A proper one."

"I want a less proper one." He pulled her close.

She returned his kiss but pulled away from his arms, agitated.

"What is wrong, Maggie?"

"We must finish this conversation, Robert. It's important."

"Mag, your father will be able to find another bookkeeper."

"I know my father can find another bookkeeper. I supposed, that is, I assumed I would continue working. In business. Your business."

Robert opened his mouth. Closed it. Rubbed the back of his neck distractedly. "You mean Henderson Mill? My father does all of the bookkeeping, for the dairy and distillery, too."

"I meant your law office."

"It's a new practice, Mag. Right now I do my own—"

"Fine!" *I sound like Becky, prim and bossy,* she thought, annoyed with herself. "Another company then."

"In Carlisle?" Robert folded his arms, looking like a man cornered.

"Yes, of course."

"Carlisle is not, well, it's not," Robert said, distressed, beginning to squirm, "Carlisle is not Baltimore."

Now Maggie was dumbstruck. *Of course it's not!* She imagined an entire town populated by Col. William Hendersons. Her stomach twisted. "Perhaps I could take the train each week." Her voice seemed to come from afar. She felt her knees begin to buckle, lurched for the back of a chair. Sat down.

He stepped toward her, his arms open in entreaty. "Maggie. Of course I'd be delighted to have you manage the law firm's ledgers. I'm sorry I didn't suggest it before. That will free me to spend more time practicing law. You will help grow the practice."

Maggie tried to return his relieved smile. But in her mind's eye she saw herself as a lone figure standing on the outskirts of Carlisle, an army of Colonel Hendersons barring the sole route into town.

~January, 1854~

The Letter

Snow raged against their windows with such force—wind-borne glossy arrows of ice and snow—that Maggie carried old linens around the house, rolling and tucking them into the rattling casements to calm and warm them. Nevertheless, Baby Webster slept peacefully, thank God. She had household bills to review, laundry drying on a rack in front of the fire, waiting to be folded, and correspondence to complete.

Given the raging storm, she particularly enjoyed the crackle and aroma of the wood fire roaring safely in its grate behind a screen. Opening and reading Philip Tyson's letter by the fire would be her reward for completing all these other necessary, mundane tasks. Robert had given the letter to her this morning before he stoically ventured out to his office. They had both expressed surprise at the letter's arrival, its delivery man stomping snow from his boots onto their porch. This on-again, off-again blizzard had taken down telegraph lines and no mail had arrived on the previous day. The letter was a double treat, considering that her dear friend and brother-in-law Philip Tyson rarely wrote. Maggie tingled with curiosity, folding each garment faster than the last until she felt she could no longer stand it.

She flung herself into the cocoon of her jade velvet chair with curved high back, angled toward the fireplace, and tore open Philip's letter. She blinked upon seeing the Washington City dateline. What on earth could Philip be doing in Washington in this weather?

> Washington 22 January 1854
> Dear Margaret:
>
> You have no doubt heard by telegraph of our sad bereavement, but as I can readily realize your anxiety to hear more, I give you a brief account.
>
> About six o'clock last evening, dear Lizzie was delivered of a daughter without the least unfavorable symptom. One hour after however, she was seized with convulsions—

Convulsions? Bereavement? Lizzie's baby? Lizzie? "God, please, no!" Margaret moaned, slipping out of the chair to her knees. She read the rest of the letter through a blur of tears.

> —which lasted about an hour. After which the convulsions were renewed with great violence and left her in a sinking condition so that it even became apparent that Lizzie was near the close of her blameless life.
>
> Feebly aware of her situation, she wished she might be spared for her dear husband and children but, as that might not be,

she said she was perfectly resigned to her fate under the confident hope she would be again united to them in heaven.

The shock was terrible to Henry & your mother, but they had become more composed when Becky and I arrived at seven this evening.

The telegraphic dispatch did not reach us until the morning cars had left, so that we had to come in the five p.m. train. Although Becky knew not the full state of the call, I had prepared her mind for the reality before we arrived. I need not tell you how keenly she feels the loss of dear Lizzie. I know not how to offer consolation in such a case: there is none but in the happy gift she delivered to this world.

The dear little infant occupies the attention of your mother and Becky as well as Henry, and I hope will prevent their minds from dwelling too much upon their loss. Mother Webster says this little girl, though small, is healthy.

I would have been glad to have given you every particular but besides having numerous letters to write tonight it is late and I must end here.

Affectionately yours,
Philip T.

Her remains will be consigned to the earth at 2 p.m. tomorrow. It could not be longer delayed.

After a few hours' paperwork, Robert could do little more than lock up the office and clear a narrow walkway outside, a path he would likely have to clear again tomorrow. He did not see the sole figure stumbling along High Street's unevenly mounded snowdrifts, coat whipping open in the wind, like slow-beating blackbird wings. All sound muffled by winter white, he did not notice until the figure was nearly upon him. When he turned, shielding his eyes from the pelting snow, he cried out in alarm as the figure crumpled at his feet.

"Margaret! What's wrong? Where is the baby? MAGGIE!"

~February, 1854~

Counterpane

Counterpane. An oddly appropriate term for a blanket, Maggie thought, given the pain of her present circumstances. She smoothed the embroidered edge of the linen sheet where it folded over the blanket. Her legs made shallow bumps beneath. Next to her, on Robert's neatly tucked side of the bed, squatted her cherrywood lap secretary, its hinged lid yawning open. Henry's wedding gift. Correspondence from Lizzy and Henry littered the rest of the bed, pages fanning out over Maggie's trembling legs.

Robert had insisted their massive basement stove be fully charged with coal, had held his hand over the floor grate. "Feel that warm air?" He had just added more logs to their bedroom fireplace. "This will keep you cozy," he had said. Indeed, her cheeks felt flushed and warm to the touch. Under her nightgown, perspiration coated her chest. Yet she could not keep her hands and legs from shaking.

"I shall read them in order, from their move to Washington City—earliest first," she said to the French mantle clock and to its odd triangular companion. Robert had placed the thermometer there as if to remind her why they could not travel to Washington City. Snow storms. Sub-zero temperatures. Trains running, or not running. Life goes on, or not.

She picked up a letter and even in the date, through his buoyant script, heard the cheerful voice of her dear brother Henry.

Washington City, Sunday Evening, March 26, 1853

> Dear Mag,
>
> I have been to church today, and it is blowing too hard for anyone to go out again with comfort. Lizzie has gone to lie down after telling me to give you her love and say that she is disconsolate—a woman's work is never done—which sounds to me like a verse I have heard before, tho' I can't remember in what poet's works I have met with it. The fact is Lizzie is suffering for want of someone to talk to, or to talk to her.

The bedroom door opened a crack. Robert's careworn eyes appeared. "I heard you crying again, darling. Are you certain this is helping you?"

She took his hand when he sat next to her on the bed. "If I cannot be *with* them, I must *be* with them, and this is the only way I know."

Robert scanned the letter, looked away. "I remember that one," he said in a distant voice. "Why does each winter seem harsher than the last?" He pulled a linen handkerchief from his pocket and wiped her brow and cheeks with it. He kissed each eye.

"Webbie and I will bring your supper soon. You must take some nourishment, Maggie. I do not like threatening you, but if you don't eat something,

Webbie and I shall be forced to occupy your bedside with much wailing and gnashing of teeth. And gums."

"Oh, no ..." she sniffed, managing a thin smile.

Robert seemed heartened. He kissed her mouth—with longing, she noted—and slipped out, easing the door closed behind him. *My neglected husband! He has been so patient. And I cannot seem to rouse myself from this bed.*

"Counterpane," Maggie sighed, laying aside Henry's letter. She stretched her fingers, spiderlike, toward the edge of the next letter. Also Henry's handwriting. Picking it up and holding it required superhuman strength. "Lord," she sighed. And left her prayer at that. Maggie recognized the date and its significance. May 20, 1853. She scanned the contents until she found the spot where Henry announced Lizzie's pregnancy in a way that was pure Henry.

> My wife, when she was first married, in spite of her household employments found time hung heavy on her hands, and I understand you do the same. I do not know what she would have done had not a lucky thought sent her to making fancy work. All kinds of curious things has she made: funny little stockings not much larger than my thumb, little pinafores, bodices, dresses, flannels, everything in miniature, and the funniest part has been the affectation of mystery with which all this is carried on. Instead of being taken to the parlor as fancy work generally is, she assiduously keeps it out of sight and seems embarrassed if anyone detects her with a piece of the work in hand. However, it seems to have amused her, and, as it turns out, these items shall soon be of considerable use. So I advise you, if you have not enough to do of other things, to follow your dear friend Lizzie's example, and take to <u>fancy work</u>.

Maggie closed her eyes. She knew three curse words. Though she never said them aloud, she thought them now, lobbing them toward heaven with all the strength her spirit could muster. In her mind's eye, she picked up rocks, threw those along with the verbal ones. Hand-sized rocks at first, then boulders, and then enormous globe-sized ones. She lifted them high above her head and hurled them until they rolled like peas to the feet of the Almighty. She wrestled from the depths of her heart bitter fragments of a prayer. "Lord. How selfish of You. To take her from us." She opened her eyes. They fell on a letter with the dateline Mt. Repose, Wednesday, June 7, 1853.

> Dear Mag,
>
> It is the intention of a number of persons to take the cars at Cockeysville station, on Monday morning next, and transfer themselves to your domicile as early thereafter as speed of the locomotive will permit. As a loving brother, I give you notice of the intended immigration in order that you may prepare for

it. According to the present understanding the party will consist of the Websters and the Tysons and will remain from four to seven days according to circumstances, most probably the shorter period.

Lizzie, Betty, and Ma are in perfect health and look forward to seeing you, as do I.

Mention of Maggie's mother brought a fresh stab of grief. Her father had died the previous year. Dropped dead. In an aisle of his beloved store. Ma soldiered on, dependent upon the frequent ministrations of Henry and Lizzie, Philip and Becky, querulous toward her absent younger daughter who had "run off to Pennsylvania." After her own mother died, Lizzie had started calling Mrs. Webster Ma. *Even before she and Henry were married, sweet Lizzie always doted on her. How will Ma bear losing her?*

Maggie could hear Robert's voice though not his words, rumbling up the spiral staircase from somewhere below, the kitchen perhaps. *And Sarai's here.* When Maggie had still been pregnant with Webster, Robert had hired the "remarkable Sarai"—his description—after getting to know her through her husband Chance, a local carpenter. The Thompsons lived nearby.

What's this—an undated letter? Ah! Lizzie's hand. Maggie frowned. She realized that it had been written just this Christmas past. December, 1853. Her hands stilled as she heard her best friend's voice echo from memory to heart.

Dear Maggie:

Knowing you would like to hear from me, I thought I could not employ a few moments better than in writing you. Ma is sitting by and seems to be quite happy in reading a very interesting book Henry gave her. The weather is very damp and the walking bad so that the children have to be housed a great deal.

We started to take a walk today. There was a turnout of old soldiers & we happened to come upon them. Ma was alarmed on my account but I felt no fear as it was the most orderly procession I ever saw and we had no difficulty in getting out of it.

Do write. My best love to all and everybody and blessings. I am as ever

Your affectionate friend,
E.

Maggie gritted her teeth against the pain of loss. It burned as if one of the red glowing logs had sprung from the grate and rolled over her soul until it was charred brittle and lifeless. *I too am an old soldier*, she thought, *and weary of the battle*. "Soldier's heart, they call it," she said aloud to the pitcher and bowl on her washstand. "Perhaps that is what is wrong with me." She groaned when she saw the last letter—from Henry, just arrived, yet already smeared by tears, both dried and those falling now.

Washington City, January 29, 1854
Beloved Sister,

Would that you, and Lizzie's other nearest and dearest ones, could be with me in the sorrowful hours. Dear Ma is still here and her presence has been inexpressibly consoling. It is useless to speak of my loss. All can see it in some degree but sense only the thousandth part of its reality. What Lizzie was to me, none but myself and the Searcher of hearts know or can know: Her influence was upon my heart, and I trust and believe it was not of the fleeting nature of human things, but like all that is pure and holy it will endure forever. Through her love it was given me to attain peace of mind, to a degree of rest in my affections, wishes and thoughts, and to an amount of happiness, which I had never expected God would vouchsafe to me, nor did I think my heart was capable of receiving.

Now that she is taken away, I await with fear the development of what yet is in store for me, though yet with confidence in the mercy of Him whose loving kindness blessed me with the gift of her love.

When I look back upon the few short years of my union with Lizzie, I see a thousand things that were intended by Providence—if I may say so—to prepare for this event, and I find reason to be truly thankful for many things that I used to lament. Among these was the want of society for Lizzie in Washington, and how can I now be too grateful for a circumstance that drew so closely the bonds of our union, and enabled me to give myself up, with so little intervention, to the influences of her mild and loving spirit. Her heart was as pure as a snowflake. There was, as I believe and declare, no stain of earth upon it. She had not a thought or a wish or a hope, as I believe, that she will fear to see, exposed on that last, great day. If the pure in heart are to see God, she is with him now.

That such a mother should be taken from her little children is a mystery shrouded in perfect darkness. But the mercy of God is manifested in many circumstances that soften the blow. The dear little baby thrives. I am anxious to give her a name that shall connect as much as possible with the memory of dear Lizzie, and I can think of none so appropriate as yours.

Remember me to Robert.

Affectionately, your loving brother,
Henry

Maggie looked away and caught sight of her swollen face in the mirror. "Stop crying," she hissed angrily. In her reflection she saw tangible grief: a dark, misshapen thing. More gently she added, "Put it away now. Others need you."

On a separate sheet, Henry's letter bore a postscript:

> Betty sends her love and encloses a drawing of a country house and little girls of her own manufacture.

Maggie cupped the tiny cutouts in her hand, gently stroking them as if they were actual tiny versions of Betty and her new little sister. She cocked her head, listening. Her eyes grew wide with wonder. "Grace speaks in a child's voice!" she breathed. She heard footsteps mounting the first stairs of the staircase, the silvery clinking of a lunch tray, her own baby, Webster, cooing his glee.

"All right then," she sighed, glancing heavenward. "I shall get up, as you say. Sorry about the rocks." She slipped Betty's cutouts back into their envelope. She gathered the rest of the letters into a stack, tucking them into the lap secretary. "If, however, I am taken from my Webbie before he reaches adulthood," she closed the secretary lid with resolve, "there shall be hell to pay!"

PART II

Thompsons & Hendersons

1861-1862, the War begins

(Carlisle)

~January, 1861~

Politicking for Peace

A relentless winter cold settled into every nook and cranny of Carlisle, the wind shoving drifts of snow up to window ledges. Horse-drawn sledges armed with plow-share blades worked throughout the day to clear snow from streets and lanes so that business and school could resume.

Web watched for Junior from the carriage since the snow had become too deep for Junior to use his shortcut through the woods. "Avast, Yancy! A Shipwreck! Ahoy, a survivor!" Web called when he spotted Junior along the road.

Under ordinary circumstances, Robert told himself, he would enjoy the yips and giggles of two boys on their way to school. These were not ordinary times. Work mounted around him: the needs of his law firm's clients, doubled with his growing political party responsibilities. Thus, buried in his work, he gave the boys little more than a raised eyebrow when their cavorting became too energetic.

With Web and Junior safely deposited at school, they continued to Robert's law office, where he gave Yancy a bundle of work documents to deliver to Maggie back at Sharon.

Concerning work, Robert and Maggie had arrived at a compromise: Maggie would do bookkeeping for the firm from an office at home. She disliked the isolation. On most of those days, during more decent weather, she would have Yancy drive her back into town to drop off completed work at the office, confer with Robert, visit with a friend, or make purchases at Ogilby's or one of the other shops.

Maggie had also begun to work as a volunteer correspondent for an organization of women politicking for peace. Yet increasingly the group took on sanitation projects that served to prepare for war, such as fundraising for more beds and supplies for the local hospital and saving old linens for re-use as bandages. The other women called these activities "peaceful engagements," insisting that the work created better medical resources for the community in any case. Maggie grudgingly accepted this inconsistency and knew the irony was not lost on any of them. As wives and mothers, they were perfectly capable of managing multiple contingencies. And wiping up messes.

She had also become a more faithful correspondent to Henry, and to Becky and Philip. In her letters to the Tysons, she disclosed her concern about Henry's sad moods and the looming war. She filled letters to Henry with cheerful, encouraging tidbits. She missed his good humor. Both Robert and she urged him to accept more work from Robert's firm, perhaps even move closer. Whether writing the Tysons or Henry, she always included amusing adventures of Web and his friend Junior. She did not mention, but spent increasing amounts of time puzzling over, an adult relationship that eluded her. Sarai Thompson.

The Thompson family had recently begun attending the Hendersons' church. Robert Thompson had purchased a pew in the rear that had been vacant for some months. Maggie ignored the eye-rolling and comments by parishioners who were scandalized by the Thompsons' presence. She overheard someone say, "Don't they know the gallery space is for them. Heavens, up there they wouldn't even have to pay!" But when one old harridan crabbed about the "unseemly ambition of that family," Maggie leveled her most penetrating gaze at the woman and replied, "Do you mean the Thompsons? Why, they are our closest neighbors."

At first, the boys had begged to be allowed to sit together. Maggie and Robert discussed it and thought that would be taking things a bit too far. The Thompsons apparently agreed, insisting that Junior remain with them and meet up with his friend after the service. So that he could see Junior, Web sat side-saddle in the pew, legs up, careful not to let his shoe bottoms soil Maggie's clothing. Maggie allowed this seating arrangement so long as Web remained quiet and attentive to Rev. Wing. In fact, it seemed to help Web concentrate. His childishly surreptitious system of winks and grins distracted Maggie, though, and on at least one occasion, she failed to stifle a laugh that drew Pastor's stare, mid-sermon.

Robert seemed to have an easy, friendly relationship with Junior's parents. Not so, Maggie.

On the Thompsons' first Sunday, after service, as Robert stood by the Henderson carriage and chatted with Chance Thompson, Maggie approached Sarai, who averted her eyes and turned. Sarai called Junior and busied herself with buttoning his coat. Maggie had tried on several other occasions, but Sarai frowned, withholding eye contact. She made it clear she preferred small talk with the two husbands, or no conversation, to any talk with Maggie.

Maggie had been drawn by Sarai's intelligence and energy, during those months when Sarai had worked at Sharon and helped care for Web and the household's domestic affairs. Maggie felt frustrated by Sarai's pulling away. Had she been this remote when she worked for them? Maggie could not remember having had a single conversation with Sarai, beyond instructions, since that time was so blurred by the emotions of new motherhood and her devastation after losing Lizzie. After Junior was born, Sarai no longer came to help with Webster. *Perhaps*, Maggie admitted to herself, *I set the cool tone. Perhaps I should keep trying.*

Sunday was the only day their paths crossed. But cool, enigmatic Sarai only withdrew more with each of Maggie's attempts. Sometimes Sarai walked away toward her home so abruptly that her husband and son would have to hurry to catch up.

Maggie did not know where Sarai shopped. Negroes tended not to frequent the downtown market unless they were doing the selling. She wondered what Sarai's market was like. What sorts of purchases might she make and place in her market basket? Did Sarai even use a market basket? The knowledge that they lived in separate worlds pulled at the edges of Maggie's beliefs and assumptions. When in town, she considered venturing into the colored section. She lost her nerve, telling herself that it would be presumptuous. For the same reason, she rejected the idea of paying a visit next door, uninvited, to the Thompson home. When she watched Webbie and Junior at the table together playing checkers, she imagined Chance and Sarai sitting at the Hendersons' table, too. *That should happen, will happen. Some day*, she told herself. *If they invite us first.*

The Hendersons entertained frequently. Robert extended most of the social invitations. Maggie hosted community meetings or sanitary committee work projects. She was only vaguely aware that her busyness further isolated her from other women. And that there was really only one woman in the community she truly desired to know.

And so, perhaps once a week, Maggie would pause whatever activity had her attention to look across the back of her property and wonder what in the world Sarai Thompson was up to.

~late March, 1861~

Two Roberts

Chance stoked and lit the woodstove in his workshop. He closed and latched the stove door, opened the draft gradually until he heard the whoosh and thunder of flame engulfing dry wood. He breathed in its aroma. Cherry wood. Mr. Robert Henderson would like that. He favored a cherrywood pipe, cherry tobacco.

Chance stood at the narrow rectangle window over his workbench and watched the dirt lane where Henderson's carriage would pull in. Henderson was a punctual man. His carriage would arrive no later than 7:28, for their 7:30 appointment on this beautiful spring morning. Sweet, clear air, vibrating with life. A robin's egg blue sky. Weather gave no reason to defer the meeting, Chance was grateful for that. He had allowed Henderson to defer until spring his final payment. He was bringing it now and would feel indebted. He was coming to Chance's office because Chance had asked him to come and allow time to discuss something he had for Henderson. His curiosity aroused, of course the father of Junior's best friend had said yes.

Chance's leg jiggled from nerves. Blood felt the carriage arrive, stood and yawned. "Stay in here, Blood. Sit. Mr. Henderson likes you, not your paws on his suit." Chance rewarded his dog's obedience with a grin and a quick scratch behind its ears as he hurried out the door.

He greeted his guest and returned his firm handshake. The two men walked the short gravel path to Chance's workshop. He held the door open. Henderson greeted Blood by patting his head. Blood rose but confined his eagerness to vigorous tail-wagging.

"Nice and warm in here. Fire smells good." Henderson reached inside his right coat pocket, withdrew an envelope addressed to Robert Chance Thompson, and gave it to Chance. Chance ran his thumb across his first name, the one he shared with this man. Chance thanked Henderson, who then reached into his left coat pocket for his pipe and tobacco, tamped some in, and lit it while Chance opened the envelope. Chance put the money into his till, separating the bills by denomination—his way of counting without offending the customer. He tucked the envelope into his ledger for entry later, marked Henderson's invoice paid, and returned it to him.

"First rate work." Robert exhaled a ring of smoke with the compliment.

"Thank you for the opportunity." Chance turned to a folded worktable, pulled it from its hook on the wall and opened it. "You admired mine, so I made one for you, Mr. Henderson."

"Call me Robert, please!" Henderson's eyes widened with pleasure at the sight of the worktable. "This is a handsome piece!" He crouched to run his hand along its smooth lacquered surface. "Why, it's cherry, isn't it? Ahhh …" he chuckled, bobbing his head in admiration. He stood and gave Chance a penetrating look, another strong handshake. "I shall take this with me. Let's see …" He reached inside his jacket again. "How much do I—"

"It's a gift," Chance said firmly. "I thought you might need it. As captain of the company."

Henderson stood puffing his pipe, still admiring the table. "It's a splendid gift. Thank you."

"Captain Henderson. Robert." Chance waited until Henderson met his gaze. "I want to join your company."

Henderson pulled the pipe away, exhaled. "Your family needs you."

"So does yours. Our country needs us more."

"The company's training is almost complete. We—"

"I've been watching your training. I catch up quick. I have my own gun. And I use it well."

Chance watched Henderson mentally rifle through the many ways he could say no. Henderson clenched his jaw almost imperceptibly. He did not break eye contact with Chance. Finally: "You have been worshipping with our congregation for some months now. Has anyone invited your family to supper?"

He knows the answer to that question, Chance thought. *Our sons are best friends. Yet we have never supped together.* When Chance did not respond, Robert shifted uncomfortably and looked away.

"See here," Henderson cleared his throat. "Yes, I could make you a soldier in my company. We are volunteers, after all. The men have high commitment; they would not resign. But acceptance would come grudgingly. Under fire, if not before." He paused. When his gaze again met Chance's, he sounded confident but looked doubtful. "My prayer is that we'll quell this rebellion quickly."

"Long war or short, I can make myself very useful."

"That's not the larger issue."

"What then?" Chance intended for his impatience to prod. *Get to it.*

"Everyone is saying this is a white man's war. There are no plans to raise colored troops."

"Everyone?" Chance further steeled himself. "Robert, you are friends with Meade. Your connections go far. I believe you have the influence to—"

"I do not know Mr. Lincoln personally. But I do know your own President does not want you to fight. Does not believe you are equal to it."

"He will be my President when I'm allowed to vote for him. What do *you* believe, Robert?"

Henderson's arms dropped to his sides, his pipe still cupped in his left hand. Its stem trembled. "Equal to fight? And vote? Yes, without question. But I don't believe any man could bear up under the mental pressure of what you propose. Even if you manage to attach yourself to a company, the other men will resent your spirit. Your own supposed comrades will try to break it. Insult you. Shun you. And if you wind up in enemy hands … Well. Why subject yourself to that?"

"Because I have no other choice," said Chance, his voice quiet with fury. "I must do this. For our sake. My son's sake. And yours. For their sons, God willing."

Henderson's mouth formed a thin line under his pencil mustache. "Perhaps if you had approached me earlier. . . . No. There is too little time. It would be too distracting, perhaps even a wasted effort if higher powers objected. Right now I must focus on my own affairs. Prepare my family. I'm sorry."

"If you won't help me, I'll try on my own. Unless you object, I'll use your name as reference."

Henderson nodded and remained silent. He turned to leave.

"Don't forget your table."

Henderson turned stiffly, a captain's look in his eye. "I assumed you no longer wished me to have it."

"Captain Henderson," Chance folded and secured the table, handed it to Robert as he spoke. "What I want is for you to use this table every day and think of me."

By the next afternoon, the air had turned frigid, numbing Chance's senses as he walked to Henderson's mill. Gusting winds bullied him head on, tried to force him off course. He raised the collar of his wool coat to the brim of his hat, pulled the hat lower on his forehead, and shouldered his way to the mill entrance. A farmer in dirt-caked boots stood waiting inside, startled when the door blasted open.

Mill machinery roared with the same intensity as the wind's, but at least, Chance mused, his ears could thaw out in this din. He took off his hat and rubbed his forehead where the hatband had pressed. A young man with a wisp of beard worked on the farmer's order. None of the Hendersons were visible on the floor. When the farmer completed his transaction and shuffled out, Chance asked to see Col. William Henderson. The clerk pulled nervously at his beard, then motioned Chance over to the steps and hurried off so that Chance mounted them alone.

He knocked once, then entered in time to see the Colonel's lolling head jerk, half-veiled eyes snap awake. He was seated behind his vast desk at an open ledger book. An empty glass and squat coal-colored bottle kept him company.

"Thompson! Was I expecting ye?"

"No, sir."

"Don't call me sir. I'm not King Arthur or any of his damn knights. Sit down."

Chance unbuttoned his coat and sat in a thick-legged wooden chair in front of the desk, resting his hat in his lap.

"Colonel," Chance began, keeping his eyes on Henderson's glazed expression. "I plan to enlist in the war effort."

"Good for ye!" William Henderson pounded his desktop with the flat of his hand. The desk's contents reverberated. "Go get those rebellious sons of guns!" The Colonel pulled open a desk drawer. "I'll find another glass and we'll drink to it."

"No, thank you, Colonel Henderson."

"No? Well then, I'll drink to it myself." When he tilted the bottle, only a thin thread of whisky trickled into his glass. He set down the emptied bottle, looking bereft.

"Colonel, I want to make some arrangements for my family while I'm gone." Chance pulled some documents from his pocket and began to unfold them. "This account shows how steady my farm has been in grain supply and cash payments—"

Henderson waved them away. "Don't tell me things I already know, Thompson. What do ye want?"

"I want to make an agreement with you that, if there's a shortfall on our farm's income, my wife can come to you to receive monthly payments of up to $35. During harvest season our family's farm will produce the goods to justify those payments. My wife's sister and her husband manage it well. But if the farm does not produce, or if costs of goods in wartime require a larger monthly allowance for my family, I want to arrange a loan with you at a fixed rate of interest to cover the difference. When I return, I'll settle any debt remaining."

"What are the banks charging?" Henderson squinted, the line of his mouth curling into a smirk. He knew the answer.

"Currently three percent. They will not fix that rate, so I am prepared to pay—"

"The banks won't loan ye the money at any rate, will they Thompson?" Henderson sawed off a laugh rusty with irony. "Idiots. They wouldn't recognize a profitable opportunity if it poked them in the ass." Henderson tore a blank page from the back of his ledger and began writing. "Done!"

"Done? What do you mean, Colonel?"

He looked up, scowling. "What do ye mean, what do I mean? Didn't ye just ask me to arrange for monthly cash payments of up to $35, when your wife requests it, and to extend a fixed rate loan of three percent to cover the loan?"

"Yes. I just—"

"Well, ye can't expect me to sit here and write out a contract if you're yammering away. It's distracting." He scowled at the paper. "Is this contract between me and ye, or between me and your wife? What's her name?"

"Sarai. S-A-R-A-I."

Colonel Henderson scribbled the name on the paper's upper margin. "Thanks, Thompson. Maybe ye can help me out by spelling some of the other big words in this contract, eh?" He glowered, waiting.

"The contract is between you and me." Chance sat rigid in the chair, anger gathering in his chest, volatile as stoked gunpowder. He counted. Bit hard on his tongue. Silently prayed.

"Here's my suggestion regarding wording for the length of contract." Henderson bent his head trying to decipher his own scrawl. "Contract period to conclude upon your return, or upon your wife Sarai's request. Specify a period of time to pay back debt, let's see, how about up to ten years?" Henderson looked up. "How's that?"

"And if it's paid off early, no penalty?" Thompson's hands relaxed on the arms of the chair. "That's fair. That's more than fair."

"Yes, it is." Henderson smacked his lips with satisfaction as he returned to his writing. "Either way, ye are going to make me some fair and square money, Thompson. And ye are going to give those damned Rebels one hell of a fight!"

~June, 1861~

Business

"We wait 'til there's good running space between wagons. Then run. Firing as we go."

"May I carry the flag?" Webbie waved a maple branch, leaves still attached to its tip.

"Careful! Stay low behind this bush. You don't want enemies to see you."

"What's good running space, Junior?"

"See that wagon? When it passes us, start counting."

"One … two … three … four … five …"

"Stop! Because the next wagon went by, see? Do you think we can run through enemy lines on a five count?"

Webbie looked at Junior, then up the length of his flag of maple leaves. "I think so."

"Know so, soldier?"

Webbie exhaled bravely. "Know so."

Junior peered through a narrow passage in the winterberry thicket that bordered the road leading to Henderson's mill. "Look!" he whispered. "Another enemy wagon approaching! Start running on One!"

"ONE!"

Two boys dashed across the road screaming numbers, one madly waving a leafy stick, the other firing his finger at a farmer's one-horse wagon loaded with barley. The horse reared over their heads. Webbie caught sight of its wild eye and froze. Junior shouldered Webbie to the ground where they both rolled onto the grassy berm on the other side of the road and lay, panting. The farmer shook his fist at them as he clattered by.

"See any rips on me? My mam will kill me if—"

"My mother will kill me more!"

The boys stood and took turns dusting off each other's backsides before heading to the mill.

They entered the front door to the oily scent of machines and men at work. Feathery wisps of seed hulls floated through the air. The boys sneaked by the front counter to avoid the wagon window where that angry farmer's face might appear.

Through another door and they were engulfed by the ear-thrumming rumble and hiss of the millstones at work. They felt it through their feet, their skin, their bones, their shivering teeth. Jaws agape, they beheld two behemoth stones grinding grain, a monstrous, roaring beast, yet wondrously mechanical and somehow tamed to do the work of many men.

"Fee fie fo fum!" Junior heard a man's growl, saw Webbie fly up into the air.

"I smell the blood of a Scotsman!" A hulking man dressed in a black coat and a black brimmed hat held Webbie diagonally across his chest and hoisted him toward the grinding millstones.

"Grandfather!" Webbie shrieked with terrified glee.

"Colonel Henderson!" shouted the miller tending the hopper. "Ground boy will spoil this here batch of flour."

"What? This fine Scot blood spoils the grain?" Colonel Henderson bellowed, suspending Webbie in midair.

"The bones, sir. Gets caught in folks' teeth. They won't like it, sir."

Colonel Henderson with slow reluctance set Webbie back on his feet. He grabbed Junior and lifted him. He roared, "What about this boy? He'd make a fine brown bran, ye think?"

The mill worker took his time studying Junior, whose legs wheeled helplessly in midair, his face taut and silent, caught between courage and desperation. Finally, the worker shook his head and turned back to the hopper. "No, sir. Same problem with the bones."

"All right then, Mr. Rutz." Colonel Henderson lowered Junior to the ground. He pushed back his hat to scratch his head. "What shall I do with ye boys?"

"Show us how the mill works, Grandfather!" Webbie giggled.

Colonel Henderson crouched to their eye level. He turned to Junior. "And what do ye want to know?"

Junior, still gulping for air, forced his voice to stay even. "You have other businesses, too."

"Indeed I do. Four enterprises in all."

"How do they all make money?"

The Colonel narrowed his eyes. "What's your name, boy?"

"Junior Thompson."

"Would your father be Chance Thompson?"

"Yes, sir."

Colonel Henderson rubbed his gray-stubbled cheek where the jowl lapped his neck. "Your father once asked me a similar question. He asked me *how* I run my businesses." The colonel's face broke into a lop-sided leer. "Yours is the *better* question." He stood. "Though it presents me with a problem because the answer happens to be a secret." He licked his lips conspiratorially. "Can the two of ye keep a secret?"

"Yes, sir!" they piped.

"Bound to secrecy then. Understood?" He squinted one eye and growled, "Or to the millstones with ye both. Ground bones be damned!"

The boys followed Webbie's grandfather as he pointed through a narrow eight-paned window to the waterwheel, shouting as he explained its power to move the rods and gears that turned the stones. He took them up a flight of stairs too narrow for his girth, forcing him to angle his body to fit. They watched as raw grain poured into a tempering bin for dampening. A man turned the mounding grain with a smart flip of his shovel. They smelled the yeasty dank odor of dry grain drinking in moisture.

"It will be ready in a day or so, to go into the hopper there," the Colonel said, pointing at a funnel-shaped bin positioned above the millstones. They peeked through cracks in the floorboards to see the runner millstone turning against the grain on the stationary bed stone. Its roar seemed tamer, their ears having accustomed their minds and hearts to it.

"Listen! Remember that sound. For a miller, ears, nose, and fingers are the most important. Any change in that sound tells ye something is amiss. And if ye smell burning, something is dangerously amiss. So keep your nose to the grindstone, boys, and your ears will also be ready to hear what they need to hear."

"A good miller must also have the touch." The Colonel, stepping sideways, led them back down the stairs to where ground grain poured from the mill shoot. The colonel caught a handful. "Ye want to know how a miller makes money?" He crouched and held his fist up to each boy's nose. "Smell that? Take a strong whiff. That's the smell of money. Now watch." He opened his fist. "See how it lightly clings together? Money. But if it's too loose or too lumpy? No good. Now this." Webbie's grandfather stirred it with his finger. "Just the right size and shape. And this." He rubbed the ground grain between his fingers. "Just the right fineness. Perfect! Now cup your hands." The boys huddled next to each other, lining up their hands to form a careful trough as if ready to receive gold coins rather than grain. The Colonel bent to pour the ground grain into their hands. "Now ye feel it, eh? Perhaps ye have the miller's touch." He straightened. "Did ye know it takes grain to make whisky? Follow me. I'll show ye."

Colonel Henderson led the boys outside and mounted his horse. He sat behind the saddle and held the reins in one hand as with the other he hoisted each boy into place in front of him. "Tall lad first. Aye, and stocky grandson up front." Junior wrapped his arms around Webbie's middle, whispered in his ear: "We're stacked like logs!" Webbie held onto the front of the saddle and nodded. "Tight fit," he whispered back. "Good thing Grandfather's got an extra big saddle." Webbie's grandfather flicked the reins. "Take us to the distillery, Stella!"

The waterwheel's boisterous splashing receded behind them. They could still hear the LeTort's water scrambling coolly over rocks, still see glimpses of rapids foaming white as the road approximated its course, curving gently downward and along some of the Colonel's own grain fields. More horse and wagon traffic traversed the broad curve of packed earth around the distillery.

They dismounted and entered through barn-sized double doors to a green-smelling room, its floor spread with damp grain. "Scotsmen make scotch whisky, Webbie. And the whole process starts with barley grown with our good pure LeTort spring water." As Colonel Henderson scooped up some grain from the floor, he licked his lips as if parched by a powerful thirst. "See? This has begun to germinate. That's what ye want from the malting floor, for the proper sugars." He wiped his hands free of grain. "When ready, it's to the kiln for drying. Then to the mill, ground to a coarse flour."

"That's called grist, isn't it?" Webbie rubbed his nose, stifling a sneeze.

"Correct, Webbie. The grist comes back here and takes a nice hot bath. Comes out looking like your breakfast porridge. Then to the washback where we add yeast. Ah, the fermenting begins! Then to the still, where the alcohol gets separated from all other stuff. Then to the barrels, for aging. Some years later, it is ready for thirsty customers to buy and drink. And that they do."

He walked them through the distillery. Even though its door was closed, the boys felt the heat of the kiln bristle on their skin. Colonel Henderson spoke briefly with a journeyman named Samuel Lande and then took the boys down to the cellar. In the dark coolness, they could smell oakwood before they saw it, harvested and conscripted into barrels.

"Smells like a forest buried alive," Junior said.

"Sweet smell of whisky money!" the Colonel said, as if Junior and he were in perfect agreement.

"This is all your proptery too, Grandfather?"

"Property," the Colonel corrected quietly, his gentleness sounding odd against his sandpaper voice. "Your uncles run the businesses. And I count the money."

They found their way to daylight and the spot where Stella waited, nibbling grass at the base of her hitching post. They mounted, as before.

"To the dairy!" Colonel Henderson urged Stella.

At the road's fork, they bore right, crossed a sturdy beam bridge, and curved round the opposite side of the LeTort, arriving at a stone bank barn next to a white clapboard farmhouse, both ringed by a whitewashed rail fence. The fence gate stood open. On their way through to the barn, they passed two wagons loaded with capped ten-gallon tin urns, their sides sweating in the heat and beaded with creamy milk drippings.

They dismounted and entered the barn's shaded interior. A wide-shouldered boy arrived and tethered the first cow to her stall with a rope at each end, one looped around her neck, the other looped around one of her legs. The boy sat on the side of the tethered leg, safer from getting kicked. When he put his hands on two of her teats and began milking, she turned to glare, still chewing. She lowed and returned to her food trough, deciding to ignore him.

"Sometimes I milk my uncle's and auntie's cows," Junior observed.

"Truly?" Webbie watched the milking process, uncertain.

"Not this many, though. They have two."

"Two is just right." Webbie counted stalls. "Ten is too many for one boy." He looked up. "May I try, Grandfather?"

"Martin Burgett, let these boys have a go!" Colonel Henderson called to the boy milking. Martin leaned against the stable wall, his eyes hooded with feigned indifference. The Colonel took his seat at the milking stool. He pulled Webbie over so that he stood between his grandfather's legs, within easy bending reach of the cow's teats. Colonel Henderson guided his grandson's hands through the proper pull and squeeze motions. Before the demonstration was over, all three of them had squirted milk into a bucket, and into each other's mouths. The boys were still giggling as they remounted Stella.

"Ready for home?" the Colonel asked.

"You said there are four businesses, Grandfather," Webbie protested. "Where is the fourth?"

"Let's go back to the main road toward Sharon and see if ye can guess."

The boys looked for buildings on both sides of the road but saw only meadows, woods and fields.

"Farming?"

"Part of the mill business."

"Wood-cutting?"

"Part of the distillery."

"We're out of guesses, Grandfather."

"Are all the wagons plain?"

"No," said Junior. "Some say 'Henderson.'"

"Aha!" Colonel bellowed.

"You mean that carrying things around pays money?" asked Webbie.

A Henderson wagon rattled by as he spoke.

"The sound of money!" crowed Colonel Henderson. "I'll drink to that!" He pulled a silver flask from an inner pocket of his jacket, uncapped it and pulled a mouthful.

"Let me taste!" Webbie craned his neck, waving his hand toward the flask.

Colonel Henderson guided Webbie's hand as he had with the milking. Webbie swallowed hard. His cheeks bloomed pink, his eyes wide with surprise. Webbie took the flask in both hands and, twisting in the saddle, tipped it into Junior's mouth. Junior sucked cautiously, tasted, spat it out on the dirt road with gurgling disgust. He heard the Colonel laugh.

"Tastes like something no boy should try!" Junior rasped, his throat afire.

"Again!" Webbie took another taste. His smile was equal parts mischief and glee.

"Just a wee bit more. That's it." Colonel Henderson retrieved his flask from Webbie, who swallowed and coughed. "Ye have a taste for it, eh?" The old man sounded pleased with his grandson.

Junior squirmed. "Money for hauling things. Is that the secret part?"

"No." Colonel Henderson drew Stella to a halt so that they could watch another Henderson wagon go by.

"See the driver? His name is Creigh. Irish. And the fellow milking, Burgett? English. Remember Mr. Rutz? German. Mr. Lande? French. Good men. With great and special talents. Thompson, where's your papa from?

"Carlisle."

"And his papa? His grandpapa? Find out your history, Thompson. Your papa got his woodworking talent from a prior generation. Another time, likely another place. Everyone thinks it's the thing, the product. Don't fall in love with the product, boys. Look for talent. And character. That's the secret."

"To making money!" Webbie crowed, proud to have grasped his grandfather's lesson. Colonel Henderson chuckled as he withdrew his flask again and drank.

"Again!" Webbie exclaimed. When his grandfather said, "Just a wee bit more," Webbie laughed, took the flask in his hands, and sipped.

On the ride toward home, Junior felt Webbie begin to roll forward drowsily. Junior tried to hold him more tightly but kept losing his grip. He grabbed and twisted a handful of Webbie's shirt, pulling it tight. Stella jounced along at a canter. Webbie pitched forward and to the side of the horse.

"He's sliding off!" Junior yanked Webbie's shirt. He heard a tearing sound.

"Eh, what?" Colonel Henderson's voice rolled dreamily from above.

Webbie's head dipped and lurched to the side. Vomit sprayed onto the horse's side and the riders' right legs, densely fouling the air.

"What? Why, oh—" The Colonel reigned in Stella to a stop. Junior sat stiffly. Webbie was still bobbing loosely between Junior's arms. Webbie's grandfather brushed off his right leg with the flat of his hand. He bracketed both boys with his arms while maintaining his hold on Stella's reins, coaxing her into a slow trot. Junior wished himself far away from the old man's gnarled and hairy hand, smelling strongly of Webbie's shame.

When Junior's hand touched the doorknob, he heard Stella wheel and race down the gravel lane toward Sharon's gate. As he opened the door Junior steadied Webbie. The door yawned wide, then was yanked open even further from the other side.

"Webster Henderson!"

Webbie smiled up at his mother, one eyelid lower than the other. He burped. Junior turned his head against the smell.

Maggie pulled both boys into the vestibule, glaring at the fading haze of dust raised by Stella's hooves. She crouched to Webbie's eye level, studying his eyes, his red-patched pale face. "Where have you boys been?"

Junior cautiously replied, "With Webbie's grandpap. He showed us his businesses."

Webbie, with sloshy glee added, "Almost threw us 'tween the mill stones! But no! No bones!"

Junior watched Mrs. Henderson's eyes go hard with anger. "He what? Webbie, are you sick? Why do you smell so?"

"He had a… a taste of whisky." Junior stepped away until his back bumped against the doorknob.

"A *taste?*" Maggie exhaled her disgust, her eyes, murderous. She looked past Junior to the door and beyond it. "Junior?"

"The taste doesn't suit me." Junior noticed where he had grabbed the back of Webbie's shirt. It was crimped and torn. Junior clenched his own shirt with both anxious hands.

"Good!" Maggie said this grimly. She narrowed her eyes, fixing on Junior, looking him up and down as his own mam would. She gentled her voice. "Junior, can you safely find your way home? By yourself?"

"'Course!" Junior's hand found the knob and opened the door. He wheeled onto the porch, galloped down its steps and, choosing the path Stella could not take, vanished around to the rear of the house to the field and their footbridge, to home.

Maggie heard the downstairs grandfather clock strike five times, its mellow baritone suffusing the near silence. She had been in Webbie's room, rocking him, and stood to carry him to his bed. The rocker still swayed, its rolling staccato of wood against wood taking slow measure of her smoothing his sheet, his blanket, his cheek, his hair, still damp from a vigorous bath and his tearful protests. As he breathed evenly in sleep, the rocker gave up the last of its movement. She stood at the second-floor window of Webbie's bedroom watching for her husband's arrival. Rays from a setting sun filled the room, illuminating everything in it with slanting golden light: a small bed table bearing a saucer and teacup from which the boy had drunk two full doses of chamomile tea; a door and an armoire door, both ajar; a honed play stick leaning against the wall; a low bookcase, with two shelves brimming, one book knocked to the floor in Maggie's haste, next to Webbie's splayed shoes and vacated socks, pants, and shirt; a square desk and chair, its surface bare but its drawer stuffed and yawning; a squat bureau, its marble top scattered with the contents of a boy's pockets; and a spindle bed, containing one flame-haired, dreaming boy.

The moment her husband's carriage pulled up to the house, Yancy's top hat bobbing, Maggie rushed downstairs to the front door and threw it open.

"What is *wrong* with your father!"

"Hello?" Robert dropped his coat and valise onto the vestibule bench, astonished by his wife's crimson anger.

"I do not mean your father's drinking. He's a lush, that's clear." Maggie lunged, gripping Robert's coat by its lapels. "I want to know *why*. Why would he give liquor to eight-year-old boys? Why would he get his *grandson* drunk? Why?"

Robert clenched his jaw, his voice. "I shall handle this." As soon as he reached for the doorknob, she knocked his hand from it.

"Oh no, sir! First you answer my question. Enough of protecting the patriarch! That old man hides in his office. In his own home! He never bothers to visit here. Enough of the family secrets! I am family, too! We, Robert. WE are your family now!"

Robert reached for her hands. "I am not protecting him—"

Maggie shoved him away. "Oh, yes! Yes, you are! See, you cannot even answer my question!"

Robert covered his mouth with one hand, fingertips smoothing his mustache. She recognized the same cowed look she had seen in her son's eyes as he gulped the last of the forced tea.

"Fine! Keep your bloody secret! Your son is sleeping. Look after him." On her way out, Maggie slammed the door with such force that it popped back open. Through its widening crack, Robert watched her leave.

"Yancy! Bridle a rested horse! Never mind the saddle."

"But a lady *never*—" Yancy swallowed the words. He heard the ire in her shout, saw the fire in her stride. His fingers worked quickly. By the time she arrived at the carriage house, Yancy had found just enough time to throw a saddle over the horse's back and fasten it. "Now I know you be in a big hurry. This horse will get you there faster if'n we fix her up right." He talked fast as he bridled the horse and held the reins ready for Maggie.

Maggie stopped her pacing, grabbed a crop, and stepped up to Yancy as he offered her a leg up. She flung herself onto the horse, leaning forward, her skirts mounding around each leg and in the back. She pressed her heels into the steel-gray mare's sides and wheeled her toward the open gate. She slapped its backside with the crop for more speed and lay low against its neck, so that, by the time they reached the gate, horse and rider were a blue-gray streak against a darkening landscape.

When Nathan answered to the pounding on the front door at Oakland, his eyebrows arched with surprise, concern.

"Mag-g-gie, what—"

"I want to speak to your father." With both hands, she attempted to rake her hair, which was blown wildly about her shoulders and face.

"I don't think he's here."

"You don't know?"

"We lead separate lives …" Nathan rubbed the side of his neck. He held a book in the other hand, one finger stuck in it as a placeholder. "It's a big house, Maggie."

She began to shoulder her way in.

"Wait." He touched her shoulder. "What time is it?" He squinted at the fading daylight. "No, he's not here. He visits Meeting House Springs at this time every day."

"The old graveyard?"

"Yes. Mag-g-gie."

She wheeled around and hurried down the steps.

"Wait! What's happened?" He followed her as she returned to her horse.

"No time now, I—" Maggie turned toward him as she spoke. Her heel caught the hem of her dress. She crumpled and fell.

Nathan caught her flailing arms and lifted Maggie to her feet, her face just a hand's breadth from his.

Maggie, your eyes. Fearless! Looking into me—Wait!—

Maggie pulled away from Nathan and gathered her skirts.

"Do you want me to come along?" Nathan's arms, palms up, still held the space Maggie had occupied.

"Yes—I mean, *no*!" She waved away Nathan, but when she hesitated at her horse, Nathan came to her side and offered his cupped hands and shoulder as Yancy had done. Maggie remounted and rode away in one fluid motion.

Nathan watched her departure, skirt and hair billowing. *I commit to memory the truth of you. The scent of you. Rosewater, wind, jellied toast. Your hair caught behind your ear, strands of fire, grazing your open lips, I am jealous of their liberty—*

He spent the rest of the evening as he had many others, trying not to think about Margaret Webster Henderson.

Maggie dismounted at the cemetery gate, hitched the horse carelessly. The gate sat at an awkward angle in a slender black fencing with gilded points that circumscribed its graveyard, an antique calligraphy wrought in iron. It was the hour before gloaming, when light gathers itself from deepening shadows, shimmering an imitation of day. As she passed through the gate, she spied him toward the center, in profile, on one knee.

To reach him, she had to weave between aging headstones, time already erasing identities, lifespans and terse final sentiments. She stopped two headstones from where he crouched. The Colonel's black hat lay next to him on the grass. His head looked frail on his body. Gray hair, thin and matted, radiated from a pale bald spot. He clutched a fistful of flowers in his left hand. With his right hand, he selected blossoms stem by stem, placing them so that they encircled the base of the headstone inscribed ELIZABETH PARKER HENDERSON. The flowers' colors reflected gemlike in the day's fading translucence: pearled lily of the valley, sapphire woodland iris, citrine daffodils, amethyst hyacinth. Gathered from Oakland's garden.

"Explain yourself!"

Only when she spoke did he look up. He pushed himself upright with both large hands, crushing flowers as they fell. He used the headstone to steady himself. He stood with one shoulder sloped toward Maggie, bearing no trace of the defiant irony she associated with the Colonel. His forehead furrowed, the squint of failing vision. No light in those bead-black eyes. Only sadness. Sadness! So unexpected on that face! And so painfully unguarded, she had to look away for a moment.

"Well?" Maggie slapped her riding crop impatiently on her skirts, gathering courage to look at him again.

"I don't—" he said. "I can't."

"That's it?"

He opened his mouth. Pulled at his chin, as if this would draw forth the words. But his hand dropped, his shoulders dropped in a half-hearted shrug.

She straightened, shoulders back, judge and jury. "So be it. You may never again see our son unless Robert and I, or one of us, is present. You are a dangerous, unpredictable man."

Maggie turned her back and walked deliberately toward the horse. She wanted her sharp words to penetrate his hard, unrepentant heart. She did not bother leaving through the gate. She used a crossbar on the fencing as toehold from which to mount her horse, tethered on the other side. Only after she mounted did Maggie allow herself to look back.

She saw Colonel Henderson lower himself back down onto both knees at the grave. His hands moved slowly, back and forth. It appeared that he was sorting through broken stems for any flowers that remained unspoiled.

~June, 1861~

Drum & Bugle

It surely was a gray day for June. Leastways, the spitting rain had stopped. Junior waited with Webbie and his parents for the parade to begin on the square, not far from that place where the Carlisle Volunteers practiced fighting, and where the young Christian men had their meetings. *Mostly they're the same men anyways*, Junior thought. His folks weren't coming. It seemed to Junior as if the whole rest of the town was there. It felt like a party. They walked by the corner where Charlie Lochman had his studio. Junior saw him up in his third-story window, fussing with his photography equipment. Junior wondered if he had gotten a shot of those girls that made the little speech and gave the little flag to Webbie's pap? *That was all right*, he thought, *but then they sang the "Star Spangled Banner" so squeaky-voice high it hurt to listen. Good thing the adults standing around decided to chime in.*

Junior could hear Webbie's parents talking, except when the train cars arrived. The drum corps started up their rat-a-tat-tat and Mr. Anderson was playing his bugle, trying to fit into their rhythm. *Sounds like a wounded cat. Somebody should tell that man to practice more.* Junior smelled popped corn. It made him fierce hungry. In ordinary times, Webbie and Junior would scout out a good treat like that and see if they could trade or just talk nice for some, but today Webbie was busy saying goodbye.

Mr. Henderson looked shiny and sharp in his full uniform, hat, sword, gun, everything. The soldiers were standing in straight lines of two columns, waiting for Mr. Henderson. *Am I supposed to call him Captain Henderson now?* "You look so pretty, my rose of Sharon," the captain said to Mrs. Henderson. He touched her hair, the breeze was taking it like a torch on a breezy day.

"Stay," she said. It seemed like she had trouble looking straight at him.

"What?" he said. "What did you say?"

"Don't go," she said.

Webbie tugged his mother's sleeve. "Mother, he can't stay. Everybody's ready. It's time."

She answered Webbie, but she was looking straight at Webbie's pap, put her hand on the captain's cheek. "Webbie, be careful what you wish for."

Webbie's pap put his hand on Mrs. Henderson's cheek and they kissed, his hand blocking the view. Junior looked away and saw a horse rear up over Mrs. Petty's yappy dog, so Junior started to poke Webbie, but he was looking at his folks like he was studying for a Teacher Brumbach test. When they stopped kissing, Webbie gave his pap the bayonet he'd made. Webbie and Junior had worked them with their knives out of some stout, straight sticks. *Mr.—I mean Captain—Henderson's staring at it like General McClellan himself done the presenting.* He picked up Webbie with one arm, the other still holding the bayonet. He kissed Webbie on the cheek and wrapped his other arm with the bayonet around Mrs. Henderson so that the three of them were one big Henderson family sandwich.

Whenever my parents do that, mam says, "With mustard on top," and I say, "No, sugar."

Then Junior remembered he had with him the bayonet he made his pap, and that's when he saw Webbie's Uncle Nathan standing on the side, in uniform, but not with the other men. "Go later, with another unit. Make the Henderson luck last a bit longer." That's how Webbie said his pap put it when he told his brother at the last minute to stay back. Webbie's Uncle Nathan was also looking at Webbie and his folks like *he* was studying for a Teacher Brumbach test. Junior walked over and gave him the bayonet he had made.

"What's this?" he said.

"A bayonet," Junior said.

"I see. I bet you made this for somebody else."

"Well, I can make another one pretty fast."

Nathan Henderson felt the tip and said, "Ow!" Then he looked at Junior and nodded his head. He gave Junior a sharp salute. Junior saluted back. Then of a sudden the men began marching. Mr. Anderson was playing a quick number that didn't sound so bad. The men stepped to its beat. Junior jumped out of the way although for half a second he thought about going along.

Junior turned around and saw Webbie's Uncle Nathan walking away. Webbie and his mam were still standing there, waving goodbye. Her dress was waving, too, like a flag. Captain Henderson moved to the front of the line, leading his men to the train. It looked like he had Mrs. Henderson's scarf tied around his neck, the ends blowing free. His shoulders were straight and dark, dark blue.

He did not look back.

~October, 1861~

Nathan

Of all women, why Maggie? Nathan had asked himself that question hundreds of times. Thousands.

He had given himself ample time to ponder the arguments against his heart's obsession. *Maggie*. Even her name taunted him, embedded with stones his tongue tripped over. Her direct manner left him speechless.

There were other beautiful women. Yet none other moved through life with such confident grace. There were other intelligent women. But who else owned her humor, leavened with empathy? *Why Maggie?* he asked again, standing there outside her kitchen door. His boots shiny with dew. A rooster was the only other fool awake at that hour.

She walked through her garden every morning. Nathan knew this. The one time of day when she was certain to be alone. He wanted his moment with her. And she the wife of his brother.

Nathan moved under a maple tree, hidden by a shadow the same shade as his uniform. When—*at last!*—she stepped outside, illumined by shimmering first light, she looked like Truth. Eyes brilliant. Mussed hair. Solemn in her courage. His nerve wavered. He steadied himself, one hand on the tree, the other on his sword's hilt. But his feet began moving in her direction.

"Nathan!"

She looked startled but not frightened. Other women might have reached for their hair, or covered their faces. Some self-conscious gesture. She simply stood there. Waiting.

"How do you like your g-g-gazebo."

"Ah, the gazebo!" Her laughter delighted him. She held out her hand and when Nathan reached her, she took his elbow. They walked into her garden through an archway flanked by tall Rose of Sharon bursting with magenta blooms.

"Poor, neglected Nathan! All the war talk, bustle of preparation, and Robert's leaving. How could we not have properly thanked you? Please forgive me, Nathan. How do I like it? I *love* the gazebo! The perfect gift! Now let's enjoy it together."

Her voice and laughter wove its enchantment, utterly devastating his heart. Henceforth, all music would suffer by comparison. As they walked, she pulled a flowered limb toward him, urging him to press his nose into its buds and breathe deeply. She mesmerized him by the gentle yet knowing way she stroked a leaf, talked about its velvet nap. She bent to pluck a grape from its low arbor. He imagined her coaxing that grape into his mouth. In his fantasy he, too, plucked a plump grape and pressed it into her parted lips. Her lips, juice-stained scarlet and moist. Instead, she ate the grape she'd picked, swallowed, wide-eyed, and swiped at her mouth with the back of her hand, as would a schoolgirl. Those lips, stained, moist. He watched them as she told him the name of every plant they encountered.

Nathan remembered none of them, save hers. Now every flower he would ever touch or smell, every berry he would taste, would be Maggie.

They sat on a pair of chairs in the gazebo, so new, it still smelled like a living tree. Nathan had not even made the final payment to Chance Thompson. Thompson had situated it centrally, on the ground's high point. The garden disclosed its views along gently sloping vistas. He had created a break in the Rose of Sharon hedge so that it framed LeTort Spring Creek, its silver waters still racing, agitated from the mill wheel just upstream.

"Are you leaving?" Her gaze traveled from Nathan's uniform to his face. Her eyes held the question patiently.

How to answer? He did not know. "Soon," he said.

She watched the LeTort. Her left hand, with its gold wedding band, smoothed the folds of her housedress, then settled next to her right hand, the one nearer to Nathan. She had nibbled down the nail of its smallest finger and stopped there. The remaining nails had tidy white crescents, crowns on the fingers of her ringless hand.

They listened to the gravelly voice of the LeTort tell its tale.

Maggie sighed. "Time goes so quickly, Nathan." She stood as if to leave.

He stood, but in panic. He was not ready. Nathan thought about giving her a kiss, a light, quick, brotherly one. He thought about running his thumb along her lip. Gently, so that she would know he was simply wiping away berry stain. In his confusion, his arms acted without orders. They pulled her to him, her mouth just there, and his kiss enfolded her stained lips. Drank them; claimed them as his.

Maggie pushed him away. Her face flushed, heated. She whispered the order. "You must never do that again!" Ferocious, that look! Sharper than any saber. She pressed the look deep and held it in place, waiting to be certain it made its mark. Then she turned, and as she took the steps quickly, Nathan noticed she was bare-footed. Past the garden's entry she ran. Maggie in flight, streaming away from him, disappearing into that cave of a house.

Nathan knew she was gone. He should have been heartbroken. Ashamed and heartbroken.

But he also knew that for one glorious moment, she had returned his kiss.

~October, 1861~

Decision

Chance propped a mirror on a ledge behind his workbench, angling it toward the nearest wall. On the wall he slipped a square of mirrored glass beneath a nail, tapped another nail into place below it, gently tapped both nail heads until they held the mirror in place. He shifted the ledge mirror a bit more until he could see his face in one mirror, the back of his head in the other.

He held his jaw by the crook of his thumb and turned it, for a broadside view of his cheek and hand together. He saw a light-skinned black man, looked into his own blue-gray eyes and still saw the black man. Chance sighed so heavily, Blood scrabbled to his master's side to find out what ailed him. Chance patted his dog, stood back from the mirror until every vestige of his hair—fuzzy kinks, shoe leather brown, with hints of Alizanna's red—were no longer in view. He closed his eyes. Waited. Opened his eyes. Now he saw a man who could pass as a deeply tanned farmer. A white man.

He was not one to study his own features, but at this moment he had little choice. Before he could change his mind, he began to shave. He picked up the razor and removed a center section of hair, from his forehead to the top of his head. "Dang, Thompson!" he cursed himself. "Why'd you do that when you could have had a nice Indian forelock? Too late now."

The shaving would take some time. He shaved the hairline above his high cheekbone and broad jaw, a facial plane inherited from his maternal African kinsmen. Chance glanced along the narrow ridge that formed his nose, its prominence creating deep settings for his eyes, distinctive cavelike features of his father's native ancestors. Those ancients, the River People of the Susquehanna, were decimated in the generation of Chance's great grandfather, White Elk. Chance assumed his blue-gray eyes must be echoes of White Elk's wife, a fiery-haired Englishwoman named Alizanna. His lips, not thin or thick, neither his father's nor his mother's, he claimed as his own. While his skin. . . .

He shaved in sections, hair mounding at his feet. He did the back of his head last. When he finished, he swept the hair into a flour sack and knotted its open end. He would dump it behind the hedgerow. Chance pulled his hat over his bald head until the brim shadowed his eyes, then he faced the mirror.

A deeply tanned farmer looked back.

Chance was waiting when Nathan arrived at the gazebo to make his final payment. Nathan immediately noticed the change in the other man's appearance. He gave a low whistle as Chance removed his hat.

"How does your wife like the new Chance?"

"She doesn't know."

"But why would you—"

"I heard you were leaving tomorrow to enlist."

"To Philadelphia, yes. But—"

"Take me along and I'll forgive your last payment."

Nathan leaned against the gazebo railing, gripped it hard. Blinked. "Handsome job."

"Thank you."

Nathan rubbed his hand along the gazebo rail's smooth facings as he considered the request. "You're asking me to help you pass."

"Yes."

"It's risky."

Chance nodded. "And I'll need an identity. Or a story, at least."

Nathan spoke slowly, studying the gazebo floor as he talked. "We have a cousin, moved to St. Louis. Talked about moving back, but he fell sick. Too sick to fight." He looked up at Chance. "Left most of his stuff behind, stored in the attic at Oakland. I could probably find—I don't know—a baptism record. Or something." He straightened. "Chance, you may come with me. Here. Take your payment."

"No." Chance slapped the railing. "You keep it. I'm certain you'll earn it many times over."

"As will you."

Nathan agreed to keep half of the money. Before parting, they shook on an early morning meeting time.

By the light of his workshop oil lamp, Chance laid his hand tools onto a length of canvas, folding over the top and bottom margins and rolling them into a bundle. His open satchel sat at his feet.

"You have a job away from home?"

Startled, he twisted round to see Sarai standing on the threshold holding a steaming earthenware cup.

She gasped, her eyes sharp with fear. "NO! No, please, Chance!" The moaning started deep within her. "No, Chance, no. Please, God, no!" The cup dropped from her hand and broke, spattering coffee and pottery shards across the workshop floor.

"Sarai—" He caught her as she stumbled forward. "We have a good amount of savings set by. You know where it's hid. And I made an arrangement with old Colonel Henderson, so you can get more, any time you need it." He stroked her back, spoke into her hair. "I must serve our country."

"Our"—Sarai shoved him—"*country*? What about our *family*? This here is my country. Right here. This land. Our child peaceful asleep in that house. We are not a family without you!"

"Sarai." His gaze gentle, but unbending. She shrieked, lunging at him and pummeling him with her fists. He turned, letting the blows land against one broad shoulder until she paused to sob. Chance grabbed her fists in his hands, enveloping them.

"Sometimes peace must be fought for. Our property, our family must be defended. Or we become property. You …" He waited until her eyes, wild with grief, returned to him. "You understand this, Sarai." It was not a question.

She nearly collapsed under the weight of her sobbing. Chance released her hands and held her. At length, her sobs ended against his soaked shirtfront, with a shudder and a sigh. This wave of despair finally subsided within her though he knew it was the first of many, and his heart ached for her.

Chance carried his wife back into the house. He gazed at the sleeping form of their son. His love poured out over him in a wordless prayer. He lowered the wick of the oil lamp on their supper table until it went out. He eased his way through the darkness to the other side of the large room, nudging past a chair and a high-backed bench facing the cast iron woodstove, to the alcove that was their bedchamber. He pulled back the curtain and lowered her onto the bed.

"Sarai," he breathed, as he tenderly undressed and kissed her. "You are stronger than any of us."

He made love to every part of her, pressing her shape and her spirit into his memory. He was a man at the banquet before a long march: feasting lavishly, surfeiting his appetite. She returned his love fiercely as if doing battle against the enemy, an army of fears.

Sarai awoke to daylight flooding past the half-open curtain. She sensed his absence instantly, felt herself overwhelmed by it, drowning in it.

She heard the sharp crack of dry wood. Her heart leaped. *Maybe I dreamed …*

She pulled herself up to see Junior shoving kindling into the woodstove. He turned toward her, smiled proudly. "Look, Mam! Pap said I'm ready to take full charge of woodpiles and the fire! From now on!"

~October, 1861–April, 1862~

Sons of War

Sarai flopped back onto her bed, eyes shut. A suffocating heaviness settled on her. She forced air into her lungs. Junior left for more wood, his small feet barely louder than a pencil tapping across the floor. She listened for Chance's return, for the dull ordinary of his footfall, and his humming, irritatingly cheerful as he muscled logs into the stove. The silly way he talked the logs into igniting: "We know you can do it! Fire! Heat! Show us what you've got!" The confident sound of his tools swaying and bumping in their leather holsters with his every move. The smell of him, arriving at their bed on a wave of heat from an accommodating fire …

Instead, she heard the huffing of a boy struggling to open the door with one hand while maintaining a hold on his burden with the other. The door creaked open, and he came in backwards, dragging a stout log, grunting with effort.

A voice within her said, *Die now. Or get up.*

"Take me now, Lord," Sarai groaned.

"What, Mam?"

Sarai sat up. She saw how the log had etched its trail into her spotless pinewood floor. She pulled a morning shawl across her shoulders, tied it, and hurried to help lift the dragging end. Junior pushed her hands away.

"My job, Mam. Don't you have your own?"

Sarai straightened and crossed her arms, pulling the shawl tighter. She ventured toward the door, took a two-handled piece of leather from a wall hook and laid it on the floor.

"Doesn't Pap use that?" She watched for his response as she moved to the sink and pumped water for breakfast preparations.

Junior nodded soberly and moved the leather closer. He rolled the log onto it and dragged the leather and its load the rest of the way across the floor. At the stove, he opened its firebox door and studied the kindling he had lit, now ablaze. Junior leaned the log against the firebox and tried lifting it in before it tumbled to the floor. He stuck his hands in his pockets, studying the room. He leaned against a footed cast iron tools cradle with hooks on its two high sides, shoving it closer to the woodstove.

"I know this is where Pap puts his boots and tool belt," he said. "But I think it'll work good for wood, too."

Junior looped a handle of the leather sling on one of the hooks. He groaned against the weight of the log as he pulled on the other handle until it looped over the woodstove door. The cradle teetered but it did not overturn. The log, suspended in the sling, was just high enough for him to lift up on and slide into the box. In his triumph, he grabbed for the woodstove door, his hand landing on the hot interior surface rather than the handle. Junior stifled a howl by stuffing his burned fingers in his mouth.

Sarai stood frozen at the sink. Waiting.

Junior slowly withdrew the two burnt fingers from his mouth. "Can I—may I have a cold, wet rag?"

She prepared one for him, watched as he carefully wrapped it around his fingers, tucking the end between them and letting it dangle across the back of his hand.

She bent down on one knee. "Junior, did Pap tell you why this is your job?"

He regarded her for a long moment. Shook his head.

"Why, do you think?"

Another long moment. "He's gone to fight in the war. Like Web's pap."

She stood.

"I have to get more wood," Junior said. She had never seen his eyes so dark. Smoldering. The very color of smoke on a gray day. "A lot more wood." He darted back outside.

Sarai wanted to yank a burning ember from the firebox and cauterize her heart. His, too. Another childhood ended too early. Instead, she talked back to the silence of the sink and water pump and the room and the land and the smoke spiraling from the stovepipe chimney. "Least he had two more years than me!" she muttered through clenched teeth. "Uh huh. Two more years."

Webbie had new chores and responsibilities, too, which kept him busy on Saturday mornings. On Saturday afternoons Webbie would arrive at the Thompsons' door, looking for Junior. If Junior still had chores, Webbie would help if he could or just watch. They would whisper their plans and then head off.

Sarai would stand by the door, watching them leave. She started counting their leave-takings. She found a slender hand-sized slab of slate rock near the woodpile and a hardened chunk of clay. She marked each departure with a small stroke and bundled each set of four strokes with a crosswise fifth stroke. In counting each leave-taking, she assured herself of each homecoming. She tucked the slate and clay into the corner nearest the door, under a cane-seat chair they didn't use. Chance's chair.

One afternoon before venturing off, the boys sat on stumps in the yard. Sarai stood inside the door's shadow and listened.

Junior had given Web one of his knives, and they were hunched over sticks, whittling. Web looked up to see how Junior was holding his knife. "We got a letter from my father." He adjusted his own grip and started up again. "Envelope said, 'Company A, 7th Pennsylvania Reserves.'"

"What'd he say?" Junior shaved the wood in short curls, blowing them off if they did not fall of their own accord. He did not look up.

"Not much. They left camp, and he's going somewhere to fight. Can't say where, Mother says it's a secret." Web blew on his wood, as Junior had done. "Did your father write a letter yet?"

"Nope."

"He left same time as my Uncle Nathan. Mother says they're with the 5th."

Junior shrugged, looked up. "Do you wish your pap and uncle were together?"

"If they stayed together, they could help each other fight. But my father's busy leading Company A. So I guess your father and Uncle Nathan are helping each other fight." Web checked the point of his stick with one chubby finger. "It's funny, our house feels smaller with Father gone. Not bigger. Smaller. How about yours?"

"Smaller," Junior agreed.

"Junior, how close do you think the war is?"

Junior looked up. "If it was close, we could hear it."

"Do you think it will get close?"

Junior squinted at Web. "That's why we're making the bayonets." Junior felt the tip of his stick, then felt Web's point. "Webbie, I think we're ready."

They pointed their sticks at the woods. "Let's get some Rebels!" Webbie shouted.

"Charge!" Junior yelled. They ran into the woods.

Sarai reached for the rock, made a mark, placed it back under the chair.

One afternoon, Webbie and Junior crawled into the big shade of their oak tree to get out of an unusually hot April sun. They lay on their backs, staring up into its layers of spring green leaves, whispering their secrets.

"That tree's kind of like the bridge we built, only it goes up," Junior heard Webbie say.

"Yeah," Junior said. "Hey, let's catch spring peepers tonight."

"I can't tonight. Mother wants me to stay home with her after dinner." Webbie sat up. "I got you a gift."

Junior rolled onto one elbow and saw Webbie grinning his cat-with-mouse-and-milk grin. "What for?"

"Today's my birthday."

Junior sat up, too. "I didn't know that. Happy Birthday. But why would you get a gift for me on your birthday?"

"Because you're my friend."

Junior punched his arm. "Thanks."

"Thanks yourself." Web rubbed his arm, still grinning. "Would you like it now?"

"Sure, why not?" Junior said, wondering if he was going to end up fooled by a prank. Except he knew Webbie never made a fellow feel bad about himself.

"It's right here."

Junior looked at the pile of acorn caps Web was fiddling with. Junior pointed at them. "There?"

Web shook his head and pointed straight up. "There."

Junior looked up into that forest of a tree, its limbs all muscled and scary.

"It's tied to a branch up top. "I can't wait for you to get your gift. You are going to LOVE it!"

Even though he sat on the ground, Junior felt dizzy. All he could do was shake his head. No.

The boys taught each other special calls and whistles. Junior repeated what his pap had told him, that Indians taught soldiers these signals. Junior asked Sarai for one of his father's old jackets, along with some scraps of yellow twill and the use of her sewing basket.

Webbie showed up with one of his cast-off jackets. After Sarai gave them a few tips on sewing, they cut the coarse twill into bars and stitched them on their jackets. They decided on the rank of captain, two bars each.

Sarai served as witness when they exchanged coats with grave formality. Web, the heavier boy, gave Junior his outgrown coat. Junior hesitated before handing over his pap's jacket. They faced each other, mirroring the other's movements. They each pulled one sleeve on. Saluted. Pulled the other sleeve on. Saluted. Buttoned the jackets. Picked up their bayonets. Extended them to touch each other's right then left shoulders. Waited. Together shouted "Charge!" and disappeared into the woods.

Sarai marked her stone. Two seasons' worth of marks. Six months since Chance left. Come October, she would select another stone to begin the second year.

~May, 1862~

Confederate Sky

New maple leaves unfurled and fluttered on their stems, asterisks across a dawning sky. At pondside, an arc of willows bent their tresses toward water's surface, a light-struck display of May's jewel green that would dull to olive by June.

Birds testified to a new day: Chirps from robin chicks urging their mother to hurry, steadfast cardinals clicking warnings to each other, songbirds casting hopeful melodies. *Such variety yet so purposeful*, thought Maggie. Nature's music, improvised yet not chaotic, keeping harmony on behalf of an uncertain universe.

Pink shimmered on the horizon. Maggie watched as it paled to the translucent butter-gray of a cloudless sky. *A Confederate sky*, she shuddered. She straightened her back in the rattan porch chair, ignoring aches and pains from the week's exertions. She reached for her porcelain cup of hot water. She sipped, pretending that it was tea and that she was not alone. The full-throated birds became chattering women gathering for a Saturday afternoon social. She imagined her son and his mates playing tag on the lawn. And in a far corner, a knot of pipe-smoking fathers, discussing the week's business affairs, with one eye on their children, looking for the opportunity to introduce a ball to their games. A gaggle of plump geese making their way across the lawn. The normal, ordinary stuff of life.

Normal. Maggie pressed the cup to her cheek, absorbing its warmth. What a remote memory! Would she ever again experience the ease of ordinary, the luxury of normal? She closed her eyes. She had come to the porch for a few moments of quiet to pray before Web awoke. All she could manage were sighs and groans, a form of prayer so discouragingly honest she did not want her son to hear it; therefore, she confined her audible prayers to these solitary dawn vigils.

She breathed deeply. Lilac mingled its fresh scent with the cloying tang of honeysuckle and pungent, mossy undertones of pond vapors. Maggie overheard a bullfrog wooing its mate. She spotted the wingspan profile of an owl, circling with breakfast before it swooped into a copse of pines and settled in for sleep. Spring peepers called out to newborn crickets. In truth, she was not alone. The earth was teaming with resurrected life.

Maggie gathered her skirt in hand and rose with a sigh. Webbie must not see she had slept in her dress again last night. She swished through the summer parlor and up the staircase leading to her bedroom. *Robert's and my bedroom*, she corrected herself, as she began undressing.

Maggie hung her garments on a door hook. She scouted in her wardrobe and found a blouse and skirt not too spotted to wear. She pulled a brush through her hair a few times, then put it down. "Why bother?" She twisted and pinned her hair into a half-hearted bun. She paused at a bedside table, picking up the framed photograph portraits Mr. Brady had done of each of the Henderson men in their dress uniforms. William Jr., looking gaunt even then. *Poor Willy. Now you are with your dear mother. No more suffering for either of you.* Nathan looked so young, so confident, the teasing dare of that dimpled smile of his. "Why, I've seen that grin on Web!" she half-whispered, surprised she had not noticed the resemblance until now. She picked up the photograph of Robert in his dress uniform, outlining his image with her finger.

Maggie thought she heard sounds of Web stirring in his bedroom, so she hurriedly finished dressing.

She would write a letter. But not here.

In his absence of a year, their bedroom had become the abode of a woman living alone. The room was cluttered with her clothing, her books, her nearly empty lotion bottles—used so sparingly these days as she could not afford to replenish them. The space looked like her, smelled like her. Only when she opened the paneled doors of his armoire could she bury her face past the sleeves of his suits and find his scent, his presence, still lingering there.

Maggie pulled on a pair of frayed, once-white slippers. She padded along the gray corridor, gliding past Web's closed door to the staircase. Its broad mahogany handrail felt comfortingly solid in her palm. She ignored dust motes visible in the slanting morning light, neglect hanging heavy in the air.

Not much bookkeeping to do, as the law firm's business was poor. Nor was the Baltimore business a source of income. After the death of Maggie's father shortly before the war's start, the business had been sold to Uncle Turnbrough, from whom she was estranged.

Her grief at her father's passing was eased by the knowledge that his physical suffering, and heartsickness over the war, had ended. Henry was helping, but there was too little work and too few clients who could pay for work, which seemed to exacerbate Henry's depression, as he still mourned Lizzie. He kept his house in Washington City. Their mother lived with him and also cared for his children. Each week, when Henry came to Carlisle on the overnight train to work Thursdays and Fridays, he stayed with Maggie and Web in the spare bedroom, returning to Washington on a Sunday train. He spoke of moving his family to Carlisle if Washington became "too fraught with risk." His government salary sustained his own family, and his Carlisle work provided Maggie with a monthly stipend. Colonel Henderson would also provide money if she asked. Which she was loathe to do.

People all over town were struggling. For that reason Maggie had kept her household workers as long as she could. As a housekeeper, Maggie was neither skilled nor motivated. As a cook … well, there wasn't much to cook anyway. Now, only Yancy remained. She could not manage without him to oversee the horses and property.

On her way downstairs, she took each step deliberately. It bought her time to think about what she would write in her letter to Robert. What new embellishments could she invent to provide a lively, cheery missive, covering up their bad-to-worse situation? On the middle landing she turned, stood taller.

Imagined Robert, just out of sight at the bottom of the stairs. In gleaming dress uniform. Waiting. Looking up. Expectant.

She moved more quickly through the empty foyer to his office door. Her hand lingered on the knob, an ornately textured brass affair, different from all the others in the house, which were variations of a milky ceramic glass. She fancied that perhaps he had slipped in somehow, on leave, to surprise her. Robert, just on the other side of this door . . .

Maggie sat in the vacant chair at his desk, easing back into its deeply cushioned leather. Old leather, trained to his shape, not hers. What was he doing at this moment? Was he still sleeping? Did he make his bed on bare earth? Or in some trench he dug by hand?

She tried to imagine battle and could not. She knew it was not the glittering stories of heroism that old men bantered about in the barber shop and women gushed over in the Women's Relief Corps meetings. For the men at war, and particularly for Robert's and Nathan's sake, Maggie had to do something to help. She could not walk away from rolling bandages. She attended Relief Corps meetings so that she could help with the war cause, but she wadded some of the cotton scrapings, and, unobserved, tucked balls of it into her ears to block out their sentimental fantasies.

She looked at the desk's rows of pigeon holes, many filled with neatly folded papers. One evening shortly before he left, Robert had brought her to this desk and explained how everything was organized. What papers she needed to know about. Whom to consult if such-and-such an issue should arise. Henry, yes, for legal matters. And others in the community who were grateful to Robert, who would be willing and able to help in certain ways, should she need help. *Here,* he said, *I'll make a list.*

She had taken the pen from his hand, set it aside and pulled him close. *Later,* she'd said.

Though she had an easier time managing the new steel-nibbed pens which contained their own founts of ink, Maggie knew Robert would enjoy a dipped-ink letter from her. She sighed and pulled the inkwell and blotter toward herself. Lifted the dip pen, his favorite.

Dearest Nathan, she wrote.

She dropped the pen as if it were a hot poker, spattering ink across paper and desk. She grabbed at the paper, checked the blotter beneath it to see if Nathan's name had bled through, stared at what she had written. She leaned over the ash bin, tore the sheet of paper into tiny pieces. Lit the pile. Watched a spiral of smoke rise. Thought of Robert lighting his pipe. *Robert, Robert, Robert.*

She would write smaller, she thought, as she dabbed with a rag at the spilled ink on the desk, several small blood-dark pools. *I'll write twice as much on one sheet, to make up for the ruined piece of paper. Write horizontally, then vertically, as Robert often does. Robert. Robert.*

Dearest Robert, she wrote. And thought of Nathan.

"Mother?" Web stood in the open doorway, rubbing his eyes. "I smell smoke."

She placed the pen in its rest hastily as if it were a shameful thing. Web climbed into her lap. He nuzzled against her shoulder as she closed her arms around him, his pajamas warm and fragrant with sleep.

"I burned a bit of paper, it's nothing, don't worry."

"What paper?"

"Oh, a letter."

"To who?"

"Whom?" A correction. A question. "I started a letter to your father. But I made a mistake."

Web's voice fuzzed, half asleep. "Teacher Brumbach says, 'Correct your mistakes and keep writing, paper is too costly to waste.'" Web rubbed his nose and yawned. "Especially a letter to Father."

"All right then." Maggie made a decision. Web would have to be a party to it, no way around that. "Webster Henderson, I promise I shall never again burn any letter—most especially to your father. In fact, we must keep letters. And other things. Records of these times. So, Webbie, will you promise to help me keep them?"

He nodded against her chest, eyes closed.

"Web, this is important. I shall keep them in the wood chest at the foot of my bed. Remember, the one with the leather straps. I keep the key here, on a ribbon around my neck. Even when you are a grown man, protect and keep them. Do you promise?" Ink stains on her fingertips. She tried rubbing them off with her thumb, without success. Traces of smoke lingered, stinging her nostrils.

"Yes, Mother." The trusting curves of his mouth, his cheeks, his eyelashes, on the threshold of sleep. "I promise."

Crossroads

1862, early battles

(Virginia, Washington City, Pennsylvania)

~August, 1862~

Meade's Orders

General Meade ducked into Robert Henderson's tent. "Have a smoke, Captain?"

"No, sir, I don't smoke." Robert saluted and pulled out his pipe.

"Neither do I. May be time to start though." Meade acknowledged Henderson's salute with a grin. It was an old joke between them. Meade sat in the empty camp chair. "Looks like you didn't sleep too well last night."

"With due respect, General, looks like you haven't slept in a year."

Meade rolled his eyes. "My girls tease me about these saddle bags. Came with the face, I'm afraid. Now your Margaret used to tell me I had a wise demeanor. How did you manage to win one of the prettiest girls in Baltimore? She's definitely the smartest." He tapped Henderson's table with a paper scrolled in his gloved hand. "I know your men have been champing at the bit for action, so I came to tell you personally. A clear set of orders for a change, thank God. Strike camp at daybreak. By the way, that's a handsome table."

Henderson took the offered paper and spread it open on his table to read. "The table? It was made by a craftsman from Carlisle. Chance Thompson."

"Tell him I'd like one." Meade stood to go, waited until Robert finished reading, then held his hand out for the paper. "Is he here, part of your company?"

"He asked to be. I told him no." Henderson rolled the orders and returned them to Meade.

"Physically unfit?"

"On the contrary, very able. But he's a colored man, sir. I told him the hard, misguided truth: the Army is not mustering Negros."

"Isn't yours a company of volunteers?" Robert heard the impatience in his commander's voice, saw the well-known temper begin to rise. The General was waiting for his reply. None came.

Damn it, Robert! I'm sick of the politics! It's *killing* us! Meade pointed to the table as he left, barking, "Tell Thompson I want one!"

Captain Henderson watched as the men of Company A—his men, now trained as skirmishers—exchanged their Pennsylvania-issued muskets for Federal government-issued Springfields. Their new weapons glinted smartly under an early August sun. Today they would march six miles southwest, from Meridian Hill north of Washington, to their new camp at Tenallytown, where they would serve picket duty. They were eager to fight, more than ready to defend their capital from any western incursion by the enemy.

From dress rehearsal to Act One, Robert thought, as he waited. He closed his eyes and remembered. *we are here now because of Bull Run. That defeat on July 21st. A patch of Virginia land just thirty-one miles southwest of here. Our nation's capital at risk. Maryland transformed into much more treacherous geography.*

As he took his position at the head of his troops and his men began to march, Captain Henderson thought of the tormented faces of the 79th after Bull Run. On a vivid summer day, with fresh legs, he would never have considered the possibility of a second Bull Run.

Or that in another year's time, only 28 of Company A's 117 recruits would still be standing.

~August 30, 1862~

Union Sky

Robert Henderson jerked awake. He blinked against smoke and exhaustion. He had done it again. Dreamt about that boy he shot at Gaines Mill. When Robert had spent his first shot, the boy was an anonymous foe. Robert had taken him as a prisoner of war. Had tried dressing his wound. Had gotten him to an ambulance wagon, where the doctor deemed him good as dead, and would not treat him. *Too much blood loss.* The boy keening with pain. Robert had found a quiet wooded spot. *Rest there, boy, on your side. Back to me.* Then spent his second shot into the boy's back. To end his suffering, that's what Robert told himself. *What was his name? So thin.* That boy's starved face would haunt him for life.

He rubbed his eyes. Oriented himself. Breastwork. Battlefield. *Here we are again.* Nearly one year after the first Bull Run. Same battered farms. Same damned feeling that Richmond—*so close we can smell it!*—was slipping away. So many men lost and captured. Too many to count. He could bring to mind faces, though. Faces he would never see again, this side of eternity. He kept a mental list of fellow officers, dead and missing. Zimmerman, died at Baltimore. Kenyon, dead at Washington. So many more. Burkholder, wounded at Gaines Mill and a prisoner. *God protect him from the horrors of the enemy's prisoner of war camps!*

His own brother. *Willy. Dead.* Robert saw glimpses of his childhood with William as if stereoscope slides, especially the image that came to him frequently these days: five-year-old Willy, struggling to hold their bundled newborn baby brother Nathan. Willy, slack-jawed and silent at the news of their mother not surviving childbirth. Tears streaming down Willy's face. Robert thought it odd that he couldn't remember seeing their father take to drinking after their mother died. *But I can remember hearing it.* The clink of bottle to glass. The thud of bottle to table. His father's voice. How it shifted from a Colonel's commanding presence to the querulous whine of a drunk. *I remember. The rasp of his criticism. The helplessness of his snoring.* Through all of that, the baby survived. Nathan was still alive.

Nathan. Freshly promoted to Second Lieutenant, Company E. Better that he serve in a different company, Robert had argued, in the illogical hope that it might cut their losses.

Robert's mind thus roamed even as his shooting joined the dense heat of battle. Private John Cuddy, another soldier from Carlisle, crouched near Robert, firing shot after shot. Then Cuddy's Springfield jammed. The air was too thick with smoke for Cuddy to see to clear the jam. Cuddy tapped Robert's shoulder and motioned toward a breastwork farther back. He began to crab-walk backwards until he reached it, to grab another gun. Robert continued firing, first on one knee, then from standing position. Cuddy scrambled back with another gun. As Robert reloaded, Cuddy shouted, "Down!" But Robert did not move.

Robert's head flew up as if he had heard startling news, and his back arched in the unmistakable way of a man who's been shot through. He fell backward. John Cuddy broke his fall. John scrambled from beneath him, bent his ear to Robert's mouth, looked up, saw Captain Erkurius Beatty at a distance. Erk Beatty froze, staring at him. Cuddy shook his head.

General Meade, who had seen Robert go down, came thundering over on his horse. Captain Beatty collected himself and ran over to them. But Meade, with Cuddy lifting, had already pulled Robert up in front of him. Meade motioned for Beatty to follow and rode away.

Robert's gun lay on the ground where he had fallen. Cuddy watched the rump of Meade's horse and then Beatty, scrambling on foot, disappear into a miasma of smoke and gunfire.

Cuddy picked up Robert's gun and kept shooting.

~August 31, 1862~

Rail to Washington

Maggie held General Meade's telegram clenched in one fist, her other hand draped over her travel bag. Her forehead rested against the window frame of a soot-streaked railcar window on the Cumberland Valley train to Harrisburg. The telegram was her passport to Robert. A talisman. *I will keep this in my sight*, she vowed to herself, *until I have seen him alive*. She would not entertain any other possibility.

"Robert wounded arriv Wash. Arsenal Hosp. Sat Aug 30." When Maggie had received the telegram before dawn on Sunday, she told the operator to relay the message to her sister Becky and husband Philip Tyson, adding, "join me Balt Sta Su aftern arriv" in hopes one of them would come. She sent a second telegram to her brother Henry in Washington, ending with, "Locate Robert meet me Wash Sta Su eve arriv."

Maggie had tried to ignore the firestorm of emotions that kept coursing through her, steeling herself with the thought, *Surprise will not be one of those feelings.* In minutes, she had finished packing the bag that waited, half-packed, readied for such a telegram. She packed a second bag for Webster and ushered her sleepy son, still in his bedclothes, into the carriage Yancy had drawn up to the front door. She hugged her son, whispering, "I'm going on a surprise visit to Father." Webster dozed, his head drifting on her shoulder. She was grateful he asked no questions. Webster would stay with Junior. Just days earlier, Maggie had knocked at Sarai's door to make arrangements in the event something like this might happen. Sarai was kind to receive Web, firm in her refusal to stay at Sharon.

Under ideal conditions, the distance between Carlisle and Washington was a half-day's horse ride. Conditions were far from ideal. Travel by horse or carriage would be too dangerous. Traveling by train was her safest option, but the most time-consuming. The trains would be crowded at all hours, their schedules unpredictable. The only route available from Carlisle to Washington looped north, then east, then south, through the Harrisburg, York and Baltimore stations. She would likely travel all day. Even under the best of circumstances, she faced eight hours of train time and hours of waiting time between trains

Maggie arrived at the Carlisle station before seven in the morning, boarding a train at 7:50. She was in Harrisburg an hour later. She faced a long wait for the North Central passenger car and roamed restlessly around the cavernous gray Harrisburg station.

It was mid-afternoon before she and others crowded into the passenger car of a train heading to Baltimore. A fine misting rain settled in after the Harrisburg stop.

The rain gave little relief from August's torpid heat. It did control the coal smoke, thankfully. A bonnet-clad country woman boarded at the York Pennsylvania station and sat next to her for the ride to Baltimore. Maggie nodded and said, "That rain means we shall not have to cough and gag our way south!"

This pleasant, broad-faced woman broke into a gap-toothed smile. She rummaged in her woven basket. From it she withdrew a stubby paring knife, offering Maggie a slice of bologna perched on its tip.

Maggie was thrilled to have the distraction of her company. Between nibbles she jabbered on about her son Web and motherhood and "How tasty your bologna is!" and "Do you have children?" When the woman, still smiling and nodding, sawed off a second slice and, in rapid-fire German, offered it up on the point of her knife, Maggie knew her seatmate had not understood a word.

An elderly man and woman sitting in the seats opposite rose, their pale faces pinched with disapproval, and hobbled to seats at the other end of the carriage. The carriage filled, but the vacant seats near Maggie and the Yorker did not.

Maggie caught a Union officer staring at her from his seat across the aisle. He tipped his hat and leaned toward her.

"I don't mind standing if you would like my seat."

"Why, Captain, I already have a seat!" He threw a look of disdain toward Maggie's seatmate, then to Maggie, and turned his head away.

Maggie looked at the woman, perplexed. True, she did have the odor of boiled cabbage and bologna. *But it's pleasant*, Maggie told herself. *And now I smell of it, too.*

The woman was stitching together bright blocks of fabric. Her quilting needle flashed with astonishing speed. The woman's tongue clicked against her one visible tooth as if counting each stitch. She caught Maggie watching. The woman held up the paring knife but Maggie shook her head. So the woman dropped the knife in her basket, fishing again until she surfaced with a small quilt, crib-sized, consisting of colorful nested squares, a diamond at its center. The woman pointed to a threaded needle fastened into one corner. She gave animated instructions in German.

"Oh no, I could not. I can barely darn a sock. I would spoil it."

The German woman fixed a thimble on Maggie's thumb, grinned and winked. Then Maggie's new friend returned to her own needlework.

Maggie stroked the puckered fabric with her fingertips and realized its entire surface bubbled with intricately decorative stitching, a different pattern raised in each color block. The background block of green fairly rustled with a thread-pattern of swirling leaves. Maggie looked out the window to see verdant pastures and forests and wildflowers roll by, gilded by a setting sun. Brilliant blue cornflowers, creamy drifts of Queen Anne's lace, bold shocks of red cardinal flowers. She looked back at the quilt and recognized the same colors. Within the green, a cornflower blue square rippled with wave stitching, and within it, a white square with ringed stitching, which had centered on it an audacious red diamond bursting with fireworks stitching. Her German seatmate nodded at the window view, grinning at Maggie, the woman's sole tooth winking, *Yes, like that.*

Maggie checked Meade's telegram, still safely secured to her belt. She studied her seatmate's technique, each tiny stitch separated by a tiny space. *If I slow it down and make the stitches somewhat larger*. Maggie stabbed through the quilt's captive layers of batting and fabric. *Now up*. When her needle emerged, a dark thread hidden against black fabric, she felt a surge of relief. But some minutes later, when she glanced at her mentor's handiwork, Maggie sighed. "Look at this! I'm ruining your quilt! Someone could catch a toenail on those stitches!"

The quilter examined Maggie's stitches and smiled, patted her pupil's hand, and motioned for her to continue. The two women sat out much of the rest of the trip to Baltimore in the silent companionship of their needlework.

To her astonishment, Maggie finished, though not without some blood shed by her fingers. *Those stitches may look ragged, but they are secure,* she thought. Her German friend had fallen asleep, with a purring snore. Every lurch frayed her patience. She clutched the sleeve of the conductor as he slid past, "My husband's life is at stake. Can't this train go faster?"

His eyes, barely open under the brim of his cap, matched his voice. Weary, condescending. "Sorry, madam. No." He moved away.

"I could run faster than this train!" Maggie moaned, exasperated.

The ride stretched into six hours, bringing them into the Howard Street Station as night fell.

When they pulled in, the Baltimore platform thronged with people and baggage. Maggie spotted Philip leaning against a gas lamppost, alone in its wan pool of light. He did not see her wave. His shoulders hunched with anxiety, face deeply furrowed. Maggie felt the quilt slipping off her lap as she began to stand. She caught it and swiveled to return it. But her German friend was gone. *Why, she must have intended for me to have it all along!* Maggie shook her head, smiling in spite of herself. *My needlework is such an abomination, the poor woman was perhaps too embarrassed to keep it!* Maggie tucked the quilt into her bag.

Philip rallied when he saw her descend to the platform. She noticed his attempt to arrange his face into a smile. "Your sister and I had a lively row over you," he said, kissing her brow. "She insisted that you needed her. I maintained it was much too dangerous a journey. We finally both agreed that you are insane to be traveling now."

"Philip, you know I—"

He cut her off with a wave of his hand. "Here—let me carry that. I've got our tickets. The next train to Washington is leaving as we speak, so let's hurry." They crossed the platform and scrambled into the B&O passenger car just before the southbound train began moving.

Maggie saved her rejoinder until they had settled into their seats. "Philip, you know I would not leave Web except under the most dire circumstances. Robert needs me now." Philip patted her shoulder but did not respond. Maggie chided herself for sounding emotional. That would not play well with her friend and brother-in-law, a man of science. She tried a different tack.

"I've telegraphed Henry. He will meet us at the station. Henry has sufficient clearance and pull that he should be able to get us in quickly to see Robert. Plus, I have this." She unfurled General Meade's telegram.

Philip lifted his hands in surrender. "What's done is done. We're here now."

He peered out of the dark patch of window, pointed. "Look at that terrain, Maggie. Even in the dark, you can see and feel its marvelous, rolling topography. I've not outgrown my fascination with the land, and the stuff it's made of …"

"Why should you? It's your life's work, your calling. You are, after all, Maryland's agricultural chemist!"

"Geology may be a young science, but, to me, it is utterly absorbing." He dimpled shyly. Maggie was proud of her friend's accomplishments. She resolved not to let her mind wander to fretful worry, imagining the worst about Robert. *Besides,* she told herself, *if I accost a conductor again, he'll likely throw us both off the train.*

"Tell me about the geological survey of Maryland you completed. Will it help the war effort?"

He lowered his voice. "The maps have found their way to both armies, of course." After a long pause, he continued. "I pray the battlefront does not venture to Washington or Baltimore. However, if it does, I further pray that accurate knowledge of the land will bring this conflict to a swift conclusion."

"How are Uncle Isaac and the rest of your family? Are they still pestering Becky and you to start a family?

Philip's lips formed an angry, thin line. He looked past her, out the window and beyond.

"I am sorry, Phil. How thoughtless of me!"

He pointed. Their window framed the shadowed outskirts of Washington, pulsing with gaslight and firelight.

"Washington's profile expands each time I see her," Maggie said, glad to change the subject.

Philip nodded. "She is a town that greatly wants to be a city."

As the train approached the station, Maggie quickly gathered her belongings. "It is a land to itself, a 'company town,' from what Henry tells me."

Maggie and Philip descended into the depot against an insistent current of people climbing aboard. *Everyone seems in such a hurry to leave the city,* she thought, warning herself not to read too much into it. She felt Philip's hand on her shoulder, protectively guiding her, heard him shout over the din, "We made such good time, I doubt Henry will be here."

As if on cue, Henry swooped up to them and embraced them in a three-way hug.

"Always the shy, backward one," Philip joked.

"Shut your trap, you pie eater. Eighty percent of that affection is meant for Maggie, the rest to you. Mind what you say or I shall reduce your allowance to five percent."

"After I have traveled all this way to see thee?" Since boyhood, Philip had retained the habit of lapsing into Quaker expressions when teasing.

"Friend of my dearest sister!" Henry gushed theatrically, planting on Philip's cheek a big, wet kiss.

"Ehhhh!" Philip scrubbed his cheek with the back of his sleeve as if back in grade school.

"Come on, you two." Maggie's laughter dissolved. She pulled at their coat sleeves. "Henry, I beg you, lead me to my husband!"

The recovery room of the hospital was immense, its air fetid with heat and medicine and wasting flesh. The tidiness of rows and columns of beds failed to mask a sea of suffering. A nurse gave Henry a lantern and some hasty directions before hurrying off. Maggie braced herself against the moaning, the missing limbs, the emaciated faces flickering into view. She was thankful many were asleep and others lay beyond Henry's circle of lamplight. As Henry led them, Maggie forced herself to smile and greet every soldier who looked up. *Courage must greet courage*, she reminded herself.

"Robert!" Maggie recognized his profile from three beds' distance, forced her way past Henry and ran to the foot of his bed. He appeared to be sleeping, his arms at his sides above the blanket. He wore a thin round-collar cotton shirt with sleeves ending above the elbow. She motioned to Henry and Philip and asked Henry to hold the lantern over the bed.

An attendant in Army uniform also standing at the foot of Robert's bed, blocked her from moving any closer.

"Quiet!" he whispered harshly. "Stay there, at the foot!"

She reached past the attendant, gently clasped Robert's ankles through the bed coverings, and did a quick physical inventory, as new parents do with infants: legs, feet and toes intact, hands and arms resting above the blanket, intact. All accounted for. The sheet spread over Robert's chest rose and fell with regularity as he breathed. Good. So far.

"His surgery is recent and he is very weak," the attending soldier muttered crossly. He made a move to usher them out. Henry approached him, whispered. The soldier shook his head vigorously. The whispered exchange heated up and lasted for several minutes. Finally, the soldier planted a chair mid-bedside, and said, irritated, "Get no closer than this." Then he backed away with reluctance, planting himself in a chair nearby, arms folded, glaring at them.

"His name is Beatty," Henry explained, jerking his thumb in the direction of the soldier. "Apparently, Maggie, when Robert was wounded, the thought of incurring your wrath struck such fear in General Meade's breast that he ordered Captain Beatty to commandeer a private carriage. In it, he carried your husband to the battlefield hospital at Centreville, then to this hospital. In fact—" Henry clapped his mouth shut.

Maggie gave him a warning glare. "Out with it, Henry. Quickly!"

Henry sighed. "Beatty tells me that General Meade is now injured as well. With a wound very similar to our Robert's."

She listened with her eyes fixed on Robert's face. "What are Robert's injuries? Tell me everything."

Henry and Philip exchanged looks. Henry spoke, low-voiced. "He took a minié ball shot, straight through. Just above his hip and small intestine. Just missed the spine—and no vital organs harmed—thank God. At first, they thought … well, on the battlefield they thought he was dead. Then he began to groan. Beatty is rabidly devoted to your husband, Mag. Raved about his courage, how he inspired his men to fight and keep fighting. If you were not his wife, he would not have let us pass." As she turned to Robert, Henry tugged her arm. "One other thing, Mag. He says that we should not remain here. He says you may have a short visit on the promise that afterward you go straight home."

She gave a brief nod and turned to her husband, as she slipped into the chair the attending soldier had placed at Robert's bedside. She whispered, "Robert can you hear me? Philip, Henry, and I are here, darling. We cannot stay long." She studied his face and the changes war had made to it. Deeper furrows in his brow. A hungry, hollowed look to his eyes and cheeks. *I must see his eyes. They will tell me everything.*

"See, Robert," she whispered, "I brought a telegraph from your friend General Meade." She held it up, then tucked it in her bag, its work complete. She pulled out two envelopes, one lettered in a child's hand. "Here's a note for you from our Webbie. And a letter, just arrived, from your old friend A. B. Sharpe. You always called him Brady." She watched his face closely. "I never could tell if that was his given name or a nickname. I am going to read them to you, darling."

She placed Web's letter on Robert's chest so that he could see it as soon as he awoke. The paper, translucent as a butterfly's wing, fluttered as he breathed. She knew by heart what it said, so she lifted his hand from the blanket and stroked it as she spoke.

"Love, here is Webbie's note. He's fine, Robert. We're fine. But we need you. Listen: 'Dear Father. I am learning to play the bugle. Mr. Peters is my teacher. Boys who play the bugle may join the army.'" Maggie drew a deep breath, stood to reach the other hand, watched the letter on his chest rise and fall and tremble. A paper wing about to take flight. "'Here is a drawing, me with my bugle. Mother says you will come home soon. Love, Web.'"

She prayed for the words to sink in. He lay so still. She could feel warmth flowing through him. Maggie let go of Robert's hands just long enough to place Sharpe's letter on a tiny bedside table and then pressed Robert's hands in both of hers, their weight familiar, reassuring. She sat on the bed, nodding to Philip and Henry to stand behind her so they could run interference with Beatty if necessary.

"Now the one from Sharpe." She had opened it earlier but had not finished reading it. Maggie had resolved to bring as many voices to her husband as it took to rouse him. She squeezed Robert's hands with her right hand. With her left hand she picked up the thin sheet of closely written text.

"This posts from Headquarters Council, Mississippi, July 20, 1862. Goodness, it took over a month to reach you! Your old friend writes:

> "I thought it would not be improper for me to write to you this morning. It is long since I heard anything directly from you, and of late so many things of interest have transpired that my anxiety

> has been doubly increased. A few days after we arrived here, I received a commission from the Secretary of War as Captain—

"Oh, that's a fine thing, isn't it dear?" Robert's eyes remained shut, his breathing shallow, but still regular. She scanned to find her place, and continued:

> "—and upon receipt of it I tendered my resignation as 2nd Lieutenant of Co. E. in the Regiment, which I considered I was bound to do, as it would be wrong to hold two commissions at the same time. But in a week or ten days afterwards I heard that the Senate had passed a bill taking away the commission of all staff officers who held them under commissioning independent of company organizations, so I sent another letter withdrawing my resignation ..."

Maggie scanned the letter, looked up. "Sharpe is asking for your help, I gather. Conserve your strength, dear. I know you live to serve! And you will be able to help in due time." She scanned the page, one eye on Robert, the pressure of three anxious men at her back. She looked up smiling. "A compliment ahead, my dear man! As only wives can make!"

> I have had two letters from my wife lately in which niceties have been made of you & your Company: and in the last she says that *Henderson & Colwell have won for themselves an immortal name.*

"Referring to your action at Charles City Crossroads. And your wound at Gaines Mill." She pressed the back of her hand to her mouth, remembering. When that news had arrived, the only thing that had kept her from rushing to the battlefield was word that it was a mere grazing wound to his right arm and that Robert had immediately returned to action. She pulled up on his sleeve, exposing his upper arm, turned it gently. Sure enough, a beige scar, about two inches long, angled just below his shoulder, a jagged melding of new skin with old. Cool to the touch. She sighed with relief. Maggie continued reading:

> You would realize what sensations this sentence has produced in my mind. I received the letter this morning and write to you before I write to her because it has led me to think so much of you & the past. It was just about this time, one year ago, that we were going to Washington, with our feet swelled in the cause from much marching and countermarching in Baltimore. It seems to me if it would not be foolish and tedious to you I would go on & tell you nearly every incident of importance from that time until I left with another regiment. But maybe we will get a chance to talk these over some time again, either in my back parlour,

> or walking round your grounds looking at the King Cong geese, game chickens, asparagus and bids of celery in your garden, with my son Dillon and your Web close by—

Maggie stopped, closing her eyes against the threat of tears. She felt Henry's reassuring hands on her shoulders. She shook her head, opened her eyes to watch Robert breathe. She forced a laugh as she read on:

> —Web holding on to his hat, which his mother insisted he should put on before he left the house!

"Can you see that, darling?" Maggie squeezed his hand, hard. "You must fix that image in your mind. You must come back to him. To us," she sighed. "How can I nurse you, dear, if you refuse to wake up?" She studied his face for a long moment before returning to Sharpe's letter.

> Our friendship began when I was a lonely boy in Carlisle fourteen years ago, without a single friend and very few acquaintances. You and your brothers showed me unusual kindness, and should it turn out that I am never to see you again—

Maggie shot up out of her chair, against the threat of breaking down. Startled, Philip and Henry took a few steps back. Beatty joined them. Maggie pressed Robert's hand to her cheek, her voice dense with emotion as she finished reading:

> —I want you to know that I have always truly appreciated your manliness of character and magnanimity, and I have full confidence that the sacrifices which you have made in leaving a happy home and lovely wife and child will be duly appreciated by your many friends and the County at Carlisle. Our country one again and blessed constitution vouchsafed to us by our fathers served as of old, and respected all over the land.
>
> What a blessed day this would be to see. May the God of battles who holds the life of all of us in His hands, grant us this privilege, but should He not, may you and I meet and congratulate each other, our duty well done, in a still happier home.

Still happier home? A swell of rage overwhelmed Maggie. Her husband, barely hanging onto life! With his deep abiding sense of duty, would he respond to a direct order?

"Robert, you must hear my voice! Our home is plenty happy! Leaving is *not* an option!" Maggie felt Robert's hand move. She pressed it against her chest. "Robert, damn it all, *open your eyes*!"

Robert's eyes opened a slit, seemed unable to focus, closed again.

Maggie covered his hand with kisses. *The heck with Beatty*, she thought, and kissed her husband's brow, stroked his cheek. Whispered, "Thank you, thank you, thank you, for coming back to me!"

She straightened. With all the resolve she could summon, Maggie turned to Beatty. "Thank you for serving your country, and my husband, so admirably. I know he will receive the best care in your charge."

"Yes, ma'am."

"May I convey any message to your family?"

"Oh, yes, ma'am." Beatty patted his jacket, found a letter of his own, and gave it to Maggie.

"I shall give it to the Wells, Fargo and Company man on the train." She slipped the letter into her bag. She pulled out the German woman's lap quilt and laid it across Robert's sleeping form, tucking Webbie's note under its top border, near his heart.

"Let's go," she said to Henry and Philip, forcing herself away from Robert's bed. One more moment and she would throw herself on it.

~September, 1862~

Room at Dusk

His first night home, Robert insisted on undressing himself. Margaret readied his makeshift bed in the center of his downstairs study, stayed just close enough to where he sat in his wheeled chair. He grunted and strained, his white shirt damp with effort by the time he removed it. She kept a discreet, vigilant silence. Fragments of his arrival came back to her.

Running to the carriage. Web racing ahead.

Two officers lifting Robert onto the ground. His legs trembling.

Web's wide owl eyes registering shock right before he sank into his father's embrace.

The officers easing Robert into the wheeled chair in the vestibule. Web grabbing the chair's handles, loudly announcing, "I'll drive!"

He can't get his pants off. Are they stuck on the chair? Maggie thought, wringing her hands when Robert waved her off. *He won't let me help. Good God! His face so twisted. The agony! He needs something. When will the doctor arrive? I can't watch.*

She didn't hear me, Robert thought. *So much on her mind.* His shirt off, he removed the smelly old bandage and managed—*finally!*—to get his trousers down, his drawers with them. They draped around his ankles and feet, to the floor. He wore nothing but his black-stitched scar. Still raw at the margins, still oozing. Zigzagging down and across his side as if he were a tin canister pried open, then forced shut. He hesitated, before asking again.

"Am I still handsome to you?"

He asked this when her back was turned, her hand lifting the curtain to draw it back and capture the last dregs of day's light. The curtain dropped. Her hand dropped. She turned her head so that he caught in profile a glimpse of her magnificent face before she could disguise her fright.

In this fraction of a moment, Robert also saw in every part of the room emblems of his manhood he could no longer command: shelves of legal volumes beyond arm's reach from this damned chair; his valise, too heavy to lift; the bed, too high to mount unassisted, in which he could only hope for a fitful sleep, nothing more.

This new thing gathered in him. Terror, metallic and dense in his mouth, radiating, overriding his pain. Even in battle, where he learned how vast a record of time and space could be eclipsed by a mere sliver of a second, even then, he had been fully confident about his capacities. And his identity. Now? His breath came in shallow huffs, which he hated. Defenseless, he waited.

Maggie came to him in a slow arc, as if extending her path through his office-*cum*-bedroom would give them both more time. From a chair-side table, she picked up his brush, the one with dense, soft bristles, silver handle tarnished now. In the room's half light, incredibly, he could see gold strands of her hair trailing from it. She pulled a chair next to his and sat, resting in the curve of its spindled back. She paused, studying his face in the same frankly curious way she had looked at him the first time they met.

Then she leaned forward and began to brush his hair. She used a firm, quick stroke. He could feel a tingling in his scalp, that paradoxical response to massage of both energy and relaxation. *She brings order,* he thought, aware of the warmth of her palm as it grazed his cheek. *Order from the mess that is.* He felt every part of himself marshal, as to arms, alert, attentive with anticipation.

When Maggie finished, she leaned back, a half-smile fluttering, creasing her face. She leaned forward quickly and pressed her lips against his mouth, matching its surprised openness.

Then she whispered, "I was going to ask you the very same thing."

~October, 1862~

Battles Recounted

"This will be your first walk outdoors. Do you feel ready?"

Maggie stood by the windowed door, autumn's afternoon light illumining her face and its seams of worry. That was the chief, and now permanent difference in her appearance, Robert noticed. A deeper, more tragic beauty. He pulled a crutch under each arm and raised himself to join her. He leaned against the wall and transferred one crutch to it so that he could free his left hand to touch her hair. When he had left her a year and a half ago, it had been one vibrant shade of ginger, a flame of hair. Now the strands in the comb of his fingers glowed gold, copper, silver: shimmering precious metals.

"Don't look at my tired old hair." She turned toward him and closed her eyes. He kissed her brow.

"I can't stop. It's like touching a halo."

"Careful then. Halos blaze. Your fingers may get singed." She laughed and followed the contour of his cheek with her fingers. Robert knew he appeared less gaunt. He was gaining back weight under her care. Maggie smiled. "Look, the boys are coming."

Web and Junior brandished sticks as they made their way across the back lawn toward the brick-walled pond, which was vacant of water and lined with fallen leaves. "Why don't you walk as far the pond? You can sit there. The boys will keep you company."

"My guards?"

"Yes."

Maggie opened the door and her husband swung himself through it.

"Here comes Father! Sit with us, please!" During this significant stretch of eighteen months, Web had grown. His body had lost its baby fat, his voice the high lilt of childhood. He stood an inch taller than Junior now, between Robert's elbow and shoulder in height. Robert sucked in a breath to stay the emotion he felt as he saw the boys' faces. He saw his own face echoed in his son Web, with Maggie's eyes interposed: a sweetness in those enormous eyes that life's hardships had not yet stolen. In the Thompson boy, Robert saw Junior's mother's face, his father's eyes. And in those eyes, an unblinking intelligence and awareness that was intimidating in one so young.

Robert drew another long breath at the thought of Chance Thompson and his failure to act on Thompson's behalf. Did his son, Junior, know? If not now, eventually he would. Would he come to hate his friend Web? For the shortcomings of Web's father?

Robert knew that Chance had left town and his family to serve in the war effort at around the same time as Nathan. Robert suspected that Chance kept in contact with Nathan. Where Chance Thompson had ended up was anyone's guess.

The boys made a space between them on the low wall. "Tell us a story from the war, Colonel Henderson." Junior's voice carried the same direct curiosity as his father's. His neck looked thin in the jacket Robert recognized as an old one of his, yet Junior's shoulders nearly filled it out. Robert himself felt undersized in his new title of Colonel, a title and role belonging to his father. Colonel William.

"As you wish, Captain Thompson." Robert stifled a groan as he sat, setting aside one crutch. The cold brickwork sent chills of pain up his spine. He straightened against it. "I heard of your bravery, gentlemen. Your brevetted rank is well-deserved."

"Tell the whole campaign, Father. Junior and I want to play-act it." Web stood and presented his stick bayonet. Junior jumped to his side. A company of two, reporting for duty.

Robert peered at them over one crutch, which he staked in the ground and gripped, to give himself more leverage over the pain. "Are those direct orders, sirs?"

"Yes!" in chorus.

"Very well." Robert cleared his throat. "Thursday, the 26th of June was a bright, beautiful day, like this one. And warm—very warm. Shade from only a few stunted trees. Malarial fever and big mosquitoes were the principal crops of the swamps of the Chickahominy. Meanwhile, a General Courts Martial was sitting in a large, quartermasters tent."

The boys scrambled to sit cross-legged in their imagined tent, swatting imagined mosquitoes. "Who was being punished?" Web asked.

"The record of that Court was never written. Because by noon the court was brought to an abrupt end by a simple announcement from its president, General Reynolds. He ordered each officer to return at once to his command."

Junior jumped up first, winning the General's role. He pantomimed the order and Web hustled to the far side of the fountain, bayonet held high.

"Within an hour, the last tent of the reserves was struck. And the first fight of the Seven Days Battle was on. General McCall and his division of Pennsylvania Reserves were entrusted with the defense of the right wing of the Army of the Potomac at Mechanicsville. As General McClellan has said, General McCall proved himself the hero of Mechanicsville."

The boys sprung into battle, their mouths agape.

"McCall held his own against heavy odds. His brave troops were within sight of the spires of Richmond, a comfortable morning's walk in the distance. The Confederates' attack on the Federal lines at this point was a disastrous defeat. D. H. Hill, a Rebel general of no mean reputation, summed up the day's work as 'a bloody and disastrous repulse.'"

Robert looked over his shoulder. No sign of Maggie, certainly not within hearing distance. Even so, when he turned back to the boys, who were crouching, their mouths still ajar, Robert whispered, "Nearly every field officer in the Rebel brigade was killed or wounded."

The boys felled a few more invisible Confederate soldiers with gusto.

"Unfortunately for the Confederates, the river crossing began before Jackson got in rear of Mechanicsville. The loss of that position would mean abandoning the line of Beaver Dam Creek, as in fact they did the next day. We were lavish of blood, and it is thought to be a great thing to charge a battery of Artillery or an earthwork lined with infantry. Do you know what a French General once said, when he looked upon the British Cavalry's charge at Balaklava? 'It is magnificent, but it is not war.'

"Gentlemen, the attacks on the Beaver Dam entrenchments, and on the heights of Malvern Hill, were all grand. But exactly the kind of grandeur the South cannot afford." Robert coughed and thought he tasted blood. He would have to time his story to match his strength.

"So it was with sad hearts the Reserves received orders to fall back. Now just here"—Robert tilted his crutch toward the boys, pointing a finger at them. "Tell me: when Jackson, with fresh troops 30,000 strong, was threatening our right flank and rear, where was McDowell?" He wagged his finger. "With his army of 40,000 soldiers, a promised part of the Army of the Potomac? I'll tell you." Robert leaned forward. "Held as if in a vice between Fredericksburg and Washington by an ignoble and imbecile hand and short-sighted command which reached out from Washington. McClellan, Napoleon-like, looked for his support in vain."

The boys looked downcast at the prospect of retreat. Robert noticed their glum faces. He could not end his story just yet. He rallied, finding a bit more strength to continue.

"It's called a change of base. That Friday morning, June 27th, I confess it did not occur to me that we were taking up the line of retreat. Everything moved so well and so orderly. The dead and wounded cared for. The soldierly bearing of the men. It seemed like a march back to our old camping ground after a hard fought battle, to dream of the victory won. It was not long till the spell was broken. Shot and shell and whistling minié balls soon sped us along. Dreams tossed like children's balls."

Web and Junior marched around the fountain, faster and faster until they were chasing each other.

Robert's eyebrows raised with his voice. "The order came again for battle! We took a new stand before we crossed the Chickahominy. Gaines Mill. Indeed, without Gaines Mill we never could have crossed the Chickahominy!"

"You saved the flag! And you were wounded there!" Web shouted. "But not bad." An aside to Junior: "The bad one came later."

"That shot grazed me here." Robert pointed to his upper right arm. "I was still able to fight. McClellan was equal to the emergency and baffled one of the greatest and most accomplished field generals of this or any other war—Robert E. Lee. General Porter fought this battle with the Fifth Corps—against terrible odds. The line of battle was already formed when the Reserves marched into positions assigned them as steadily as if on dress parade. Regiment after regiment advanced, relieved regiments in front, in turn withstood, checked, repelled or drove the enemy and retired, their ammunition being exhausted, to breathe a few moments, to fill their cartridge boxes again, to return to the contested woods."

The boys made fierce explosive noises, spit flying as they wielded their weapons. Robert squeezed his eyes shut against the pain. He struggled to stand, clutching both crutches.

"Parts of the line were driven from its ground but only to receive aid and drive the enemy back. The woods were strewn with heroic dead of both sides. Multitudes of wounded and dying painfully sought every hollow affording some momentary shelter from incessant—pitiless—fire. Vastly outnumbered, the Reserve Corps did its part. Nonetheless, we fell back. Not in as orderly a manner as marching to review. It was a movement without orders."

Robert opened his eyes. The boys had quit running and stared at him, at his shaking. Robert stiffened his limbs to get through the finish. "There was a gentle slope reaching from our battle line to the Chickahominy. I can now see the little log building just in the rear of where the brave Captain Easton fell with his shout ringing in the ears of his bold soldier boys: 'This battery can never be taken but over my dead body. Pour in the double canister boys.' The battery was taken. Easton's dead body was beneath it. It was at this log building I last saw David Haverstick, who with others of Company A had taken shelter from the storm of bullets. Haverstick was killed. Here Hooker lost his arm. We hurried, more anxious to make a good retreat than a bad fight. By this time we had learned how to … change base.

"It was a saying of the boys, when they saw a comrade of another command not gotten up in soldierly style, 'that fellow is badly demoralized.' Well, a good many soldiers of the red, white and blue were rather off color. Especially in the thunder of heavy gunfire. One fine officer, Colonel Robert, rode up alone and with drawn sword shouted 'Halt!' Of course, it was idle as the wind, and, as he knew me before the war and could afford to waive rank on occasion, he asked, 'What does all this mean?' I said, 'Go and see.' In a moment, his horse was faced to the rear—without even a last farewell! I do not mean this disparagingly of Colonel Robert. He was a gallant officer."

"Gallant!" Web waved his hand in an excited salute. "That means brave!"

"Yes. Nevertheless, the battle was fought and lost. A gallant charge of Meagher's fighting Irishmen. They held back the enemy so that we could safely retreat. The capture of General John F. Reynolds was keenly felt by his first brigade. But the fact that he was a prisoner in Rebel hands marked the spirit of the Reserves and nerved every arm to do and to dare 'til the end."

"The end!" Maggie pronounced, her voice carried on the breeze over his shoulder. "Fellows—excuse me—I mean officers, please help me get Colonel Henderson back to his barracks."

"But Mother! He has not yet told us about the biggest battles!" Web looked at his father, whose face had turned a bluish pale. "When you're feeling better, Father? Tomorrow maybe?"

Col. Robert Henderson nodded. Web tucked himself under his father's right armpit, his arms around his father's waist. Junior stood on his left. Robert gripped the boys' shoulders, Maggie carrying the crutches, and they slowly walked him back to the house.

"Chair or bed?"

"This chair … fine," Robert gasped as the three lowered him. He sank against its high back, grateful for its cushioned comfort. He sat facing a window that afforded a view beyond lawn to the woods, shedding spirals of leaves: amber, rust, cinnamon, butter, lemon. *Peace. No, a semblance of peace.* He could taste it. Feel it drumming through his veins. *How, with this broken body, can I help preserve it?*

"Boys, come to the kitchen with me. I have toast and milk for you." Maggie gave Robert an assessing gaze before adding, "I'll be back with tea for us."

When Maggie returned with two cups of precious tea, trailing curls of steam, she placed one to his right, on a small table between their two chairs. "With your laudanum dose dissolved in it."

"Thank you." His hand so shaky the cup chattered in its saucer.

"You spare no gory detail."

"You want me to spare them," Robert's pinched voice stating, not asking.

"Yet you make the brutality sound so romantic," she growled in disgust. "Tell me about the letter."

Robert could feel the letter's weight in his coat pocket. It had arrived just this morning. He had not had time to answer and file it.

"You were correct. It's my new appointment. From President Lincoln himself. Provost marshal." He swallowed the tea in searing gulps, willing the laudanum to cut his pain.

Her voice flat. "And when do they expect you to start?"

"When I am physically able." *Did she just growl again?*

"So this is how it will be?"

"What, Margaret?"

She stood and paced in front of the window, arms folded. He caught whiffs of her perfume, closed his eyes to breathe in its tonic.

"Do you remember the nicknames my mother used to call us?"

He nodded, half-smiled. Both tonics taking effect. "War. And Peace."

She stood in front of him. "I never found them amusing."

Robert erased the smile. "She did not mean them to be."

"Yet I knew thee. I knew full well thy ideals about the Republic."

Ironic, the way she lapses to the Quaker manner of speech when she's angry.

"And I knew about thy certainty that warfare is both a noble and necessary means to defend it." Maggie leaned over him, her hands bracing on his chair's armrests. Her breath warming his cheek. Her voice low, intense through gritted teeth. "I am grateful this means no more battlefield for you. But now you must induce how many more men to enter into battle? I am not one of thy young, green recruits, Mr. Provost Marshal. I am thy *almost-widow*! Sick unto death of war. Half-starved by it! Before thou tells those boys—or any young men—another glory story, I need to hear the truth." She stood straight, her voice rising. Fire in her eyes. "We both need to hear thee tell it. I believe our future depends upon it!"

Robert's eyes jerked wide open. Was she threatening to leave him? "All that I told them was true."

"The rest of the truth, then."

"Maggie, I would risk my life again. For you, for—"

"I know, my dear. I am in no way questioning thy choices or valor." She dropped to her knees, was hugging his. "Please, Robert. Only my ears will hear. I will not repeat it to another soul."

Robert returned the emptied teacup to the table. He cupped her elbow with his right hand. He placed his left hand on his shirt below the ribcage, over the bandaged and stitched hole in his body. He could feel the wound's angry heat through all the swaddles of cloth. Soon it would need to be changed again, thick with the yellow-orange stench of pus and blood. He caught her gaze and fixed upon it. Saw his reflection in her eyes: gaunt-cheeks, his beard stubble and hairline edged with gray.

"Before the worst battles, each soldier will write his name on a slip of paper and pin it to his chest so that his body can be identified." Through the window, Robert saw colors swirling through the air in such gorgeous waves they seemed to mock his grim report. He fixed his gaze on a bare-limbed tree the way sailors spot the horizon, to avoid seasickness and cure their homesickness for land.

"Rotting flesh so befouls the air there is no escaping it, not even during sleep."

She closed her eyes, lowering her head to his lap.

"The pressure is relentless. Our leaders are so grieved by the annihilation of so many good men and officers they sometimes bicker over authority and orders like children. Meanwhile, our men are so desperate to fight and to win and to return home that they will follow a reckless fool more readily than a cautious genius. At Glendale—" his voice caught. He steadied it, looking longingly at the empty teacup. Rubbed his lips, already dry. "There at the Charles City Crossroads, I was the reckless fool. How many men did I kill? Only God knows. During the Gaines Mill battle, there was a mud-caked boy …" The boy appeared to him now, as he often did these days, during nightmares and day terrors. And always—indelibly!—with Web's face imposed on the broken little body. Robert had urged him to lie on his side, facing away. *Close your eyes, think upon some happy thought.* He could not confess aloud—not yet!—his grim choices: watch him suffer or relieve his suffering with a bullet.

"Maggie! Dear Maggie. Without those ideals and comradeship forged behind the earthworks, there would be only hell. Hell and hopelessness."

He stroked the fine hairs at her temple, tucked them behind her ear. He traced the shape of it, a delicate seashell of flesh. He longed to draw close, hear the cleansing ocean roar of her heart. But his body could no longer bend in that way. She sighed deeply and gathered herself to stand. "More tea?"

"Hot spring water is fine." He hesitated. "Fresh dressings in the bedroom?"

"Yes, yes!" Hurry filled her voice as she carried the teacups back to the kitchen. "Do not attempt it on your own. I shall be right back."

Robert loved hearing her skirts rustle. He now took such pleasure in the most ordinary household noises. Carpet static. Floorboards sighing underfoot. Spoon clanking against kettle, feeding his soul and body, no matter how thin the contents. Muffled voices: the hum of Maggie's lower register, the cheerful percussion of the boys. Every burst of laughter and excited chatter restored a bit more of his heart.

"Thank you. Even for the terror. Oh, God, forgive us," he whispered. "Now we know."

Gettysburg Thunder

1863, Refugees
(Carlisle and Lancaster)

~late June, 1863~

Night Terrors

Maggie awoke in the deepest part of night, reaching over to the empty side of the bed. *Robert. Stranded in Harrisburg. Under orders not to return home.* Her hands went protectively to her swollen stomach, feeling her unborn baby kick. Was that her own heart, also pounding in her ears? There. Again: sharp, insistent rapping at the downstairs back door. Real, not dreamt. Had the Confederates arrived and caught her unawares?

Nonsense. Soldiers don't knock, she scolded herself. She rolled heavily out of bed and felt her way across the bedroom, grateful for pale stripes of moonlight filtering through the shutters. She wrapped a shawl over the dress she slept in, pausing at the washbasin long enough to dash its tepid water on her face. *Stay alert,* she mentally warned her shadowed image in the mirror.

The knocking again, louder. Impatient. She padded downstairs in stocking feet, feeling her way through the drawing room to the kitchen. Pounding now. Fist against wood. Maggie lit an oil lantern and positioned it on the floor so that it illumined the pantry door entrance. She picked up a stout axe handle, practicing the swing that would split open the head of an intruder.

She firmed her voice: "Who's knocking?"

"Sarai Thompson."

Maggie yanked open the door, axe handle clattering onto the brick flooring. "Sarai! What's wrong? What's happened?'

Sarai answered calmly, her voice almost flat. But her eyes were wide with fear. She clutched a wooden box that nearly covered her chest. "Rebels coming."

"How did you hear this, Sarai?"

"Lord told me. In a dream."

Robert's evening telegram had instructed her "when necessary" to seek haven with his Lancaster relatives. Maggie had heard rumors that Confederate troops might breach the Mason-Dixon line and enter Pennsylvania. But when?

"Come in, Sarai."

"No, ma'am, I just come to warn you. And, uh ..." She stroked the lid of the box, now cradled under one arm. "And ask leave to hide this on your property. I reckon our home most likely be looted by Rebels. Seemed to us these valuables got a better chance of survival here than at our place. Or on the road."

"Certainly, Sarai. What are your plans? For you and your boy?"

"Load the wagon. Go." She shrugged.

"Let's go together. Strength in numbers. We have relatives near Lancaster, the Hagers, who will give us safe haven for a while."

Sarai looked at Maggie, eyes lingering on her very pregnant belly. *She rarely looks at me,* Maggie thought. *She looks over my head, or at the ground. Beautiful eyes. Shades of purple at the center, or is that the lantern light?*

"Yes, we go together." Sarai's mouth formed a line of grim resignation. "Chance told me I must look after you and your boy in your husband's absence."

"You have other family here, too …"

"My brothers and my sister's family going on back to Baltimore for the time being."

"Perhaps you prefer going with them?"

"Better if we travel separate." She looked at the ground. "They may not be coming back."

Maggie did not know what else to say.

Except, "Let us load the carriage, then." Sarai slipped back into the darkness before Maggie could add … *What? Goodbye? Thank you? No time to spare, for words or anything else.*

Most of the belongings Maggie intended to take were already packed in leather and canvas bags (clothing, toilet items, books, pencils and paper) and crates (fresh fruit and vegetables, pickled and preserved food, jugs of water). She changed out of her spent clothing. She quickly towel-bathed with a soaped cloth and the basin of cold water. Over fresh undergarments she tied pouches filled with U.S. coins, paper currency and some gold pieces she had hoarded for this event. She dressed in her loosest-fitting plain cotton clothes, snug only at her pregnant middle: white round-collared shirt, long blue skirt, tan vest.

She woke Webbie. While he bathed and dressed, she folded their bedclothes into tight rolls, pillows at center, and secured them with twine.

Daylight skimmed the horizon. She walked over to the carriage house, where Yancy slept. Before the war, he had lived on the Henderson property in the summer months and spent winters with relatives in Maryland. Now Sharon was his year-round dwelling. He was already up and shuffling toward her. Sarai must have alerted him, too.

Yancy called out, "Gonna stay here, Miz Henderson. Keep an eye on the place."

Maggie stopped in her tracks. "That is too dangerous, Yancy."

He shook his grayed head slowly, with authority. "Nobody want to bother with a old man. Gonna go see about the horses now." Yancy turned back toward the carriage house and barn.

"The large carriage, Yancy. And if your mind is made up, at least stay in the house. You'll be safer."

Maggie saw Yancy's shoulders straighten as he turned.

"Got a few weeks' supply of root vegetables and preserves in the cellar?"

"Yes."

He gave her a penetrating look.

"All the bedrooms on the second floor. That right?"

"Yes."

He scratched his head. "All right then," he spoke slowly. "Maybe I'll bed on the first floor. In Mr. Henderson's office. Got a window with a clear view of the pike. I'll see 'em afore they sees me. That room be close to the basement stairs. I and my things can go down there right quick. Down there, you can listen to the floorboards talk. Hear 'em comin.' Hear 'em leavin.' Plus they's an exterior entrance good for—" Yancy did not finish. Instead, he turned and walked away, the matter settled.

Sarai slipped into the Hendersons' barn. Here and there, moonlight pierced vertical gaps between its broad oak boards and beams. She breathed in the vanilla pudding smell of that fine hardwood, spoke low. "This barn could stand another hundred years. Would the Rebs dare burn it?" She sighed. "What looks so secure. Well. Leastways the foundation might survive."

She hurried over to where hay was mounded. She bounced on each stout floorboard until one wiggled. Sarai reached under hay, feeling for a latch. *There.* She shoved the mound with her shoulder until she had clear access to the trap door. She lifted it and saw a short set of stairs disappear into the void of the barn's cellar. She felt along the underside of the door's rim until her fingers came upon a metal ledge of shelving. *Good. This part not as likely to burn.* She slid her treasure box there, its carved S a deep moon shadow. The box fit neatly. Sarai lowered the hatch and covered it completely with deep layers of hay. She smiled in spite of herself.

"Thank you, Junior. And Webbie," she said softly. "Hope your secret hiding place stays a secret."

~late June, 1863~

Sarai & Maggie

Webbie was dressed and sat at the kitchen table, finishing the breakfast that Maggie had fixed for the two of them. Cooked oats and a special sweet treat: toast slathered with cherry preserves. Food packed for the journey from their dwindling supply would be bland and basic by comparison: dried beans for soup, dried venison and beef, dried currants, walnuts, apples, salt, biscuits. Stout crockery, including jugs of water. No glass jars, no perishable foods. Maggie stood to eat her slice of toast and sip hot water as she watched her son ladle the hot cereal into his mouth. Hair rumpled, his eyes still half-hooded with sleep, he seemed like any other eleven-year-old boy. *Not anxious*, she reassured herself. Webbie looked up at his mother. In that moment, Maggie realized she was tapping her foot on the wood floor, telegraphing her own worries in double time. She sat down and smoothed her son's hair.

"Ready for our grand adventure, Webbie?"

The boy nodded and focused on his cereal.

"Would you like some cherry preserves in your cereal, too?"

He shook his head. "Almost finished," he lisped through a mouthful of cooked oats.

"Me, too." *Strange,* Maggie thought, *how during the most significant moments of one's life, there is so very little to say.* She wanted to gather her son in her arms and hold him and not let go. She fought the urge. No more foot tapping, she scolded herself. She missed Robert. He worried over her pregnancy, hated being stranded in Harrisburg with the baby so nearly full term. And now this hasty exodus by bumpy carriage ride. . . .

"Yancy probably has the carriage drawn up and ready. We should begin loading our things."

Webbie broke into a grin and shook his head. "No carriage. We're going in Junior's big ole covered wagon!" He noticed his mother's surprise and waved his arm toward the pantry door. "Look outside!"

Maggie made her way over to the door, dodging the packed crates and bags littering the kitchen floor. Through the door's small square window she did indeed see a covered wagon with two horses she did not recognize. She saw Yancy standing by one of the horses, stroking it as he talked to Sarai. The Thompsons' dog sat near Yancy, ear cocked to their conversation.

"Yancy told me to load our things." Webbie stood at her elbow holding a crate of provisions. "Starting with the food." He elbowed his way past his speechless mother and out the door. She composed herself, picked up a box and followed him.

Sarai saw her coming and turned to climb up onto the buckboard.

"Yancy, I asked you to bring our large carriage."

He looked away, squinting at the house, and the Pike beyond.

"Webbie! Up here!" Junior Thompson's excited face appeared at the opening in the canvas at the back of the wagon. "We get to bunk in the back!"

Webbie held the crate up to the wagon's rear access. Yancy, sitting on the wagon's foot ledge, grabbed the crate and passed it to Junior. Junior disappeared into the wagon with the crate. Webbie loped over to the kitchen to fetch another crate. Just that quickly the man and boys had organized the packing chore.

Maggie started to approach Yancy, hesitated. She turned and instead approached Sarai, already perched on the buckboard.

"We should discuss the route we're taking to Lancaster."

Sarai shrugged. "Not much to discuss. Only one way to go. I'll take the turnpike through Mechanicsburg and the whole way over, cross the river by the Harrisburg bridge."

"Let me drive, then." Maggie felt frustration rise. "I know how to drive a wagon!"

"There's no need, Miz Henderson."

"You are in control, is that it, Sarai? I am to follow your lead?"

Sarai looked into the wagon. In a low voice, she said something to Junior in the back before climbing to the ground. She took her time. When face to face, Sarai's expression sent a shock of dread through Maggie, who had never before seen such raw contempt.

"You the leader, Miz Henderson? That's fine. Where'd we be at this moment? You up in that feather bed," Sarai pointed to Maggie's upstairs bedroom window. "And my son and me'd be two mile down the Pike by now."

Maggie heard throat-clearing, turned to see Yancy standing at her elbow, nodding at Sarai and looking pleased. "Wagon's loaded."

Sarai whistled and Blood trotted into view. "Yancy, can you look after our dog for us?"

Yancy bent to scratch behind the dog's ears. Blood cocked his head toward his mistress, a question in his eyes.

"Yancy, that r-r-reminds me," Maggie stammered. "I need to fix a bed for you in my husband's office."

He nodded toward a bedroll on the ground. "Got all I need right there."

"That looks like an Army blanket," Maggie blurted out.

"Navy!" Webbie's voice, high with excitement, his face and Junior's bobbing around the back corner of the wagon. "Yancy fought in the War of 1812. He has a million stories!"

"Lake Erie," Yancy volunteered. He winked at the boys.

"I simply mean that you should have a proper bed!" Maggie heard the angry quaver in her own voice.

Yancy picked up his bedroll, called to the dog, and started for the house. "Don't have one now. I am accustomed to sleeping on the floor. No need to worry, ma'am. Like this I can keep a watch ready and good." He gave a short wave and disappeared through the pantry door and closed it. Blood followed as far as the porch, dropping onto it with a sigh. He peered back at them.

Maggie realized with a shock that she knew nothing about how Yancy lived. Or Sarai. Her own son knew this, and more. She felt bewildered. She looked at her empty hands, dropped them to her sides with a shrug. Maggie said to Sarai, "Where do you want me?" then amended, "I'll sit next to you. Ready to relieve the driver."

~late June, 1863~

Sarai at the Reins

Sarai wiped her brow without letting go of the reins. *Our horses got that wagon moving right quick. Morning sun moved quick, too, from warm to hot.* The boys crawled to the front and poked their heads out. Junior pointed to the road they had just traveled, said "Look!"

Webbie said, "More and more wagons on the road. Leaving, just like us."

These travelers have nary business or pleasure on their minds, Sarai thought. Every carriage and wagon was bearing a full load. Word of troop movement traveled fast, and Sarai's dream was affirmed by a river—no, a flood—of women and children on the run. Sarai held the reins tense, already felt her insides quivering so violently it took all her energy to keep her terror from showing on the outside.

"We must look novel, two ladies on the road," Maggie Henderson said, staring at the horses' rumps all the while. Sarai hated the proper way her voice sounded. Like she was play-acting.

Yeah, she thought. *One of them look like she ready to give birth to a big ole watermelon.* Instead, Sarai said, "Look around you. There's plenty of other women on the road. Ladies? That's another question."

"Sarai, you seem angry."

She looking at me too calm, Sarai thought. *Maybe her insides roiling, too.*

Maggie's tone came down from on high. "Have I done something to offend you?" she said.

"Offend me? No. Takes a lot to offend me."

"Why the anger, then?"

Sarai thought on how to answer the question. Before she could respond, Maggie added, "Or maybe you're nervous because I was your employer? Just forget about that. We're on equal footing. Two ladies on the road, right? Don't worry, there are no rules."

Sarai slapped the reins so she would not have to slap someone else. The horses shifted to a faster trot, throwing Maggie backward. She almost fell from her seat. The world zipped by in a green blur. Sarai felt a little sorry on account of the baby. She could hear the wagon contents shift. *Boys'll be fine.*

"Hey!" Maggie's muffled voice came through the hat that covered her face. She righted herself, pushed her hat back. "Why did you do that?"

"Do you seriously want answers to your questions? Because I'm four behind already. Don't be adding a fifth."

"I was just trying to make you feel at ease. I—"

"Make … me …?" Sarai's voice came to a halt. It would take a couple of lifetimes to untwist that one. So she settled for, "Well, I got a few questions of my own. Be you a lady of the road? Or the Queen of the road? Seems to me the Queen the only one who gets to say there ain't no rules. So if you be Queen, I say 'Yes ma'am' and shut up. If you ain't, then stop flapping your lips because you do not know what you're talking about. There *be* rules. Lots of 'em."

Maggie looked as if she had been slapped. "Such as?"

"Rule One." Sarai slowed the horses because wagon traffic was getting thicker as they got closer to the first tollgate. It also meant she could look Maggie in the eye. "Don't touch me."

"I didn't lay a finger on you!" Maggie sputtered.

Sarai answered back, "Your shirt's touching mine. You setting too close. This buckboard uncomfortable enough without you crowding me."

They were sitting on a folded up blanket to soften the bouncing for her and her baby. Maggie moved over, offended. "How's that?" she said.

I see you eyin' me through those slitty eyes, Sarai thought.

"Rule Two," she said. "Leave my son alone. Don't touch him. Don't boss him. Just leave him to me. I'm his mam. Leave him be."

"When did I ever—" Maggie tried to interrupt. Sarai kept talking.

"You are right on one count, this ride of ours go way beyond employment. I'm here out of obedience. To God, and to my husband, who directed me to look after you."

"God, eh?" Maggie's voice crackled.

"That's right. So, Rule Three. When we aren't riding together we stay separate. I do my business, you do yours."

Something in Maggie's voice softened up. "Sarai, I was hoping we could be friends."

"You don't really mean that. Besides, I can never be friends with a white woman. You could never be friends with a black woman."

"And why not?"

"It's just not the natural order of things. We're too different. Too much history, too much pain. Too much water, too little bridge."

Maggie sighed. Her voice came out low. "That is a lie from the pit of hell."

Sarai reared her head back, shouted: "You don't know a damn thing about hell!"

"Now who's the queen?" Maggie shouted back.

"Mam?

"Mother?"

Two voices together. Came out "Mamther?" The boys' faces appeared, looking confused.

"What're you fighting about?" Junior asked.

"We're just figuring out how things are going to be , Son," Sarai said.

"Huh?" Webbie said.

Sarai felt a sudden bit of shame. If he were here, Chance would scold her for setting a bad example. But she could still taste blood. She couldn't quite manage to strap down her tongue. "I know what." She tried to make her voice cheerier. "Maybe Miz Henderson would like to tell us about a time when she was friends with a Negro woman, who weren't her slave nor worker making her life all easy."

Wagons now slowed to a stop, a long line stretching way out in front and behind. Maggie fell silent. Far off, they could see the pitched roof of the toll-man's house. The sun had settled directly on their heads. A layer of sweat came between Sarai and her favorite blue flowered cotton dress. The women went silent so long Sarai was hoping the boys would get tired of waiting to find how the fight turned out and go back inside of the wagon, which was stuffy because they weren't moving, but it still had shade. But they didn't move.

"Call me Maggie, please," Maggie said finally, sounding as tuckered out as Sarai felt. "It was a church meeting. A Friends meeting. On Sharp Street ..." she began.

~summer, 1837~

Meeting on Sharp Street

My parents attended First Monday meetings at the home of Friends—some call us Quakers—who were also close personal friends. Mr. and Mrs. Isaac Tyson lived on Sharp Street in Baltimore. 'Twas my earliest remembrance of a meeting. I recall my sister was sick, and Mother said that my brother and I could come along because there would be other children to play with. I took with me a doll and a book. As it turned out, there was just one other child, an older boy, Philip Tyson, son of our hosts, who was ten at the time. Henry was nine and I was eight, but mature for my age, as they say. "I do not mind that there are just boys," I told Mother. "Please keep the doll for me. I will only need the book."

We occupied a study filled with leather-bound books and dark-browed furniture and paintings that to me became windows that framed glimpses of other worlds. The gas lamps created dramatic light and shadows that fired my imagination. The boys did not seem to notice. They had spread a fine collection of wood blocks on the wool rug and were arguing about what to build.

"Why not build the Capitol in Washington City?" I said.

They looked at me for the first time.

"I have a drawing in my book of what it's supposed to look like when it's finished. We can use it."

Henry looked at Philip. "Let's do it."

"May I help with the dome?" I asked.

Building a dome is rather tricky. We had to work together and, as we worked, we found our conversation weaving into some serious topics. Since both families were Friends, we fell upon the subject of meetings.

"I find Quaker meetings to be boring," Henry said.

"They can be long," I agreed.

"I know one meeting that is definitely not boring," Philip declared. "In fact, it is probably in session right now."

"Where?" we asked.

"Right across the street. Listen. You can hear it." Philip ran to a street-facing window, lowering the upper sash to the summer air. We could hear singing and shouting. Negro voices.

"That cannot be a Friends meeting," I said.

"Maybe it's a pub," Henry suggested.

Philip looked indignant. "That is a Friends meeting! We shall go and that will settle the matter."

Before we had a chance to agree or bow out, Philip spoke to the housekeeper. "Please tell Mother we are taking a walk and will be back within the hour."

We ventured out to the street, toeing the curb until we spotted a break in the carriage traffic. Philip led us like an adventurer unleashed. He opened the door and hurried us through it, stepping past two greeters without a heartbeat's hesitation. He even tipped an imaginary hat to one of them, an impossibly tall man with a long thin face that ballooned when he smiled. The man tipped his stovepipe hat and winked at his partner, whose eyes popped at the sight of us.

We found three unoccupied seats in the very back of the room. I sat next to a Negro girl whose eyes held such frank curiosity. I told her my name and she told me hers. We tried to talk but mostly we looked each other over. We were dressed similarly, in simple long gray dresses and bonnets, that was the Quaker way in those days. We had a lot to take in around us, too: every bit of space packed with people and the heavy yellow light of oil lanterns. The men and women were singing, accompanying themselves with rhythmic claps and foot stomps, some seated, some standing, all focused as if part of one voice, one mind.

Philip, Henry, and I began to catch on to the rhythm and melody, blending in. Voices began dropping out as we sang along until the room became completely silent, save for our voices, which lingered in that instant. I felt my face redden. Henry and Philip blanched.

The impossibly tall man had moved to the front of the room and was pointing at us. At Philip, to be precise. His voice, so deep it vibrated the dense air, caused us to tremble.

"Art thou of the Tyson family?"

"Yes." Philip's jaw jutted bravely.

"Would the late Elisha Tyson be thy grandpappy?"

"Yes."

The room erupted in a riotous chorus of Hallelujahs, Praise the Lords, and the name Elisha Tyson ricocheting from one tongue to the next. We found ourselves swarmed by hands and levitated from our seats toward the front of the room, next to the tall man, who dropped to one knee so he could get a better look at us. He waved the crowd silent with his hat.

He said, "What be thy name, son?"

"Philip." Philip introduced us, and I was pleased he remembered my name entire: Margaret Turnbrough Webster.

The tall man asked, "Do thy friends know about thy grandpappy?"

Philip hesitated, then shook his head no.

The man stood and addressed the crowd. "Who cares to enlighten these young ones about Elisha Tyson?"

We heard a woman's voice, fragile yet determined. "I kin speak about him." The crowd parted to yield a woman whose half-smile illumined a round, age-weary face.

The tall man stepped back as he introduced her. "Mrs. Mary Wilson, thank you."

"Thank you kindly, Mr. Harford." Wiry coins of dark hair peeked from her bonnet, a crown within a crown. She said, "My membry's not so good, but I remember Mr. Tyson as clear as anyone or anything. Mr. Harford, thou must chime in if I miss a part." She pulled her shawl tighter and began a story I shall never forget.

When Mary Wilson was just a little girl, she and her brothers were taken from their mamma in Africa by slave traders. I remember Mrs. Wilson passed the back of her hand across her eyes. "I was maybe thine age," she said, pointing to me. When I was older, I learned that our country had abolished selling slaves newly from Africa, but that little girl and her brothers were taken all the same.

They arrived in Baltimore and were taken in the slave trader's carriage to the public house outside of town. That evening, Mr. Tyson rapped at the door, and, when the men saw him, they drew their weapons because they knew who he was. Against those guns and knives and brutes who cussed and threatened, there stood Mr. Tyson with nothing but his courage. His faith, too, and that's not nothing. That's something. Mrs. Wilson said he shoved his way through and had no trouble finding them because he had been there many times before. Elisha Tyson helped them out of their chains and took them to safety. Then the sheriff went back to the public house and rounded up every last one of those evildoers. At trial, little Mary Wilson and her brothers were found free and guiltless. But their persecutors went to the penitentiary for the full term for their crimes.

Then Mrs. Wilson looked at Philip. "That was nigh on thirty-one years past. Thy grandpappy set me and my brothers in a good home. We got some proper education and made a proper wage. Now I have a family of my own. Not a day goes by that I fail to think of Mr. Tyson and thank the good Lord for him and bless his whole family. See, child, it takes only one person with the courage to stand up and make a world of difference."

Mary Wilson concluded her story to a flurry of amens. And Mr. Harford told us there are many other stories like hers. "Thousands from our community paid proper respects at his coffin," he said. His own children viewed the funeral procession from their rooftop. The streets were filled in every direction.

Mr. Harford paused to see if Philip wished to say anything. Philip stood silent. To his credit, he did keep his eyes fixed on Mr. Harford and Mrs. Wilson. My heart felt full; I am certain his overflowed, yet he maintained his composure.

Mr. Harford added, "One thing, though. Mr. Elisha Tyson could not abide our form of meeting." He threw his head back and let loose a throat-full of laughter and said that more than once Mr. Tyson had come over and actually scolded them for the noise of their meeting. Sometimes he even snuffed out the lamps! Mr. Harford told us we could come back and visit any time. "Just don't snuff out our lights!" he said, and the whole meeting broke out in laughter and applause. The body of worshippers parted for us as it had for Mrs. Wilson. As we passed, many hands touched us, and from many mouths came blessings too numerous and overwhelming to remember.

Once outside, Philip hurried us back to the house before our appointed curfew. It was an evening lit only by street gas lamps, carriage lights, and a few stars. Yet I found myself immersed in light, many hued: intense greens, blues, golds, indigo and red. The light seemed to transport me across the street and bled away once we entered the Tysons' home. I said nothing to Philip or Henry about the light. Partly because I was stunned to silence. Partly because I did not want to bear the grief of not being believed. Perhaps also because I wanted to savor the experience privately, a secret joy. Ever since then, whenever I feel especially weighted by the world's cares, I summon the memory of that meeting and the intensely hued light and immediately rekindle breathtaking joy.

Back in the library, we stared at each other and paced with nervous energy, too excited to know what to say. An occasion so momentous seemed to require commemoration of some sort: a blessing or sacrament. I grabbed my book, and, with all the solemnity I could muster, I held it out and touched the forehead of each boy. Then I held the book over my own head and lowered it a bit too strenuously. It landed with a thump.

"I knight thee … and thee …and me …" I intoned, "the three musketeers!"

"Here, here!" Philip and Henry cheered, delighted to have regained their voices.

Philip and I became lifelong friends. I introduced him to my sister and, as you know, they wed.

Just a few years ago Philip and I recollected our meeting house experience. On impulse I blurted out about seeing the multi-hued light. He took both my hands in his and searched my face. "Maggie," he whispered. "I saw it, too!"

Philip, Henry and I attended more Sharp Street meetings, sitting with other children. I became friends with the girl I met, Ester Tilghman. I began the practice of slipping a small chapbook story into my Bible. Ester and I put our heads together and pretended to share my Bible. We were really silently reading the popular little story. We took turns turning the pages. Sometimes we did not finish, so Ester took the chapbook with her. Next time, I would bring another one. She began bringing me cut-out figures. Little boys and girls constructed from wallpaper and bits of fabric. Children of all colors. They wore vivid costumes and had fanciful bodies and features, paper fringe eyelashes and intricate hairstyles that I believe Ester fashioned from real hair. Ester and I never had much time to talk. Ours was a friendship of companionable silence. The reading became a sort of communion.

One day my mother came into my bedroom and found the Bible stuffed with those lovely Ester dolls. She frowned as she pulled them out of the book.

"Margaret," she said, "Bibles are costly! Thou wilt ruin the binding! Where did all these come from?"

She insisted on knowing about the dolls. I was reluctant and told her the minimum.

"They are gifts from a friend," I said. She gathered them and began leaving. I clutched at her skirt and screamed, "Mother, please! Give me back my dolls!"

"I shall find a proper box for them," she said, not pleased with my tone. She pulled my fingers from her skirt, one at a time. I can still feel my nails clawing ghost trails into the velvet nap of that skirt.

I never again saw the dolls. Not long after that, my mother insisted that we were old enough to join the adults during their First Monday meetings. And so the next time I saw Ester …

Maggie seemed to be trying to figure how to end her story. "Oh, I know just how this story ends," announced Sarai. "Little Maggie's in her papa's store, or warehouse or farm somewhere, and she spots the face of her friend among all them female slaves. And that's why she works so hard at the abolition job she so proud of. To free a slave girl good at making dolls."

Maggie looked at Sarai, her eyes begging for a different response. Sarai looked away. *I won't tell her about my sister Ester. And how Maggie's darky friend was likely one and the same person. It makes me half-crazy to think of them two as friends.*

Instead Sarai brought up the thing that was making the other half of her crazy.

"You don't remember me, do you?"

Maggie's look went puzzled. She laced her fingers together on her lap and waited.

"You woulda been six. I woulda been five."

Sarai watched Maggie's face while she rifled back through her earliest memories, looking for any that included another brown-faced girl. When she found it, she lit up from the inside. Her hand went up toward Sarai's cheek, stopped short, palm out, when it remembered Rule One. She pulled her hand back, laced her fingers around her knees again, sat curled like that on the buckboard, lost in the memory.

Sarai was remembering, too. And she was pretty sure their memories matched up.

We was playing dolls that Sabbath morn, before the ceremony. We found each other in the cut-flower garden by the barn. We played in that sweet-smelling morning light that fills the world with possibilities. She had two dollies, gave one to me. I had on my Sunday hat which I spread on the ground. The dollies picked flowers together, made the hat look so so beautiful. As did I, when I quick put on the hat after Hettie called my name. We hopped up from our fun, ran away from that Eden place and into the world adults had created, not knowing we could never again run back.

Junior stuck his head between Sarai and Maggie and said, "So, Miz Henderson, you knew my mam *and* my Auntie Ester from when you was, I mean, were a girl!"

Maggie looked confused. Then Webbie said, "I'm hungry!"

The wagon ahead pulled away. It was their turn to draw up to the tollhouse. The sign on its side had numbers and letters written large. *Does Maggie know I cannot read?* Sarai thought. *But my Ester can read.*

The toll man studied them up real good and stretched out his hand to Maggie.

"This is your time to shine, Miz Hen—uh, Maggie," Sarai said, turning her face to spit over the side of the wagon. "Somebody gotta pay the toll."

Maggie's cheeks turned red. "Just give me a bit of… privacy." She shooed the boys to the back of the wagon and crawled in. *Fetching money from a pouch in her undergarments,* Sarai guessed. When Maggie came grunting back out all mussed up she put the money on the seat, between Sarai and herself.

Sarai picked up the paper money and handed it to the man. He fingered it, looked them up and down again, and made a big show of giving the change back to Maggie. "Expect a long delay at this bridge. You ain't gettin' to Lancaster before nightfall."

"All these vehicles are local folks heading east?" Sarai's voice buckled with frustration.

He shook his head. "No, it's not just local folks. Word is, Union forces are gettin' set to burn the bridge down there between Wrightsville and Columbia." He motioned them on. Sarai drove the wagon off to the side of the road. *Need time to think.*

Sarai and Maggie got quiet again. Burning that bridge was a desperate act. It left this bridge as the only safe escape route left. If troops ever crossed this bridge, it would mean only one thing: the enemy had come north with the state capital in their sights. Maggie looked toward Harrisburg, where her husband was marooned.

Sarai spoke up. "We have a decision to make. We have a couple hours left of safe summer daylight. Dusk no time to be on the road."

Maggie said, "We should find a place where we can eat and overnight."

They agreed for once. "Plenty of roadside taverns along the way. But not all of them have space for a wagon," Sarai said.

"We stop when we find one?" Maggie asked, lifting the reins that Sarai had been holding loosely, and adding "Now is a good time for me to relieve you and drive the wagon."

Sarai nodded, then shook her head. She was staring at the reins in Maggie's fists. "Might be better for me to take the reins," Sarai insisted. "Those're my horses and they be touchy."

Maggie flicked the reins. "I have plenty of experience—" The horses whinnied and bolted, jerking the wagon back toward the jammed-up road.

Sarai grabbed the reins and stood, setting her legs wide, shouting, "Whoooa there! WHOOOA!" Maggie gripped the seat edge. The boys shouted from the back of the wagon. The horses came to a sudden stop, just a stitch or two from the road's edge. Maggie called to the boys, who shouted back that they were fine.

After that, Maggie did well enough driving the horses and kept her silence for the most part. *And that be a big accomplishment for her,* Sarai thought, *a woman who gets so much pleasure from running her mouth. I think maybe she was praying to her God.*

My God.

Our God.

Dusk was settling by the time they found a small tavern with some space in its side yard. Sarai climbed down to get the horses settled and secure. Maggie crawled down and half-staggered toward Sarai, holding her pregnant belly and stretching the stiffness from her legs.

"You must want some relief from the travel," Maggie said. "I know I should like to find a latrine. Would you like to go first?"

"No, you go."

"Really, I don't mind," said Maggie.

They watched the boys climb out of the wagon, shoving and laughing their way toward their mothers. Sarai rocked from one foot to the other. *Oh, I mind.*

"Well, perhaps I can just go quickly. Then you can go," Maggie said.

Sarai pointed to an outbuilding behind the tavern. "You can set in there. The boys can find their own spots." Sarai directed the boys toward a clump of trees and bushes just past the outhouse. They ran ahead. "Watch out for the poison ivy!" she called after them.

Maggie stopped at the outhouse. "There is only one here."

"I'm following the boys."

"No, come ahead, Sarai. It's fine. You're with me."

Sarai stopped. She stared at Maggie. "It is not fine. Don't you know that? Go!"

Fire in her eyes, Maggie yanked open the door. Her other hand flew to her mouth and nose, but not soon enough to stop her shriek.

A man's voice roared, "SHUT THE … BLOODY … DOOR!"

Maggie let the door slam shut and nearly fell backward before bumping against a tree, holding her stomach. Sarai disappeared behind a tangle of bushes, laughing. She watched as Maggie walked wide of the outhouse and looked anxiously toward the trees.

When Sarai emerged from the bushes, Maggie went into the woods. Before long she and the boys returned.

"Look!" Webbie cried. He and Junior held something in their hands. "Peaches!"

~late June, 1863~

Roadside

Maggie made her way through the tavern jammed with people and found the tavern owner. He gave an outlandishly high price, Maggie thought, to provide them with hot meals. In fact, he seemed sheepish about it and gave them permission to camp overnight. He charged a few cents extra and filled their water jugs. For a few cents more, he allowed them to take their horses to his water trough and hay bin. They could help themselves to some peaches, he added, as well as wood for a cook-fire.

While Sarai watered and fed the horses, Maggie worked on the fire. She found the parts for a spit and hung on it a small iron pot, partly filled with water pumped from the tavern keeper's well. She was searching in the wagon for the salt pork and beans for soup when she heard Sarai shouting. Alarmed, Maggie hurried out, in time to see Sarai running down the slope from the peach trees. Suddenly Sarai's feet flew out from beneath her and she went tumbling down the rest of the hill, her flowered cotton dress ballooning to reveal her undergarments and flailing legs. Maggie ran to her as Sarai landed near the base of the hill.

"I must have slipped on them ground peaches," Sarai gasped, raising herself up on one elbow.

Maggie helped Sarai to her feet. Maggie said, "I heard you shouting. Why?"

"Lord's mercy!" Sarai huffed. "Woman, you just about made our supper in my chamber potty!" Still catching her breath, she added, "Not to worry, though. I did just rinse it out for the boys."

"Not worry?" Maggie groaned. "What should I not worry about first? The possibility of making us sick over supper? Or maybe getting arrested by the sheriff for reckless driving?" Her voice went up with every question. "Or maybe he'll arrest me for attempting to peep at the private business of men in privees!"

Sarai shook out her skirt, swiping at peach and dirt stains with her handkerchief. Maggie heard the boys choking on their laughter and saw that Sarai was managing to keep hers tucked in.

Maggie ached to laugh, too, knowing it would be a relief. But the humiliation, added to her worry, got the upper hand. She avoided Webbie's eyes as she waddled past the boys, leaning on her pride like a bent walking stick.

Supper consisted of soup made in a proper pot, fresh peaches, and cold water straight from the tavern owner's spring-fed well. They spread their bedrolls in a semi-circle around the fire. Stars littered a clear night sky. A honeysuckle-scented breeze promised comfortable sleeping.

Maggie fell asleep almost as soon as she settled onto her pillow. Moments later, it seemed, she was awakened by heavy breathing and the stench of sotted breath. Someone was groping her through the blankets. "You looks lonely in yer bed," a man's voice growled.

Before she could utter more than a muffled cry, Maggie saw a burst of fire and heard the gut wrenching clang of bullet against metal. Their cook pot! She heard the ominous click of a cocked revolver. Heard Sarai's voice snarling, "Back off, stranger! I give a good warning shot. And an even better drop dead shot!"

Maggie heard the intruder stumble away. Her heart pounded in her ears. She heard Sarai let out her breath as she uncocked her firearm. "Thank you," Maggie gasped.

The snarl was not entirely gone from Sarai's voice. "Go to sleep!"

The next morning, back on the road, Sarai sat in the driver's seat and the boys rode shotgun. Maggie felt grateful for the interior space, alone with her still-racing heart. She had never before been attacked. She detested feeling vulnerable, weak. *What a brutal, chaotic world. What a protected life I've led.* She felt shame over her naiveté. She thought of the many faceless, vulnerable ones traveling in the wagons all around them: war widows; fatherless children; persons sick, aged, or alone.

Men living on the battlefield. Dying there.

War paths. Peace paths. The same old tragicomedy playing over and over, through the ages.

The tavern owner proved to be correct. It took hours to gain access to, and then cross, the vehicle-swarmed bridge.

~June 28, 1863~

Assignment

Chance Thompson sat hunched behind the riverbank earthworks, his fingers drumming his elbows, surveying the expanse of covered bridge over a sullen Susquehanna River. The old man sitting at his side gave a low whistle.

"That is one handsome covered bridge."

Chance nodded. "Longest one in the world, they say."

Earlier in the month, news had traveled fast of skirmishes with Rebels north of the Mason-Dixon. Chance had volunteered to meet up with the 27th Regiment out of Harrisburg to help with the risky and delicate task of arranging explosives to set the bridge afire. Another man would have the honor of lighting the fuse. *No matter. This Negro has endured much in life,* Chance thought as he looked at the Old Head. *He deserves to be the one.* As a back-up plan, Chance had helped members of the Pennsylvania infantry militia coat a section of bridge supports with pitch tar and crude oil from a refinery just across the bridge on the eastern bank, in Columbia. He stood ready with a torch, if ordered to ignite the bridge. Judging from the curses of the militia men arranging the explosives, things did not seem to be going smoothly.

"Chance, how do you manage to go where you want, in this war?" the Old Head wanted to know.

Chanced smiled rather than answer.

He remembered vividly the day Nathan and he had reported for duty in Philadelphia, for service in the 3rd Pennsylvania Reserve Infantry.

The mustering officer had looked from Chance to Nathan and back down at their paperwork. "You two are related?"

They both gave short nods.

"That's your real name?" The officer glared at Chance. "Thompson?"

Chance met his gaze. "Yes."

"He brought his own g-g-gun." Nathan, talking a little too fast.

The officer glared at Nathan. "Does that guarantee he knows how to use it?"

Before Nathan could respond, Chance lifted his rifle to his shoulder and shot a crow sitting on a pole some 100 feet distant. The crow fell to the ground, raising dust.

The officer wrote in his logbook and handed papers to Nathan. He waved them on. "Next."

"What about his papers?" Nathan pointed his thumb toward Chance.

The officer grabbed Nathan's paper, scribbled something across the bottom and handed it back.

Nathan squinted to read: "Attended by Robert Thompson."

"You'll both get food, munitions. My advice?" The mustering officer gave Chance a long look and jerked his head toward Nathan. "Stick with him. Next!"

Nathan looked ready to answer back, but Chance shook his head and nudged him to keep moving. No one else asked to see their paperwork after that. Chance and Nathan were both provisioned and trained as privates. They were stationed first at Easton, then at Harrisburg. Just one day after the 7th Pennsylvania Reserve Infantry, with Robert Henderson's company, had moved on from Harrisburg to Washington. Nathan and Chance spent so much time together, the other soldiers in their company nicknamed them "the Twins." *All those months of drilling and waiting*, Chance remembered. *Not a cross word between us. But once*. They had still been in Washington, preparing to break camp and head south to Tennallytown, Maryland.

"What are you going to say to your brother when we catch up to him?" Chance asked.

"Nothing!" Nathan growled. "He doesn't know we're here. Doesn't need to know!" He spat, walked away. From July until December, their regiment lagged behind Robert's until their winter quarters. Nathan kept track of Robert's whereabouts so as to stay out of his way. Once, Chance even heard Nathan deny he was related to the officer with the 7th's Company A.

"Ain't you from Carlisle, Pennsylvania, too?" the curious soldier had asked, almost dropping his hand-rolled cigar when Nathan stalked off.

Together Nathan and Chance had seen so much hard action the battles bled one into another. They did not part ways until word came that the Rebels were threatening the Pennsylvania border. Nathan stayed with the regiment as it headed north and west. Chance worried about his family's safety and headed north and east. He carried with him the outer trappings of a Union soldier, and without an official muster, he could not be considered missing from duty. Now Chance found himself back in Pennsylvania, crouching next to the Old Head and some other local militiamen on the eastern side of this magnificent covered bridge, just forty-five miles from home.

Chance had the habit—from youth, not soldiering—of scanning his environment for signs of trouble. He noticed movement across the river just outside the village of Wrightsville. Then artillery fire split the air. Streets emptied. Locals had been warned to stay indoors. The movement turned into a stomping gray wave of Rebel soldiers racing toward the bridge. Chance felt his flesh crawl as he sprang to his feet.

The Old Head lit the fuse. A hiss was followed by acrid smell, a muffled boom, and the chilling crack of stone columns giving way. The bridge swayed a bit, yet it remained intact. And the Confederates charged closer.

Col. Frick brayed the order to torch. Chance and others scrambled onto the bridge, reaching down to the oily wooden piers. His torch barely made contact before the fire leapt straight up, singeing his sleeve, heat sizzling his eyebrows and skin. Then he raced away from the bridge, along with the rest of the militia, east, toward the huddled factory town of Columbia.

Within seconds, the bridge transformed into an accordion of fire. Chance and the others watched as first lines of Confederates arrived on the opposite river bank and stood immobile, their shouts silenced by the sight of the great bridge collapsing.

Sparks blew west, settling onto rooftops in Wrightsville, so tinder-dry in the summer's heat that they, too, burst into flames. The men in gray watched the townspeople swarm out-of-doors to douse the fires. With no Union troops to fight and no bridge to cross, the Confederates set about helping the townspeople save their homes.

~June 28, 1863~

Lancaster

Early in the evening. Maggie, Sarai, and the boys finally arrived at the base of a steep dirt and gravel lane that led to the home of Robert Henderson's cousin, Olivia Hager. The Hagers' two-story brick home west of Lancaster straddled a bare hilltop and was situated for its river view. They owned the dry goods store in town.

Olivia's husband had also joined the Union troops, and so it was an anxious, thin woman and her two children who stood at the doorway to greet their visitors. Webbie helped his pregnant mother out of the wagon. Sarai followed. Junior scrambled to tie the horses to a hitching post. Olivia's voice came to them, high and threadbare. "Robert wired to say you were coming. Didn't mention how many."

Olivia scratched her arm in the habitual way of someone whose skin is long past itching. Her fingers, Sarai noticed, had worried the skin into red-rimmed scabs. Olivia saw Sarai staring. "Biting bugs love me. Around this time of year, mosquitoes love me almost to death. They come up here all the way from the river, believe it or not." She looked past them, shaded her eyes. "Seems to me they could find a better meal closer to home. But just look at that sunset!"

They looked. The sun spread its flaming carpet of orange and rose across the western horizon. The Susquehanna River shimmered gold in its wake, reduced to a slender band stretching north to south until the land's contours hid it from view.

"Due west, set into the trees you can see towns like beads on string," Olivia said. "Wrightsville. York. Hanover. Just over the horizon, Gettysburg. See those bumps to the northwest? Those are your South Mountains, Maggie." Olivia turned, showed a tired trace of a smile. "You've come a long way."

Maggie hugged her. "Thank you for taking us in," she began. "We're sorry to impose—"

"No, no." Olivia used her scratching hand to wave away the thought. "You're not imposing. Plenty of room. We just need to rearrange things."

Olivia's eleven-year-old daughter Kathleen stood at her mother's elbow, a smaller, paler version of Olivia. Olivia's son Daniel, aged eight, ran to help the boys with the horses. "We can spend all night together! All day, too!" he crowed. Junior and Webbie looked at the boy indulgently, as older brothers might.

"Why don't we camp outside between the wagon and the house," Junior said. Danny's thin face stretched wide, smiling in anticipation.

"Oh, boy. Yeah!" Webbie agreed.

The boys decided to take turns standing guard at night.

"And help with chores during the day," Maggie added.

"So now we have the Lancaster-Carlisle Boys' Militia?" Sarai teased. She exchanged a moment's glance with Maggie, then looked away. The nickname stuck. From then on, the mothers called for the "Boys Militia" to come for meals or chores.

Maggie and Sarai pulled bags from the wagon. Each woman loaded up her shoulders and hands with things to carry. Olivia ushered her guests up a central flight of stairs and into an expansive bedroom with a handsome four-post mahogany bed and a brass day bed. "The two of you will be comfortable here, I think."

"This is your bedroom!" Maggie protested.

"Daniel's bed is fine for me. I can gather some clothing from my room and we shall share a bureau drawer."

Kathleen's eyes darted around the room. "No." She fixed her gaze on the big bed. "You need your sleep, Mama." She reached out to feel the tufted bedspread, her fingers brushing lightly across its white cotton ridges. "You need to be in your own bed. Papa's bed!" Her voice rose before it broke into sobs. She turned and ran out of the room, shoving past the women.

"Fine with me," Sarai said, her arms folded. "No way I'm sleeping in that bed!"

Worry stitched Olivia's face. "We work long hours together, Kathleen and I, keeping the store going. Any change seems to disturb her so. That's the most she's spoken in days," Olivia sighed. "Weeks."

That night Olivia and Kathleen slept in their own bedrooms. Maggie and Sarai bunked in Dan's room. His wood-frame bed was too narrow for even one adult of any size. They pushed the bed into one corner so they could spread their bed-rolls on the floor of the little room. As they moved the bed, something beneath clattered loose. Where the bed had been, a small open-faced box lay exposed, its collection of odds and ends scattered. The sorts of things an eight-year-old boy would treasure.

They carefully picked up each item.

"A tooth. No, two teeth." Maggie dropped them in the box.

"Used to be a penny before a train flattened it." Sarai held up a smooth disc of copper.

"Obviously not the coin that bought this—" Maggie gave one toot on Dan's tin whistle.

"He likes to carve." Sarai examined a small knife, then the small figure of a bear. "Good work for a eight-year-old boy. His papa must've taught him."

"Yes, James Hager has a knack for carving. He likes to do animals. Robert has a few of them."

"Hmmm," Sarai studied the bear carving. "My Chance has the knack, too. But not the time." She looked at Maggie. "You said Mrs. Hager is your husband's cousin. On his mother's side, that right?"

Maggie nodded. She picked up Danny's daguerreotype of his father, pressed into a small tin frame, and passed it to Sarai.

"I can see that. Because the men don't look at all related, do they?" Sarai said. "Your Robert and her James, I mean. James is stouter and shorter."

"By at least a head," Maggie agreed. She repositioned herself cross-legged on her bedroll, her lavender cotton nightgown billowing and settling around her pregnant belly. "Both our families came to this part of the world before the Revolutionary War. Robert's family settled in Pennsylvania. Lancaster first, then Carlisle. My people started out in Spesutia, then Baltimore, Maryland."

"Spesutia?" Sarai echoed. "Sounds like a town I should know."

"Robert and I discovered that, two generations back, our family lines touched. I am named for a great aunt, Margaret Miller, whose first marriage was to James Armstrong Wilson, and her second, to Matthew Henderson. My great aunt is Robert's grandmother."

Sarai was examining something that looked like a flat tapered stone, turning it over in her hands, fingering its edge.

"What about your family, Sarai?"

She shrugged. "That be one of the things you lose to slavery. Your past." Sarai held up the object she was examining: an arrowhead. "Like the maker of this Indian point. We know he existed. Just don't know anything about him." She nested the arrow point in her palm, rubbing it as she sorted through her thoughts. "Chance knows his line, though. His people were free." She looked up again. "Spesutia. That's where his line begins, least what he knows of it. Don't know all the names, but I do know one. White Elk. Chance talks about him enough."

"White Elk?"

Sarai heard the surprise in Maggie's voice. She held the point up again before dropping it into the box. "That's right. Chance has Indian blood."

Maggie opened and closed her mouth, struggling to speak. "White Elk of Spesutia?" she repeated. "He is our ancestor, too."

Sarai looked surprised, then skeptical. "This man, White Elk, took a white wife with an unusual name."

Maggie nodded. "Alizanna."

The room filled with silence. Sarai's fingers clenched her bleached cotton nightgown, twisting at it, threatening to tear it. Finally she spoke, saying each word carefully as if conceding. "Our families are related through marriage. And blood."

More silence. Then came a low knocking at the door. Maggie opened it to find Olivia holding a tray and wearing a secretive smile. She slipped into the room. "Quickly, Maggie, close the door!"

Olivia placed the tray on the floor. She handed Wedgewood blue porcelain cups and saucers to Maggie and Sarai. "War has stretched our provisions thin. But I found this English tea in a canister that I thought contained dried herbs," she explained, chuckling as she unwrapped a teapot from its quilted cozy and poured steaming tea into each cup. "Silly to be so excited over a bit of English Grey's Tea! But you see, Kathleen's birthday is coming up. I could not even think about how to celebrate. Until I was surprised by my tea discovery. So I thought, 'I'll use some of the molasses I've been saving and make molasses cake cookies.' I had the time, so I made them tonight. They'll keep just fine." She unwrapped a linen napkin to reveal a soft round of cookie, still warm, its sweet, dark aroma filling the small room. "They will go wonderfully with the tea, don't you think? A nice birthday surprise for Kathleen?"

Maggie and Sarai nodded, each breaking off a piece to taste. Its goodness melted on their tongues. They moaned their appreciation. Maggie urged Olivia to join them. But their host stood and excused herself. "I am wrung out. You must be, too. See you in the morning."

They sat across the tray from each other, sharing the cookie, which Sarai divided into halves. Maggie refilled Sarai's teacup.

"Sarai," Maggie asked gently. "Who hurt you?"

"You should never ask a question if you don't want to hear the answer."

Maggie pushed the tray aside and moved closer.

"I want to hear the answer. In fact, I may already know the answer."

Sarai blinked hard. Her face took on the haunted look of a girl resolving to be brave. When at last she spoke, Sarai's voice emerged young, frightened.

"I had never seen a bed so grand and a cover so white as that one. 'Til the one we seen here today. It looked soft and inviting. I loved touching it. Vast like the sea. 'Sea of dreams,' that's what I'd say out loud. He laughed. 'I hear you have a birthday coming.' 'Yes, I'll be twelve,' I said. 'Come look,' he said, opening a big chifforobe next to the fireplace. 'Pick out something to wear on your big day.'"

Sarai twisted at her gown as she remembered. "I knew 'twas the mistress's closet, recognized her things. I wasn't a tall girl, but she was very short. Still her things mostly too big for me then. There was a scarf, almost big as a shawl. Flowers so vivid you could almost pick 'em. I could see me wearing it and it gave me gooseflesh, but I didn't say nothing. He saw me looking, though. He lifted that lovely thing off its hook and put it round my shoulders, turned me to face a long mirror so's I could see my whole self. Took my breath away. 'Beautiful,' he said, looking straight at me in the mirror, so's I'd know he meant me, not just the scarf. 'You could wear this as a skirt. He took it off my shoulders and tied it around my waist. He moved his hand down my front to smooth out the wrinkles. 'See how pretty?' he said. 'So pretty.'

"His hand found my privates through the fabric and touched me. Made my blood flow hot and shameful in a way I didn't know I could feel.

"I wanted to get away from Master, but he pressed me tight against himself. I couldn't move." Sarai turned her face away. "He had me on that bed. Everything happening was right there in the mirror. I had to close my eyes against them awful expressions he was making. Wanted to stop up my ears with my fingers so I couldn't hear them grunts and moans of his but he had my arms pinned down to my sides. Then he stopped sudden like he woke up from a bad dream, or heard something. I felt him loosen on me so I broke away and ran."

Maggie's voice was hoarse with fury. "Who? Turnbrough? My uncle did that to you? *Our* uncle ..."

Sarai glared. "He's no uncle to me! He's nothing! When it happened, I hated him. Felt too ashamed to tell a soul. And yet my little girl's heart wanted to believe he thought I was beautiful. And later, when he told me he loved me … he was the master, after all. See how twisted up a heart can be?

"After a while I figured out that, when the mistress went into town to shop, the master would come looking for me. Tried to hide at first. The others thought I was trying to get outa my chores so they called me out. Every time, after, he'd give me some little thing or other that he bought or had made."

"Outrageous!" Maggie said through gritted teeth, doubling her fists in her lap. "Our families must be told! Amends must be made!"

"Amends? How? Fight a war, maybe?" Sarai's eyes hooded. "My mama knew. In fact, that's how I learned what kept that bedspread so white.

"One afternoon he hurt me particular bad. Soon as I could, I slid off that bed. Turned around, saw I left a patch of blood on the spread. He got agitated. Said I had to take the bedspread off, run it to the laundry, wait while the laundry woman cleaned it and dried it by fire or oven, then bring it back and make the bed. 'Hurry. Hurry!' So I run to the outbuilding where the laundry gets done and saw the laundry woman that day is Hettie. My own mother! She took one look at that bedspread and knew what happened. I never saw such wild in any human eyes. My knees were shaking, I thought the whipping of a lifetime was mine, for sure. Instead she took the whipping out on that spread. Wailing and weeping as she labored. Lord, she scrubbed and strangled that fabric 'til not a speck of her daughter's blood could be seen. Hung it above the oven. Told me to wait. When it was dry she flung it at me and disappeared, don't know where. No time to find out either as I had to make that infernal bed 'fore the mistress got home.

"After that, I didn't much care whether I lived or died. Started doing foolish things, crazy things. Before, I knew better than to wear that scarf when the mistress was around. After, I wore it on purpose, right under her nose. Her eyes bulged. Whole face got red. Nothing more. Then one day I was outdoors strutting in that scarf when she come by. Looked her in the eye, dared her: 'How do you like my handsome shawl?' Just that fast, she yanked it from my shoulders and threw it into the pigsty. She hissed at me like the devil snake: 'That's where you belong, too.'"

Each woman looked stricken, unable to bear the weight of another word. In the gathering silence they took turns restoring each of Danny's valuables to its home. Sarai lowered the lid back onto the box.

"Maggie, you knew something of his ways, eh? Even a child is known by his doings. Bible says that. So you probably knew something on your uncle." Sarai studied Maggie's ashen face. "Answer me straight, Maggie: Were you the girl who witnessed my sale?"

Maggie nodded slowly. "What can we do, Sarai?" she whispered. "What can *I* do? Say the word and if it is in my power, I will do it."

Sarai held her tongue as she considered the question. Her voice surfaced, dangerously calm. "Do you folks still have them slave papers? That's something I surely would like to see."

~late June, 1863~

Cellar

Yancy chuckled to himself in spite of the darkness and the June heat. "Come a time they'll call ye Noah. Not Yancy," he said to himself. He wiped his brow with a dark blue kerchief already sodden with sweat. "Noah, sure enough." He sat on a footstool in the cellar of Sharon. A slanting crack of light where the exterior double doors met was his only clue that daylight still lingered.

The ladies had left Carlisle by wagon on Wednesday, the 24th. Robert Henderson would remain in Harrisburg. Yancy spent two feverish days re-organizing the cellar's contents in high stacks along each wall and in a rough-looking configuration of stalls, leaving an open center space. Into that space and the stalls he spread a thick layer of straw. Into each stall he secured a bucket for fresh water. He placed his bedding nearby, flanked by sweet smelling hay and a sack of oats.

At the opposite corner he stationed a chamber pot and wheelbarrow for his waste, next to a deep, empty cart, into which he would shovel the beasts' waste. "Good thing I have an old man's nose," he sniffed.

Rumors of the Confederates' advance flew up and down the Pike. On Friday afternoon, June 26, the old sailor had felt the vibration of advancing troops through his leather boot soles, confirmed by Blood's whining and pricked ears. Yancy begged and pleaded and cajoled as he led first one horse then the other remaining horse into the dank mouth of the cellar, soothing their skittish negotiation of the six broad concrete steps leading into it. The dog lay down in front of the two horses in their makeshift stalls, which seemed to reassure them. Yancy had decided against bringing chickens into the cellar. Too noisy. Too smelly. "Aw, let the Rebs have ye, if they must!" Instead, he had gathered several days' worth of eggs and hard-boiled them. He had placed them, along with some apples, in a metal box to deter scrabbling rats, and set it in a cool spot, near the water and his bedding, where he could find it in the dark.

Yancy piled leather goods on the ground next to his footstool. Most required repair or polishing. Here, he could light a work candle without detection. It would give his sleepless fingers something to fuss over during the pitch-black, drawn-out nights.

Yancy started awake. Hoof beats had crowded his nightmares and now beat the ground outside. He rubbed his eyes, remembered where he was and why. A weak sliver of light outlined the cellar door. Saturday, he remembered, but morning? Or later? Thuds of boots hitting the ground, breaching the porch, entering the house. Yancy's charges, made restless by the strange sounds, whinnied. He stood between the horses to soothe them, softly instructing Blood, "Be still."

Long minutes of footfall, around and overhead. Silence. Invaders' boots making their way back outside. A sudden rattling at the cellar doors. Yancy stiffened, every nerve alert. Blood barked—Yancy's hush came too late.

Light flooded onto a vacant portion of the straw-laden floor. Spurred heels clattered halfway down the steps. A gloved hand appeared, probing the dank air with a rifle muzzle.

"Show yourself!" Deep voice. Heavy South.

Yancy felt a quickening of spirit. He opened his mouth, said, "Behold! A certain lawyer stood up, and tempted him, saying, Master, what shall I do to inherit eternal life?"

The soldier advanced another step, barked, "Show yourself, that's an order!" Sounding less certain, he added, "And how did you know I am a lawyer?"

Yancy kept his eyes on the gun and the boots as he spoke. "Jesus said, What is written in the law? How readest thou? The lawyer answered, Thou shalt love the Lord thy God with all thy heart, and with all thy soul, and with all thy strength, and with all thy mind; and thy neighbour as thyself."

The soldier took another step down and peered into the darkness, his face visible, eyes not yet adjusted to see. "If you are a Christian, show yourself and you have nothing to fear. But Christian or no, I'll shoot you if forced to!"

Yancy took a step toward the light but still outside of the Rebel's line of vision. He could see the soldier was an officer. Yancy spoke again. "Jesus said, Thou hast answered right: this do, and thou shalt live."

Yancy stepped into the light and caught square the captain's gaze. The Rebel raised his weapon. Yancy, unblinking, said, "But the lawyer, willing to justify himself, said unto Jesus, And who is my neighbour?"

"What are you doing down here, you crazy old fool?" a tremble betrayed the soldier's voice. His weapon seemed to sniff the air around the question. Yancy, unmoved, took his time.

He said, "There's a distillery just up the road. Barrels of whisky stowed there. No need to bash the door. Key's to the right of it. Under a rock."

The Rebel held his firearm until it wavered. He drew back suddenly, mounting the stairs backward. Slammed closed the cellar door.

Several heartbeats later, Yancy heard horses and riders pounding a whooping departure in the direction of Henderson's distillery.

July Thunder

On the morning of Wednesday, July 1, the Hager household awoke to deafening silence. No carriage traffic. No buzzing insects. No human voices.

The boys scouted outside and returned breathless, reporting that they could see nothing, no one moving on the road or landscape below. The household gathered on a second floor balcony facing west to scan the horizon.

No birds flew across an impassive beryl sky. Distant toy-tiny villages lay still, as if unoccupied. No sign of river commerce broke the ribbon surface of the Susquehanna.

"Calm of a dead sea," Webbie intoned, transfixed.

"Feels like we're the only folks left," Junior said.

"In the whole world," Webbie agreed.

Olivia clapped her hands to ward off the silence and gloom. She announced, "I plan to close the store tomorrow so we can celebrate Kathleen's birthday!" They all trooped downstairs and went through the motions of dressing and eating breakfast. Like their other meals, it was made from their pooled food resources. Olivia and her daughter climbed into their buggy and rode into town to tend store. Dan stayed behind, tagging along or pitching in as the others moved through their day in the roiling silence.

In the afternoon they felt, or heard, a crackling in the air, like lightning. They raced to the balcony for a look. But there was nothing to see.

The next morning, on the Second of July, Olivia rose early to attend to breakfast and final preparations for her daughter's birthday. One by one the others shuffled into the kitchen. They had fallen into a rhythm of living together that felt both comfortable and comforting. Sarai refused to venture into town, though.

Just as well, Olivia thought, glancing from Sarai to Maggie. *I am happy to have their company. But not yet ready to entertain the town's commentary.*

Outside, the boys reinforced their fort with crates stacked at one end of the wagon and armed it with a growing pile of rocks. Kathleen stood at a front parlor window to watch them while the mothers set a table for a birthday tea and supper. The house gave a shudder, accompanied by an ominous rumbling.

"Did you feel that?" Olivia gripped the back of a chair, her face blanched.

The women called the boys indoors. They raced upstairs to the balcony. Dread seized them as they watched a haze of smoke gather on the horizon, slow, malevolent.

What they heard was unearthly. Not individual voices of gun or cannon, but a distant steady roar rising up as if some monstrous Leviathan, unstoppable, was ravaging the land. In spite of the July afternoon's muggy heat, the children shivered. The mothers gathered them in their arms, attempting to calm them.

At length, they shuffled inside for the special meal Olivia had prepared. The sound followed them. Glassware quivered. Sarai had lost her appetite. Maggie ate ravenously, then lumbered to the porch, holding her pregnant middle with one hand, covering her mouth with the other hand until she could lean over the porch rail and vomit. The children picked at their meals, even the special molasses cookies. Sarai challenged them to a "spoon and swallow" contest, gamely chewing until Kathleen cleared her plate and was declared the winner. Olivia nodded to Sarai gratefully and patted her daughter's hand. Kathleen thanked her mother with a brave smile, which the girl shared briefly with Sarai before looking away.

The mothers worked at keeping their fears to themselves as they acted out ordinary tasks. Even the quiet moments seemed tightly coiled. That evening in the dark privacy of their dark beds, each mother clasped her hands in silent prayer and begged that the firing would cease. Yet in their fitful dreams the battle raged on.

Startled awake on the morning of July 3, their hopes were dashed.

On that day, Friday, terror gathered with a menacing smoke cloud that spiraled up from the center of the western horizon, demonizing their waking hours. Windows rattled in their frames. Word came to them that the conflict raged in the village of Gettysburg, less than forty-five miles away. Their eyes and noses began to burn. Was it their imaginations, or did artillery smoke—the smoke of many big guns—truly reach their nostrils?

Both house and ground quivered intermittently. Webbie and Junior gathered more rocks in a second large pile, near the front wheel of the covered wagon. The three boys took turns climbing onto the wagon's high seat to keep watch. Square jawed, Junior came to Sarai and asked to have her rifle, for the purpose of defending them. Sarai gently assured him that if the time came when defense was required, he would have his chance with the gun.

On July 4, they awoke to silence so overpowering, their ears rang. A light rain commenced. People began using the road again. The Hager household held towels over their heads and stood along the roadside to talk to passersby. Rumors flew that the Yanks were chasing the Rebs back to Virginia.

Rain fell harder, and steady. They retreated back to the house. The mothers felt too numb to be comforted by the news.

"Is the battle really over?" Kathleen asked.

Dan, sucking on his fingers, withdrew them just long enough to ask, "Is the war over, too?"

Some refugees had already loaded their wagons and begun the trek homeward. That night everyone under the Hager roof collapsed into a dreamless, exhausted sleep.

On July 5, Sarai, Maggie and the boys awoke to ringing church bells. After breakfast, they loaded the wagon and said their goodbyes.

Olivia Hager stood outside the house at the top of the lane, waving one of the towels still damp from yesterday's rain. Her children stood with her, their sad, resigned faces mirroring hers. "Fare well!" she called. "Fare well!"

The wagon started back for Carlisle, Sarai at the reins, Maggie seated next to her, hearts leaden, dreading the ruin awaiting their return.

The road was filled with travelers hurrying toward Gettysburg, some with empty carts. Ebullient with victory, they noisily expressed their hopes to profit by harvesting souvenirs from the bodies of dead soldiers.

~July 5, 1863~

Fare Well

Junior and Webbie sat in the back of the wagon and waved to Danny. He poked himself in between his mother and his sister, and they all three waved goodbye. In his other hand, Danny held tight his stick bayonet Junior and Webbie had helped him make and stuck out his chest, proud to be the man. Everybody in the wagon waved until Olivia and the children shrank from view.

Then Junior said what Webbie was thinking—which happened a lot. "Glad we didn't have to fight for real."

"Me, too," Webbie said. "We're just boys. Sticks break."

They saw every kind of thing with wheels on this road. All bump and rattle and stuck to the ground, sometimes even stuck in the ground. The boys talked about all the things wrong with them, made a list, even.

"Lots of these problems would go away if things on wheels were smaller," Webbie said.

"How small?" Junior asked.

"Boys and girls sized," Webbie said.

"Oh," Junior said, and he got that look on his face when thinking about a new idea. "Is that the only thing you'd change? Just the size?"

Webbie had to think about that. It was easier for him to think while he drew so that's what they did. That's how the secret book got started. Webbie drew on the left side, Junior on the right. They looked at each other's drawings, looked outside at real wagons and carriages. Before long, Junior and Webbie had carriages that looked like balloons and others with birdlike wings that could fly over water and land.

They were making changes to one of their flying carriages when they felt the wagon slow down and heard Junior's mother shout their names into the wagon. She sounded angry-scared, so they looked out the front, fast. Sarai was driving the horses with one hand and waving the boys forward with the other. Webbie's mother was leaning back awkwardly, with her eyes closed and her hands crossed over her stomach. The blanket she sat on was darkly wet.

"Mother!" Webbie said loud but not too loud. He did not want her to hear the scared in his voice. She didn't answer. She was moaning though.

Sarai said, "Junior, get up here next to me and take the reins. I'm gonna slide back where you are, and Webbie and me are gonna bring his mama back and lay her down."

Junior scooted up and did as his mother said. Webbie had never seen Junior drive a wagon before but it did not surprise Webbie he could.

"Is my mother—" Webbie started, but Sarai was trading places with Junior and pulled Maggie into her arms.

Sarai said, "Hold your arms open wide, Webbie. You are going to catch hold of your mama when I lower her to you."

Webbie caught his mother and held her leaning against him like he was her pillow. Junior's mother climbed into the back, spread their bedrolls out and helped Webbie lay his mother on them.

"Web, go to the back of the wagon and find a full water jug, a knife, two basins and some towels."

"Is Mother having the baby now?"

Sarai nodded yes and tried to smile at Webbie, but he thought she looked like she was going to cry or even run away.

Webbie crawled back to get those things, all the while watching what was happening to his mother. Sarai propped Maggie's legs on a couple of bags and her arms hung down loose so her body looked like a wide M. Webbie brought water and basins and towels to Sarai and was going to sit next to Maggie, but Sarai said, "No, Webbie—I need you to go to the back of the wagon again. Keep a watch out for—" She squeezed her eyes shut and moaned like she was having a baby, too. She opened her eyes and looked at Webbie, and she looked calm. That made him feel better. She said, "Web, can you find a book and come back to the spot right where you're setting now and read to us?"

"Sure!" Web said. He went back to the box where Junior and he had stashed some books and picked out *Moby Dick*. When Web sat at his mother's shoulder, she was groaning, her eyes still shut, and Sarai's face was all hot and perspired. Her hands looked to be working fast and hard with a basin in front of her and the wet towels. Web just started reading where his father's read-aloud left off a long time ago, where he liked to keep the bookmarker even though he had read the whole book already. Several times.

"You cannot hide the soul," Web read. "Through all his unearthly tattooings, I thought I saw the traces of a simple honest heart; and in his large, deep eyes, fiery black and bold, there seemed tokens of a spirit that would dare a thousand devils."

Right then, Web's mother screamed like a thousand devils were after her. He started toward her, but Sarai shouted at him to keep reading, that Web had to keep reading to help the baby be born.

"My, oh, my," said Sarai, with her eyes wide, wide open. "This baby loves reading, I can tell! Set there and read! *Read*!"

So Web did, and the more he read, the more his mother groaned. And the more she groaned, the louder Web read, Sarai grunting, too, her clothes and arms a scary mess. But Web kept reading and of a sudden all the hot loud sounds and smells and mess went quiet. He could hear the wheels on the road and the creak and sway of the wagon. And something else.

A tiny, tiny, tiny little cry.

Sarai cut the cord connecting daughter to mama and held this child for an eternal moment. *This the first newborn baby I ever held, though I've had two of my own. The one I never got to hold, as it was took from inside of me by master before it*

ever got to breathe the clean bright air. And the one I was afraid to hold, my very own Junior, lest a worse fate befall him.

Yet there Junior was, strong and smart and well, driving a wagon into their future. And there, right there in her hands, this babe, like a shiny precious egg. Sarai bathed the child and wondered, *Are all newborn babies golden*? Her hair, her skin, she swore even her eyes when they blinked open for an instant. All wiggly golden.

Maggie was spent, her eyes closed. Sarai looked at Web, his mouth open and speechless, his eyes wide with wonder. "Help me bathe your sister. Gently, gently," Sarai whispered. "Then we dry her, that's right. Gently, gently, so your mama can hold her." All clean, the infant daughter was a marvel to behold. Sarai bundled her in a dry towel and showed Web how to hold his sister. "She's very fragile," Sarai said. "You know what I mean? Like a fresh egg."

Web laughed at that. Sarai helped him lift the baby onto his mother's bosom. Maggie's eyes blinked open. With the first sight of her tiny baby girl, Maggie's face became joy and gratefulness so pure, it made Sarai's eyes water.

"Junior!" Sarai shouted. "How far?"

He turned his head, called out over his shoulder, "Almost to town."

Sarai wanted to shout, *Hallelujah*! That's only natural, as witness to a miracle. Instead, she yelled, "Don't go home! Drive straight to Dr. Davies on High Street!"

~July 2, 1863~

Defending Round Top at Gettysburg

Dense veils of artillery haze hung in the air. Nathan could no longer see the tip of his own rifle. Unconsciously, he had begun to rely on his hearing. At the mill, just by listening, he could always tell when machinery needed attention. Some subtle shift in the machinery's vocalizations—a bit of whine in the humming, say—would clue him to trouble. He could follow the sound with his eyes closed if need be, through the motes of grain dust, right to the troubled spot.

Crawford's division had orders to support Col. Vincent's brigade in holding onto a hill called Little Round Top. Nathan, near the end of the line, got separated from his comrades during the chaos. He scrambled ten paces to a boulder, where he squatted for cover. He felt the incline with his feet. He closed his eyes, cocked his head, listening. Opened his eyes. The thrum of gunfire roared heaviest to his left. Certain death. If he circled to his right and stayed low ... yes, he could crawl sideways, like a crab. Take his time ... listen ... crawl. He advanced with one arm outstretched, his fingers scanning the earth for clues. Grass turned to muddied boot prints. Fallen bodies. *Listen.* Groans of the dying.

As he crawled, time stretched and bent. Minutes became hours, hours dissolved into seconds. His fingers touched bare skin and recoiled. He drew close and saw two bare feet, the bloody torso of a Confederate soldier, his revolver still smoking in his open palm. His nose blown away. Nathan took the revolver, checked its chambers—loaded, but for the one bullet spent—and continued crawling. His fingers finally made contact with the cool surface of stone. Another boulder. He felt out its dimensions. High enough for cover. Good. He visualized the motions that would come next, calculating how many firings he could cram into each fraction of a minute with his new repeating rifle, which Chance had been able to purchase and smuggle to him, before leaving. Fourteen to twenty rounds a minute. Dozens of rounds before he'd have to pause to blow out the powder buildup. He could count on this gun's accuracy. He did not have to wait until he could smell the enemy's stinking breath. If his rifle jammed or he spent all its ammunition, he would use the revolver and pray.

Nathan began his assault. Almost immediately, he heard groans and thuds of men and arms falling to the ground. He continued firing instinctively, shocked by how close they fell, how the ground beneath him shuddered as they landed. He became a machine, relentless: *lever-cock-fire, lever-cock-fire, lever-cock-fire, lever-cock-fire.* He crouched in a deepening puddle of blood, sticky and dense, and not his own. Sometimes the moans ended in sighs as if receiving a gift.

Several rounds sliced through dead air. He loaded seven more metal shells into the Spencer's tube magazine with rapid efficiency. Nathan fired again into dead air. Should he forsake his cover and advance? He felt an odd heat to his right, rolled onto his left shoulder and fired. He heard a hoarse cry, its owner's weapon clattered against a nearby boulder. Nathan braced his rifle on the ground and fired. At close range, the impact sounded like a grain sack exploding. He heard a strangled plea: "Mary!"

Nathan paused. The voice again. "Tell … Mary." He knew he should fire and finish the job. "Our baby." Nathan raised himself to his elbow, rifle cocked. The air between them thick. He pulled into a wide-legged crouch no higher than the boulder and crab-walked one foot forward. The man's face loomed into sight, mud-smeared beard framing a grimace of vengeance. Nathan did not see his adversary's firearm but heard the click low to the ground. Then a hot bright light, like the Second Coming. The enemy's gray coat sailed across the void, a cloud covering Nathan.

"Bastard!" the bearded man croaked.

Wilderness

1863–1865, later battles
(Pennsylvania, Virginia)

~July 4, 1863~

Doctor

The assistant surgeon in blue moved on his knees from body to body among the Union dead and dying, a bandana masking his nose and mouth against the stench. Feel for a pulse, lower the eyelids. *Mother was right, I should have become a priest*, he told himself. This one shuddered slightly when the doctor touched his eyes. After too many twenty-hour days his motions had become so automatic that he almost missed one barely alive.

"Do you want to live, son?" He said this under his breath, more a test than a question. If a brave soldier could muster the will to answer, the medical officer would muster his own will and fight for the life. This one did not respond, except for the tremor arcing through his limbs. The assistant surgeon opened up what buttons and cloth remained from the soldier's scorched uniform. Too much missing flesh. Too much blood lost. The surgeon moved on to the next.

Except that he had come to the end of the blue uniforms. He looked around. An expanse of dead to be buried. Then a bare patch of grass. Then an expanse of gray uniforms, half-dead prisoners of war, some still moaning. He pulled himself up, dragging behind him his bag of implements and meager remains of medicines in a child's wagon he had salvaged from the previous town. What was the name of that place? He couldn't remember. Farmland on rolling hills. So green. Plump German-speaking girls, smiling to cover their fright. Their offerings of warm bread. Just baked. His empty stomach roared in protest.

The medic dropped to his knees next to a hatless Confederate soldier whose breathing came in shallow rasps. His coat was buttoned tight and low around his waist and, odd in this heat, he wore his pants pulled up over another pair of trousers. The tight wrapping may have saved this soldier's life. The surgeon considered the bloodstain soaking through. He removed the outer pair of pants. The doctor decided to cut away the bloodied section rather than removing the second pair, blood-soaked. He cut deftly, using his other hand to guide the knife through the sodden fabric and away from the patient's flesh. *Odd*, he thought. *These are Union trousers*.

He suctioned away some of the blood for a better view of the damage then gave a low whistle of disbelief. He looked up, saw the nurse assigned to him working nearby. She had labored hours at least as long as his. He shouted, stumbling over her name. "Miss—" *Which one? Oh, yes.* "Siddon, Miss Siddon!" She turned and hurried over. The assistant surgeon started talking and directing even before she arrived.

"We've been seeing more wounds like this. The shooter missed bone, see? Nothing broken, just scorched and burned, which actually cauterized the skin here. And here—uh, that's right, there's just a bit of chloroform left, enough to daze him perhaps, but we can still prep for surgery." He set to work as soon as she wiped down the instruments with a cloth and passed them. "Yes … we'll debride here, start stitching up … here. . . . God help me, I don't know whether it's worth it to leave a remnant, given risks …" He looked up to see Miss Siddon's thin shoulders shaking, yet her face composed, wide-eyed.

"Are you all right?"

She opened her mouth, closed it.

"Get some stretcher bearers so we can get him to the hospital tent," he said gently. "And more lint packing and bandages for this wound."

After she scurried away, the medical officer asked quietly, "Do you want to live, son?"

The soldier's eyes opened. Startlingly blue. "Yes," the patient whispered. "Don't you?"

The assistant surgeon chuckled his reply. A long-forgotten warmth of emotion animated his spirit.

"You'll lose this pair of trousers. Don't worry, I'll get another pair for you from a dead Reb. We estimate there are almost 6,000 of your wounded left on the field for us to tend. And you, still alive. You're a lucky Reb." As the doctor lowered the chloroform-soaked mask near his face, the soldier resisted it.

"Reb?" he protested. "I'm a Second Lieutenant, 36th Pennsylvania. Army of the Potomac—"

"Easy there," the doctor soothed. "What's your name, Lieutenant?" He slowly lowered the mask.

"Nathan. Nathan Henderson," came the drowsy reply. The patient squeezed shut his eyes, and though he made no further replies, the assistant surgeon sensed he was still listening.

"Some Rebel loaned you his coat to get you shot up, eh? Or did you fall behind the enemy's line and borrow the uniform to get out?" He worked with speed and precision, prepping the wound for surgery, making small talk as he worked until Miss Siddon returned with the stretcher bearers. The doctor hustled alongside them as they got Lieutenant Henderson to a just-vacated space in the hospital tent. He prepared the first length of linen thread. Blood-spattered straw crunched under his boots.

"Blasted hot day for doctoring, eh?" he said, still making small talk for the patient's benefit. "Don't mind Miss Siddon. She's a fine nurse, you'll meet her again soon enough. If you want to live, this surgery is necessary, do you understand? We'll save what we can anyway. Go ahead and groan, this must be agony, bless you. You're a brave lad. Poor fellow …"

~July 4, 1863~

Blinding Pain

Nathan woke up to blinding pain. He groaned and squeezed his eyes shut. His fingers groped at his left side looking for the neck of a bottle.

"We took it away, Lieutenant." Nathan opened his eyes to the smiling face of a young woman who introduced herself as Miss Hannah Siddon, a volunteer nurse at the corps' temporary hospital. "Medical director's orders. Says the overuse of alcohol with wounded soldiers is deplorable. Want something for the pain?" she added rhetorically, motioning to the nearest medical officer. When that did not work, she turned back to Nathan.

"Would you please scream? I know you don't wish to. Would you do it for me, please?"

Nathan did his best to obey nurse's orders, keeping his gaze on her smile. The medical officer hurried over, hair disheveled, his sleep-deprived eyes deeply circled. Wordlessly, he filled a syringe, administered morphine, and moved to the next bed before Nathan had stopped screaming.

Miss Siddon peeled back his bedsheet exposing his left inner thigh. She carefully removed blood-soaked dressings, gently swabbed his flesh with water and iodine, and placed fresh lint dressing onto the stitched wound.

"You are going to be fine, Lieutenant Henderson," she said. "The surgeon said you are very fortunate there's no damage to bone. You were shot at close range, so there was a lot of surface damage and bleeding. Bleeding's the thing. That second pair of trousers probably saved your life."

Nathan noticed the exhaustion her smile couldn't mask. As she moved away to catch up with the medical officer, Nathan caught her wrist.

"I can't tell from the bandage. Would you please find someone who can come tell me about my injury?

Her smile vanished. She gently pulled her wrist from his grasp. He felt himself redden, embarrassed to realize how roughly he had gripped her. She looked away, then adjusted his bedsheet before meeting his gaze. "You are one of the fortunate ones."

An emaciated soldier in a bed across the dirt aisle wanly pleaded with Miss Siddon, "Don't go … It is so good to see your smile." His red face gleamed with fever. Whether typhoid or gangrene, it did not matter now. *He is dying, just as my brother Willy did, and Miss Siddon knows it*. This intuition came to Nathan unbidden.

She spoke gently to the fevered man. "Who should you fear, eh? God draws near. The angels sing their welcome. You will never be hungry or tired or in pain anymore." She stood at the foot of his bed.

Nathan listened to the man's breath come in irregular, surprised gasps until it stopped altogether. The nurse motioned to the medical director, who swept by long enough to add the deceased soldier's name to his list. Miss Siddon closed the man's eyes and drew the sheet over his face. She whispered to the medical director and nudged him toward Nathan's bedside. She hung back.

The medical director fixed his weary gaze on Nathan and spoke without preamble. "The surgeon was able to salvage enough of the penis that you will be able to urinate. But the testicles are … gone." The man glanced away briefly, cleared his throat. "We were able to use a catheter, so the urethra does not appear damaged, though you may have a good deal of pain at first when you urinate. Your right leg is secured and bandaged to support the sutured areas until they heal."

After the medical director and Nurse Siddon left, Nathan stared up at the ceiling of the hospital tent. It was draped with cedar and pine boughs. Boughs also scattered on the floor, as fresheners, and to cheer the place. They were failing on both counts.

Slowly, painfully, he raised on one elbow to view the tent entire. End to end, rows of beds diminishing to points at the far end, too many to count. He saw a continuous flow of stretcher carriers enter with wounded men, looking for available cots. He watched as a pair of carriers found his newly deceased aisle-mate. They set the stretcher on the ground, laid the dead man next to it, and lifted the wounded man onto the bed. They placed the dead man on the stretcher.

"You got any room for me in that buggy?" Nathan called out weakly, his voice frayed.

One of the attendants heard him. "You don't want to go where this guy's headed."

Nathan closed his eyes, whispered his response. "How do you know?"

The attendants disappeared through the open tent flaps into the blinding daylight to bury the corpse and find another body, dead or alive.

Nathan watched the medical director make his way back through the tent, jotting notes, making his tallies. Then Nathan spotted a man who looked familiar. His surgeon. Nathan called to him.

"Good to see you awake and looking better, Lieutenant."

"I suppose looking better means anything better than dead."

The doctor chuckled. "How may I help you?"

"I know you're busy, doctor. Just four things. First, thank you."

"You are welcome."

"What day is it?"

"Saturday. July 4."

"Were we victorious, sir?"

The doctor smiled grimly. "The bloody devil of destruction occupied Gettysburg's battlefield for three hellish days. But yes, we count it a victory." He looked over his shoulder, distracted. "What is the fourth item?"

"I want to return to active duty. And I do not wish my injury to be reported."

"Now see here, Lieutenant, I am under orders to—"

"You must count the wound, of course. But I do not wish my name to be associated with it."

The surgeon shook his head. "That's five items."

Nathan held his gaze.

"Very well. We can observe your progress here, upon which your release to active duty depends."

After that exchange, Nathan did not again disturb the medical personnel. In another day his bandages would be changed and he would be helped to his feet by a male volunteer—not by Nurse Siddon, who never reappeared. Nathan was given a broken length of plow handle as a crutch and taught how to rehabilitate by walking. His first destination: the "sink," an open pit latrine. When he urinated, it burned like fire, spraying bloody orange flames across the pit.

In a week, he would overhear that Miss Siddon had contracted typhoid fever. The same disease that had claimed so many soldiers, including his brother. In three months, he would learn of Nurse Siddon's death. On the same day, he would receive clearance to return to active duty.

But on this particular day, he began the arduous work of forgetting Gettysburg. It became a lifelong struggle, a battle in which, ultimately, he was not victorious.

~July 5, 1863~

Supper

Junior guided the horses through Sharon's gate and along the lane to the house. The wagon rolled to a stop with a sigh.

Yancy emerged from the carriage house, saw Junior with the reins, and a Well-look-at-you! grin spread across his face. The smile vanished when he heard a baby's cry. He hurried to the wagon as fast as his lopsided gait allowed.

"Mr. Robert, he rode to town this morning. He be back soon, for sure."

Web held the baby while Junior and Yancy helped the mothers down. Then Web handed the baby down to Yancy, who held her for a long look, his lips moving, and passed her to her mother's cradling arms for a few moments. Then Sarai carried the baby while Web helped his mother into the house and her bedroom.

"Those Rebs went easy on the house, Miz Henderson," Yancy called out. "I think they recognized you from your portrait. Knew you was a southern lady." Maggie and Web stopped to look at Yancy. Maggie's knees buckled. Web tightened his hold on his mother. Yancy nodded. "Took all the food, though."

"Thank you, Yancy." Maggie grasped the porch rail and smiled weakly. "Robert insisted on that portrait. Glad to know it finally earned its keep."

After Maggie was safely in bed, Web helped Sarai swaddle the baby in her crib. "Let them both stay abed as long as they can," she whispered. Web remained in the nursery to watch his sleeping sister and listen for his mother, resting in her bedroom.

When Sarai emerged from the house, she found Junior helping Yancy tend the horses. She saw some of herself in Junior's face, some of Chance in his build. His movements, the confidence with which he held himself, and spoke, and listened, these qualities belonged entirely to Junior.

"Junior, I'll be right back."

He waved to show Sarai he had heard. She walked to the barn, still standing though the land around it was marred and muddied by hoof prints, as if a stampede had passed through. One barn door yawned open. Sarai stepped inside.

The barn's floor was scraped bare. The floor hatch lay flung open. A scattered handful of hay was the only clue as to what the barn had once contained.

That, and Sarai's treasure box, upended and empty.

"My husband, Chance Thompson, say that by this agreement money is available for me here." Sarai did not know the young man with glasses behind the counter. He didn't look like any Henderson she had ever seen. She had never been to the mill before. The noise of the place gave her a crushing headache. The clerk pushed at his glasses, looked at the paper she held to face him, looked at her.

"Where does it say that?"

Terror shot through her. She clenched her entire body against the humiliation. Her mind scrambled for footing. "Are you saying you're not gonna give me my money?"

The clerk straightened. His round cheeks looked not quite adult. Unblinking. Not answering.

She clipped the tremble out of her voice. Now more anger than fear. "Let Colonel Henderson know I'm here. That I need to speak to him."

"Sorry, little mama. Colonel Henderson's not here. He's sick. I'm in charge today."

"I am not your mama," she said in her sternest Mama voice. "I need $35 today. Read for yourself."

He tapped the document with his finger. "May I borrow this?"

"Of course not!"

He withdrew his hands so they were both below the counter, out of sight. "That's a lot of cash. I can't give you that."

She folded the paper once and put it back into her black drawstring purse. "Tell Colonel Henderson that I was here. And that I pray he's soon feeling well again."

Sarai strode out stiffly and kept walking until she felt certain she was well out of sight. She left the road for the woods and came upon a cluster of broad, low tree stumps, the felled trees still waiting to be cleared. She doubled over, fell onto one of the stumps as if it were her own roots that had been severed. Her stomach seized and growled with hunger. Humiliation. Sitting there, she groaned and rocked. But she found no relief. She opened her purse, found with her finger the signature she knew belonged to her husband. She stroked it and moaned, "What now? What now?"

Sarai sat there until the sun sank toward the trees lining the horizon and the cold numbed her. She stumbled back to the road in gray light. Saw the moon begin to rise as she made her way home. Words formed, coming to her lips in a whisper.

When she arrived home, Junior sat at the table, wide-eyed in front of a short candle, which smoldered more than it gave off light. He had set two plates, placed on them thin slices of apple. Sarai counted in a glance, five slices each. She sat down and ate one.

"Shouldn't we pray first?"

"You pray, Junior."

"Lord, thank you for protecting our house from the soldiers. And for this food. And for bringing Mam home. Amen."

Sarai looked from her plate and its meager fare to her son's grateful face. "Amen."

They took their time eating the apple. "What were you saying when you came in, Mam?"

"Was I saying something?"

"Your lips were moving. Like I do sometimes when I read to myself."

"Oh." Sarai pressed her thumbnail into the last piece of apple. "Yes." In her mind's eye she glimpsed the barest crescent of a moon in an invisible sky. "I was saying over some words that just come to me."

"Tell me, Mam."

Sarai closed her eyes and said,

"Road which way you going?
Hill how far you rise?
Moon why you be smiling
Whilst your sister stumble by?"

Junior rubbed his arm to warm up his feelings. "That's a good poem, Mam."

"Is it?" Sarai blinked. "What's a poem?"

"I'll show you one in my book. Let's write yours down, Mam. Maybe you'll make more."

Sarai sat back in her chair while Junior cleared the plates. She blinked at her purse, its drawstring still threaded around her wrist and through her fist. She opened it and with great care pulled out the contract.

"Junior, we got some other reading to do first."

~May, 1864~

Mass in Spotsylvania

After the Wrightsville bridge burning, Chance had made his way west. He resisted the enormous urge to go home. His assignment—his calling, as he understood it—was not yet complete. He caught up with Nathan's company, and they directed him to a town east of Gettysburg. Chance located Nathan at a hospital in York, where he was recuperating. When the hospital staff thought Nathan was ready, Chance and he reported for active duty together.

At Gettysburg, Nathan had been serving as an aide de camp to General Crawford. The General had commended Nathan's heroism and made him first lieutenant in March of 1864.

In early May of 1864, they marched headlong into a bewildering series of battles that would later be called "The Wilderness." And wilderness it was. Even at noontime, dense forest yielded an eerie half-light. Brambles and undergrowth ripped holes in the clothing and patience of the soldiers. Back at camp, Chance and Nathan had to put up with the jeering and spitting of a Confederate prisoner, in exchange for gleaning information about the roads that threaded through the area, more trails than true roads. That knowledge helped them and other members of their company escape with their lives.

Meanwhile, when Robert Henderson began his duties as provost marshal of Cumberland, Perry and York counties, Colonel Bolinger assumed leadership of Robert's former company of men. On May 5, the first day of the Battle of the Wilderness, Bolinger lost track of the rest of the Fifth Corps, advancing his Company A so far ahead into the woods and enemy territory that they found themselves surrounded by Rebels. They were captured and marched to the Confederates' rear at Orange County Courthouse, Virginia, then south, to prison camp.

"We're heading *south,*" Nathan said low. They marched by starlight and the trembling glow of a waxing moon.

"Not a retreat!" Chance did not hide the excitement in his voice. "We're moving forward!" He could hear snatches of song up and down the line of men. On other marches, the footfall of divisions on the move had sounded to Chance like an enormous grinding machine, ready to consume anything caught in its maw. But on this balmy May night, the footfall of many men and murmur of voices had the buoyant sound and feel of celebration, of imminent victory. Each step took them deeper into Virginia. Closer to Richmond.

Nathan marched with a rolling gait, accommodating stiffness and a dull, thrumming pain, residuals from his Gettysburg wound. He spoke rarely these days. On this night, he was little more than a shadow moving next to Chance.

Chance had developed the habit of watching Nathan for signs of weariness. When he saw his friend beginning to falter, Chance would slip the rifle from Nathan's shoulder and carry it for him. Other soldiers noticed the gesture. "Let them think what they will," Chance said, the first time he did it. Nathan nodded his response, too weary with pain to speak. The others admired their fighting abilities and had long since grown accustomed to this odd pair of soldiers. They were battle-hardened survivors, only days away from mustering out with the rest of their contingent of Pennsylvania Reservists. And they felt on the verge of achieving a glorious finish.

One of the Carlisle soldiers of Scot descent began singing a wartime love ballad, in a wistful baritone.

Ye want to fight the foe, lad,
I maunna grudge ye th' right.
For with a Scot like ye lad,
They'll sure gie up th' fight!
But I'm waitin for th' day lad,
When th' heather blooms again,
And th' bagpipes play once mair lad,
For the ranks o' Scottish men.

Along a road called Brock, their movement slowed down. By midnight, they had reached a place known as Todd's Tavern. There, in the darkness, Chance and Nathan overheard a blistering exchange between two senior commanders.

Nathan strained to hear. "That's Meade's voice," he whispered. "He's furious! Bet his eyes are popping out of his head! But who—"

"He's grilling Sheridan," Chance said.

A soldier ahead of them turned and whispered, "Meade caught the cavalry sleeping. Just told Sheridan seven different ways to go to hell!"

Another soldier wheezed, "If hell's where we're headed, this road's as good as any."

At dawn, they heard gunfire. Robinson's Union division was attacking Fitzhugh Lee's Confederate States cavalry. Chance and Nathan's division was still in stop-and-go marching formation. It was maddening for these soldiers to stand by idly while a battle raged. A young soldier named McPherson, a Roman Catholic from Maryland, spoke up. "This isn't Mass, but we may as well pray." A murmuring of prayer commenced, underscored by restless feet. Their prayers slipped into silent litanies as the line started moving again.

Robinson's men, guns roaring, managed to break through, but a torrent of grape and canister shot from Rebel artillery pushed them back. It was afternoon by the time Nathan and Chance entered the fight. Crouched side by side, they fell into a rhythm of alternating reloading so that they kept their rifles continuously firing from their earthworks into those of the Confederates, at some points a mere 100 yards distant. Confederate guns answered furiously. The ground near Nathan and Chance became littered with Union dead. At times their comrades would fall against them as they went down. Chance and Nathan took turns checking whether the soldier was wounded or dead. They shouted for litters to carry the wounded to the rear. They piled up the dead and fired from behind them.

By early evening, Sedgwick's Sixth joined their corps. At seven p.m. the men rose up from their barricades in a united attack, dashing into a deafening roar of artillery.

In fighting mode, Nathan blocked out all noise, experiencing combat as intensely silent. The wall of men charging in front of him fell away under enemy fire. He did not think about the soft lumpy surface underfoot, that he was marching over a carpet of bodies. His repeating rifle could best a smooth bore musket five times over and kill a man 300 yards distant. He braced and watched for a gap in the men just wide enough to shoot through. The setting sun, casting long shadows over the field, illuminated a gap. He began firing. Firing and reloading became automatic. Nathan kept firing until hoarsely shouted orders to fall back pierced his concentration. As he loped backwards, pausing only to fire, he looked around for Chance and spotted him dragging a wounded soldier along with him. Nathan crouched and ran the short distance between them, offering cover fire until they reached a Union breastwork.

Chance dropped to his knees and lowered the wounded soldier, a corporal. Immediately, two soldiers from the Fourth Division US Colored Troops met them, lifted the wounded officer onto a litter and carried him to the rear. Chance crawled back to his spot next to Nathan behind the earthworks. Nathan had fixed his muzzle into a deep notch in the breastwork. His hands fired with smooth efficiency. The rest of his body was trembling.

Chance cupped his hand to Nathan's ear. "Fall back! Fall back!" Nathan turned his head, his eyes still focused on the field of battle. The movement of men and Chance's urgings jarred him into motion, and he joined the retreat.

"Can't stand the waiting!" Nathan said through gritted teeth. It was shortly after noon. They had just finished a meal of beef broth, beans. Nathan spit out the coffee, snarling an insult about the brew. Other soldiers took his gruff talk as nerves. Chance knew Nathan's pain was spiking higher and that Nathan, adamant about finishing his last days of enlistment in active duty, refused to do anything about the pain.

A young colonel, Emory Upton, had strode by, heard Nathan's remark and recognized him. "Henderson? Artillery? Bring a few of your best men and come with me. Sixth Corps, special orders."

Those orders took them to a position where they could see the Confederate line at a spot presumed most vulnerable. Nathan and Chance joined 5,000 men in twelve regiments forming four lines.

Upton's plan to break the Confederate line was simple and unconventional: these soldiers were to run like madmen without firing and try to breach the enemy line. They would form a human arrow, waiting until the last minute to fire.

"Run like madmen? We can do that." Nathan flashed a wicked grimace at Chance.

"We surely can."

The order to charge finally came at six p.m. The men roared as they raced across the field, firing their voices into the surprised expressions of the enemy at a spot called Mule Shoe. When he reached the enemy line, Nathan shot rapidly and, when he needed to reload, first used his rifle butt in defense. Out of the corner of his eye he saw a pair of Rebels rush at Chance, then saw him go down. They dragged him out of sight. Nathan fought his way over to where Chance had disappeared. He spotted Chance flat on his back, pinned to the ground. One of the Rebel soldiers hacked away with a knife, their backs to Nathan. He took aim. One shot. Two. They crumpled. Nathan threw himself to the ground near Chance and snatched away the Rebels' dropped weapons, just in case. Chance was on one knee and then on his feet, one arm pressed to his chest. Bleeding. With his other hand, he managed to fix his bayonet to his rifle. By some miracle, they made their way out of that hellish chaos and back to the remaining body of Union fighting troops, now badly cut down. No reinforcements in sight. Enraged and frustrated, Upton reluctantly ordered retreat.

As they pulled back, it began to rain. Under cover of night, they cleared the field of Union dead and half-dead. Rain fell in sheets. "Minié-balls from heaven," said one soldier, only half joking. They squatted around nearly-quenched, hissing fires, coats pulled over their heads. Yet they could still hear the moans of wounded Rebels left on the field. Some called out to God. Women's names floated over the field, along with cries for Mother, begging her to bring a drink of water. Thirsty. So thirsty.

Nathan knew Chance was somewhere doctoring his hand and had not let Nathan see it. By the time Chance returned, he had missed a meal. Nathan had saved some for him and urged him to eat. He saw that Chance had wrapped his thumb and every finger on his right hand.

"How bad is it?"

"I'll live." Chance gnawed at a piece of hard tack, sipping water in between bites.

"You look pale. Very white."

Chance glared at him.

After that, they watched the downpour in silence.

At 4:30 a.m., rain dissolved to a mist shrouding the dawning sky. Another order came and they attacked. Once again, they broke through Confederate lines. Ammunition gone, Nathan and Chance fixed their bayonets and killed many men. They brawled hand to hand. Day broke, revealing minute-by-minute horrors and opportunities. Rain started up again and pummeled them. By mid-morning the enemies were wrestling each other in the mud, blood thickening around Rebel barricades. Dead Confederates lay next to waterlogged powder. Those Rebels still living battled back with their fists. Nathan saw Chance stabbing men left-handed with his bayonet, punching them with his right, with what appeared to be a bloody stump. *Intimidating*, Nathan thought. *I'll have to try that trick.*

The spot became well named the 'Bloody Angle.' The melée lasted twenty-four relentless hours. When the Confederates finally fell back to a hastily constructed new line of earthworks, reports confirmed almost 9,000 Union left dead on the battlefield. Rebels casualties were estimated at 8,000 with 3,000 prisoners taken at Mule Shoe.

Devastation to the land surpassed even Gettysburg: not a single tree or even blade of grass appeared intact.

Nathan stumbled with Chance to a surgeon's tent. Nathan was cut and exhausted but with no serious wounds. Not a shred of bandage remained on Chance's right hand. Could the surgeon, they wanted to know, salvage any part of the bloody pulp that was once his fingers? The surgeon, grim-faced, refused to answer.

After the surgeon had done what he could, Chance said goodbye to Nathan. Nathan said simply, "I'm staying to fight." He pressed an envelope into Chance's good hand. "Paper and pencil. I don't plan on using them."

Chance nodded once, turned, and started walking northward. Toward home.

~May, 1864~

Slave Graves

Chance awoke to light piercing his eyelids. He opened his eyes to a canopy of leaves. He sat up, felt dizzy, lay back down. Pain roared from his hand. His mind felt slowed by it. After some moments, he pieced together where he was and why.

He had left with seven days' provisions for the three-day (God willing) journey home; Nathan and their unit's quartermaster saw to that. Packets of hard tack and dried beans, a full canteen, his bedroll, clothing, rifle, munitions, and a sheet of oiled canvas he could lie on or crawl under, depending on weather's demands. No official muster, therefore no muster pay. When Chance stopped to rest by the roadside and opened up the envelope to fish out one of the pencils, he saw money Nathan had tried to give him earlier but Chance had refused.

Chance found a more private spot in a woods behind a hedgerow of privet and wild berry brambles. On a bare patch of earth, he shook out the envelope's contents. He used his bandaged knuckles to count the money back into the envelope. It took a painstakingly long time to do so. He counted out far more than the amount Chance had given Nathan for help in getting into the Army. *Must be half of Nathan's soldiering wages*, he guessed, shaking his head. He took the pencil between the knuckles of what were once his fore and middle fingers. After several attempts—the pencil kept slipping from his grasp—he managed to write the money total on the envelope's inside flap and stuff it back into the pocket inside his jacket.

By dusk, Chance had reached Fredericksburg. He followed a knot of colored men and women as they made their way to the north end of town, to a war-battered, brick African Baptist church situated by the Rappahannock River. They set to work at cleaning up some of the debris in the gutted space that had once been a sanctuary. Chance offered to help. They studied his Union soldier's uniform, the features visible from below his cap, including his hair, which Chance had begun to let grow out. They cautiously agreed to accept his help. Conversation kept to a minimum. Chance labored alongside them as a stranger. None of them seemed to have the energy to satisfy their curiosity.

As they prepared to leave, one of the women asked if he had a place to stay. He pointed to a small stand of trees that had not been felled or defaced by artillery and asked if it would be all right for him to bed there. She glanced at the others, a few shaking their heads. "Too exposed," one man grunted. They walked a short distance around the edge of town to a tree-shaded, gated cemetery. "If you mean to sleep outside, reckon this will do," the woman said, holding the gate open for Chance.

Morning. Chance tried again to sit up. Scenery spun round him, then settled. The headstones looked dizzy, too. *Mourning.* Some had been damaged or downed, and re-seated. Several freshly dug graves occupied one corner. There were unmarked graves too and graves with sticks hitch-knotted together to form cross markers. Some of the stones bore first names only and a date of death. No birth date. Slave graves.

A grief seized his spirit with such force that he had to close his eyes against it. Chance lay back on his bedroll. It was as if the pain in his hand had moved to his heart and settled there. His shoulders seemed weighted to the ground. Grief. Anger. Shock. Yes, and fear. Thoughts slipped darkly through his mind, unbidden. *This would be as good a place as any to die.*

"Lord!" he grunted, rolling onto his uninjured arm. The furies still locked him down. Even his eyes seemed pinned shut. "Lord!" Through clenched jaw, gritted teeth. His lips barely moved. But his eyes flew open.

One arm's length from his face sat a mound of something carefully wrapped in a white cloth. He pushed himself up on one elbow and reached for it with his injured hand, pulled it toward himself. The cloth was oozing something, the bottom felt damp. He sat splay-legged to open it, unfolding each layer with a slow hand, revealing a fragrant small round of brown bread. Soft. Still warm to the touch. Its baker had knifed a slit through its middle. Chance could smell the butter dripping from its edges. He felt butter coating his fingertips and thought about the hands that churned it. He smelled his fingers. Tasted them. Rubbed them against his cheek so the fragrance would stay with him for a few miles. He sank his face into the loaf, consuming it entirely, in big, grateful mouthfuls. *This is my body, given for thee.* He thought about the journey ahead as he folded the cloth and funneled the last crumbs into his mouth, then swallowed a few long draughts from his canteen. Chance was tempted to keep the cloth with him as a gift, a talisman. But he noticed it was the sort of cloth a practical woman like his Sarai would put to good use. He fished some money from the envelope, folded it into the cradle of cloth and laid it at the foot of his sleeping tree. He gathered his things, craned to look at the sky. Still very early. He would meet laborers on the road at this hour. *Keep your cap low, eyes straight ahead, and keep walking.*

A wordless, tiny seed of a blessing fell from his lips as he passed from gate to road. Chance wondered where on that scarred, sacred ground it fell, and how it might grow.

PART III

At Home

1864–1865, as the War ends

(Carlisle)

~spring–summer, 1864~

Visitor at Daybreak

Junior woke while the world was still dark. He sat on his bed, eyelids heavy, listening for signs of day. Not even the birds were awake. He tugged up his woolen socks, yawned. He would keep on the long drawers he wore to bed. They were clean. He sniffed his undershirt: clean enough. He felt for the clothing draped on the rail at the end of his bed and went through the half-asleep motions of putting them on. His shirt with the round, tight collar, too tight, but no holes, so wearable. He pulled on his heaviest dungarees, useful for work. He stood to tuck in his shirt, grunted to force button into hole on his too-tight pants. Pants too short, a grayed inch of sock showing. His toes felt for and found his boots, and he pulled them on.

He paused when he heard his mam shift in her bed, sigh. Junior smiled when she resumed her soft snoring, the sound reassuring him. *Mam's a sound sleeper*. He tiptoed to the stove and quietly, efficiently stoked it from wood he had stacked before going to bed. Blood lay nearby, listless with hunger and age. He opened his eyes but did not otherwise move.

A sliver of light so frail it could have been either setting moon or rising sun glimmered through the window. Junior angled toward it and lit a pine cone wrapped in an old scrap from the saved paper box. Junior placed the glowing tinder into its nest of wood, adjusted the draft and heard air whoosh round the wood like contagion, an instant before the logs burst into stunning brightness. Junior allowed himself a few moments before the fire. His clothing warmed, passed the warmth to his body. His stomach growled, protesting, *Warmth alone is not enough!*

He shuffled over to the sink and pumped frigid water into his cupped hand. Sip, pump, sip, pump, sip. A knot of stale bread lay swaddled in cloth on the counter. He unwrapped it, picked away at the moldy spots, broke off a piece, bit off a mouthful and swallowed. Dry. Tasteless as dust. He had to pump and sip another handful of water to relieve the sour rawness of his stomach's disappointment. He lifted his jacket from its nail hook and pulled it on, along with the gloves stuffed in its pockets. He stuffed the remaining lump of bread into his pocket.

Outside, he trudged to the woodpile, log carrier rolled under his arm. Frozen ground crunched underfoot. No snow, just dark, brooding hardpan as spring refused to appear.

What month is it, March? This Fall it would be three years since his father left. The days looped over on themselves like links in a chain with no end in sight. He had a dream about chain, *what was it? Oh, about a workhorse, plodding in a circle pulling a heavy load.* His harness was chain, not leather. In the dream, Junior drew closer to pet its nose but pulled back startled when the horse slowly turned its gaze to him. The horse had Junior's face.

A rustling stirred the shadowed hedgerow skirting the woods. Too loud for a bird or small animal. Junior stopped to peer into the woods. A pair of slanted yellow eyes glowed back at him. Junior's body stiffened. When he heard the snarled growl, saw a wild canine jaw flash open to bear its vicious teeth, Junior's legs failed him. He dropped to his knees.

Wolf reared and leaped.

Junior averted his eyes, hooded his fear. "*Sadahǫsiyohsda!*" He hissed the word. Forced into his voice warning. Authority. "*Sadahǫsiyohsda!* Listen!"

He heard Wolf land a few feet away and lope uncertainly on its massive paws.

"No chickens left. No jerky either. I do have a crust of bread. Some for you, a few bits for your family."

Junior eased the bread out of his pocket. He heard Wolf's panting. Tossed the bread toward its stinking breath.

Its jaw snapping, Wolf caught the bread in midair.

"*Sadekhǫ:nyah o:nęh?*"

Wolf whined as if uncertain how to answer Junior's question.

"Well then, don't eat it now," Junior advised. "Take it to your family. *Desaehdat!* And do not stop until you are home."

Wolf growled. More for show than intent, Junior thought because its mouth was busy with that dry rock of bread. He heard the leaves brush back as Wolf trotted away.

Junior exhaled loudly, releasing pent-up fear and breath. He saw an angular animal limping toward him, then break into a run.

"Blood! Poor fella, I haven't seen you run like that in—

Junior heard something running behind him, recognized Wolf's rasped panting before he had time to turn. Blood charged past Junior, knocking him to his side. Junior turned in time to see Blood bury his jaws into Wolf's neck. They stood locked for a long moment. Wolf struggled to shake off its relentless, bone-thin attacker. Blood's body snapped and fluttered like a rag in wind. But the dog held on, his jaw obscured by Wolf's fur and oozing blood. They dropped to the ground in a snarling blur. The wrestling froze. The animals lay entwined, panting. Wolf on top. Panicked, Junior shouted "Blood!" He saw the dog writhe, and the furious battle resumed, both animals struggling to their feet. Junior heard a single bark, ending in a plaintive yelp. Wolf backed away, limping, as Blood collapsed.

"Blood!" Junior's voice barely broke a whisper. His entire body was trembling.

Wolf crept away, bleeding from its neck, and disappeared into the woods. Blood lay listless, a patch of his shoulder darkly matted.

Junior stood up, dazed until the spinning in his head slowed and the world stood still once again. "C'mon, fella. Can you walk?" Junior coaxed Blood to his feet.

Junior loaded wood into the carrier and trudged back to his house. Blood limped close to his side. Junior felt wetness in his pants, urine trickling down one leg. He would tend to Blood's wound first. Then he would have to change into his other pants, dry but dirty. And rinse out these. *Is Mam awake? Worrying about some wolf is the last thing she needs*, Junior told himself. By the time he reached the door, he had settled on a story about tripping, landing in a puddle of skunk-smelling water.

Blood stopped a few feet from the house. When Junior heard the dog fall, he dropped his load of logs by the door. He ran and lay down next to Blood, whispering in his pricked ear, "Well done, Blood. Good fella." They lay together for a long time, Junior's face buried in the dog's familiar fur.

Junior rose and got a spade. He found a spot some distance from the house and dug as deeply as the thawing earth permitted.

It would have to be at school, after the whipping for his late arrival, that Junior worked out the part of the tale about finding Blood dead.

Webster told his mother that Junior had brought no lunch to school for two days straight. On the third day when Junior dragged himself home from school, he found Webster's mother sitting in the rocker by his mam, who was still hunched in bed. A meat-fragranced pot of something simmered on the stove. Whatever tantalizing food was in it, his stomach turned itself inside out leaping for it.

"Fix yourself a bowl of soup," Mrs. Henderson said, as she leaned over to wring out a cloth into a basin of water next to the bed and smooth the cloth onto his mam's forehead. "Your mother has a fever. How long has she been ill?"

Junior shrugged as he slurped soup from bowl to mouth. "She's in bed a lot."

Mrs. Henderson went to the cupboard where Junior had found his bowl and took another one. She ladled into it broth from the pot. She pumped some cold water into the bowl, found a spoon and stirred it. She angled the rocker close to the bed and cooed, "Junior is here, Sarai. Have some soup." Sarai did not respond.

"Junior, do you have an extra blanket?"

"Yes, ma'am."

"Good. Bring it to me, please." Junior pulled his own blanket from his bed. Mrs. Henderson folded and rolled it, handed it back to Junior. She spoke softly. "I am going to lift your mother up. When I do, slide this behind her. We will not be able to feed her unless she's sitting up."

As Maggie lifted, Sarai groaned, her head rolled toward Junior, eyes still shut. Her lips were cracked and covered with dried spittle. Her breath smelled like Wolf's. Junior quickly slid the rolled-up blanket into place and stepped away.

"Well done, Junior. Go have some more soup. I think Sarai will take some of this. Especially if you are eating, too."

Junior heard his mother moan again, and looked away, toward the fire. He admired the way flames, visible through the flue door slots, rippled in a myriad of patterns, flashing shades of orange, yellow, white, even slits of blue and green. He heard his mam choke and gurgle. Heard her swallow once. Twice.

"Very good, Sarai!" Mrs. Henderson sounded proud of his mam. He devoured more soup, hoping Webster's mother did not notice when he choked and had to wipe his face, his eyes.

After his wife had hurried off to help Sarai, Robert Henderson managed to contact Junior's Aunt Ester, who had remained in Maryland after fleeing Carlisle in advance of the Confederate invasion. Ester arrived at the Thompson home the next evening with more food, all huff and bustle. Junior braced himself for a scolding for not telling anyone about Mam. He could imagine Auntie Ester shaking her finger, her voice careening around in that loud sing-song way. But she looked at him with kindly compassion. After Web's mam left, Auntie Ester turned to Junior and said, "We're moving back here now, for sure." When Ester patted his head, he shoved her arm away. Ester's face squinched up in hurt surprise.

"Sorry, Auntie," he said gruffly. But it seemed to Junior that she should know better. Who dares to pat the head of the man of the house?

After that, Web's mother and Ester took turns nursing Junior's mam. One day he came home to see Mam sitting in her rocking chair. He rushed to hug her, but she held her hands up in warning.

"Save up your hugs, Junior," she smiled feebly. "When I'm better, you can give them to me all at once!"

With the snow gone for the season, Junior could take the shortcut every day now. He walked with Webster, who considered a ride to school too babyish. Besides, their legs were long enough to take them to school faster than a carriage by road.

On one of these mornings, Junior said, "I spoke to Wolf last week."

"Aw, you're full of lye soap!" Web's eyes widened with his grin. "Really, Junior? What did you say? What did the wolf say? Tell me everything!"

Junior explained what his pap taught him, adding, "Wolf's not used to people talking back to him. I think it surprised him. Also I have something to show you." Junior stopped walking.

"Did Wolf come back?" Web's eyes darted along the forest edge as he asked this.

Junior toed a patch of dirt. "Once!"

"Whoah! What did you do? I would have climbed the oak." Webster slapped his cheek. "Wait, can wolves climb? They can't, right?"

"I didn't do anything. My back was turned," Junior said. "Blood did it."

Web searched his friend's face for the rest of the story. Junior stood mute, his eyes combing the ground longingly as if he had lost something precious there. Web looked down and realized that they stood on a recently dug mound. He sank to his knees.

"Oh no! This is where Blood's been?" Web patted the earth gently. "Poor fella." When he looked up at Junior, Web's eyes were watery with loss. Junior had never before seen his friend weep. He bent down next to Web and put his hand on his back. Though Junior had no tears left, the rise and fall of Web's shoulders as he sobbed eased Junior's aching heart.

"Blood!" Web cried. "Such a good, brave dog!"

Sarai watched the mail carrier gallop away. She held the package lightly in her palms, as a fragile, worrisome thing. She made out the name *Thompson* scrawled on its face. The rest of the loopy writing, gibberish. She had learned lots of printed words from Junior's books but had not yet taught herself how to decipher what he called cursive writing.

What could be inside? Something from Chance? Something *of* Chance? Had something happened *to* Chance? The package trembled, she could not control her own shaking. She hurried it into the house, onto the table. It stared at her, a square-eyed thing. "No!" she moaned. "Don't let it be that!"

She crouched so that it could not see her, rocking and holding herself. What to do? Bury it? But who knows what poison or danger it would release in the soil of her fearful neglect? She stood suddenly, pinched its corner between her thumb and finger and tossed it into her iron cook pot on the unlit stove. Closed the lid on its pot, tight.

Good. Out of sight, out of …

She busied herself in the garden and Chance's workshop, where she managed some income, doing repairs to cane and upholstered furniture. Anywhere except in the house; she did not want to be near that devil package.

When Junior came home, Sarai intercepted him at the door. "Come! I got something to show you." She led him over to the pot, directed him to pull off the top very slowly.

"Mam! What's a package from Gettysburg doing in our cook pot?"

"Careful! Who knows what sorrowful news it bears?"

"Do we know a Mr. Firestone in Gettysburg?"

Sarai's eyes bulged. She shook her head.

"Only one way to find out, Mam."

"All right then," she whispered, hugging her elbows tight. "Go."

With his pocket knife, Junior sliced open the package at one end and peered inside. "Just some papers, Mam." He pulled them out and put them on the table. "This one's a letter." He began reading, "Dear Thompsons, we are sorry it took so long for us to write—"

Sarai stared at the document lying on the table and squeezed Junior's arm. "The deed!" she breathed in amazement. "It's our deed! Lost …" She smoothed its torn edges, touched each of the myriad new stains and scars it bore. "Now found!"

Junior kept one eye on his mother as he finished reading the letter. "Mr. Firestone says he's a farmer and he's been too busy to return it." Junior put down the letter. "He found the deed on the battlefield."

"Oooohhhhhhhh." It was more song than moan. She could not seem to stop gazing at the document, caressing it. When Sarai turned to Junior, her face glowed. "It's a miracle of the Lord's doing! Just think on how that farmer found our *deed*, Junior! And the gracious way he took the time to send it back to us. And in the midst of all his own troubles he surely has if he be farming in that godforsaken place." Her smile warmed Junior like seeing a long-lost friend. She unfolded her arms toward her son.

"Got any hugs stored up for me, Junior?"

Later that week Junior came home from school to find his mam leaning against the sink, whistling softly. She was washing and peeling potatoes. "Potpie for dinner." Sarai winked. "Go see if Web and his papa are hungry."

Webster's mother sat at one end of their table, chopping carrots. A stack of papers sat at the far end, with two chairs drawn up. Lizzy lay sleeping on a blanket at her feet.

"Grownups have homework, too?" Junior asked, half-teasing as he stole a glance. He saw some names and dollar amounts. Not much else.

"Maggie and me just working on something," Sarai answered, looking pleased with herself.

Junior's and Webster's mothers began to take walks together. To get back their strength, they said.

On their first walk, they invited Junior and Web along. Ester sat at the Thompsons' table with Baby Lizzy in her lap. She held Lizzy's tiny hand and together they waved the group on their way.

Sarai carried her black purse. They walked to the mill. "I'd like to go in," Sarai said.

Maggie nodded. "Boys, let's stand right here." As they waited by the roadside, the three of them watched farmers arrive with their crops and leave with fat grain sacks or pockets fattened with cash.

When Sarai came out, she wore a wide smile.

Her purse looked fat, too.

After school ended, summer heat arrived full force. One day, Junior slept until almost midday. Then he hurried into his clothes, grouchy and behind on his chores.

He made his way toward the woodpile but froze in his steps, startled by rustling. He scanned the forest's perimeter. With the advent of warm weather, he had forgotten to look out for Wolf. In full daylight, he would not be able to see Wolf's eyes glow. He scanned for tufts of fur disguised among the chaos of vines and underbrush.

Something crashed into the open, a tall break in the undergrowth, leaves flying; a man stumbled into Junior's path.

The man looked familiar, his arms folded in, slightly hunched, soldier's hat pulled low, backpack bulging, rifle slung over his shoulder. Junior recognized the backpack before the face, which eased into a dazed smile.

"Pap!" Junior cried.

The man drew a breath, tried to straighten. "You got tall, Son."

Junior stood stock still, his legs would not move. His pap lurched forward, opened one arm, and folded Junior to his chest. *Pap's breath smells like Wolf's.* Junior felt shame to have that be his first thought to greet his pap's homecoming.

They walked toward the house in silence. *What's the proper thing for two men to say to each other after such a long absence?* Junior wondered. "Blood's dead."

Pap stopped walking. He brought his left hand to his chest. It hovered there as if it forgot what to do next. "He was an old dog," Pap said. Then he cupped his hand around the back of Junior's head.

"Sorry, Son."

Sorry? That's it? Junior stared hard. But Pap was moving again, and the back of his head didn't much care if it was getting stared at.

"What's your mam doing?"

Junior walked faster to catch up. "Making lunch."

"Good!" Pap called back, a foolish grin on his face.

Mam had been carrying a tinware bowl generously filled with potatoes to the stove. As Junior and Pap walked in the door, the bowl clattered to the floor, bald potatoes tumbling and scattering in all directions. Pap stood there, arms still folded, still slightly hunched. Junior caught one glimpse of the hungry way they stared at each other, then he turned and bolted from the house.

Junior dashed through the woods, crossed the bridge in two leaps and battled halfway through green stalks of chin-high corn. He crouched down, his own arms folded over his chest, and, as joy and grief tumbled together, finally and at last, he wept.

Late afternoon rays shot through the trees by the time Junior made his way back home. His house looked different: slightly off-center, a grayer stain to its siding.

Light glinted from its two front windows, the front door stood cracked open; the house looked as if it was smirking at Junior. He heard their laughter. When he reached the front steps, he heard his mam's voice clear, half-saying, half-singing, one of her poems:

Rosebud don't be discouraged
Leaf don't turn on me
Stone give me a foothold
'Til in full flower I be.

Junior stepped through the open door to see his pap sitting at a table spread with food. *This must be all the food we have in the house!* Junior thought, irked by the wastefulness.

Pap wore a sock over his right hand. *How strange,* Junior thought. Everything was strange to Junior. "Come in , Son," Pap grinned. "Where've you been?"

"I've been—" Heat rose in his chest. Junior looked at his mother, radiant with joy. "We've been … *surviving*!"

Junior stalked past the food, past his father and mother, and lay across his bed. He ignored all attempts by his parents to rouse him. He turned his face away from them and closed his eyes. He tried not to pay any attention to the sound of them eating, their excited whisperings. After they ate, they left the house. "For a walk!" they called out to him.

It seemed to Junior that he lay awake for a long time, listening to the memorized creaks and shudders of his home. He did not hear his parents return. He had slipped into a sleep ruffled by dark thoughts, darker dreams.

~early spring, 1865~

Can no dog go in it?

Chance bent over Junior, watching as the boy sanded a book cabinet. Chance loved watching his son's skills unfold. Chance was passionate about his trade. He loved teaching it, fortunately, since others had to do what his right hand could no longer accomplish.

It was early spring, 1865. One long winter had passed since his return home, and business was picking up. Everyone, it seemed, needed to rebuild. Most were eager to erase the signs of a receding war that had come crashing through their town, so dangerously close to ruin, and more and more people had the money to do so. Chance was content. True, his mind raced with all the work needing completion under deadline. Yet he felt well prepared to manage the business and those working for him. Negro troops had been actively recruited and trained in Philadelphia for over a year, so there were not as many available workers. But enough. Chance could afford to take the time to model for his son the craft of a business that would one day be his own. Even—and especially—the painstaking details, such as the slow, patient task of sanding. Chance could slow his racing mind to the tempo of the sanding block as his son worked it and let its prayer-like rhythm help mentally loosen a knotty challenge into a solution.

"That's right, Son. Go with the grain. A nice, smooth movement. Good. Right up to the carved edge. But not on it. We use a different sanding tool for that. Very nice." Someone knocked at the workshop door, a firm, loud thumping.

"Why did you stop, you tired? Already?" He nudged Junior, teasing. Chance walked to the door and opened it.

"General Henderson. We were not expecting you. Come in!"

Robert Henderson stepped into Chance's workshop, walking stiffly to hide his limp.

Chance had heard that Henderson's valor and wound during the second Bull Run had garnered him brevetted brigadier general status. Henderson was still serving the 15th district as its Provost Marshal.

"How is the recruiting effort?" Chance knew the answer, swallowing hard at the irony that Henderson refused to help him enlist. Betrayal has a metallic taste.

"Oh, well enough. Some trouble with bounty jumpers, but that's to be expected, I suppose." Henderson met Chance's steady gaze, then looked away.

"I understand there's talk of a judgeship."

"There has been talk," Henderson nodded. "Hello, Junior. I will report your industry to my son. It may inspire Web to double his efforts in our office."

The two men stood facing each other in wobbly silence. Henderson cleared his throat. "Chance, could you join me outside? I would like to consult with you on a matter of some importance."

"Junior, you all right with finishing up this piece on your own?"

Junior held the sanding block with both hands. He looked from one man to the other as if deciding whether to allow them to leave. He returned to the deliberate work of sanding.

Chance held open the door for Henderson. "Any word from Nathan?" He could scarcely believe ten months had passed since he had left Nathan on that Virginia battlefield near Spotsylvania. With no word from him since.

"No, he does not write." Henderson averted his eyes. "No news must be good, I suppose. Let's walk."

Henderson glanced around at Chance's property as if for the first time. "You have added to the house, the workshop. Your land, your crops, all look to be thriving. Were you much affected by looting from the Rebels' occupation? No? Good. We suffered the most loss at the distillery. Thinking of selling that business anyway.

"Gracious, Chance, how long has it been since I last visited with you here? This Rebellion certainly has a way of interrupting things."

Chance nodded. "We were fortunate there was so little damage to our property. Somewhat more damage in town."

"Fortunate. Yes." Henderson rubbed his clean-shaven jaw. "Chance, have you ever noticed how one loner can spot another a mile away? We have that in common, I believe. We are both also men of faith. You hold yourself to a high standard. That tends to isolate a man, does it not?"

"I suppose."

"For example, you could worship at the African Methodist church and be a leader there. But you choose to attend our stuffy old Presbyterian congregation, where people barely give you the time of day. I don't know why you choose to worship in such a dismissive, isolating environment. But you put up with it. And I am glad for it. So is my family. We are a better church, a better family, for knowing you. I believe you are, like King David in Hebrew scripture, a man after God's own heart."

They had matched each other's stride and were walking at a comfortable speed, when Chance asked, "Why do you?"

"Eh?" Henderson turned and slowed his pace, expecting a thank you, not a question.

"Why do you choose to worship in such a dismissive, isolating environment?"

"Why, we've been—for years we've been, uh …" Henderson stammered, realized he could not answer the question, and retreated to his earlier theme. "We also have, uh … military service in common. Have you talked to anyone about your war experiences? Other than your wife?"

Chance shook his head. "Not even."

"Neither have I. Not much." Henderson coughed as he pulled his cherrywood pipe from a pocket inside his suit coat. "I do not smoke much these days, but this old pipe still gives my hand something to do." He rubbed its smooth bowl with his thumb as they strolled. "We both saw active duty, and I am sure you shot your fair share of the enemy. As did I. Who on earth knows how many men we killed? Not always men, either. Boys." He squinted past Chance. "There was one boy, barely older than our sons ..." he paused, shaking his head. "I wounded him. At Gaines Mill. Took him prisoner. Tried to get him to safety, to some medical attention. He was too weak. Terrible pain. Poor boy. He suffered for hours. That's all I could take."

"Suffering and killing are part of war."

"Indeed. It strikes me that many biblical heroes also killed. David. Moses. Paul." Henderson gave Chance a long look. "As I watched that boy die, it occurred to me that I had killed a man, even before the war. Because if we take seriously what our faith teaches, that Jesus died for our wrongdoings, then that makes us all murderers."

Chance nodded. "God's grace. It's the only way out of the hole we dig for ourselves."

General Henderson jabbed the air with his pipe. "Supremely true."

Chance felt baffled by the conversation. "You have something to discuss?"

Henderson scratched his brow along its deep furrows and looked at Chance, who could see worry in the general's clear blue eyes. "I ask you to please listen to what I have to say and not immediately respond."

Chance stopped walking. "All right."

Henderson stood, fingering the stem of his pipe. "You know the spot on the wooded section of the Conodoguinet Creek that is being cleared? For residences, and some commercial purposes, too, I think."

"Of course. The old 'Can-no-dog-go-in-it' Creek. I just drew up an agreement to build one of the homes." Chance wondered whether his voice sounded normal. He felt a tremor begin deep in his chest.

"Good. Congratulations. Then you know some construction has already begun and with the spring rains—heavy this year, were they not? Yes. Well, I heard—that is, I overheard—the sheriff say that some bones were discovered. Human remains." Henderson looked straight ahead, not at Chance. "They did some investigating, to try to identify the deceased, the details of which in this particular case I am not privy. I suppose that by sizing up accounts of missing persons and the bones themselves, the sheriff suspects they may be the remains of a gentleman named Graysom. I believe he was a friend of yours, and so I am certain this news comes hard to you. Emotional shock and loss come hard for men, don't you think? No less hard than for women, I am sure. Though somehow the ladies often seem better able to handle it in the long run. Allow the proper time to process, to let it play out." Henderson cleared his throat. When he started back up, his voice was slightly deeper.

"In any case, I heard a rumor that will be doubly shocking. Just a rumor, mind you. That you may know something about his death." Henderson began walking again, more slowly. Chance fell into his rhythm. The men stopped at the creek that formed a boundary of their properties. "Ah," exclaimed Henderson. "What a clever footbridge. Did our boys engineer this?"

Chance nodded numbly. When he saw that Henderson was not looking at him, Chance cleared his throat. "Yes."

Henderson had already begun walking across it. He turned and faced Chance, his arms lifted in delight. "What ingenious young men we have! Oh, I am so pleased to learn about this very serviceable little bridge between our two properties. It's a longish walk, otherwise." He turned toward his own land. "I can just barely make out the boys' footpath through the cornfield. A few cornstalks sacrificed for the cause. Not too costly a measure, though, for a proper shortcut."

"How long?" Chance's voice sounded more like a croak.

"What? Oh ..." Henderson shrugged. "I think that's different for every investigation. Each one is unique. However, I do think there's wisdom in waiting." He gave a short salute of a wave and walked the path through waist-high corn. Chance watched him the entire way, until, thumb-sized, Robert Henderson arrived at his home and disappeared into it.

Sarai took the news without tears. Calmly, almost, Chance observed with admiration and some surprise.

"What are you going to do?" They sat at the table. Chance had closed the shop and given his son the rest of Saturday off. Junior had run off into the afternoon's slanting golden light, whooping with pleasure. Sarai smoothed the tablecloth with her palm. "What are you going to do, Chance?"

"Guess I'll go to Henderson's office on Monday. Tell him I need a lawyer." Chance closed his eyes, pressed his temples between his palms. "The man's let me down in the past. Yet I trust him more than any other attorney. Who else could I ask to represent me?"

Sarai shook her head slowly. "No."

Chance looked at her. Waited.

"No." She folded her hands in her lap and looked at him, her mind made up. "He is already taking your case, Chance. He already advised you. He told you to wait. That's what you should do."

"Wait?" Chance's eyes widened. "Wait for the sheriff to show up at my door? Humiliate me in front of my wife, my son? Wait to be thrown into jail? Wait for white man's justice to throw the dice?" His fist thundered on the tabletop. "Above all other arguments against waiting, I am guilty! It's agonizing, Sarai! I can't bear it!"

"You can bear it," she said quietly. "You been bearing it ever since you done this terrible thing. 'Consequences have a sharp edge.' You remember saying that to our son? Yes, the consequences are harsh. It's taken a toll on you. I see that now. Keeping it even from me." Her voice trembled as she sighed, but held. "Graysom lost his life. Come what may you likely gonna spend the rest of your life repenting and regretting. That's your nature. And I do believe them consequences fit the crime."

Chance buried his face in the palms of his hands. "Sarai. No matter what I do, or say, it does not seem this weight will ever lift from my shoulders."

Sarai leaned forward. "You know what this reminds me of? When I got back to Carlisle, looking for the box of valuables I hid, and they was gone? My only table linens. My papa's picture and watch. Our deed. Our most precious belongings. Gone! Months later, a letter arrives by post from Gettysburg. I could not believe my eyes. Some hard-pressed farmer finding our deed on the body of a Rebel soldier. And if that ain't miracle enough, he has the decency to return it. Impossible! Yet there it was, a mere slip of paper. All tattered. But made *whole.* No linens though. No matter! When you came home to me, I said, 'Thank you Lord, you returned to me everything what matters. Forget the other stuff. They're just things.'"

He reached for her hands. When his fingertips touched hers, his voice cracked. "Wait?"

"Yes, my love." Sarai turned over his left hand and stroked its calloused palm. "Wait."

Web observed how visitors changed when they stepped across the office vestibule of Henderson and Webster, attorneys-at-law. Their anxious haste relaxed in the confident aura of the law office's dignified order. Rows of books filled each shelf of the bookcase, their spines in precise alignment. Some attentive hand had combed the fringe on each end of the Persian rug so that it lay flat and straight. Perhaps the same hand—his mother's—that kept the firm's business ledger.

Now it was up to Webster to manage the appointment calendar. Clients stepped from the doorway into the rug's thick pile and soundlessly followed it to divan or wing chair or side chair. Another long oriental carpet, glimpsed from the inner reception door as it sat partly ajar, ran a path to Robert's office and back office area. No crass sound of leather on wood floor, or creaking hinge, or raised voice. On the hour and half hour, the grandfather clock occupying one corner announced the passage of time in its reassuring, felted bass. Whether visitors sat, stood, or paced—and regardless of their level of distress upon arrival—the reception space of Henderson and Webster's law office soothed them into hopeful expectancy.

Webster Henderson sat on a stool at a law clerk's high desk, which sat just outside the open door of his Uncle Henry's office, and facing the entrance at the opposite corner of the room. Webster, a long-legged, wide-eyed thirteen-year-old in a handsomely understated new suit and collared shirt, brushed an unruly lock of hair out of his eyes. To Web's affectionate gaze, the office looked like his father: distinguished, larger than life, approachable, if not entirely knowable.

For several days now, Web had been coming to his father's office straight from school. He changed into a fresh shirt and the suit and worked until suppertime when he and his father would ride home together in the two-person carriage. Webster's role was to announce each visitor's arrival to his father or uncle. If Web knew his father was not already with someone, and an appointment arrived on time, the son ushered the visitor into his father's inner sanctum. Web would inform unscheduled visitors of the attorneys' availability, and the option of scheduling an appointment on another hour or day.

Web's real job, however, was to listen and observe. He watched his Uncle Henry prepare papers for court. When his mother arrived with the books, Web observed as she reviewed columns upon rows with tidy notations, murmuring her way through complex combinations of numbers, letters and calculations, depending on the book and task. He listened as his father discussed his plans for a particular case.

He noticed how a visitor's manner revealed volumes about the individual. Web became particularly adept at reading subtle nuances in his father's reaction to people: a tightening around the eyes; a particular set to the jaw; a stiffness to the straight planes of his back and shoulders; the warmth or coolness of words chosen. Web's interest in the law grew, not because of his interest in the subject, or the profession, but because working in the office made him realize that his father reserved a warmth and familiarity meant only for the son. Webster Henderson wanted to be wherever his father was, doing what he was doing.

Carlisle's sheriff wiped his feet on a mat outside before entering and crossing the rug directly to Uncle Henry's office. The sheriff slanted his eyes toward Web and whispered something in Uncle Henry's ear. Uncle Henry's eyebrows raised ever so slightly. His facial expression remained fixed, sober. He stood and, without looking at Web, disappeared into Robert Henderson's office. The sheriff stood in front of the wall bearing framed diplomas and certificates and military commissions. His gaze seemed to settle on Robert Henderson's brevet as Brigadier General. The sheriff rocked slightly on his feet, from ball to heel.

Uncle Henry reappeared, followed by Robert Henderson, who motioned for the sheriff to enter. Web noticed the stiffness of his father's bearing, the bearing of a military officer. After his father's office door closed, Web turned to his uncle with a question, knowing it would go unanswered.

"What does the sheriff want?"

Uncle Henry put down his pen and cleared his throat. He picked up a neat stack of letters, addressed and sealed. "Webster, it is time to take these to the postal office. Be sure to check the postage on each. The postmaster will charge to the firm's account." His dark-slitted gaze waited for Web to comply.

Web slid from his stool. He suppressed a schoolboy sigh. Realizing he must manage his emotion in an adult fashion, he straightened his back, shoulders, and face as he imagined his father might. He took the mail from his uncle and strode out the door.

Working for his father and completing schoolwork after suppertime pushed Web's playtime with friends to the weekend. He was not the only son to be helping his family by working. He noticed that many of the schoolboys his age—including Junior, the McCormick twins, Yacob Faller—took on new work responsibilities.

It made Web and his friends feel grown, important. And something else. Like adulthood was rushing toward them.

On Saturday morning, Web joined his parents in the kitchen. His mother cracked eggs into a porcelain bowl, salted them, beat them with a wooden spoon, and poured them onto the hot iron skillet on top of the stove. She talked to her husband while she worked, as he caught up on reading the previous evening's newspaper. Nearby, Lizzy hummed and cooed and rocked in a long-legged chair, banging its armrests with her dimpled fists.

"It has been a while," Maggie said, nudging the scrambled egg with the spoon's blunt edge.

"A while since what?" asked Web.

"Since a dead body was found in our vicinity," Maggie tapped and scraped, sizzle and heat, wood against iron. "Odd, and sad, how war can desensitize one's spirit to the notion of death."

"Who died?" Web prodded. "Where?"

"Oh, a fellow named Ransom. No that's not it. Graysom. Mr. Graysom. You probably did not know him, Web. He had no wife or children." Maggie used a second spoon to scoop cooked egg onto plates warming on the other side of the stove. She shook her head. "That Conodoguinet has some nasty spots."

"Sheriff turned the case over to the coroner." Robert's voice sounded clipped, coldly distant. Web felt a chill prick the hairs at the back of his neck.

"Accidental death. Says right here." Robert jabbed the newspaper with his index finger, then turned the page.

Web and his mother looked at each other as she served the eggs. But for the sound of newspaper pages turning and folding, and Lizzy's chirping, they ate in silence.

~early April, 1865~

Oakland

It was late afternoon by the time the train wheezed into the Carlisle station. Four years had passed since Nathan had last seen it. The station looked shrunken, age-worn. He could make out forms of people on the platform. A group of men, five or six of them. He knew by their nervous listlessness where they were bound. *Some of Robert's recruits*, he thought. *They don't look like volunteer soldiers. Must be bounty pay jingling in their pockets. By the time they reach Philadelphia it will be past dark. No matter. They still have a few more long training days before the summer begins shrinking again. Then fighting. Then, God willing, Peace. Or winter.*

Nathan stepped onto the platform where they slouched, smoking and waiting. Their eyes slanted down his uniform from his civilian's jacket to his weapons to his mud-crusted boots. A train attendant shouted for passengers. Nathan watched the soldiers board.

"Good luck, fellows."

None turned around. One of them sniggered. A thin, high voice said, "Like yours, old man?" They laughed and ducked into the car.

Nathan glared at windows too sooted for him to see in. Fists in pockets. The left one clenching the thin bills of his muster-out pay. The right flexing, debating whether to bolt back into the car and start swinging.

"How old are you deadbeats? Twenty-eight? Thirty?" Nathan barked at the blackened car as it rolled away. "Come back in October for my birthday party. Oh, that's right, you *can't!*" he screamed over the steam engine's whistle. He watched until the train, no larger than his smallest finger's nail, rounded the curve and disappeared, its smoky entrails already vanishing.

"I'll be twenty-six," he croaked.

Nathan could not see his own flushed face. He did not notice that startled onlookers whispered and stared at him. He shouldered his rifle and haversack and pushed past them, toward home.

The house had been built much earlier than Sharon, in simpler, less monied times. No gate welcomed visitors onto the sod-and-pebble lane. A lone oak tree stood at its entrance, straight-trunked and solid. A hand-carved sign bearing one word, OAKLAND, hung from a rusted cantilevered pole fastened to the oak.

I watched Papa make that sign. Nathan dropped his sack, remembering.

He had just planted the tree. I sat next to it, playing in the upturned earth. Nathan could see his father standing at a sawhorse table, scooping out letters with violent haste as if the wood was poisoned. *He worked bare armed. I admired his muscles. Wait. He was talking. Said ... He ... said,* "This tree's four. Same as you. Oak is the strongest tree alive." Nathan remembered his father swatting woodchips from his own hands. *They fell into my lap. I gathered them into my palm, added some dirt, stirred with my finger. Inhaled deep. Tasted.*

Nathan placed his hands on the trunk, fingers wide. It would take at least two more sets of men's spread hands to completely encircle it. His hands slipped down, down until he was on his knees, then on his face; he turned his cheeks to the earth, first one, then the other, then face down again, lips touching soil at the feet of this oak. He closed his eyes and breathed in: the sharply bitter smell of the land mingled with the sweet vanilla smell of oak. His earliest memory.

He used its trunk to steady himself as he stood. He leaned against it, considering the dark, hulking house and which door to enter. He picked up his things and made his way across the lawn to the back entrance, near the small parlor where his father used to drink himself to sleep in the dark. Nathan entered quietly. He reminded himself that his father slept with a gun. And that he had been a good marksman once upon a time. He heard snoring, was surprised by how soft it sounded.

"Father?" Still snoring. "Father!" A snore ended with a phlegmy gag and coughing.

"Father, I'm home." Nathan's confident voice. He stood in the parlor doorway, the room's window shades drawn against the fading daylight. He could just barely make out the outline of a man in an armchair.

"Good for ye." A muffled reply. The voice sounded much frailer than he recalled.

Nathan waited. Began, "I remember what you said."

Shifting in the chair, groping, hand bumping a glass.

"Father, I remember what you said. When you planted that oak tree."

"Long time ago."

"Yes. Twenty-two years."

"Strongest tree alive." The old man moved, groaned.

"That's what you told me. You also said, 'Young oak starts out …'" Nathan paused. Facing his father brought his old speaking difficulty to mind. His stutter had disappeared on some battlefield. *Will it return on this one?*

"'A young oak starts out growing its roots strong,'" you said. "'Its trunk straight. Up top you don't see much at first. If an oak makes it to age five, it'll likely live to 105.'"

"Find a Lucifer, will ye? I can't see the damned things."

Nathan found some matches on the side table next to his father. He struck one against the rough edge of the remnant of granite his father used as a striker. He lit the lamp on the side table. "You told me all the things that could kill off an oak. Disease. Deer and other critters. Lack of the sun's light and warmth. Or it could die from thirst. 'But never loneliness.' That's how you said it. 'An oak tree will root itself deep and wide and doesn't mind standing alone.'"

"Strongest tree alive." The Colonel's voice, airy, almost wistful.

"And then you told me all the things it could survive. Disturbed places. Earth tremors. Fire. You told me, 'Oaks like fire because it kills the other trees, makes room for the oak to live. New wood rises up from the scarred and charred, with thicker skin.' You patted the bark to show me that's what you meant by 'skin.' Told me it couldn't make its acorn babies until it was twenty or more years old. And that my birthday was at the end of acorn season."

"I can't see a damned thing! Where's the lamp?" Colonel tried to stand, stumbled back into his chair. "Didn't I ask ye for a match?"

Nathan lifted the lamp and moved it toward his father, its glow illumining different facets of his father's crumpled form. The old man's glazed eyes stared straight ahead. When Nathan held the lamp directly in front of him, his father lifted his hand as a shield against the light.

"Papa. Did you plant that tree for me?"

Nathan listened into silence so deep he could hear an upstairs clock ticking from the far side of the house.

"She told me to plant it on your birth date. Didn't actually get to it 'til a few years later."

"Who? Mama?"

The distant clock chimed six times.

"Forty-year-old women should not have babies!" He tapped his empty glass querulously.

"Do you blame me? Do you blame mama's death on me?" Nathan's voice rose with each question.

The colonel's fingers fumbled along the table's lamplit surface. A pause, and a gurgly "Ahhh." When the struck match flamed, the colonel snorted. Lit a cigar. Its orange glow illuminated two of his fingers, a corner of his mouth. "Ye look like her." His voice, already flat, went flatter.

"Father. I've been gone to war. Four years!" Nathan shrieked, the lamp tipped perilously as he put it back on the side table. He could not control his shaking hands.

"Four years. Sounds about right." Colonel's smoking voice huskier, but calmer. "Root ball'd be too big otherwise." Clock ticking wove itself into his rasping breath, laboring from his chest. He pressed his free hand to his heart.

"Back then, ye smelled like her, too. I couldn't come anywhere near ye for the longest time."

Nathan stalked out of the room, stormed out the front door. He took the porch stairs two at a time. Dropped his haversack and rifle at the foot of them. He loped across the lawn to the tool shed by the barn. Jerked the door handle. It fell off in his hand and the rotted door groaned open. He felt inside, caught the familiar broad shape of an axe, lowered, and double handed it. He broke into a limping run toward the tree.

Nathan was already drenched in sweat by the time he thrust the axe deep into the tree one last time, knocking loose a V-shaped section from its trunk. The tree yawned and cracked against its loss. Shivered. Began to tilt, to sigh, to bow.

Because nothing stood in its way but its own form, the oak tree surprised Nathan by how meekly it gave in, cushioning the fall with its own branches covered with unfurling leaves. The tree exhaled as it landed. The only other sound was a creaking rip, wood against iron as the OAKLAND sign twisted and fell.

Nathan found the loose slab of wood that was the sign. He felt its deep carving, each letter an island. Heavy to lift. Still dangling from its rusted rod whose broken end came to a fierce point. *Good.*

He found the V section he hacked out. Cut clear to the heartwood. *Good.*

Nathan thrust the pole into this slab of wood, dead center. Lifted it to his chest, the pole levered against his gun-toting shoulder. Night clouds rolled across the moon, shrouding its light.

He limped and stumbled all the way to Sharon, pausing at its kitchen door. Chest heaving. He stood a door's width away. Dropped it.

Tomorrow, when she opens the door for cool morning air, it will be the first thing Maggie sees.

~Sunday morning, April 9, 1865~

Front Porch at Oakland

"Are you coming to church!"

Nathan heard the edge of command in his brother Robert's voice. Robert stood stiffly impatient in full uniform, taking charge of the entire front porch. Maggie appeared frozen at his side, her breath caught, an exquisite statue of bronze hair, alabaster skin peeking from the high neckline of a maroon satin dress cascading full from her narrow waist over a crinoline skirt. Even the carriage and hitched horses in the lane beyond seemed to stand at attention. Web sat in the carriage, immobile in profile as if listening for instructions.

"Father left for church already." Nathan stood, holding the front door ajar with his shoulder. He finished tucking his shirt into his pants, looking Robert over, buying time for both of them. He knew that Robert had come by the night before, but that was several hours after Nathan had downed the oak tree and then a considerable amount of Henderson whisky. "Staying longer, this visit, Robert?" Surprised by the evenness of his own voice.

"At least you're upright. A major improvement over your drunken condition yesterday."

"What do you want, Robert?"

"You heard me! Church!" Robert's voice thundered, each word a shot. Robert's hand, Nathan noticed, was flexing, restless.

Nathan stepped onto the porch. He was in easy range now. He stood half a head taller than Robert but his brother the General did not seem to notice.

"Is this the way your family welcomed you back, Robert?"

Maggie moved swiftly. "Welcome home, Nathan." She touched his face with one gloved hand and kissed his other cheek. Nathan felt the warmth of her fingertips through a fine web of lace. The heat from her lips still burned even after she stepped back.

Robert, verbally reloaded, firing, "You expect a hero's welcome, is that it? Nathan, what the devil is wrong with you? You gave Maggie a fright! Dropping that—that butchered tree and sign at her kitchen door! I found the axe you used, last night, right here on this porch! You ruined the heart of Oakland! That magnificent tree! Why? So shapely and vital, it must have been twenty years old—"

"Twenty-two."

"Nathan! That was *Mother's tree!*" Robert's voice vibrated with fury.

Nathan heard Maggie take a nicked breath. Her hands held each of her own wrists. Self-manacled.

"No," Nathan said.

"What?" Both of Robert's fists clenched.

"No, that's my tree. The old man told me. And no to church. With you."

"Do you have any notion of what you've done?" Robert seethed. "You fool! That oak tree stood for something! Our family. Our heritage. Our life! It was a living thing that you mauled, that you destroyed. And so crudely!"

Nathan felt something within him slip from its moorings. He heard the agitation in his own voice. "You don't understand, Robert. It's not—"

"Understand? This is what I understand: My wife had to witness the evidence of your wanton brutality!"

"Your wife." Nathan looked at Maggie and found it impossible to look anywhere else.

"Yes, my wife! What is the matter with you, Nathan? This is strange behavior, even for you."

"Robert!" Maggie cautioned.

"You side with him, Maggie? You approve of this behavior?" Robert glared at her. Maggie looked in Web's direction, but Robert did not give her time to respond. He turned back to Nathan and lowered his voice, though still as fiercely in his control as his eyes, his fists.

"As you wish. Stay at home. You need rest, that's clear. Do not hurry back to the mill. Father and I have managed this long without you."

Nathan cut in, "I'm fine! I'll be at the mill tomorrow!"

Robert held up a hand to silence him. "Calm yourself! You have had your differences with Father. Probably best to take a few days, let this whole affair cool off." Robert's tone sounded somewhat more reasonable. Nathan saw his brother arranging his expression into an indulgent condescension. But he could not maintain it. Robert rubbed the back of his neck. Irritation crept back into his voice. "Why lay that awful destruction at our doorstep?"

He could not bear his older brother's domination any longer. Nathan knew exactly what would break Robert. How to break free.

"I'm in love with Maggie."

All color drained from Robert's face and knuckles. It flew to Maggie's cheeks, spreading like a bruise, darker even than her dress, to a violent red. Her eyes widened and grew liquid—*with, what? Not surprise. Relief?* Robert's arm drew back. Nathan waited for his jaw to take the blow, for his head to fly back against the door frame. The blow and its consequences would splinter his skull or the door frame, likely both. *Or perhaps Robert will draw his sword and whip it across—where? He won't kill me. Slice my cheek. The one she kissed.*

Robert lunged forward. He grabbed Maggie's elbow and spun her around. He pulled her toward the steps and down. *A retreat!* Nathan was dazed by surprise. *The attack will come later.*

Maggie stopped on the middle step. She wrested her arm from Robert's grasp, surprise also favoring her.

"Never mind." Maggie stood at ease, looking at Nathan full on, unblinking. Nathan did not move. *Those eyes! They spell the terms of my surrender though they call it a truce. What sweet, unrelenting strength of will! Poor Robert. We both are vanquished!*

Maggie gathered her skirts with both hands, a step away from Robert. Before she turned toward the carriage, she spoke again. "Never mind, Nathan. It's just a tree."

Web watched as his mother climbed into the open carriage next to Lizzy, opposite him, her face turned to the side. His father took charge of the horses and started them away. Uncle Nathan shook his fists, yelling something drowned out by the gravel under the wheels and the carriage's squeaks and bumps. Then he charged into the house and slammed the big door.

Web wanted to talk to his mother, but she put her hand up to her face like a horse's blinder. Lizzy crowded into her lap and pulled at her arm, but his mother sat still as stone and kept her face covered.

Web opened his mouth to say something but then closed it again. *Sometimes it's hard to find the right words to say,* he thought. *Especially for a boy talking to adults. Especially when the adults are covering their faces.*

~Sunday afternoon, April 9, 1865~

Sabbath Peace

The carriage ride after church began in heavy silence. Robert drove the horses as always on Sundays, as Yancy attended services at the African Methodist Episcopal Church. It was Webster who had insisted on taking Nathan home.

Web sat next to Maggie, who held Lizzy. They faced Nathan, who slumped in the seat closer to the driver's bench, his eyes closed, head back, face slack with exhaustion.

The carriage was so small, Maggie found it nearly impossible to avoid Nathan's face, so she watched Web as he studied Nathan's pants, ghosted with stains.

"Is that your blood?" Web bit his lip.

Nathan's eyes flew open and searched until they found Web.

"Some. Mostly the other guy's," Nathan said.

"Why did you wear this Rebel uniform to church, Uncle Nathan?"

"It was a gift from a soldier I killed."

Web leaned forward, earnest. "Uncle Nathan, you're a grown-up," he said.

"Yes." Nathan returned Web's unblinking gaze.

"You should know that you're not supposed to pull your pants down in front of people. No matter how badly it hurts."

"You're right. I should know better."

"I understand why you did it, Uncle Nathan. But how did you know the preacher was talking about that too, before you came?"

"What do you mean, Web?" Nathan asked.

"What Preacher Wing read from the Bible about being naked in church."

Maggie held Lizzy tighter. She saw Nathan lean forward, say to Web, "Tell me."

Webster tapped his lower lip, a gesture Maggie had often seen Robert make when he was trying to remember something.

"A man named Zekiel said it. He said it was time for love and so God covered us with his skirt when we were naked in church."

"God's skirt," Nathan echoed.

Web kept his owl eyes on Nathan. "I thought you were going to shoot Grandfather."

"Webster Henderson!" Maggie kept her voice low but shot a warning glance at Web.

"What was that?" Robert slowed the carriage, twisting and calling over his shoulder, "I can't hear what you're saying. Everything all right?

Nathan answered his nephew. "Never, Web. I would rather hurt myself."

"Are you going to hurt yourself?"

Nathan's unsmiling laugh ended in a small sighed groan. He looked at Maggie as if seeing her for the first time. "God's witness, Web. I hope not." Maggie gave Nathan a penetrating glance before she returned to tucking Lizzy's hair behind her ears.

Web looked at the stick Nathan clenched, its point trembling in the air.

"My friend Junior Thompson turned twelve today. He made that bayonet stick. Did you kill any Rebs with it?"

"No, Web. All the men who saw it were so afraid they ran away."

"Whan away!" Lizzy cooed.

"That's enough, Web! No talk of killing!" Maggie's voice sounded shrill, angry, and much louder than she intended.

"What is going on back there!" Robert thundered. He pulled the carriage off the road. It jounced to a stop. "Maggie! You're riding up here with me!"

"It's all right, Robert!" Maggie called out. "Not enough room for Lizzy. It's safer here." But Robert had already jumped to the ground and turned toward them. She saw him reach inside his coat, into the pocket where he had stashed Nathan's sidearm after they took it from him in church. Maggie gasped. "Robert—"

Robert's hand re-appeared, clutching a white handkerchief. He wiped perspiration from his livid face. "Get out of the carriage, Nathan!"

"You're going to make me walk?"

"Get out of the carriage!" Robert barked.

"Yes, sir!" Nathan rolled his eyes, smirking.

Robert lunged into the carriage and grabbed Nathan by his jacket lapels, yanking him out and onto the ground. Robert pinned Nathan's shoulders. Nathan did not resist. Robert's breath came in ugly grunts as he pressed one knee into Nathan's chest.

"Hit me." Nathan's voice, calm.

Maggie saw Robert's fist hurtle down. She heard bone crack, saw Nathan's head swivel sharp toward them, his eyes latching onto hers. Calm.

"Again."

Maggie screamed. Robert buried his fist into Nathan's cheek, knuckles grinding, a gruesome sound that tore through Maggie. Webster scrambled out of the carriage. Maggie struggled to follow, her skirt hem caught. Lizzy began to cry. Webster tossed the stick to the ground. He clung to his father's back and shouted, "Ahoy, ahoy! That whale's my uncle!"

Robert swayed onto his heels, eyes unfocussed. Fist cocked in midair.

Out of the carriage and standing, Maggie swayed, too. Lizzy clutched at her skirts, sobbing. Maggie's throat felt raw from the scream. "Web!" she croaked.

Robert slowly rose, easing Webster from his back. The father looped one arm around his son and brought him close, the boy's head cupped by those bruised knuckles, the father whispering something.

Nathan's mouth lay open, his jaw at an odd angle from his face, cheek to cold earth. One of his blue eyes was swelling shut. He stretched out his hand, palm up, fingers wide, toward Web and Maggie and some distant shore.

"Ahoy," he sighed.

Robert often received visitors at home. But never on Sundays. A strict rule. "The Sabbath is a family day," he insisted.

Even so, for the past several weeks Yancy had begun to pay a visit every Sunday afternoon. Usually he arrived after they had finished the big midday meal. When Maggie answered the door, he would give her a brief nod and the shyest of smiles, covering his chest with his hat, its brim crumpled in both fists.

The Hendersons took their Sabbath day family meals at the round table in the kitchen. Given the events of this particular Sunday, they had arrived home later than usual. Maggie stood in front of her stove, trembling. She had not even finished preparing the meal when Yancy arrived at the door. Robert invited him in.

No! Maggie clenched her heart against competing emotions. *I want to be left alone! My family to myself!*

This morning. In church. Nathan exposed himself.

Then, on the ride home—Maggie shuddered at the remembering.

Webster and Robert had helped Nathan to his feet. Robert had returned to the carriage driver's seat in silence. He held his arms out to receive Lizzy, then stretched his hand to help Maggie onto the narrow seat next to him.

But the waiting that followed was what Maggie found herself thinking about. Robert had waited while Webster walked with Nathan back to the carriage; while Web climbed in, then Nathan slowly eased himself into the seat. Robert had not looked back. Maggie had not dared to look. When the carriage had ceased rocking from its passengers' entry, Robert signaled the horses to continue toward Oakland. Nor had Maggie turned to watch Nathan enter the house. She had heard his boots tread each porch stair with firm deliberation.

Maggie transferred hot food from stove to dishes with unsteady hands while Robert took each dish of steam-trailing food and ferried it the short distance to the table. They steered away from each other, avoiding eye contact.

Yancy teased Web about being "unusual quiet" until the boy finally smiled. Maggie heard Web whisper, "Not supposed to tell." Yancy eased a spare chair between Web and Lizzy, who sat in her high chair. Yancy wiggled his finger at Lizzy. She clapped her chubby hands and laughed. He began swapping stories with Web, the old man as adept in listening as he was in spinning yarns.

Web shot both hands in the air. "Teacher Brumbach got from floor to chair in one leap! She did!"

"A mouse? Or other critter?"

"Other critter."

"You gonna make me guess?"

Web nodded, grinning.

"Squirrel? Chipmunk? No?" Yancy rubbed the stubble on his chin. "Lessee. Well, I seen that Knight boy do some skunk trapping."

"That's right!" Web howled. "Terry Knight brought his trap, with the skunk in it, right up to her desk!"

"No!" Robert and Maggie said at once. They had taken their seats with an awkward space between them.

"Bet Teacher had some choice words," Yancy said, chuckling.

"We weren't so sure about her words," Web answered, mashing his potato with the back of his fork. "They were all in German."

Toward the end of the meal, Maggie obliged Robert's request for a second piece of apple cobbler. Yancy swept his thumb through the air, jabbed himself in the stomach, and said, "From there to here, Robbie."

Robbie? Maggie looked up.

Robert and Yancy chuckled over the joke. Web had gathered water glasses from the other place settings. He was entertaining Lizzy by tapping them with the tip of his knife, working out a tune.

After dinner, Robert rose stiffly with the aid of his cane. Yancy walked with him to his office. They closed the door behind them.

On other Sundays, Maggie had assumed they spent these sessions planning their work schedules for the week. Before the war, Robert would visit with Yancy at the carriage house or in his room above it. *Come to think of it,* thought Maggie, *they still do that, too.*

She cleared the table. Web wandered off to his room. Maggie carried Lizzy to the counter next to the sink and picked up a damp cloth. She wiped the baby's mouth and hands, then tossed the cloth into the sink, onto a pile of dishes. She carried Lizzy to her tall chair, positioned a safe distance from both sink and the stove, so that Lizzy could watch her mother clean the dishes. Maggie placed into her daughter's lap little twists of bread. Lizzy giggled, shaking her fair curls with delight as her chubby fingers explored these edible playthings.

Maggie poured hot water over the stack of dishes. She dipped a cloth into the water and lifted it out by one drenched corner, waiting for it to cool a bit before rubbing it with soap and cleaning the dishes.

Robbie?

After Lizzy was settled into her crib and asleep, Maggie left the nursery door open a crack and slipped down the stairs, pausing at Robert's office door. She heard muffled laughter just before she turned the knob. The door swung open silently to a view of the men's backs. Yancy sat in Robert's leather armchair, Robert in his desk chair, which was swiveled close to Yancy. Robert's head bent toward the elder man and Yancy was ruffling Robert's hair with his knuckles, saying, "Is that so, Robbie?" with teasing affection.

"Is what so?" Maggie stood very still just inside the door.

Yancy drew his hand to himself and looked away, toward the fireplace, where logs had burned to embers.

"I always said—" Robert started, raking his fingers through his hair. "I always said that, if we were still children, I could just wrestle Nathan, and that would settle everything. Now I've done it."

"Settled what? Do you even know?" They remained silent. She counted fifteen clicks of the mantle clock. She inhaled. "Robbie?"

"Margaret. Have a seat. If you like," Robert said.

"If I—like? Why do I feel the odd person out? As if I am intruding? What is going on?"

"I could ask you the same," Robert said hoarsely, staring at his boots.

"You ain't intruding, Miz Henderson. 'Course not," Yancy said low. "It's just that we go back a ways." He turned to Robert. "Robbie, maybe I should—"

"Willy sat in that chair. Right there," Robert blurted. He pointed to a high-backed armless rocker, its threadbare upholstery faded from red to a grayed pink. Just an aged, battered furnishing Maggie had wanted to get rid of, had actually discarded, several times. Robert always rescued it and put it back into that same neglected corner of his office.

Yancy shook his head and gave a low whistle. "Never thought on that before. No arms on it 'cause that's an old-time nursing chair."

"Poor Willy," Robert said, flat-voiced. "Not even six. In the back parlor at Oakland. He sat straight up. Rocking slow. Scared. Holding the baby." Robert rocked absently.

"Baby?" Maggie tried to imagine the haunted, hollow-eyed expression of her late brother-in-law on the face of a round-cheeked five-year-old.

Robert was breathing sharp, pale around the eyes, lips pressed closed. He sat forward in his chair. "That baby would not stop crying."

"What baby? Nathan?" Maggie guessed.

Both men stared at the chair.

"I was almost fourteen," Robert said. "It should have been me, holding the baby."

"You were with your mama," Yancy said.

"Mother! She was screaming. I can barely remember her face. But I can still hear her screams." Robert closed his eyes.

Maggie wanted to comfort him. But her feet seemed frozen in place.

"Sit in this here chair." Yancy stood up, gesturing, urging her into the leather chair. "Please."

Once Maggie was seated, Yancy hobbled over to a stool and perched on it, facing them. Maggie took Robert's hand in both of hers and squeezed it. He squeezed back before he pulled away. His eyes remained closed. She noticed Yancy's gentle watchfulness over Robert. Yancy softly clapped his hands and kept them together as if catching and holding a moment in time.

"Nathan was born late Fall. Or early winter, you could say. Yes, 'cause there was a heavy snowfall, come early. Doc made it to the house anyways. Miz Henderson didn't make it, though." Yancy wheezed as he exhaled. "'Twas a miserable hard delivery."

"Where was her husband?" Maggie asked, her voice tight. Memories of her dear friend Lizzie dying in childbirth came flooding back. Maggie was having trouble breathing.

"Now that's a right interesting question. Robbie say he wish he knew. I say, better not to. Anyways …" Yancy ran his fingernails along the stool's base. "Doc say he would notify the undertaker. He say his Sorries and left. Colonel musta left right after."

"He left the boys alone?" She stared at her husband. "Robert, how long was your father gone?"

Robert shook his head. Opened his eyes halfway. Looked at Yancy.

Yancy said, "Y'see, I was working for the Colonel then. Long before, we was sailors together. Served together, in the 1812 conflict. Friends. True friends. Right up 'til he left." Yancy rubbed his palms on his legs.

"I lived in town at that time. Made it in to Oakland the next morning. Early. Front door swinging wide open. Slammin' shut in the wind. *Strange*, I was thinking, and runned on over and all through the place. Nobody home! Then through the back winder I seen the barn door's open, too. Lanterns lit, swaying. Dangerous, with the hay in. I runned over there, fast as I can go. Oh my!" Yancy's voice caught. He wiped a palm across his eyes. Kept it there.

"I seen them boys crouching low, huddled together. Jackets on and they still shaking cold. And there was little baby Nathan. Ooh, Lord, he wrapped in a blanket, ends dragging down. His brothers holding him up to the teat of that cow, Robbie working the teat. Nathan sucking, his little hands blue with cold, milk dribbling down his tiny cheeks. Lord, Lord! That cow looked at me with eyes so deep, so sad. Like she knew."

Yancy clapped his hands again. His gaze settled on a corner of the ceiling. "Anyways. Took a while for me to get those shivering boys something to eat and then into they own beds. The Colonel's Missus had a cradle ready for the babe. Baby Nathan fell right to sleep in it. Yes, he did. I went down the road a-ways to a farm. Farmer's wife found a wet nurse and hurried over to see about the boys."

Yancy looked at Maggie. "Whilst I went to see about the Colonel. Found him in the saloon. Now I know what you're thinking. But he was not a drinking man. 'Til then. Filled glass set there on the table, next to a empty bottle. Along with his pistol, not unusual in them days. Colonel sat there, nodding off. I picked up the glass and tossed that whisky in his face. He stared at me, blinking, wiping his face like a man regretting his baptism.

"I picked up his pistol. Held its butt near his head. Ready to use it if need be. 'I never took you for a coward,' I say. He gave me a long look. I seen lonely eyes before. Never like that. Finally he gets up. Stumbled on home. I'm behind him the whole way. Coaxing, like he's a mule or some beast like that."

"That's when he bought the distillery." Robert's voice, thin. "So he could do his drinking at home. And plenty of it."

Maggie stood next to Robert. She rested her forehead on the top of his head. Closed her eyes. She heard the door click closed as Yancy left. She felt the rise and fall of her husband's breathing.

"Robert, I am so confused. Frightened. You are my true north. I need you! Am I not your soul mate? Why these visits with Yancy? Should you not be confiding in me, your wife?"

He gripped her hand as if he would never let go. She could feel his pulse in her fingertips, telegraphing his fears.

"My private talks with Yancy. They date back to my childhood, Mag. When I married you, I tried my best to limit them. Some things, a young wife, a young marriage, should not have to bear."

"Robert. You can share any burden with me. Our love makes that possible. And our trust requires it. Your deepest secrets should be shared with me, not with someone else who—"

He looked up at Maggie. His grip on her hand loosened, but held.

"Maggie, I just did. This is the first time I have spoken of my mother's death since it happened. It is a sad, old tale. But what Nathan said on the porch! And did! And that look in your eye." Robert shook his head. "Share my deepest secrets with you? Maggie, can you? Will you do the same?"

Robert stood. He waited for her response.

"Yes, of course," Maggie began, and stopped. She felt her face flush. *I should say something else,* she thought. *But what to say, when there is nothing to tell?*

Robert dropped her hand. As he gathered his hat and overcoat, she saw his jaw and hooded eyes cast their verdict and it frightened her. *Say something!* She urged herself. *But what?*

Robert glanced at his pocket watch. "I'd better hurry. I promised Web we would go to the playing field." He paused at the door. "Today is Junior Thompson's twelfth birthday. Chance has some special gift for his son. He asked me to take Web to the field so they could share it."

The dejected stoop of his back was so unlike Robert it scared her even more. Maggie rushed toward him as he opened the door. "Wait! WAIT!"

Just past Robert's shoulder, Maggie saw Web standing pressed against the wall, eyes fearfully wide.

Robert looked from his son to his wife, then put a hand on his son's shoulder. "Web, your mother and I will finish our conversation later, after we come home. Let's go. A promise is a promise."

Today is Junior's twelfth birthday, Chance thought. *And everything is going wrong. Terribly wrong.*

He had no idea how to make it right, or what to say to his son. He had to start somewhere. Some small bit of talk.

Father and son walked the shoulder of the road leading to the big field at the edge of town. The horizon sprayed gold from a setting sun, purpling sky. *Looks like Junior's cheek,* Chance thought. *He's probably thinking the same thing.* Their jackets flapped open in the breeze. Chance transferred his walking stick from his good hand to his bad one. He squeezed the stick as hard as he could, exercising what little flexibility remained.

"Were you surprised I could catch and throw with this hand?"

Chance knew Junior was angry and hurt. And that he avoided looking at his pap's damaged hand. Chance switched the walking stick again and placed his bad hand on Junior's shoulder, watching as he waited for his son's response to the question. He admired Junior's muscular and upright carriage, the square of his jaw—even now, when set against his pap—premonitions of manhood in a child still young, still growing.

When Junior finally turned, he looked straight into Chance's eyes, unblinking.

"No. Seems to me you get to do just about anything you want to."

Chance thumped Junior's shoulder, ignoring the sarcasm. "That's how you seem to me, too. Anything you set your mind to do, you can do it."

Junior shrugged off his father's hand. His gaze shifted. A grin stole across his face. "Web's here! With his pap!" Junior glanced sideways at Chance, then broke into a run.

Webster spotted Junior and ran toward him. They collided in the air, gleeful, rough-housing over the ball. Robert Henderson cupped his hands to his mouth, his call of "Happy Birthday" floated after them as they ran to the playing field, passing the ball to each other. Other boys appeared from all directions. By the time Chance Thompson reached Robert Henderson, a huddled crowd of boys was busily organizing into teams.

Chance stood apart from Henderson, some four feet and four years' worth of distance. He spoke into the space between them. "I'll have to thank Web for coming. And putting the word out."

"Easy to do. Tell a few boys about a ballgame, in a blink every boy in town knows. Faster than telegraph."

"How's Nathan?"

"What a morning!" Robert tilted his head skyward as if trying to empty his mind. "He's at Oakland. And he's swearing off whisky. At least that's what he says today. After his outrageous behavior at church and—well, I suppose he'd say anything."

Robert wore a black felt hat with a black silk band and a black overcoat, neatly buttoned over a gray suit and pressed white shirt. Professional attire, but with the air of a man in mourning. He attempted a smile. "Fortunately, good news travels fast, and we have genuine good news today."

"You're right, a ball game is a boys-magnet."

"Oh," Robert scanned the boys at play. "What I meant was, your son's birthdate is now and forever linked to another auspicious event." Robert's sideburns and eyebrows were turning gray, Chance noticed. His eyes, the precise color of the sky framing him, looked eager.

Chance glanced from Robert, to the boys at play, and back to Robert, waiting.

Robert's voice crackled with excitement. "We just received word! Today, April 9, 1865." He thrust his pipe high in the air. "Lee surrendered!"

Chance closed his eyes, turned away from Henderson. Before he turned back, he masked his emotions so that Robert could not see his trembling joy. Chance stuck out what remained of his right hand. Robert shook it vigorously between both of his.

"Congratulations, soldier," Robert said. "Your courageous service record is fulfilled in victory."

Chance freed his hand, held it up. "This is the only record of my service."

Robert's face crumpled. "I am sorry. Keenly sorry, Chance. It is a travesty of justice I will regret to my dying day, as I am"—he paused, strained at the words—"I am responsible for not acting on your behalf."

Chance's jaw tightened. He turned away from Robert. They watched the game in vibrating silence. Boys battering each other, laughing.

Robert's voice, hoarse. "Chance Thompson, will you forgive me?"

The question felt to Chance as if it signaled his death. His life flashed before him, embodied in the son racing with a ball across the field, moments of both sweetness and sacrifice, about to be counted and summed in his reply. He turned to Robert.

"I want the bones of Quincy Graysom. I intend to give him a proper burial. The headstone will make it clear how he died, and by whose hand."

Robert pressed Chance's shoulder. "Now see here, Thompson, don't do anything rash. Think of your family—"

"Why do you assume I am the killer? So far as anyone knows, you were the last person to see him alive."

Robert's hand dropped. "How dare you threaten me!" he growled.

"See how quickly the human heart turns? From needing forgiveness, to needing to defend and avenge what's ours." Chance shook his head. "We're all such selfish creatures. 'Stiff-necked.' That's how the Good Book describes us." Chance scratched the ground with his walking stick. "It happened just that way. I went from defending to avenging so fast. It doesn't take more than a moment to kill someone."

"No. No, it doesn't." Robert winced and pressed his hand to his side as if against a spasm of pain.

"We can't have forgiveness without truth, Robert. You told me that God-honoring men chose to kill. Paul and David and Moses, you said. As if that justifies what we have done! God have *mercy*! Did their cover-ups succeed? No. The biblical record shows that one of those men lost his life. One lost his kingdom.

And one spent years wandering, never seeing the land promised to him. Promised to *them*. Cover-ups have consequences."

Robert saw that Chance, with his stick, had scrawled into the dust.

QUINCY GRAYSOM

"We can't have trust without truth, either," Chance continued. "If we lie about something like this, how can anyone—especially our children—ever again trust us? Why should they?"

As he spoke, Chance scratched into the dust more words.

KILLED BY HIS FRIEND
CHANCE THOMPSON
OCTOBER 20,1860
John 15:13

"I want those bones, Robert. I'll be going to see the sheriff tomorrow, to collect them."

"Let me go with you. Represent you."

Chance paused long before he nodded his assent. He rubbed out what he had written in the dirt. He cupped his hands to his mouth and shouted Junior's name. Junior looked over sullenly. Someone tossed the ball back to him and Junior fell into a slow trot, to a place on the road behind his father; about four feet and four years' distant.

"What are you doing here in your office?" Maggie stood in the crack of Robert's open office door. Her hair disheveled, her face swollen from tears and the shock of her savagely beaten son. She was holding something. A towel, stained with her son's blood. Holding and twisting it.

"Looking up a scripture verse. John 15:13."

"We might lose our son, Robert! He needs you! Is it something you plan to read to him?"

"Not tonight." He recognized the verse, one he had memorized as a child. Robert closed his Bible, balanced it on his knee as he spoke: "Greater love hath no man than this, that a man lay down his life for his friends." He looked at Maggie with glazed eyes. "Lee surrendered today."

"I know." Maggie rubbed her throbbing temple, her eyes half-lidded with exhaustion.

"Margaret. I killed a boy close to Web's age. At Gaines Mill."

"Oh, Robert." Maggie bowed her head against the door frame.

"He was a Rebel prisoner, stick thin. Lost a lot of blood. I didn't have to shoot him. I put him out of his pain. That's what I told myself."

"What was his name?"

"I don't know." Robert stared at his hand, flexed the trigger finger. "Why didn't I ask his name?"

Maggie groaned. "Children soldiers on the battlefield. Violent children in the playing fields. God help us!"

Robert grabbed the Bible and stood. "There is something—" he said distractedly. "Something I must do tomorrow."

He returned the Bible to its spot on the shelf.

"Order a monument for the boy. Erect it here in Carlisle. Explaining how he died."

"Gall *durn*!"

Tree bark razored Junior's legs so bad he used the only cuss words he knew. But it sounded so silly and useless for the task, he didn't repeat it, even though he had the moonlit dark all to himself. The bag he packed with his going-away things sat at the foot of Web's tree. *I, Junior Thompson, twelve years old today, cannot leave until I master this tree.*

The full moon poured its milk-light down the tree onto Junior, every branch edged in light, legions of leaves shushing and slapping him. He got almost six feet off the ground but couldn't find another hand-hold.

"Jimmy cricks!"

His arms started to weary. "Web, for once, I wish I had your ridiculous long monkey arms." Junior said it angry to chase away his fright. *Angry. Grrrr!* He wrestled the tree trunk and—*What do you know!*—he was a few feet higher, with a sturdy branch within easy grasp. Junior pulled up … and up … and up … height making his heart bump loud enough to wake any birds still there. He reached a crotch in the tree and a break in the oak's leafy cover. It almost looked as if lightning or a strong wind had broken off the very top. *Must be right where Web sat when he—*

Holy of holies. That is some view. Spectacle-tacular, Web would say. The whole world in miniature. Moonlight bathing me, I never felt so. ... so powerful! Junior stretched out along the stout branch. His hand bumped into something covered by leaves. Tied with rope, round and round the object and the branch. *It's got to be! Got to be the gift Web left for me.* Junior almost dropped the rope and the gift. He scooted both toward his chest, caught the rope with his mouth, and tucked the gift under his chin. He stayed that way until he was sure of his hold. He leaned his back against the upright trunk, which didn't budge. *I'm nothing to it, a mite, a passing thing barely worth noticing.* When he felt steady, he took the gift in his hand and tore off its paper wrapping with his teeth, which had done its job protecting but fell away easy, like a flurry of moths, weakened from weather's drubbings.

Spyglasses. The kind with two eye-holes. Binoculars!

Junior felt like Marco Polo with fistfuls of gold.

He used them to look around in every direction, the world soaked in moonshine. It occurred to him all of a sudden: *I can't see colors at night! I'm seeing as Web sees: all darks and lights, blacks and whites.* He looked at everything all over again, more carefully this time. He wondered how hard it had been for Web to carry his gift up so high in this tree. Since it was wrapped, he did not even have a chance to take his own good look around. *How many nights did it set up here, alone, wasting all that enjoyment? Waiting to be shared by two boys?* He felt dizzy and almost slipped off the branch. He gripped harder.

Junior could imagine Web wrapping this gift good and thick, then climbing the tree. Tying the gift in place. *Checking that it's tight and safe, ready for me to find. That grin of his that can't barely keep a surprise tucked in.* The sadness rose up in him like a fever. *How many days did he wait for me to make good on my promise? Did he go to bed at night disappointed? Each night, did his disappointment nibble off another bit of hope?*

The idea got into Junior's head that a gift this special must have some sort of power. And not just for seeing things. *Like prayer, you don't even open your mouth and God gets the message.* He held up to his lips the look-into-it end of the glasses.

He whispered, "Webbie. I want to make stories."

The moon's caught in that eyehole glass, peeking at me like it's waiting to hear what I got to say next.

"I don't want to kill and polish no more trees."

Junior looked straight down.

And he felt like Captain Ahab. Atop Moby's nose.

The binoculars had a strap. Junior looped it around his neck. It took a long time to turn himself around so that he faced the trunk. With his eyes open he froze. *Can't move!* He decided to grope his way back down the trunk with his eyes squeezed shut. He edged downward carefully, carefully, peeping open an eye when necessary and squeezing it shut soon as possible.

He didn't know how far he was from the ground when his hands and feet slipped at once, and he free-fell through the air.

Junior landed on his feet, jolting so hard his knees buckled. He heard a popping sound. His knees burned bad, one wobbled a little, but he limped off most of the pain and thought, *Better than landing on my head.*

Which way?

Just away, he told himself. *My father used his fist against me. Same fist that killed his friend.*

I used to know so many things. Now I only know that.

Chance knocked twice on the front door at Sharon, but no one answered. The door was not closed or latched and so each time he knocked it opened wider. The third time he knocked, the door swung open two shoulders' widths. Chance stepped into the vestibule.

Voices drifted to him from upstairs.

Chance kept his eyes on the staircase. He kept his one and a half hands in plain view and at his side. He stood still, even though every nerve in his body screamed, *Move!*

Stair treads beyond his line of vision began squeaking under the weight of an adult. A groan of pain, a step, then another groan. He saw the slippered feet, the robe, the long, blue-veined hands of a man appearing as Robert Henderson made his way down the stairs.

"Where are you going?" Maggie's voice called after him, thick with anguish.

Robert groaned with the effort of turning to reply, "Latch. Door."

He twisted back to face the stairs and caught sight of Chance. Robert Henderson grabbed the balustrade with both hands and collapsed against it, his mouth wrestling over each gulp of air. He shook his head slowly.

Chance brought his hands together, holding them up toward Henderson in a flat-fingered prayer. He said, "Junior's missing. We figure he's here."

Robert's whole body trembled. He squinted past Chance's squared shoulders, past the door ajar, into the night-soaked world. He shook his head again. Kept shaking it as he doggedly made his way back to his son's bedroom.

~nighttime, Sunday, April 9, 1865~

What the Child Did

Junior threw his book sack over his shoulder and walked. His jaw remembered the punch his pap gave it after church. His bones remembered the bully boys' thrashing. And how Web trusted Junior's arms to carry him, which gave them extra strength. Junior's arms remembered other, earlier aches, piled one on another like all the logs he had ever split and fetched. How light his mother's head had felt when she lay sick and her eyes refused to open. Holding Blood, with one cheek buried in his fevered fur, listening to the dog release his last bit of love and breath as a sigh.

The evening smelled wind-rattling, canine wild. Maybe Wolf was waiting nearby, watching him with those yellow eyes. Junior tried to run in the dark but his legs scarcely worked, stuck in a slow motion like happens sometimes in a bad dream. Dense darkness of field and woodland gave way to houses and street signs.

His hand reached the knob of the church door, and he pushed the door open. The only light inside came from one tiny window. He had to go in, but his legs were scared. He looked to the side and saw someone sitting in the darkness, watching. An evil person, evil eyes throwing shadows on shadows. Junior needed to walk right past where that man was sitting. Not moving or talking. Just sitting and staring at Junior, trying to scare him off. Junior put both hands on the smooth neck of the pew his pap had made, felt its perfect smoothness, slid his hands all the way over to that man. Junior looked him in his evil eye and said, "What you want?"

The man disappeared.

Junior moved up the aisle toward the front, the space where the cross sits and only the preacher stands. It was empty but full of presence. As he got closer, he felt a warmth, a glow to the space. Darkness slipped away. He stopped.

Not supposed to go up there, I'm just twelve, still just a boy.

Someone said, "Come on, Junior."

When he stood up on the high place and turned around to look, instead of empty space, he saw people all around him, everywhere, the forgotten, the voiceless, singing,

The time of jubilee has come
Prepare the way of the Lord!

He opened his mouth, but no sound came out. His throat was as tight as drum skin. He tried again and squeaked out one word.

"Help."

He turned and started walking without knowing where his feet were taking him.

Until he arrived at the one part of town that was like him. Which was the one part he did not know.

Stars were clear and close. A torn-off cloud flat-topped the moon. It felt like a holy place, like he should pray. But he didn't because it felt like God was right there, walking right next to him, keeping him company. *And you don't need words for that.*

Dark-rimmed houses were all asleep on this side of town. He crossed the square onto the street where the Negro folks lived. This part of town was wide awake. Orange light swirled from windows. Music, voices singing, shouts and laughter floated from closed doors. These houses hugged together, kept each other warm.

Celebrating. What? I remember. Lee's surrender. Peace is coming. Peace and freedom at last.

Other people walked the street, bumped into Junior, laughing, nodding their excuse me's. Some arm-and-arm, some stumbling to the next house. Some sitting on porch stoops, calling out. He heard his name. When he turned, he saw a clutch of folks, dark on dark. Only their outlines showed, haze-edged by a gas streetlamp.

For the first time, he understood how, and why, people walked in bunches. Lived in bunches. Even why children played in clusters, boys here, girls there. He knew his was the only brown-skinned family pew-sitting at the First Presbyterian Church. *So what, it's our church. Now I see the difference between Choosing, or just Allowing Things to Be. I, Junior Thompson, am growing up in a family of Choosers.*

Something light hit his shoulder. He picked up a crumpled wad of paper, opened it, and saw it was one of Teacher Brumbach's assignments, scribbled out. He looked up and saw a lone person sitting halfway up a forlorn-looking set of porch steps. Trembly circles of light from both house and street were just bright enough for him to see her.

"Abigail, what're you doing here?"

"I live here."

"Here?" Junior climbed to within a step of her, to better see. Abigail looked to be all angles. She had a tiny lick of a smile on her face. *Her skirt's too short and thin for spring and nighttime,* Junior thought. She had her skirt bunched up above her knees, her legs popping open and shut, like her knees were clapping.

"What're you thinking, Abigail? That ain't ladylike."

She snapped her knees together. "Isn't, Junior. Isn't ladylike." She tilted her head. "I could ask you why you don't live here. But I don't ask a question when I know the answer."

Something about the set of her jaw made Junior look closer, at her face, her hair, her eyes, her lips, until he realized something about her pap. What his skin color might be. And what that said about where he, and she, came from.

"Does your pap live here?"

She shook her head. "Lancaster," she said, saying it "LANE-kissed her," the way local folks do. "What are you doing here, Junior?"

He knew better than to say "Nothing" or "I don't know" to Abigail. She would just keep pressing. Better to change topics.

"What's your best subject in school, Abigail?"

"Grammar." She sat a little straighter. "And spelling."

"That's right. In the spelling bee, nobody could best you. Least favorite?"

"Arithmetic."

"That's my best."

"I know, Junior."

"Grammar's my least."

"Well, that's obvious." She was smirking now. "What's that thing around your neck?"

"Binoculars! Web gave them to me." Junior held them up to his eyes. He caught a smeared, too-close glimpse of the front window. Then he saw Teacher Brumbach's face float into view, scary-fierce, looking like a monster. He put down the binoculars. "Listen, Abigail, maybe we could—"

Teacher Brumbach's voice rose from inside the house, loud, rough. "Abigail!" She said it like always, in two beats, without the first "i."

Abigail got up, weary. "See you at school, Junior."

He turned to head back up the street. He didn't expect to do that. Nor for Abigail to say, "Thanks for stopping by."

Then he heard, "Wait!"

When Junior turned around she was a flat, clear-edged shadow, her arms at her sides. "I heard Web and you talking in the schoolyard on Friday." Her fingers were wiggling. "Remember? You two were laying on your backs looking at the sun with your eyes closed. Remember what you said?"

"What?"

"Web asked you what colors you saw with your eyes closed. You said black. Now, you know that's not true, Junior Thompson! Why did you lie like that?"

Junior began shuffling backward.

"The truth is you can see orange, yellow or pink or red, even. All sorts of colors. Same as he should be able to see on the insides of his eyelids. But not black! You won't see black unless you're blind, Junior! Why did you lie to your friend?"

Abigail jabbed her fist onto one hip, thrust her chin out. "Each year my mother lists you as white, did you know that? Lists me that way, too." Her voice got loud. "Who do you think told her to do that? And don't say your father!"

Junior limped away fast. Then ran. With a stitch in the running because his knee hurt.

"Those silly spyglasses won't help you see! It's only skin, Junior!" She called after him. "Only skin!"

Junior didn't stop running until he reached the Hendersons' back porch. He slid down against the porch rails, his chest bumping heavily. As he sat there gulping air, he took a good long look at the house, the face of it, looming large. He saw the way each roofline see-sawed its way to Web's window. He had seen Web climb up the side of that house lots of times, sometimes at night. He reckoned the distance from ground to window ledge. *Not as high as the oak, that's one good thing.* But he would have to climb the trellis like a ladder. *Will it hold my weight? Will those thorny winter-tough rose canes share the space?* Then there was the matter of the porch roofline. He would have to grab the edge, lift himself up. Climb over the peak to reach the narrow, steeper part of the roof leading to Web's window, which Web claimed he always left unlatched. Open it, and drop in.

Or he could try to find an unlatched door, probably be discovered and made to leave. At this hour, that was most likely. And so, the greater risk. He traced a path in the dark air with his finger, again and again, his heart beating in his ears as he called to mind, step by step, the spectacle of Web doing it.

Mrs. Henderson must have heard him. She hurried in, tying the sash of her night robe, saw it was just Junior, and sat down next to him, sorrow written all over her face. She didn't light a lamp because, even though they sat there in the mostly dark room, there was a bright wash of light from the full moon. It poured through the window right above Web's bed so that Junior could see his face clearly, so badly beaten and swelled up, it was hard for Junior to look. Mrs. Henderson rubbed the back of his head a little bit, softly, gently, trying to soothe Junior. And it did.

"Can he hear us?" Junior asked.

"I think he can. It's hard to tell, but yes, Junior, I think he can hear us."

Junior whispered in her ear, "Is he going to live?"

She looked at Junior a long time. Gently, the same way she rubbed his head. *I've seen her look that way at Webbie lots of times and now at me. Like I'm her son. Another son.*

"The doctor's not sure, but I am going to say yes. 'Hope is the evidence of things unseen.' Ever hear that, Junior? Let's hope together."

They sat there for a while, hoping. She said, "Junior, when he wakes up, Web might not remember you. We might have to start all over again, in many ways. You are still friends, nothing changes that. Maybe you could start helping him now. Talk to him. Tell him things as if it's the first time he's hearing it. I don't know, maybe you could pretend it's your first day together. Or something like that."

When she said that Web might not remember him, Junior began to shake. He thought about life with his friend. Web not remembering any of that hurt Junior as much as looking at Web's messed up face. Worse. He felt the trembling go straight up his body to his eyes. *Oh, no. Not gonna cry. That's the last thing Web needs, is me setting by his bed, blubbering.*

"I'm going to leave now," Mrs. Henderson said, "and give you two some private time." She closed the door behind her.

From his book sack, Junior pulled out the binoculars. He put them under Web's hand so he could feel them. Junior knew he did not have to say he had climbed the tree. Web would know. *I won't tell him how I tried to run away. Walked myself in a big old circle. Right back to his bedside. Besides I can't talk right away. Least not with my mouth.* So he talked to Web with his spirit.

You're Web Henderson. You're my friend. My best friend! You're Web Henderson, my friend my friend my friend my friend MY FRIEND, he kept saying until he was shouting in his spirit and it came out of his mouth in a whisper. Finally, Junior saw a red spot on Web's cheek. That blush he would get when they were just boys and he was really excited about something. That was how Junior knew he had Web's attention.

"I know how you love stories, Web," he said aloud. "If I tell you a story, promise you'll wake up. I know you will, 'cause you always have to know how a story ends. We'll be characters in this one, Webbie. I'll use our real names, okay? It'll be more exciting."

Junior thought about how to begin.

"My name's Junior Thompson. I'm twelve years old today," he said. "My pap's called Chance and my mam's name is Sarai."

Junior kept his eyes on that flush of life on Web's cheek.

"I'm telling you this story because it's your story, too."

ACKNOWLEDGEMENTS

This journey with *Soldier's Heart* has not been a lonely one. I am indebted to friends and fellow travelers who helped capture places and voices with authenticity. My heartfelt thanks go to early readers and cheerleaders Jim McClure, Christine Lincoln, Dr. Janet Avery, Jeff Hines, Jim May, Steve Feldmann, Connie Snyder, Dr. Bob Davis, Jeff Beard, Rebecca Countess, Joyce Fodor, Robert Kinsley, Linda Phelps, Amy Oblender, Bill Schintz, Stephanie Newland, Barbara Cole, Stephanie Seaton, Alisha Lippi, Leslie Delp, Arlina Yates, Andy Anderson, Michael and Eloise Newsome, James Harris, Dr. Robyn Maitoza, Patricia Hickman, and Susan Breen.

For sharing their expertise and insights, special thanks go to Betty J.L. Curtis, a descendant of the Caleb Thompson family, who arrived in Carlisle in 1900; and to Ruth E. Hodge, author of *Guide to African American Resources at the Pennsylvania State Archives.* In military research I was guided by the expertise of the U.S. Army Heritage and Education Center's Dr. Richard J. Sommers (retired) and Jessica Sheets; and Manassas Museum Specialist, Jim Burgess.

Two writers groups generously listened and critiqued: Liz McKnight and the West Shore writers group, and Lisa Lawmaster Hess and the York writers group. I'm thankful for the insights of The Salvation Army's outstanding writers and editors, and the encouragement of Lt. Colonel Allen Satterlee and Warren Maye, along with my York Corps colleagues. You would not be reading this book without the encouragement of my intrepid editor, Lynne Cosby, and my agent, David Fessenden and WordWise Media. I am grateful to Eddie Jones, Ann Tatlock, Meaghan Burnett and the Lighthouse Publishing of the Carolinas team, for their steadfast support.

At all times my family cheerfully cheers me on. Frank, Andrew, Dan, Annie, Olivia Michele, and Mary Janice: you are simply the best. I love you.

A Hebrew poet wrote, "My heart is stirred by a noble theme;
I address my verses to the king;
My tongue is the pen of an expert scribe." (from Psalm 45:1, Complete Jewish Bible)

It is a love song. And a battle song. So too I praise the Eternal King whose Theme never ceases to inspire.